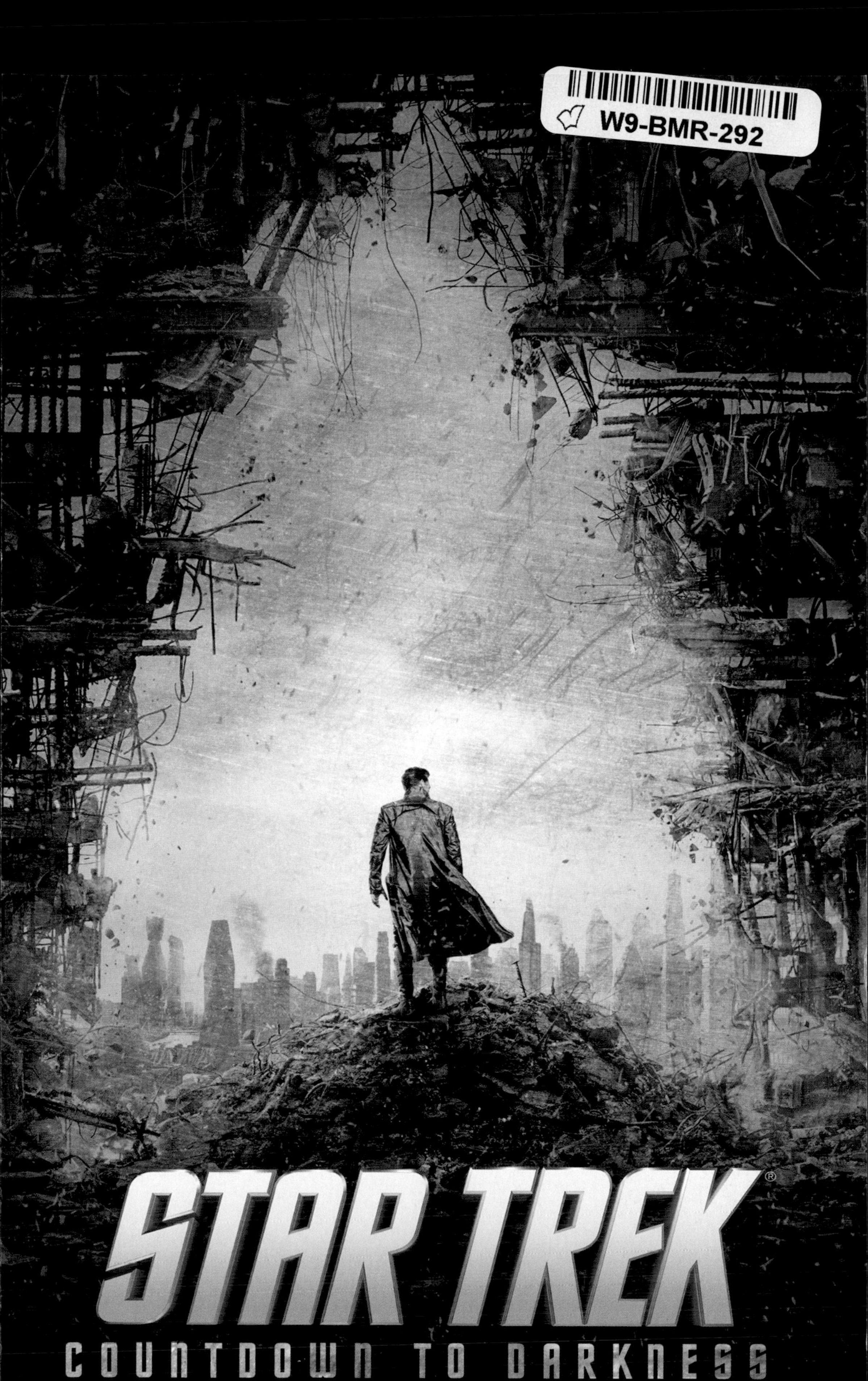
STAR TREK®
COUNTDOWN TO DARKNESS

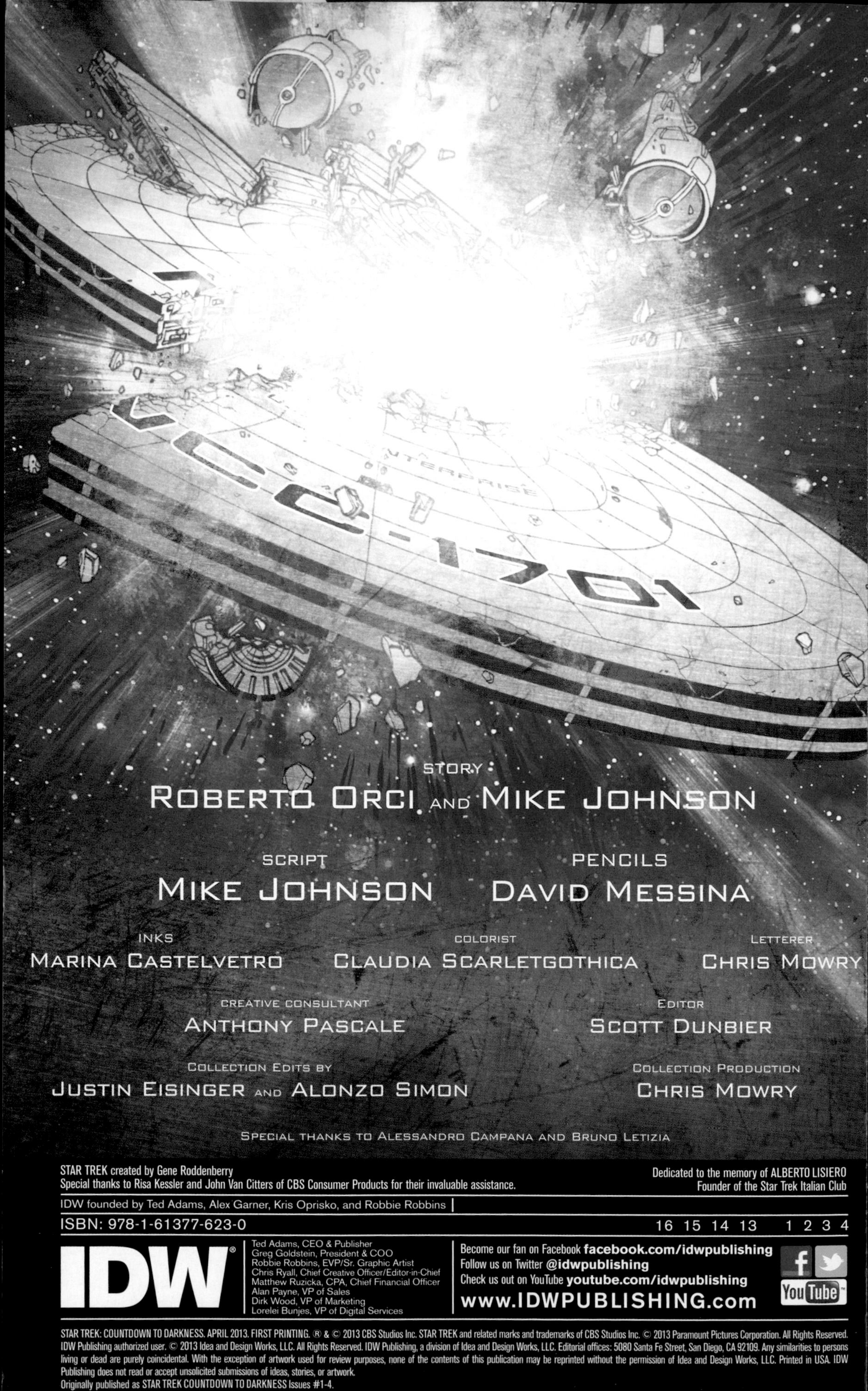
NCC-1701
ENTERPRISE

STORY
ROBERTO ORCI AND MIKE JOHNSON

SCRIPT
MIKE JOHNSON

PENCILS
DAVID MESSINA

INKS
MARINA CASTELVETRO

COLORIST
CLAUDIA SCARLETGOTHICA

LETTERER
CHRIS MOWRY

CREATIVE CONSULTANT
ANTHONY PASCALE

EDITOR
SCOTT DUNBIER

COLLECTION EDITS BY
JUSTIN EISINGER AND ALONZO SIMON

COLLECTION PRODUCTION
CHRIS MOWRY

SPECIAL THANKS TO ALESSANDRO CAMPANA AND BRUNO LETIZIA

STAR TREK created by Gene Roddenberry
Special thanks to Risa Kessler and John Van Citters of CBS Consumer Products for their invaluable assistance.

Dedicated to the memory of ALBERTO LISIERO
Founder of the Star Trek Italian Club

IDW founded by Ted Adams, Alex Garner, Kris Oprisko, and Robbie Robbins

ISBN: 978-1-61377-623-0

16 15 14 13 1 2 3 4

Ted Adams, CEO & Publisher
Greg Goldstein, President & COO
Robbie Robbins, EVP/Sr. Graphic Artist
Chris Ryall, Chief Creative Officer/Editor-in-Chief
Matthew Ruzicka, CPA, Chief Financial Officer
Alan Payne, VP of Sales
Dirk Wood, VP of Marketing
Lorelei Bunjes, VP of Digital Services

Become our fan on Facebook **facebook.com/idwpublishing**
Follow us on Twitter **@idwpublishing**
Check us out on YouTube **youtube.com/idwpublishing**
www.IDWPUBLISHING.com

Originally published as STAR TREK COUNTDOWN TO DARKNESS Issues #1-4.

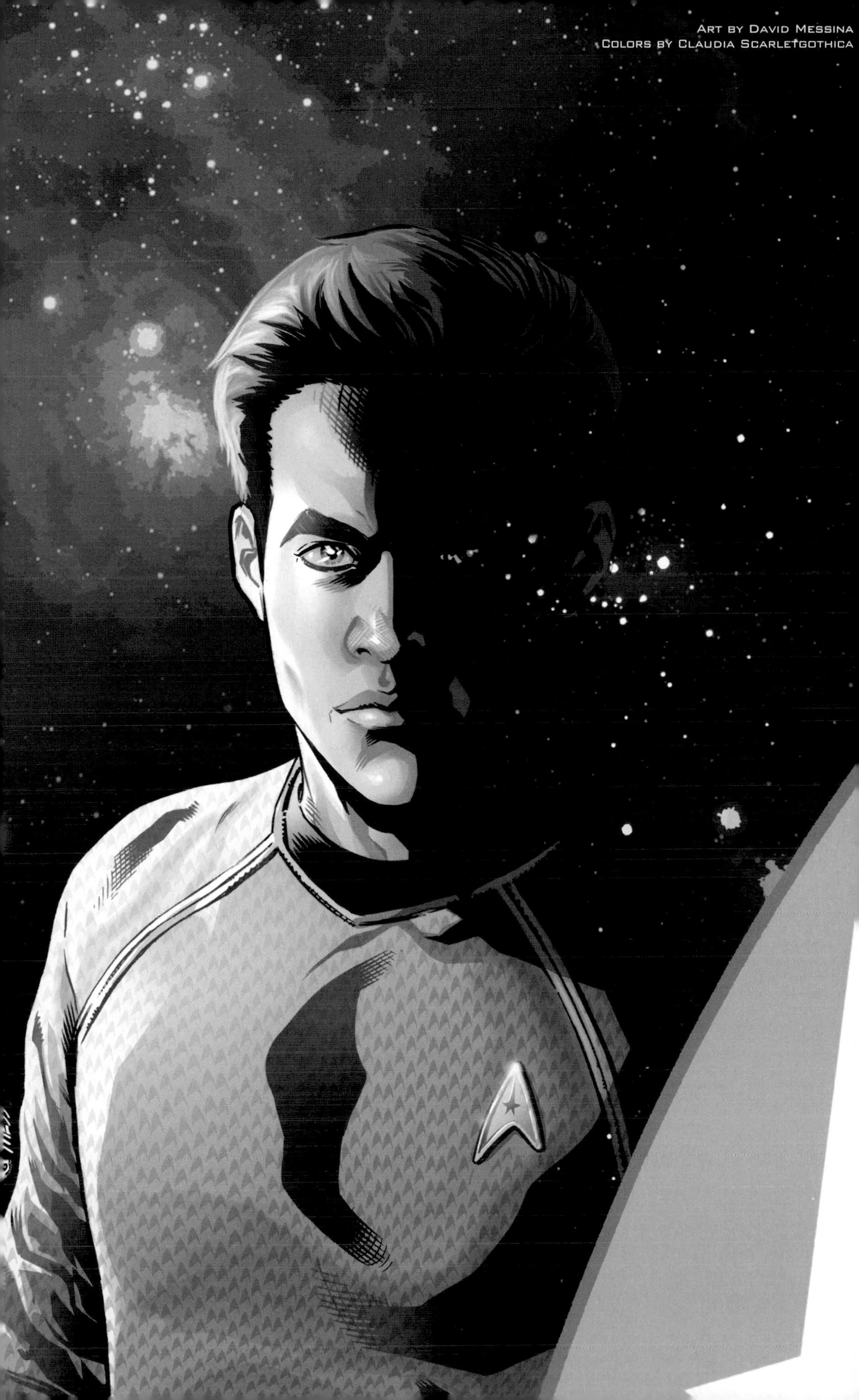

Art by David Messina
Colors by Claudia Scarletgothica

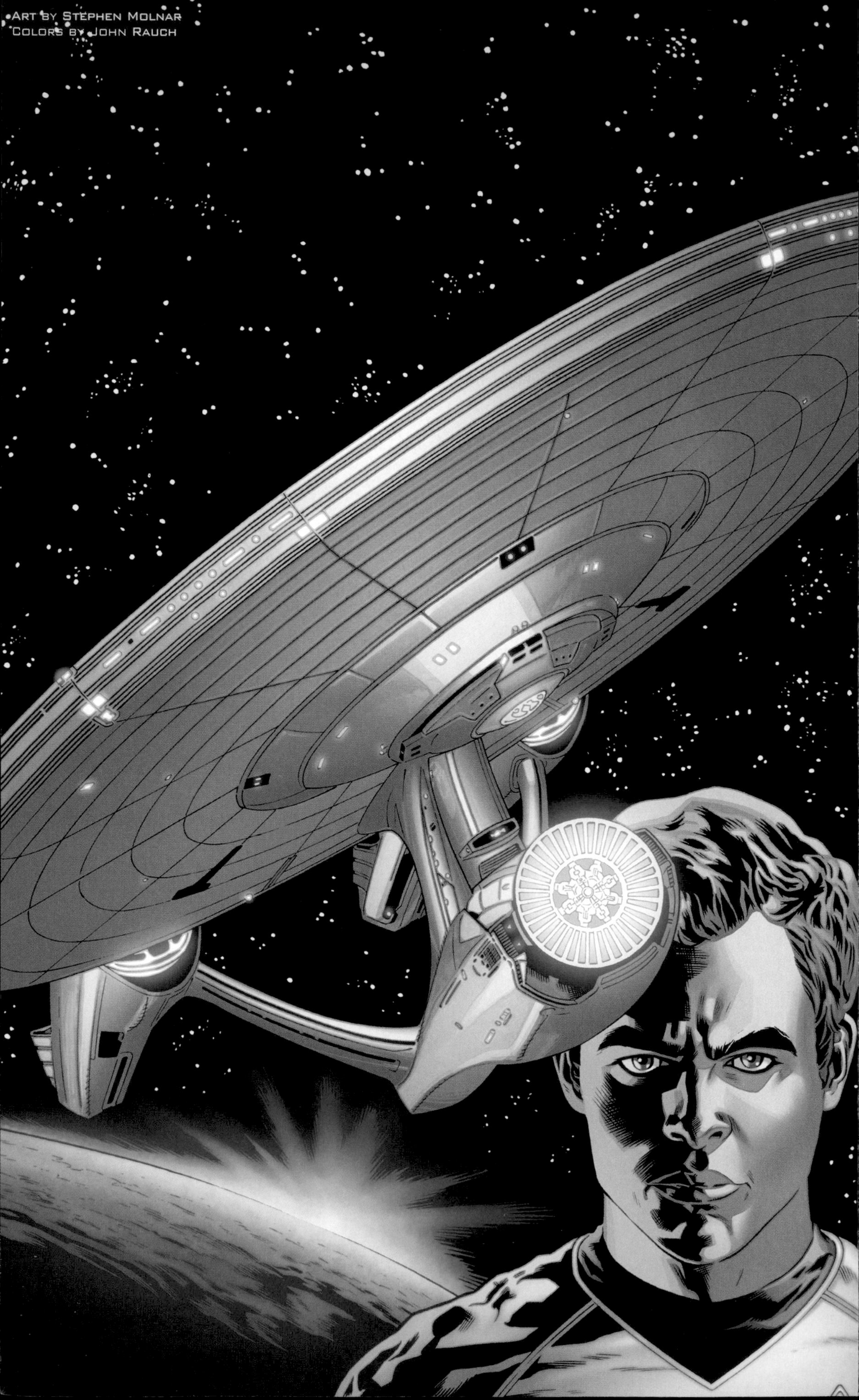
Art by Stephen Molnar
Colors by John Rauch

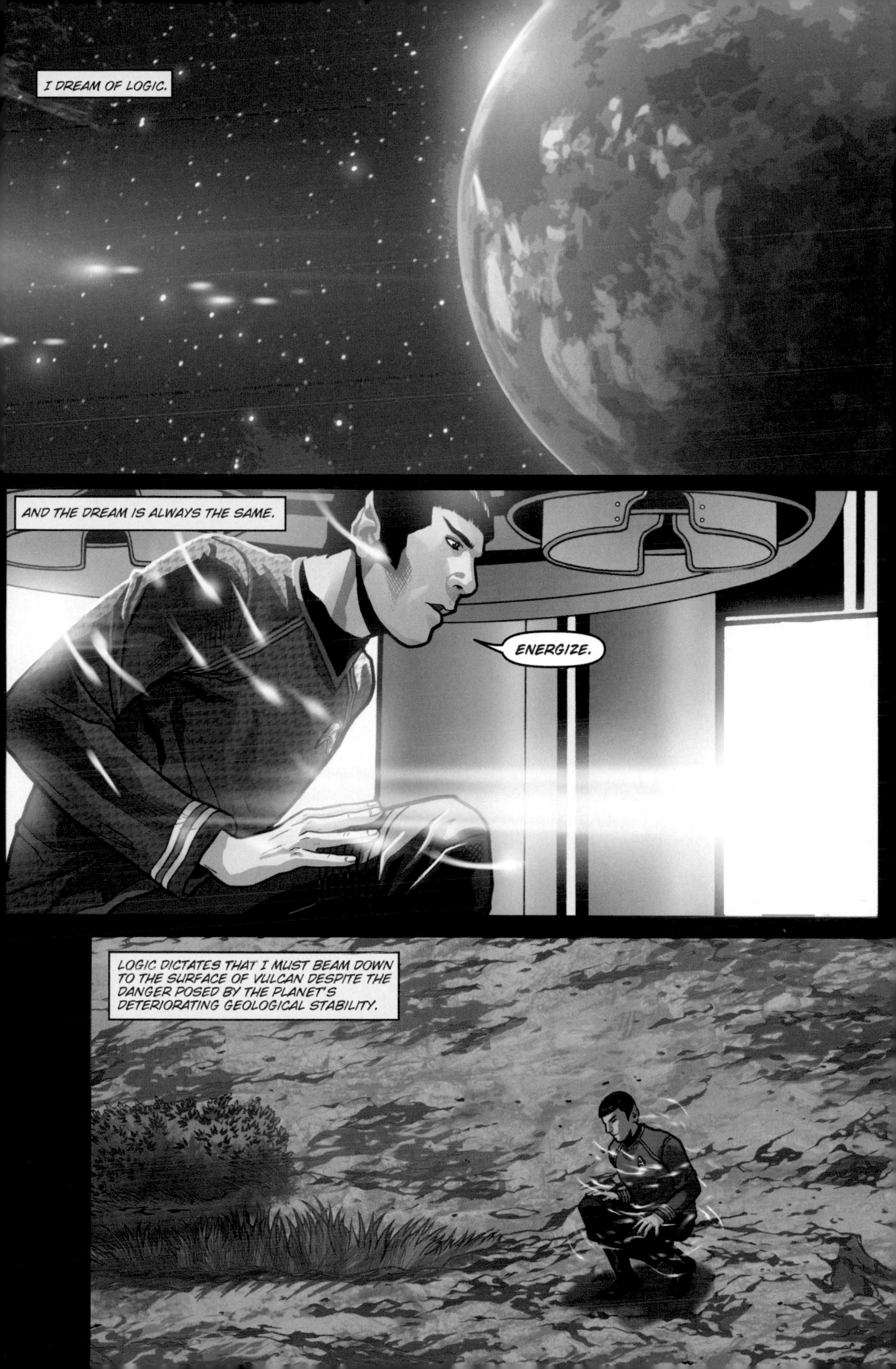
I DREAM OF LOGIC.
AND THE DREAM IS ALWAYS THE SAME.
ENERGIZE.
LOGIC DICTATES THAT I MUST BEAM DOWN TO THE SURFACE OF VULCAN DESPITE THE DANGER POSED BY THE PLANET'S DETERIORATING GEOLOGICAL STABILITY.

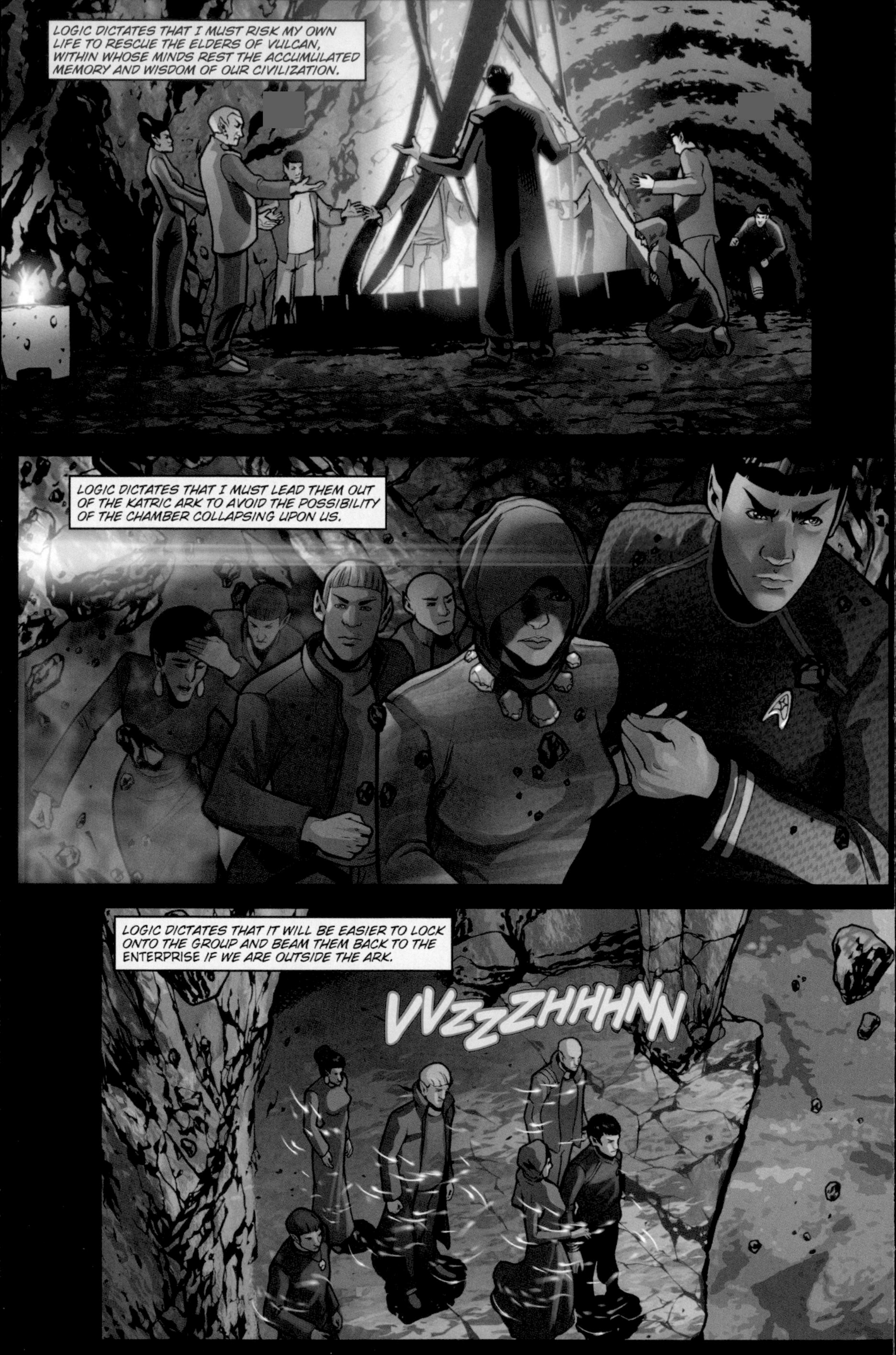
LOGIC DICTATES THAT I MUST RISK MY OWN LIFE TO RESCUE THE ELDERS OF VULCAN, WITHIN WHOSE MINDS REST THE ACCUMULATED MEMORY AND WISDOM OF OUR CIVILIZATION.
LOGIC DICTATES THAT I MUST LEAD THEM OUT OF THE KATRIC ARK TO AVOID THE POSSIBILITY OF THE CHAMBER COLLAPSING UPON US.
LOGIC DICTATES THAT IT WILL BE EASIER TO LOCK ONTO THE GROUP AND BEAM THEM BACK TO THE ENTERPRISE IF WE ARE OUTSIDE THE ARK.
VVZZZHHHNN

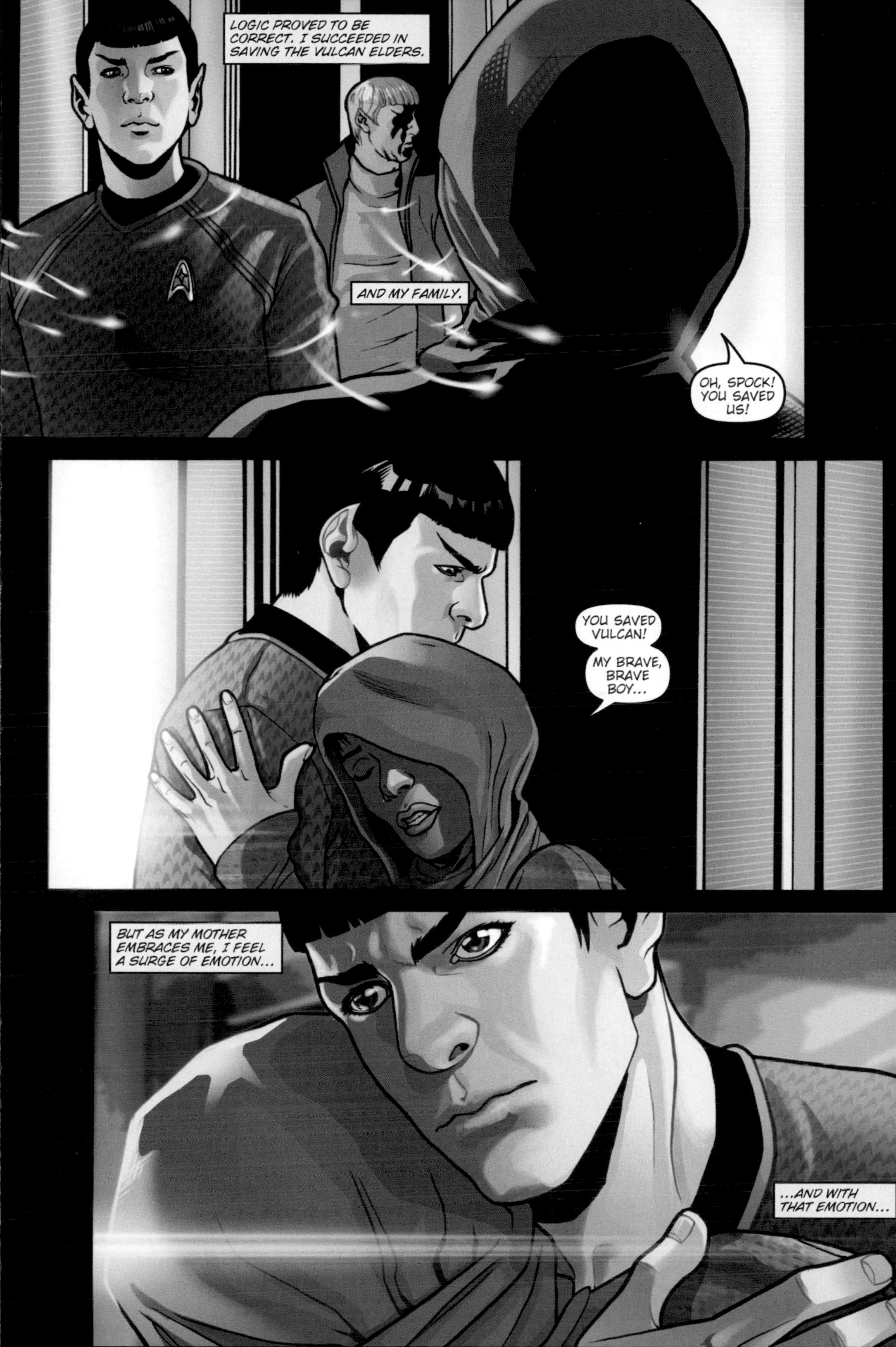
LOGIC PROVED TO BE CORRECT. I SUCCEEDED IN SAVING THE VULCAN ELDERS.
AND MY FAMILY.
OH, SPOCK! YOU SAVED US!
YOU SAVED VULCAN!
MY BRAVE, BRAVE BOY...
BUT AS MY MOTHER EMBRACES ME, I FEEL A SURGE OF EMOTION...
...AND WITH THAT EMOTION...

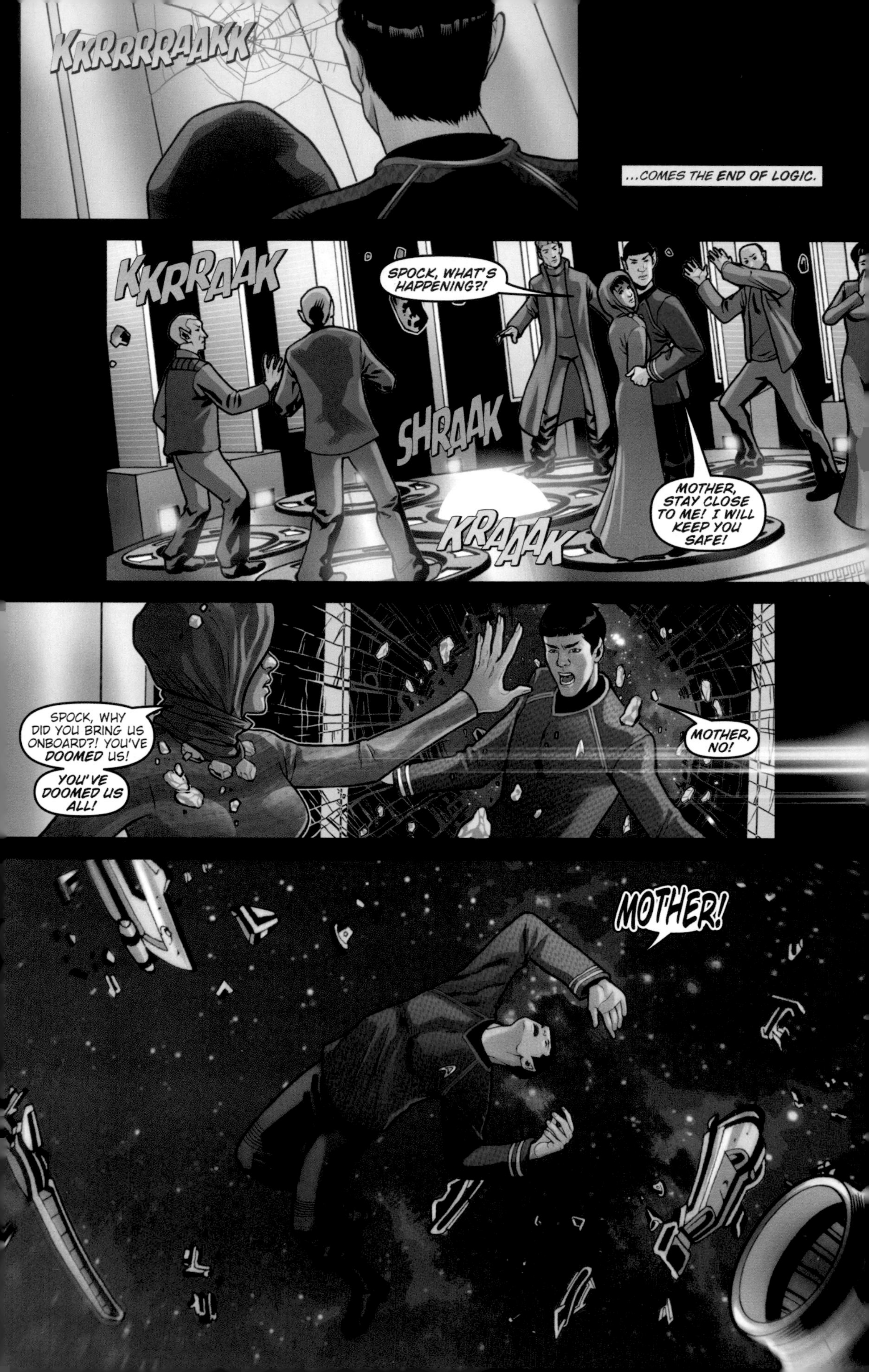
KKRRRRRAAKK
...COMES THE END OF LOGIC.
KKRRAAK
SPOCK, WHAT'S HAPPENING?!
SHRAAK
KRAAAK
MOTHER, STAY CLOSE TO ME! I WILL KEEP YOU SAFE!
SPOCK, WHY DID YOU BRING US ONBOARD?! YOU'VE DOOMED US!
YOU'VE DOOMED US ALL!
MOTHER, NO!
MOTHER!

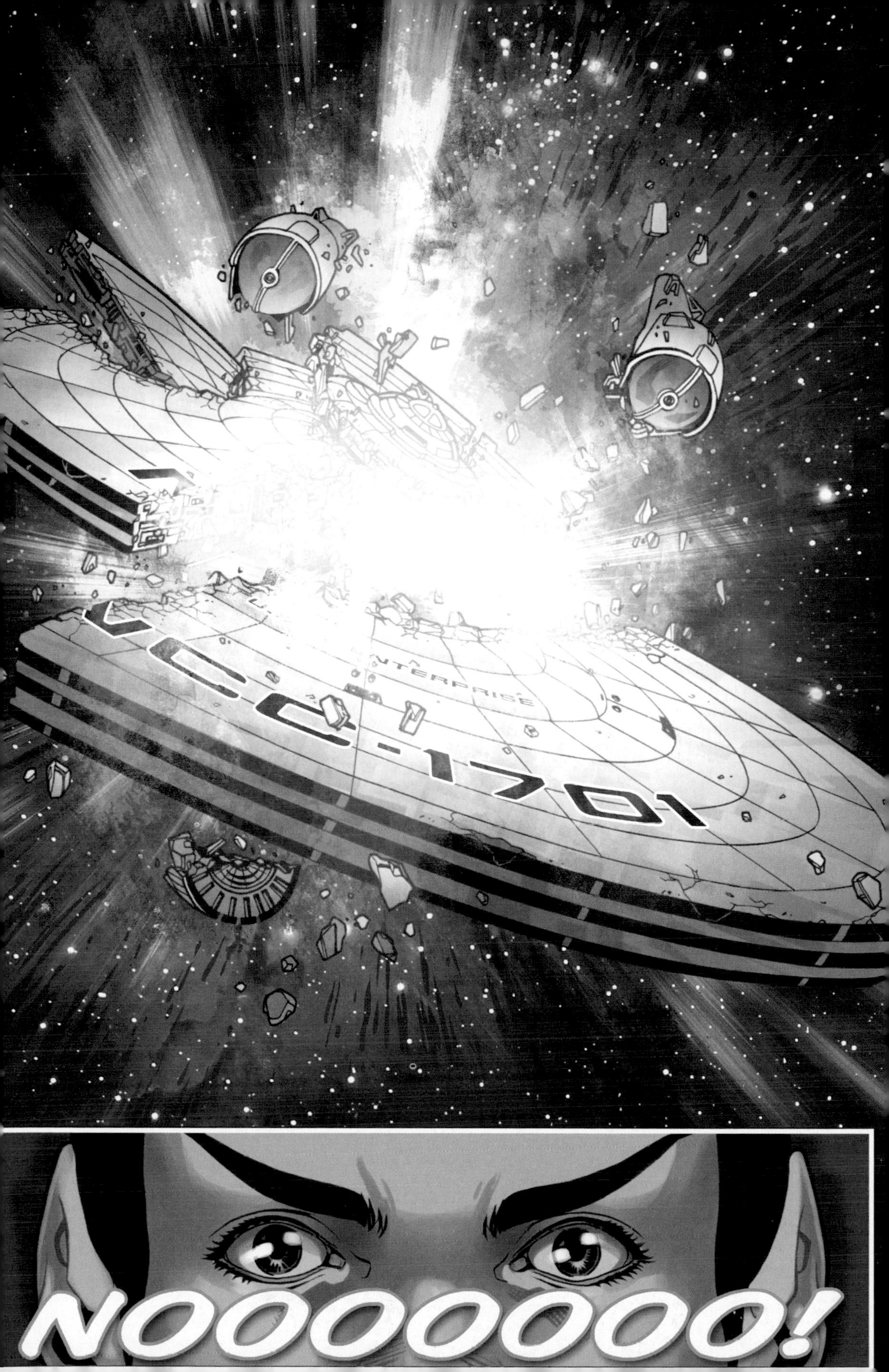
NTERPRISE
CC-1701
NOOOOOOO!

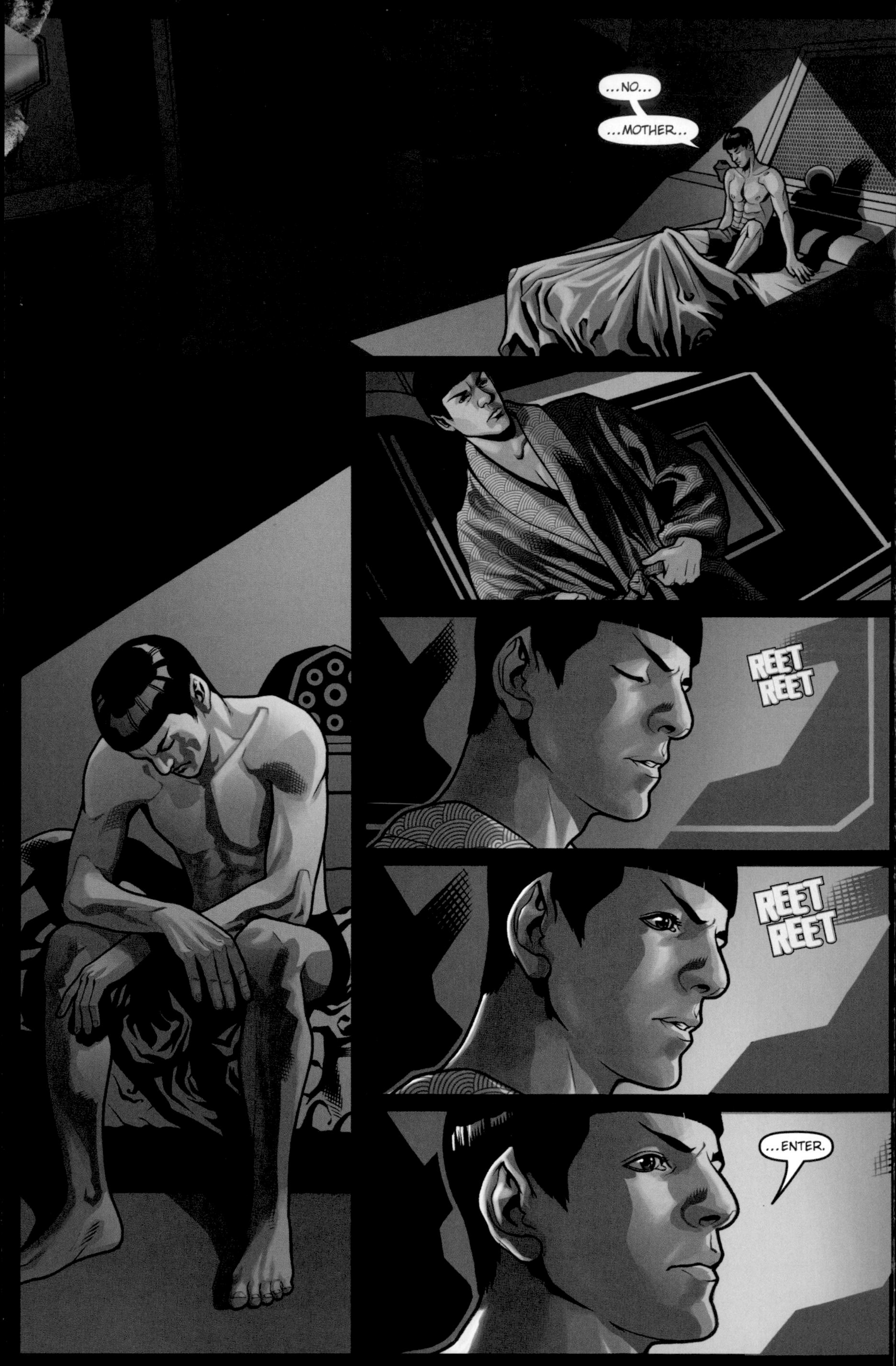
...NO...
...MOTHER...
REET REET
REET REET
...ENTER.

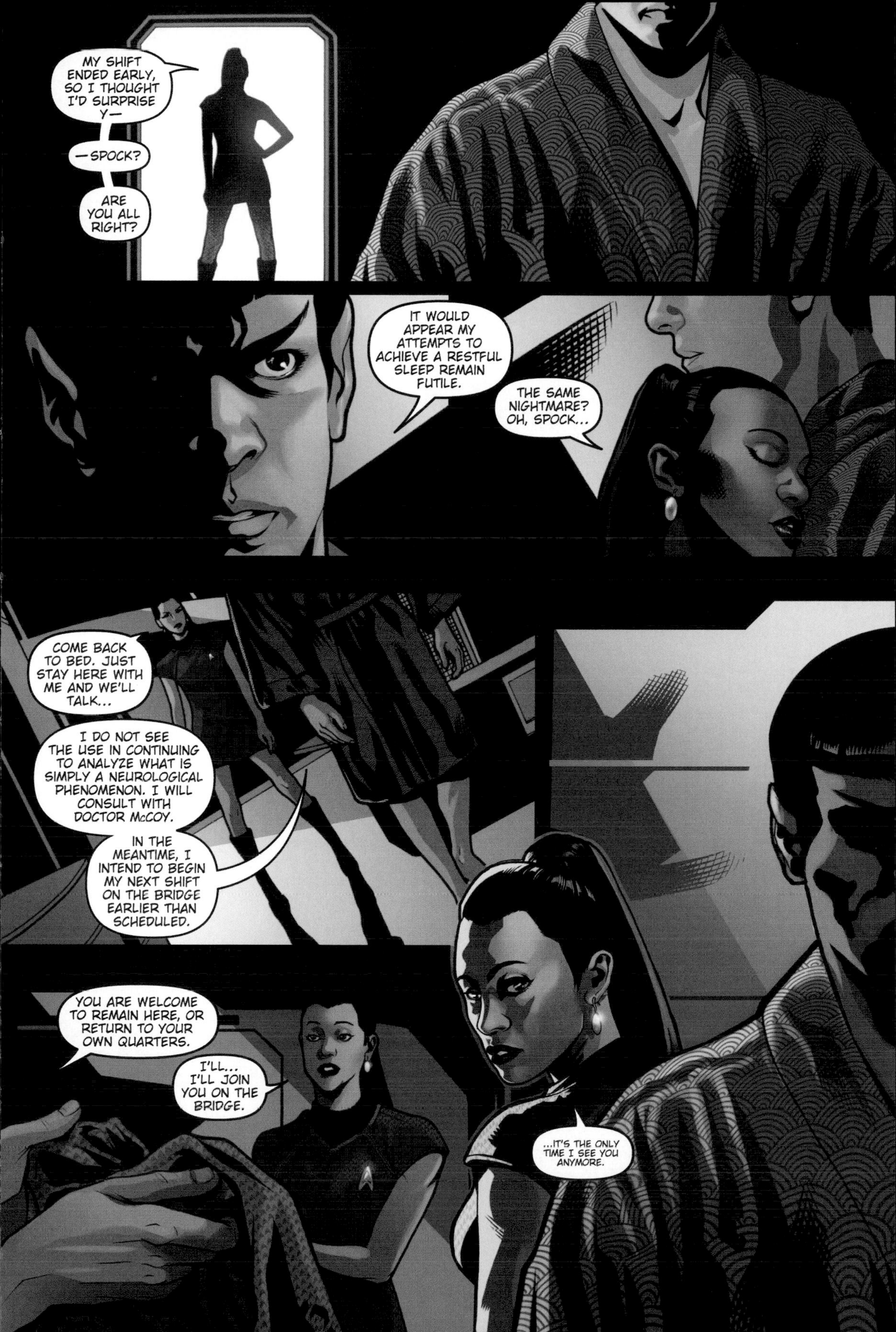
MY SHIFT ENDED EARLY, SO I THOUGHT I'D SURPRISE Y—
—SPOCK?
ARE YOU ALL RIGHT?
IT WOULD APPEAR MY ATTEMPTS TO ACHIEVE A RESTFUL SLEEP REMAIN FUTILE.
THE SAME NIGHTMARE? OH, SPOCK...
COME BACK TO BED. JUST STAY HERE WITH ME AND WE'LL TALK...
I DO NOT SEE THE USE IN CONTINUING TO ANALYZE WHAT IS SIMPLY A NEUROLOGICAL PHENOMENON. I WILL CONSULT WITH DOCTOR McCOY.
IN THE MEANTIME, I INTEND TO BEGIN MY NEXT SHIFT ON THE BRIDGE EARLIER THAN SCHEDULED.
YOU ARE WELCOME TO REMAIN HERE, OR RETURN TO YOUR OWN QUARTERS.
I'LL... I'LL JOIN YOU ON THE BRIDGE.
...IT'S THE ONLY TIME I SEE YOU ANYMORE.

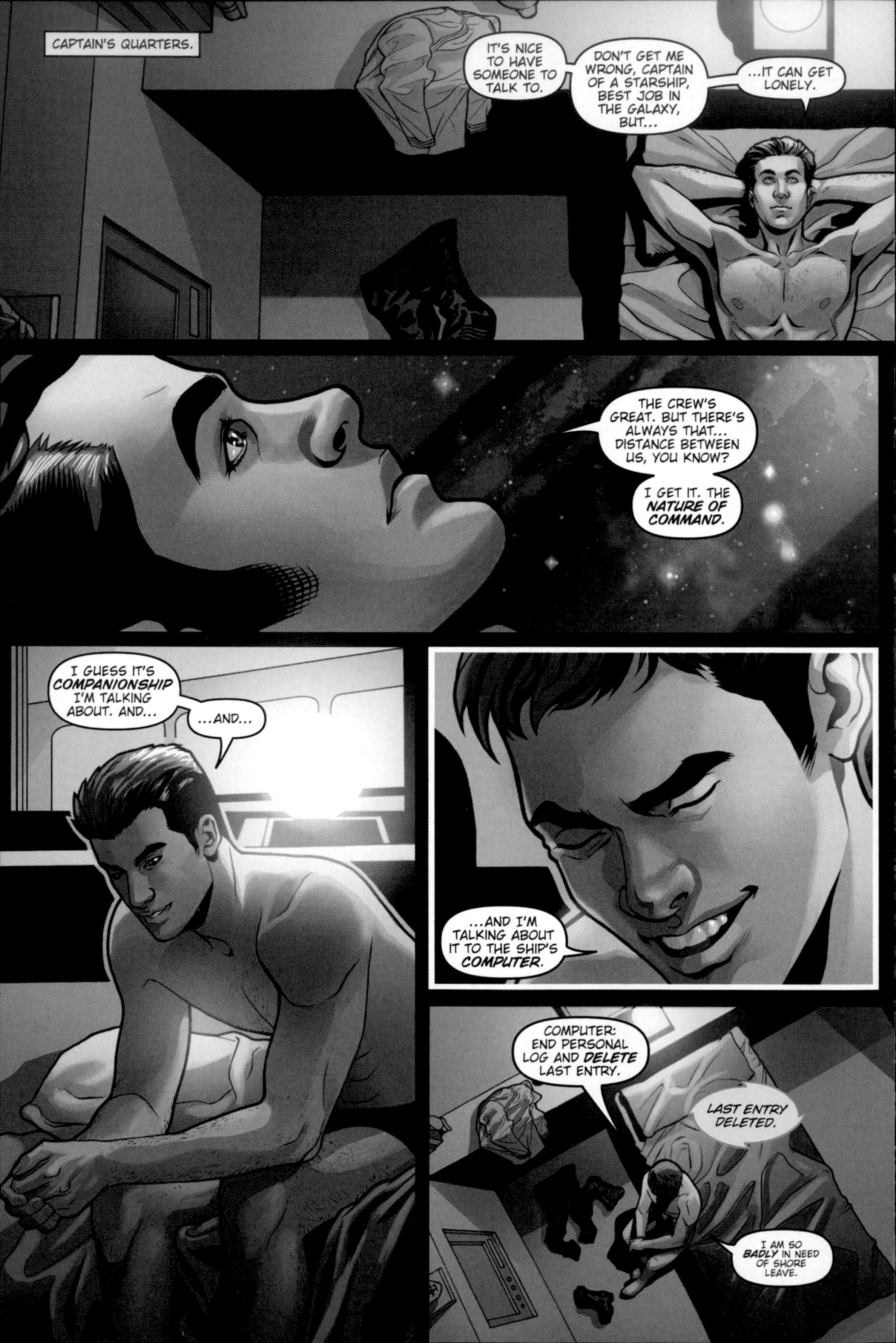
CAPTAIN'S QUARTERS.
IT'S NICE TO HAVE SOMEONE TO TALK TO.
DON'T GET ME WRONG, CAPTAIN OF A STARSHIP, BEST JOB IN THE GALAXY, BUT...
...IT CAN GET LONELY.
THE CREW'S GREAT. BUT THERE'S ALWAYS THAT... DISTANCE BETWEEN US, YOU KNOW?
I GET IT. THE NATURE OF COMMAND.
I GUESS IT'S COMPANIONSHIP I'M TALKING ABOUT. AND...
...AND...
...AND I'M TALKING ABOUT IT TO THE SHIP'S COMPUTER.
COMPUTER: END PERSONAL LOG AND DELETE LAST ENTRY.
LAST ENTRY DELETED.
I AM SO BADLY IN NEED OF SHORE LEAVE.

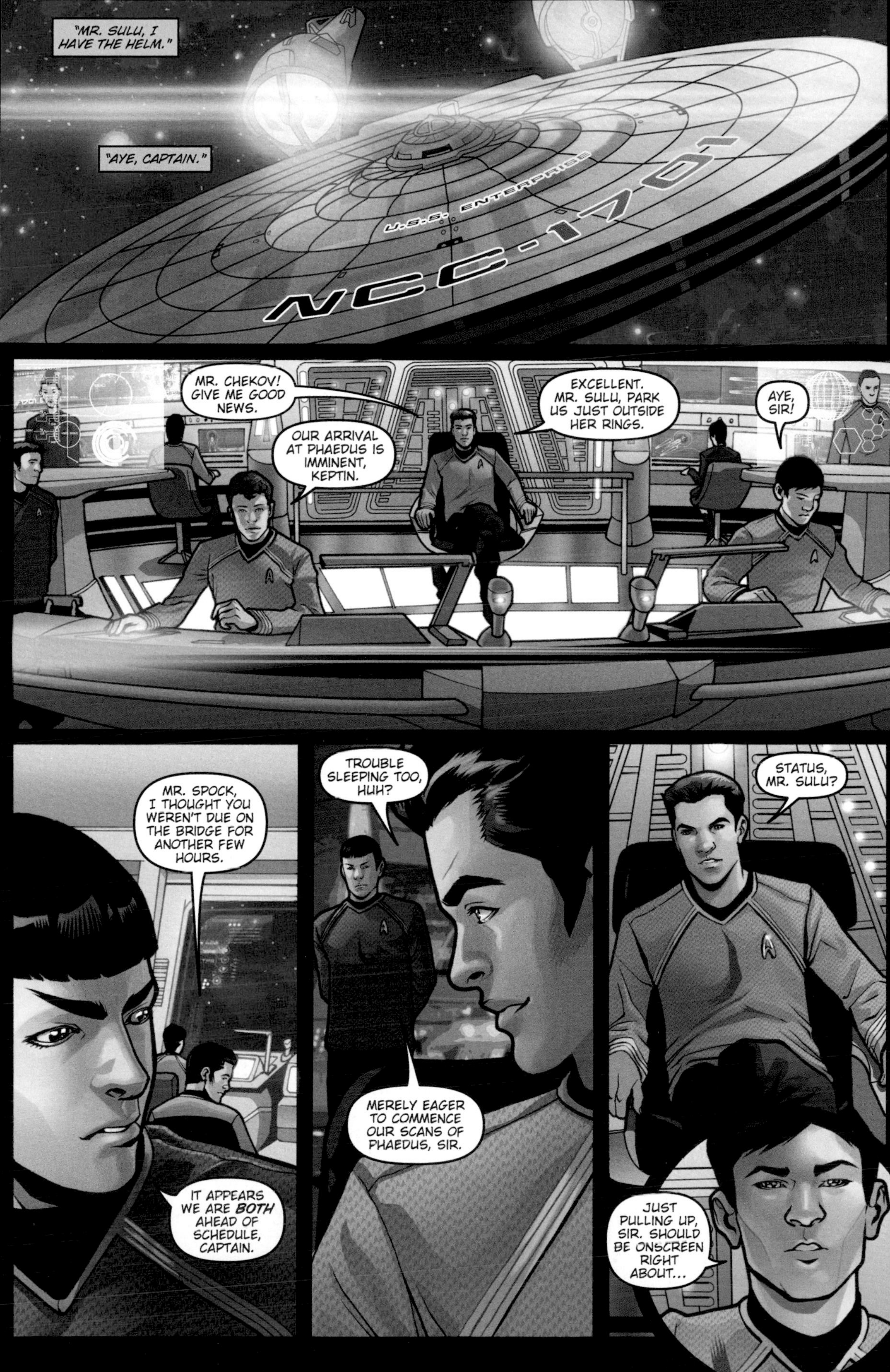
"MR. SULU, I HAVE THE HELM."
"AYE, CAPTAIN."
U.S.S. ENTERPRISE
NCC-1701
MR. CHEKOV! GIVE ME GOOD NEWS.
OUR ARRIVAL AT PHAEDUS IS IMMINENT, KEPTIN.
EXCELLENT. MR. SULU, PARK US JUST OUTSIDE HER RINGS.
AYE, SIR!
MR. SPOCK, I THOUGHT YOU WEREN'T DUE ON THE BRIDGE FOR ANOTHER FEW HOURS.
IT APPEARS WE ARE *BOTH* AHEAD OF SCHEDULE, CAPTAIN.
TROUBLE SLEEPING TOO, HUH?
MERELY EAGER TO COMMENCE OUR SCANS OF PHAEDUS, SIR.
STATUS, MR. SULU?
JUST PULLING UP, SIR. SHOULD BE ONSCREEN RIGHT ABOUT...

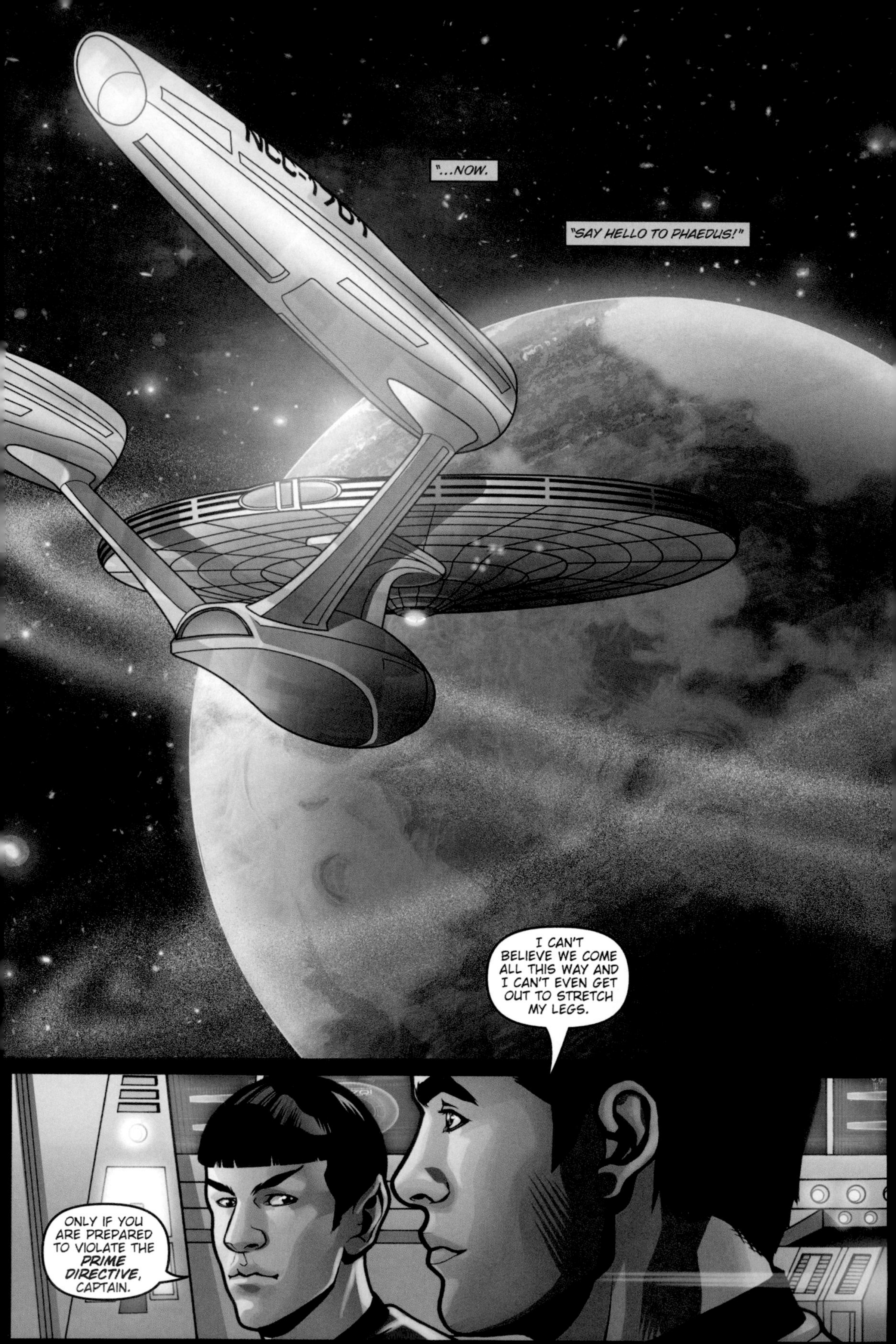
"...NOW.
"SAY HELLO TO PHAEDUS!"
NCC-1701
I CAN'T BELIEVE WE COME ALL THIS WAY AND I CAN'T EVEN GET OUT TO STRETCH MY LEGS.
ONLY IF YOU ARE PREPARED TO VIOLATE THE ***PRIME DIRECTIVE***, CAPTAIN.

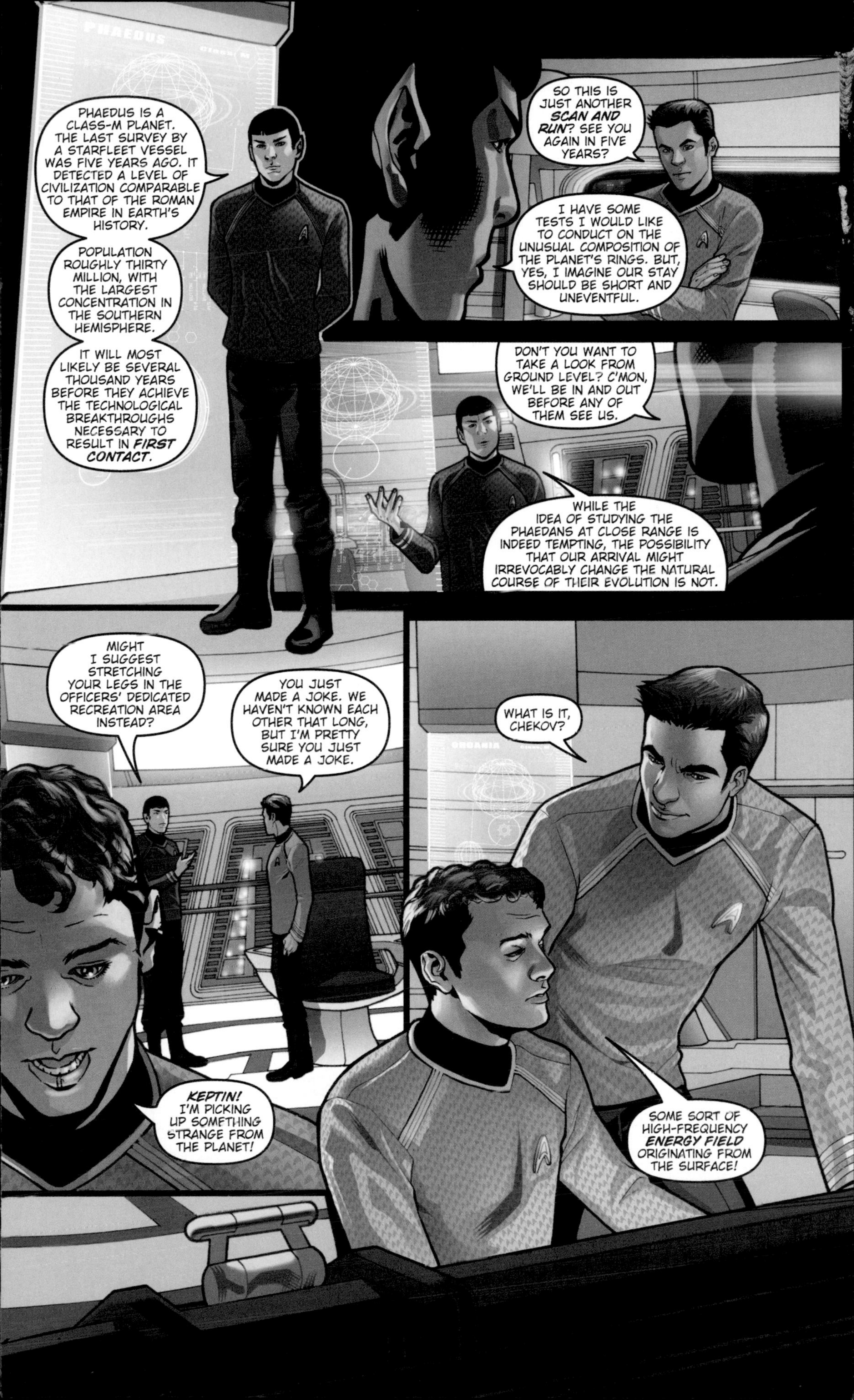
PHAEDUS
PHAEDUS IS A CLASS-M PLANET. THE LAST SURVEY BY A STARFLEET VESSEL WAS FIVE YEARS AGO. IT DETECTED A LEVEL OF CIVILIZATION COMPARABLE TO THAT OF THE ROMAN EMPIRE IN EARTH'S HISTORY.
POPULATION ROUGHLY THIRTY MILLION, WITH THE LARGEST CONCENTRATION IN THE SOUTHERN HEMISPHERE.
IT WILL MOST LIKELY BE SEVERAL THOUSAND YEARS BEFORE THEY ACHIEVE THE TECHNOLOGICAL BREAKTHROUGHS NECESSARY TO RESULT IN *FIRST CONTACT*.
SO THIS IS JUST ANOTHER *SCAN AND RUN*? SEE YOU AGAIN IN FIVE YEARS?
I HAVE SOME TESTS I WOULD LIKE TO CONDUCT ON THE UNUSUAL COMPOSITION OF THE PLANET'S RINGS. BUT, YES, I IMAGINE OUR STAY SHOULD BE SHORT AND UNEVENTFUL.
DON'T YOU WANT TO TAKE A LOOK FROM GROUND LEVEL? C'MON, WE'LL BE IN AND OUT BEFORE ANY OF THEM SEE US.
WHILE THE IDEA OF STUDYING THE PHAEDANS AT CLOSE RANGE IS INDEED TEMPTING, THE POSSIBILITY THAT OUR ARRIVAL MIGHT IRREVOCABLY CHANGE THE NATURAL COURSE OF THEIR EVOLUTION IS NOT.
MIGHT I SUGGEST STRETCHING YOUR LEGS IN THE OFFICERS' DEDICATED RECREATION AREA INSTEAD?
YOU JUST MADE A JOKE. WE HAVEN'T KNOWN EACH OTHER THAT LONG, BUT I'M PRETTY SURE YOU JUST MADE A JOKE.
KEPTIN! I'M PICKING UP SOMETHING STRANGE FROM THE PLANET!
ORGANIA
WHAT IS IT, CHEKOV?
SOME SORT OF HIGH-FREQUENCY *ENERGY FIELD* ORIGINATING FROM THE SURFACE!

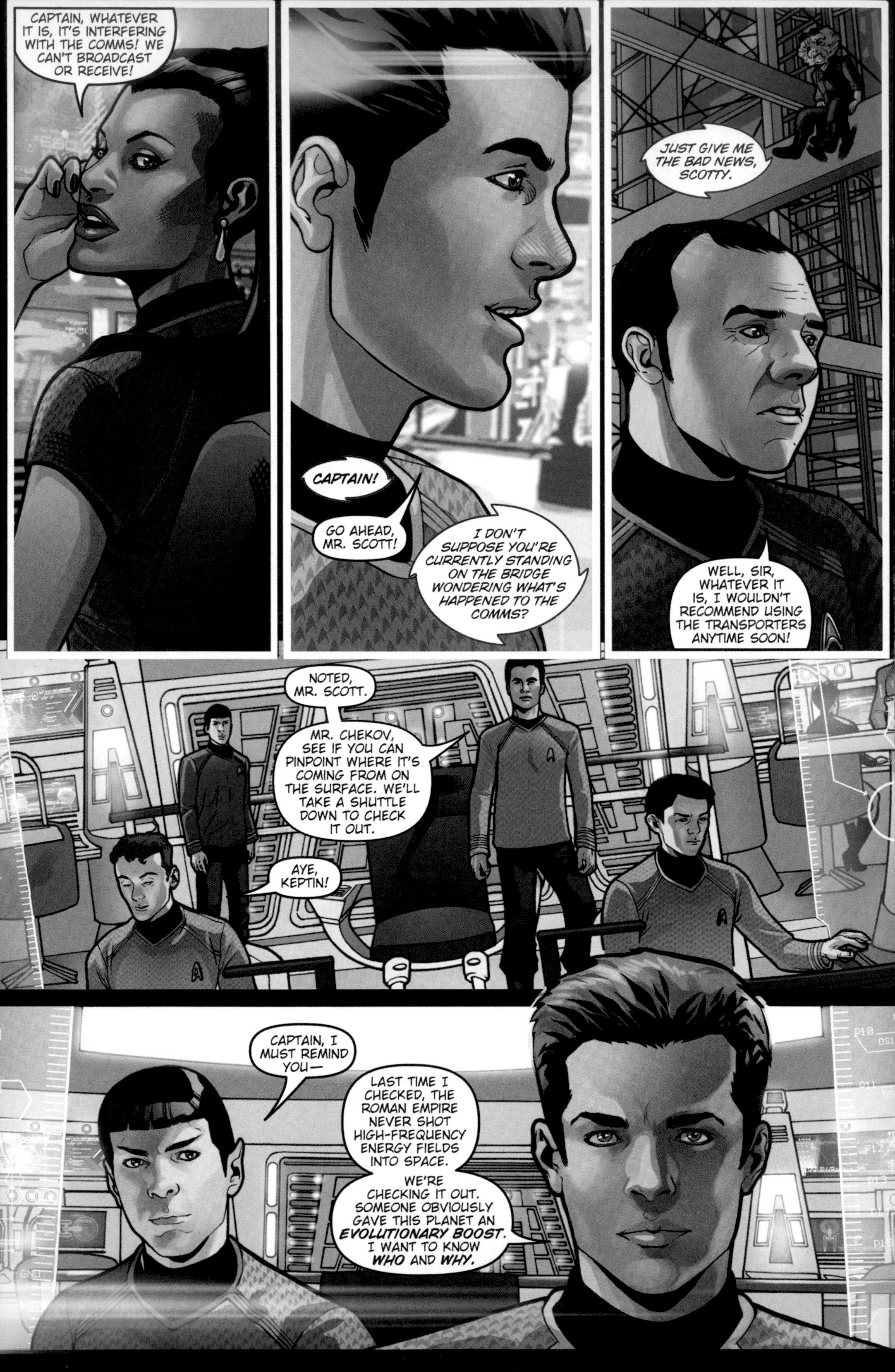
CAPTAIN, WHATEVER IT IS, IT'S INTERFERING WITH THE COMMS! WE CAN'T BROADCAST OR RECEIVE!
CAPTAIN!
GO AHEAD, MR. SCOTT!
I DON'T SUPPOSE YOU'RE CURRENTLY STANDING ON THE BRIDGE WONDERING WHAT'S HAPPENED TO THE COMMS?
JUST GIVE ME THE BAD NEWS, SCOTTY.
WELL, SIR, WHATEVER IT IS, I WOULDN'T RECOMMEND USING THE TRANSPORTERS ANYTIME SOON!
NOTED, MR. SCOTT.
MR. CHEKOV, SEE IF YOU CAN PINPOINT WHERE IT'S COMING FROM ON THE SURFACE. WE'LL TAKE A SHUTTLE DOWN TO CHECK IT OUT.
AYE, KEPTIN!
CAPTAIN, I MUST REMIND YOU—
LAST TIME I CHECKED, THE ROMAN EMPIRE NEVER SHOT HIGH-FREQUENCY ENERGY FIELDS INTO SPACE.
WE'RE CHECKING IT OUT. SOMEONE OBVIOUSLY GAVE THIS PLANET AN EVOLUTIONARY BOOST. I WANT TO KNOW WHO AND WHY.

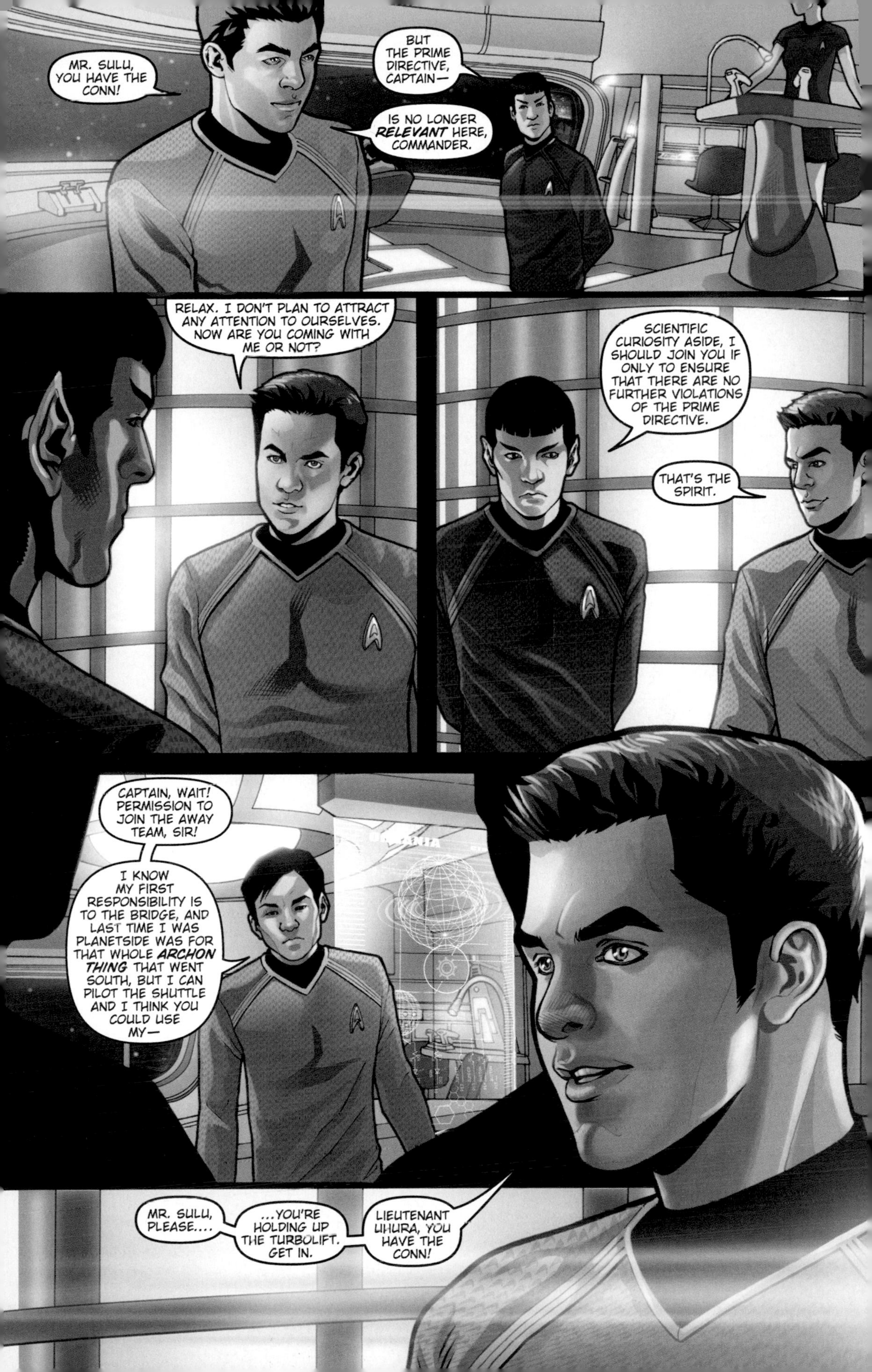
MR. SULU, YOU HAVE THE CONN!
BUT THE PRIME DIRECTIVE, CAPTAIN—
IS NO LONGER RELEVANT HERE, COMMANDER.
RELAX. I DON'T PLAN TO ATTRACT ANY ATTENTION TO OURSELVES. NOW ARE YOU COMING WITH ME OR NOT?
SCIENTIFIC CURIOSITY ASIDE, I SHOULD JOIN YOU IF ONLY TO ENSURE THAT THERE ARE NO FURTHER VIOLATIONS OF THE PRIME DIRECTIVE.
THAT'S THE SPIRIT.
CAPTAIN, WAIT! PERMISSION TO JOIN THE AWAY TEAM, SIR!
I KNOW MY FIRST RESPONSIBILITY IS TO THE BRIDGE, AND LAST TIME I WAS PLANETSIDE WAS FOR THAT WHOLE ARCHON THING THAT WENT SOUTH, BUT I CAN PILOT THE SHUTTLE AND I THINK YOU COULD USE MY—
LIEUTENANT UHURA, YOU HAVE THE CONN!
MR. SULU, PLEASE....
...YOU'RE HOLDING UP THE TURBOLIFT. GET IN.

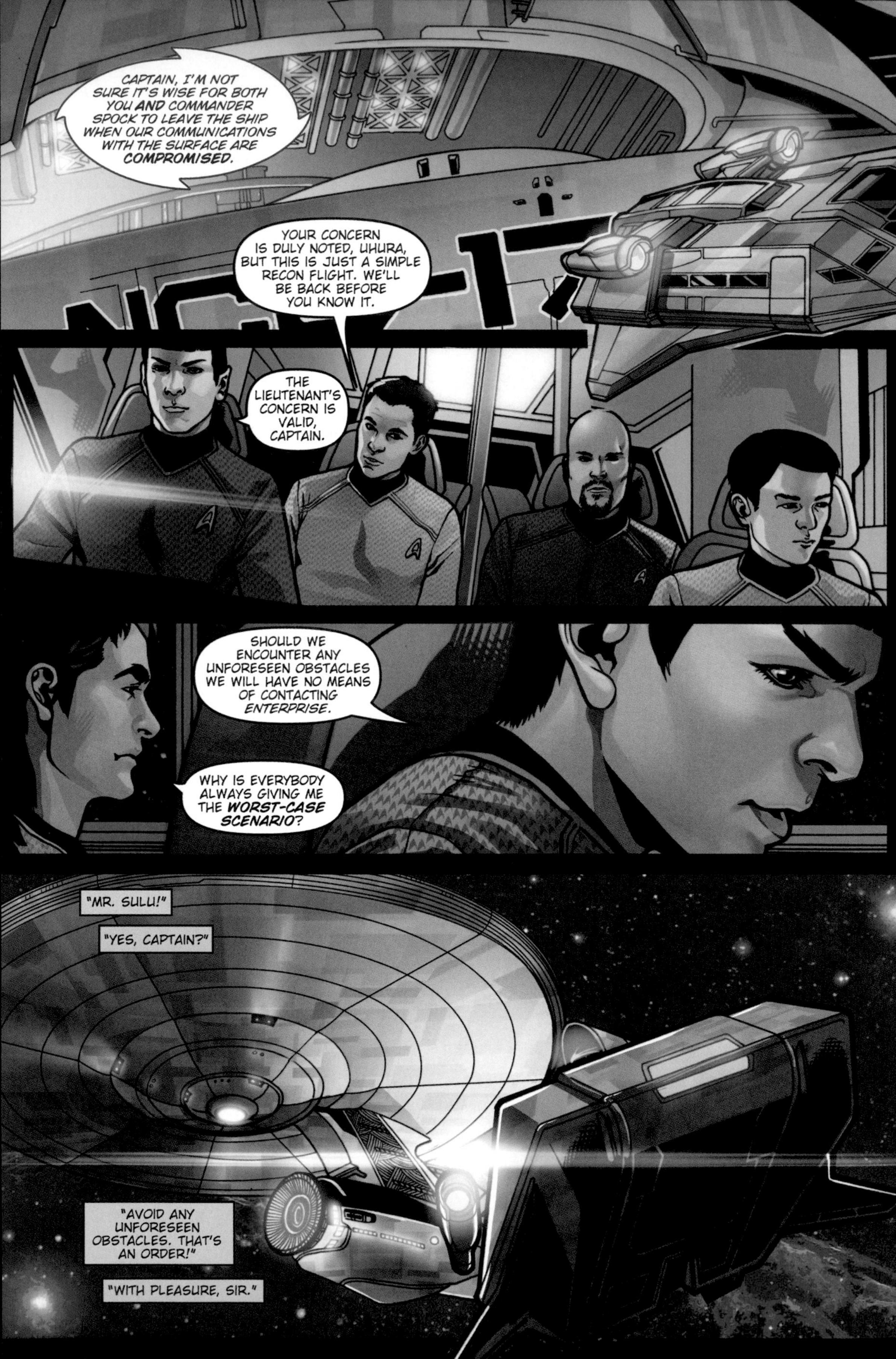
CAPTAIN, I'M NOT SURE IT'S WISE FOR BOTH YOU AND COMMANDER SPOCK TO LEAVE THE SHIP WHEN OUR COMMUNICATIONS WITH THE SURFACE ARE COMPROMISED.
YOUR CONCERN IS DULY NOTED, UHURA, BUT THIS IS JUST A SIMPLE RECON FLIGHT. WE'LL BE BACK BEFORE YOU KNOW IT.
THE LIEUTENANT'S CONCERN IS VALID, CAPTAIN.
SHOULD WE ENCOUNTER ANY UNFORESEEN OBSTACLES WE WILL HAVE NO MEANS OF CONTACTING ENTERPRISE.
WHY IS EVERYBODY ALWAYS GIVING ME THE WORST-CASE SCENARIO?
"MR. SULU!"
"YES, CAPTAIN?"
"AVOID ANY UNFORESEEN OBSTACLES. THAT'S AN ORDER!"
"WITH PLEASURE, SIR."

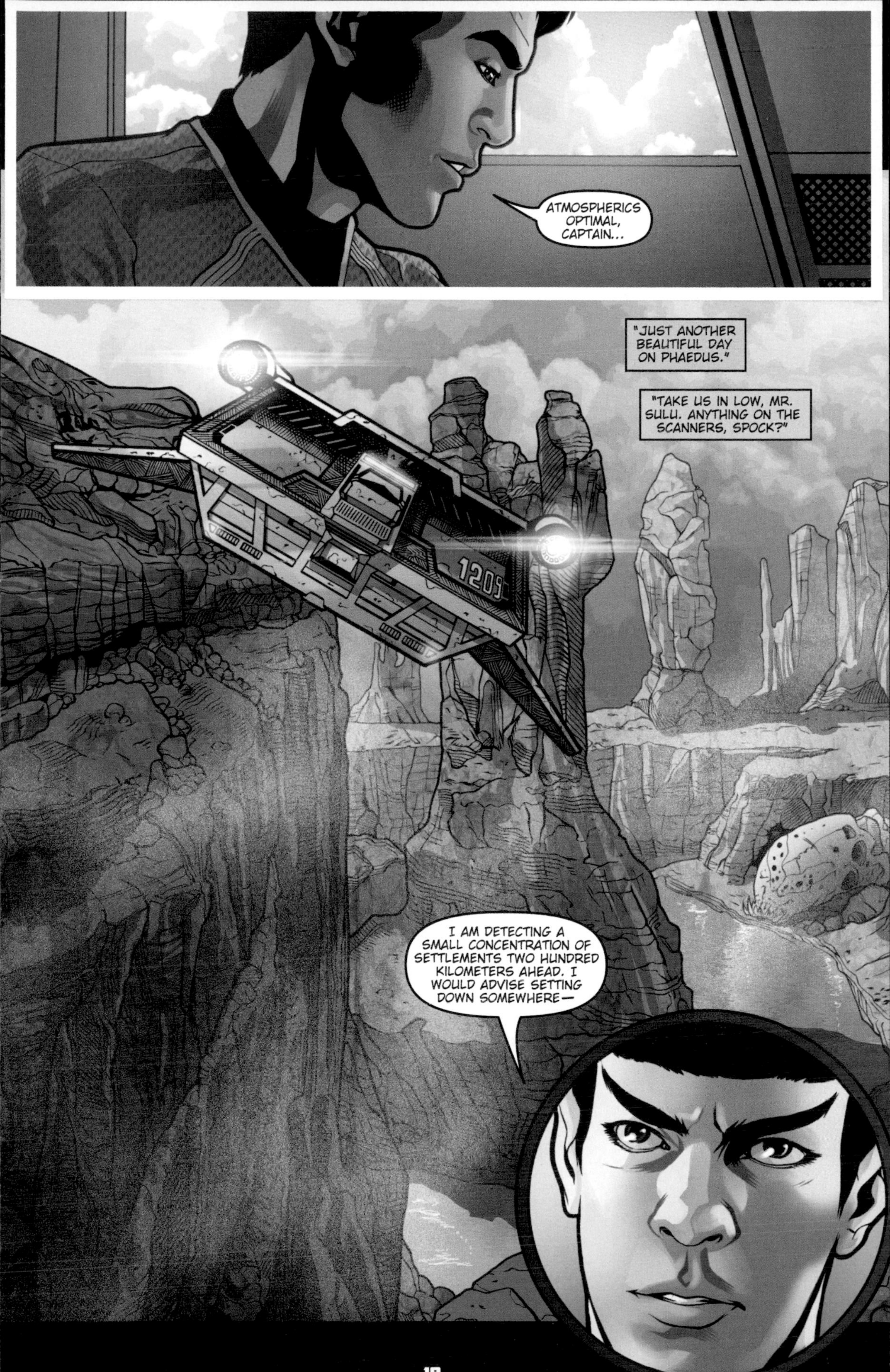
ATMOSPHERICS OPTIMAL, CAPTAIN...
"JUST ANOTHER BEAUTIFUL DAY ON PHAEDUS."
"TAKE US IN LOW, MR. SULU. ANYTHING ON THE SCANNERS, SPOCK?"
1209
I AM DETECTING A SMALL CONCENTRATION OF SETTLEMENTS TWO HUNDRED KILOMETERS AHEAD. I WOULD ADVISE SETTING DOWN SOMEWHERE—

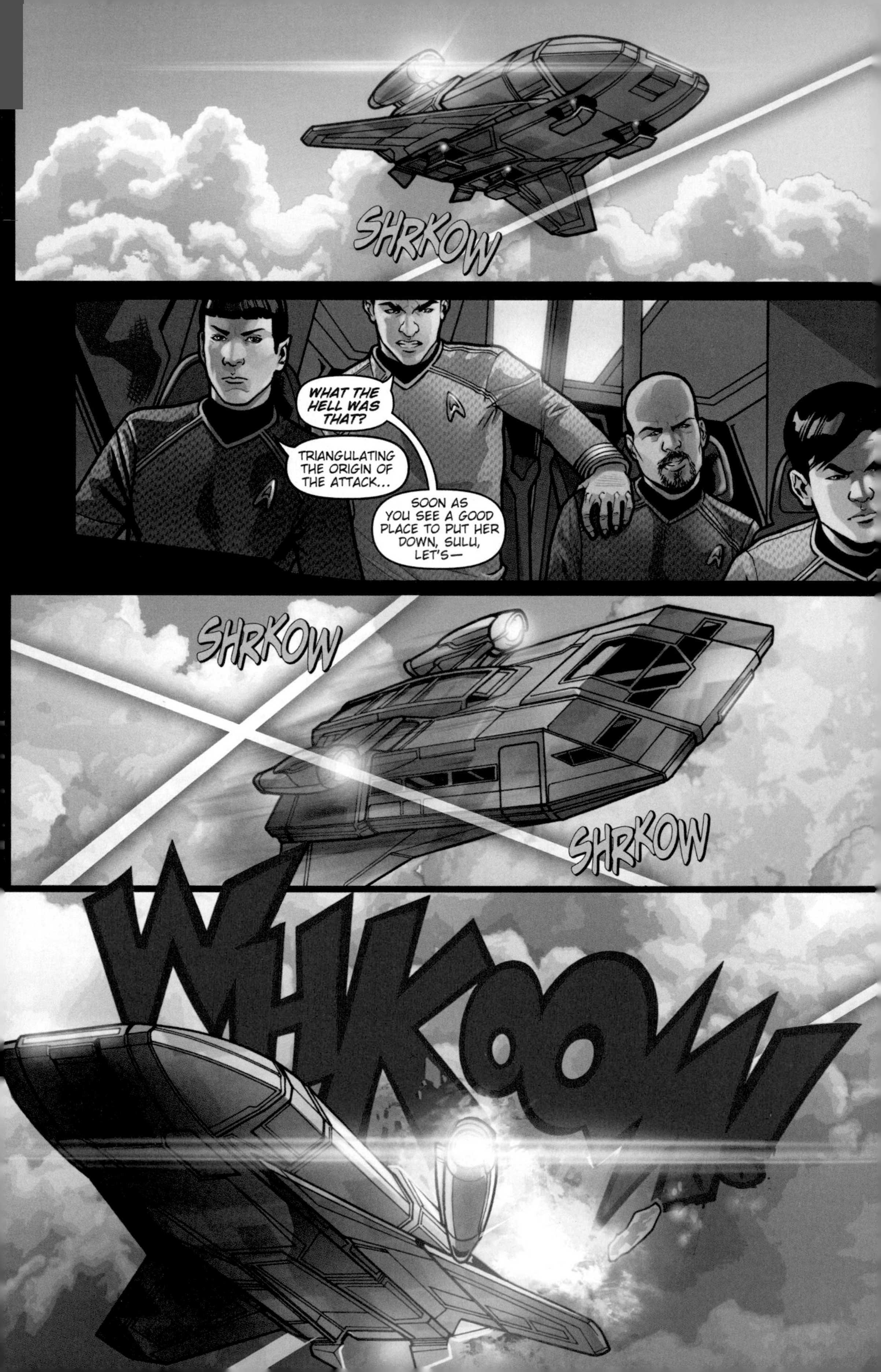
SHRKOW
WHAT THE HELL WAS THAT?
TRIANGULATING THE ORIGIN OF THE ATTACK...
SOON AS YOU SEE A GOOD PLACE TO PUT HER DOWN, SULU, LET'S—
SHRKOW
SHRKOW
WHKOOOM

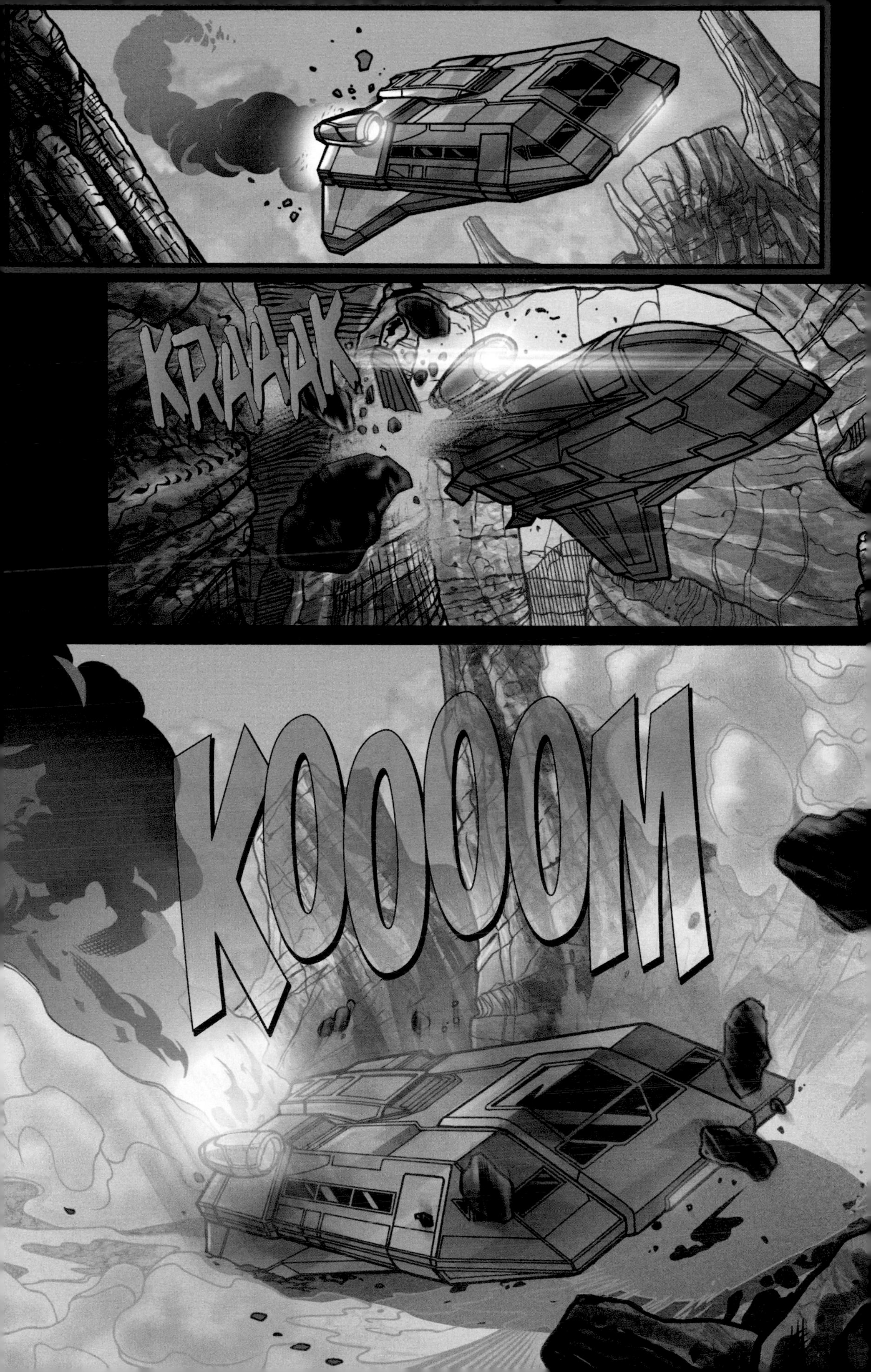
KRAAAK
KOOOOM

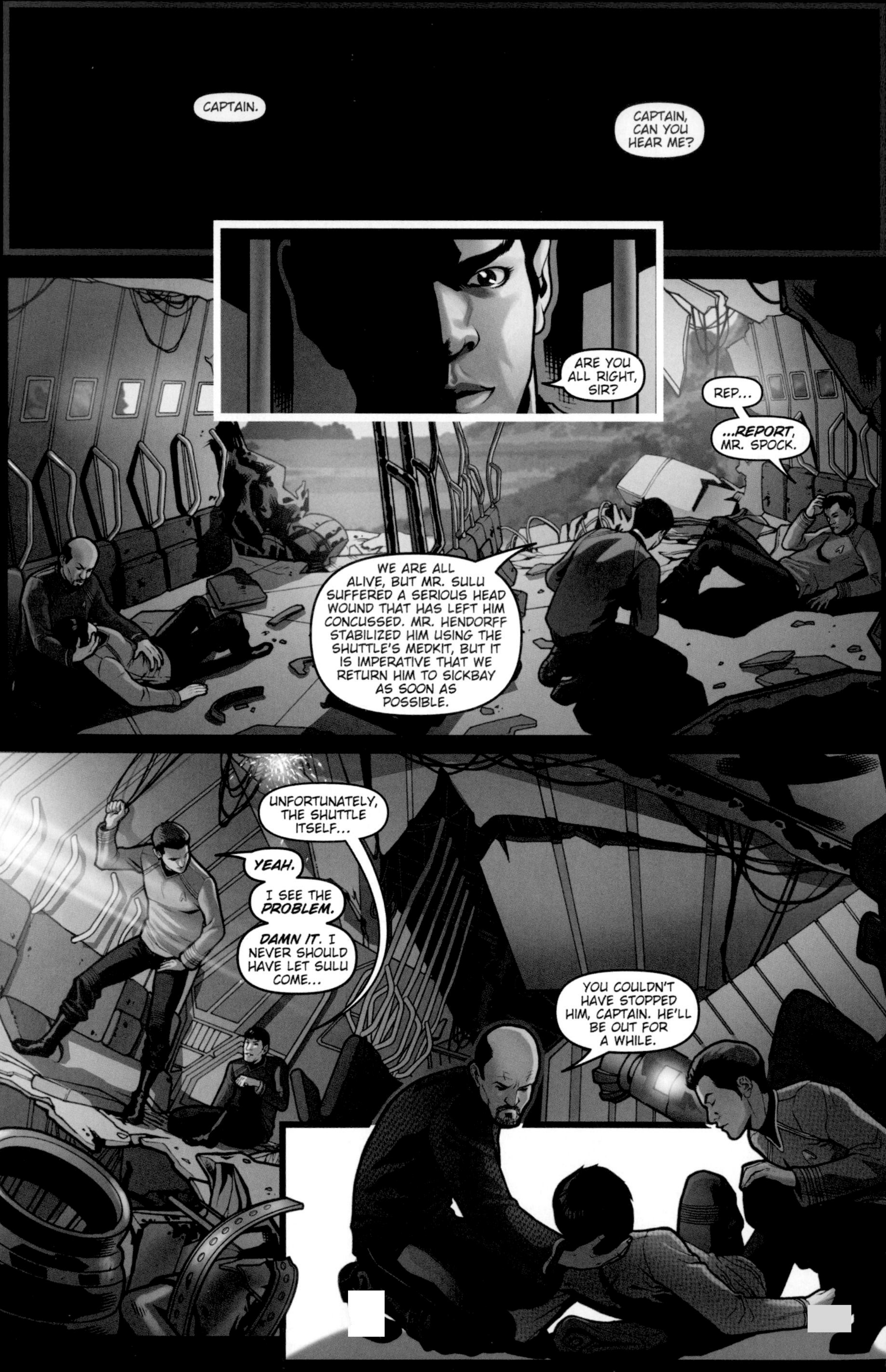
CAPTAIN.
CAPTAIN, CAN YOU HEAR ME?
ARE YOU ALL RIGHT, SIR?
REP...
...REPORT, MR. SPOCK.
WE ARE ALL ALIVE, BUT MR. SULU SUFFERED A SERIOUS HEAD WOUND THAT HAS LEFT HIM CONCUSSED. MR. HENDORFF STABILIZED HIM USING THE SHUTTLE'S MEDKIT, BUT IT IS IMPERATIVE THAT WE RETURN HIM TO SICKBAY AS SOON AS POSSIBLE.
UNFORTUNATELY, THE SHUTTLE ITSELF...
YEAH.
I SEE THE PROBLEM.
DAMN IT. I NEVER SHOULD HAVE LET SULU COME...
YOU COULDN'T HAVE STOPPED HIM, CAPTAIN. HE'LL BE OUT FOR A WHILE.

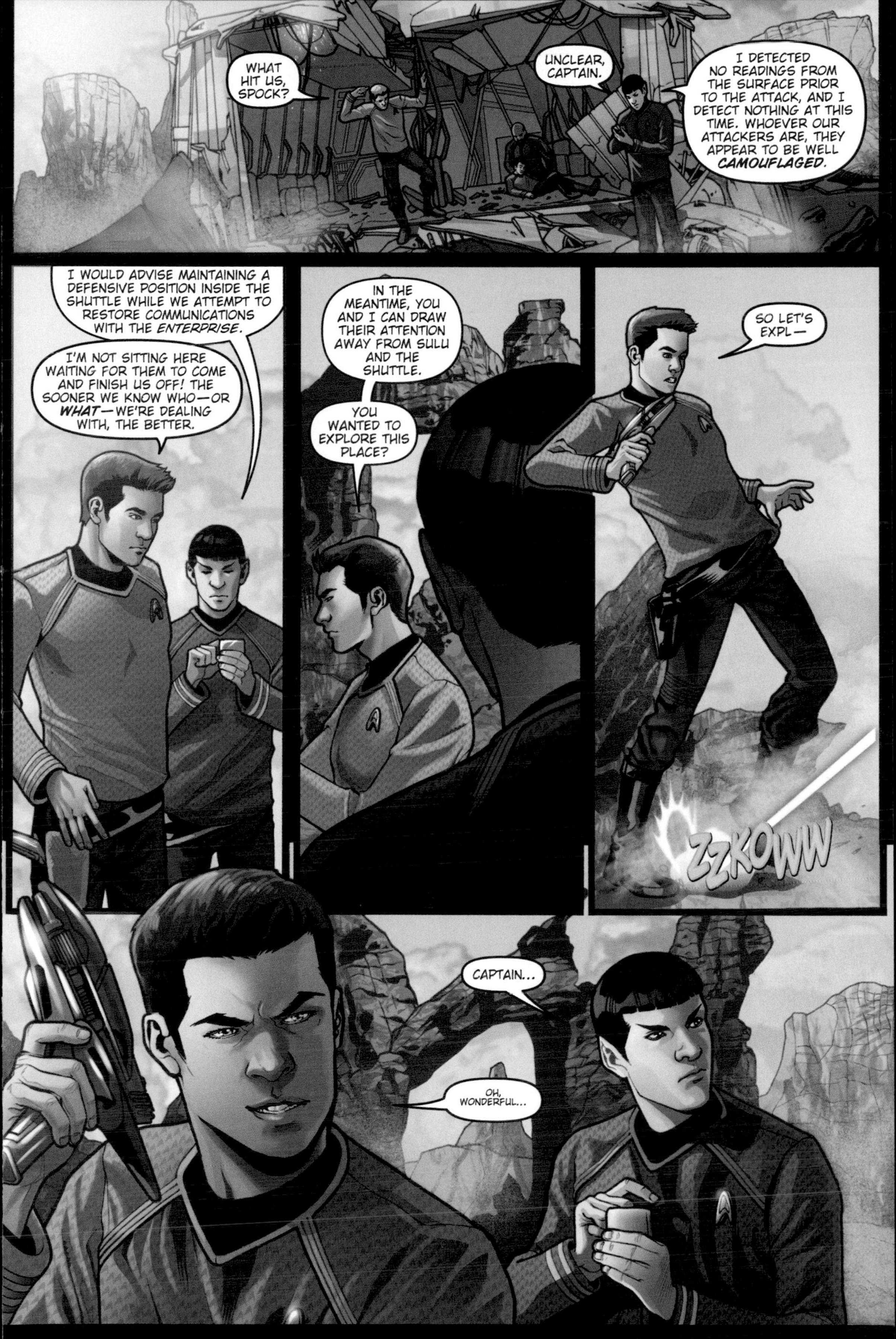
WHAT HIT US, SPOCK?
UNCLEAR, CAPTAIN.
I DETECTED NO READINGS FROM THE SURFACE PRIOR TO THE ATTACK, AND I DETECT NOTHING AT THIS TIME. WHOEVER OUR ATTACKERS ARE, THEY APPEAR TO BE WELL **CAMOUFLAGED**.
I WOULD ADVISE MAINTAINING A DEFENSIVE POSITION INSIDE THE SHUTTLE WHILE WE ATTEMPT TO RESTORE COMMUNICATIONS WITH THE *ENTERPRISE*.
I'M NOT SITTING HERE WAITING FOR THEM TO COME AND FINISH US OFF! THE SOONER WE KNOW WHO—OR ***WHAT***—WE'RE DEALING WITH, THE BETTER.
IN THE MEANTIME, YOU AND I CAN DRAW THEIR ATTENTION AWAY FROM SULU AND THE SHUTTLE.
YOU WANTED TO EXPLORE THIS PLACE?
SO LET'S EXPL—
ZZKOWW
CAPTAIN...
OH, WONDERFUL...

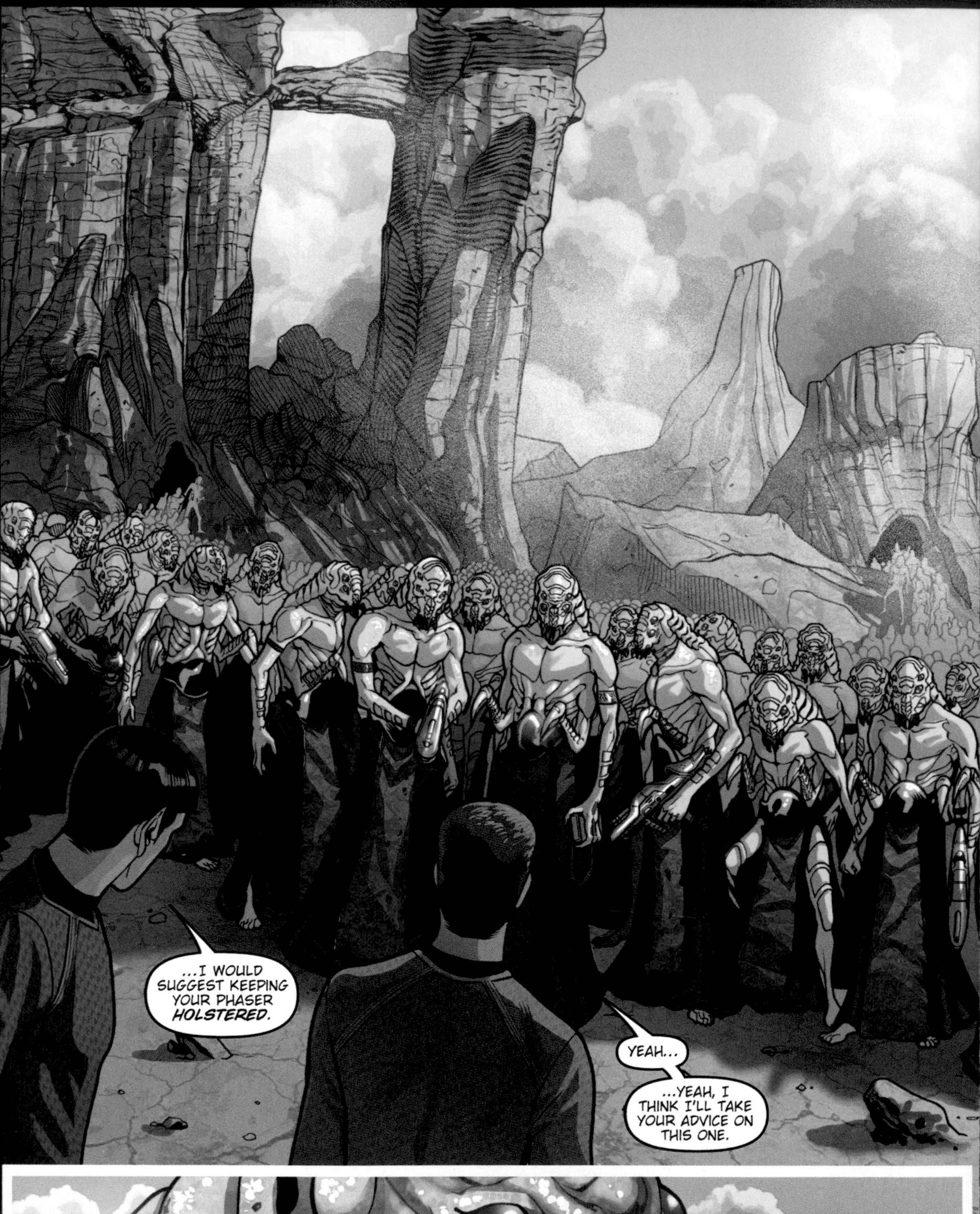
...I WOULD SUGGEST KEEPING YOUR PHASER **HOLSTERED**.
YEAH...
...YEAH, I THINK I'LL TAKE YOUR ADVICE ON THIS ONE.

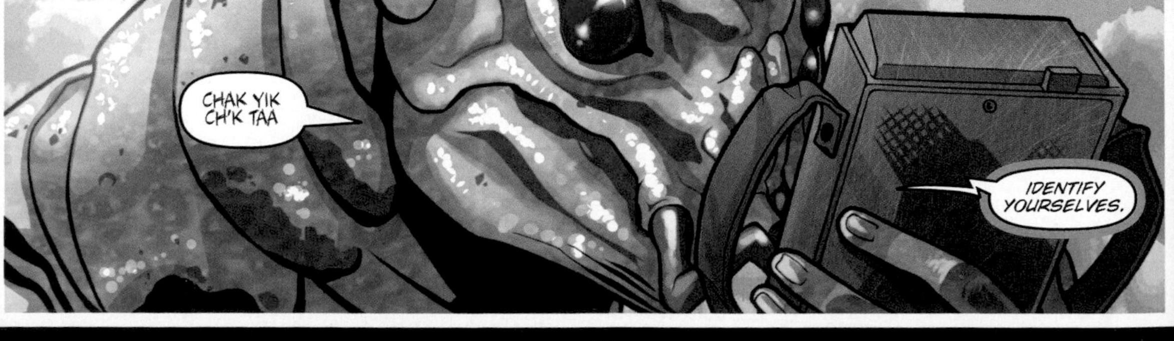
CHAK YIK CH'K TAA
IDENTIFY YOURSELVES.

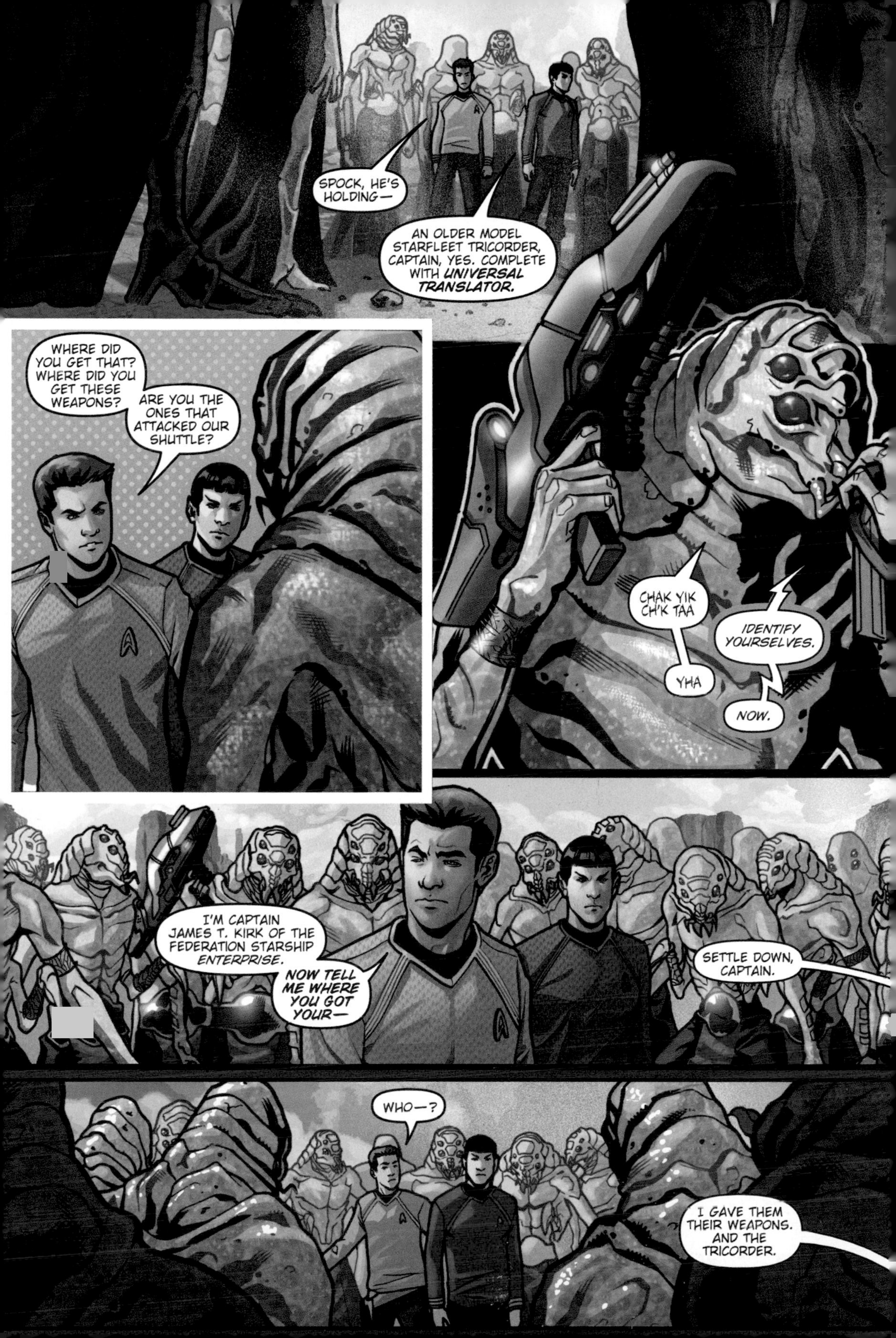

SPOCK, HE'S HOLDING—
AN OLDER MODEL STARFLEET TRICORDER, CAPTAIN, YES. COMPLETE WITH UNIVERSAL TRANSLATOR.
WHERE DID YOU GET THAT? WHERE DID YOU GET THESE WEAPONS?
ARE YOU THE ONES THAT ATTACKED OUR SHUTTLE?
CHAK YIK CH'K TAA
YHA
IDENTIFY YOURSELVES.
NOW.
I'M CAPTAIN JAMES T. KIRK OF THE FEDERATION STARSHIP ENTERPRISE.
NOW TELL ME WHERE YOU GOT YOUR—
SETTLE DOWN, CAPTAIN.
WHO—?
I GAVE THEM THEIR WEAPONS. AND THE TRICORDER.

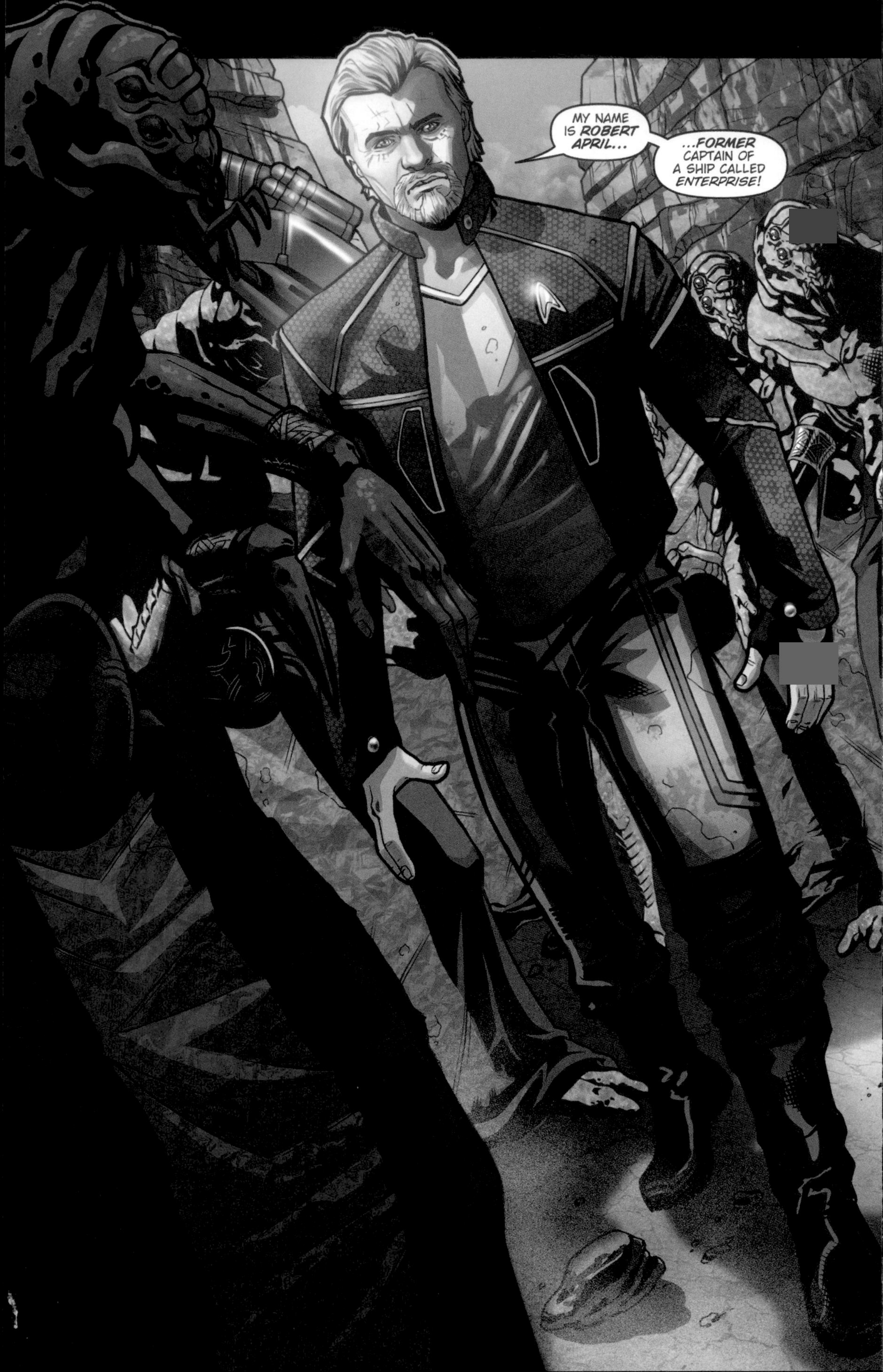
MY NAME IS ***ROBERT APRIL...***
*...**FORMER*** CAPTAIN OF A SHIP CALLED ***ENTERPRISE!***

Art by Erfan Fajar
Colors by Stellar Labs

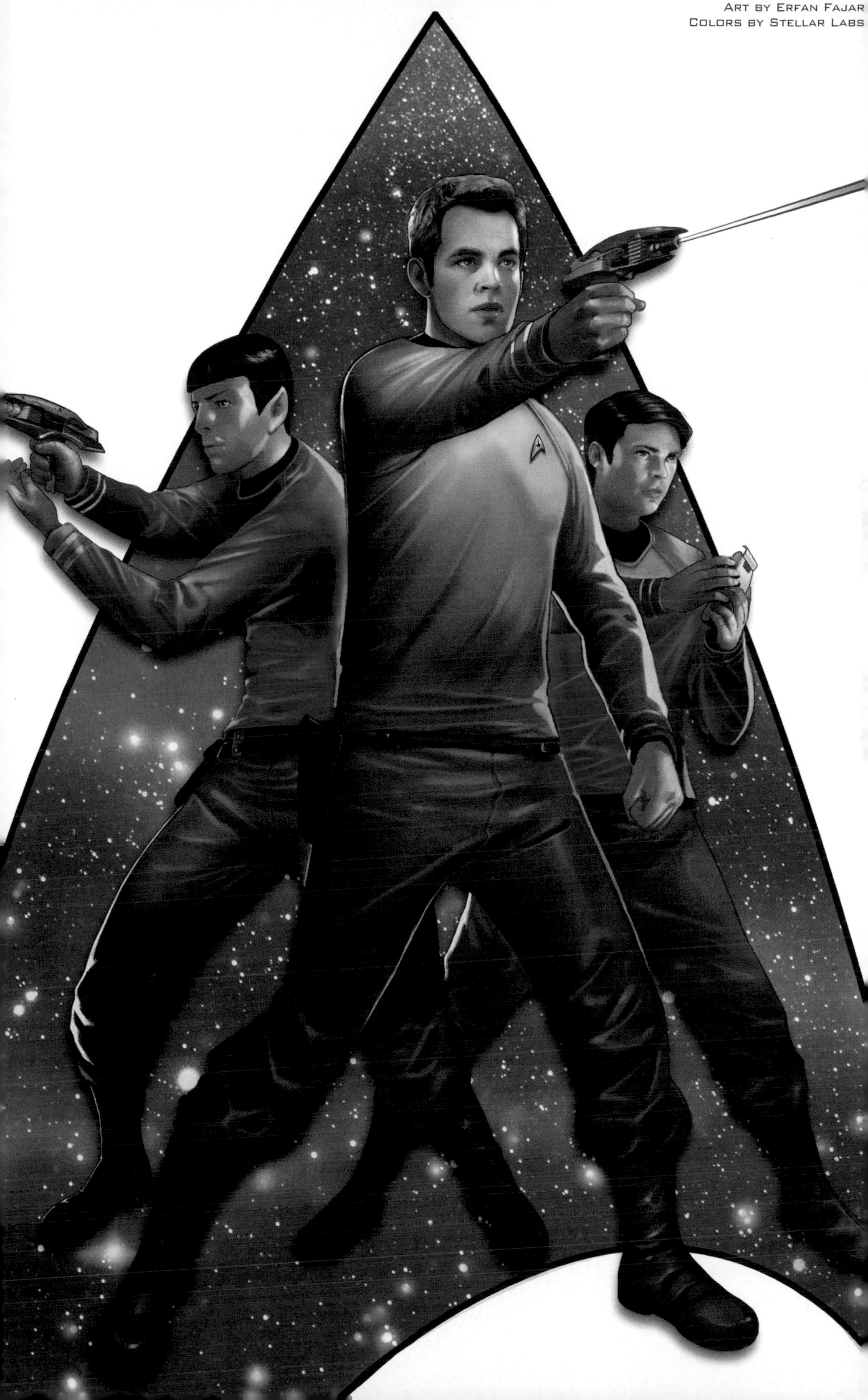

Art by David Messina
Colors by Claudia Scarletgothica

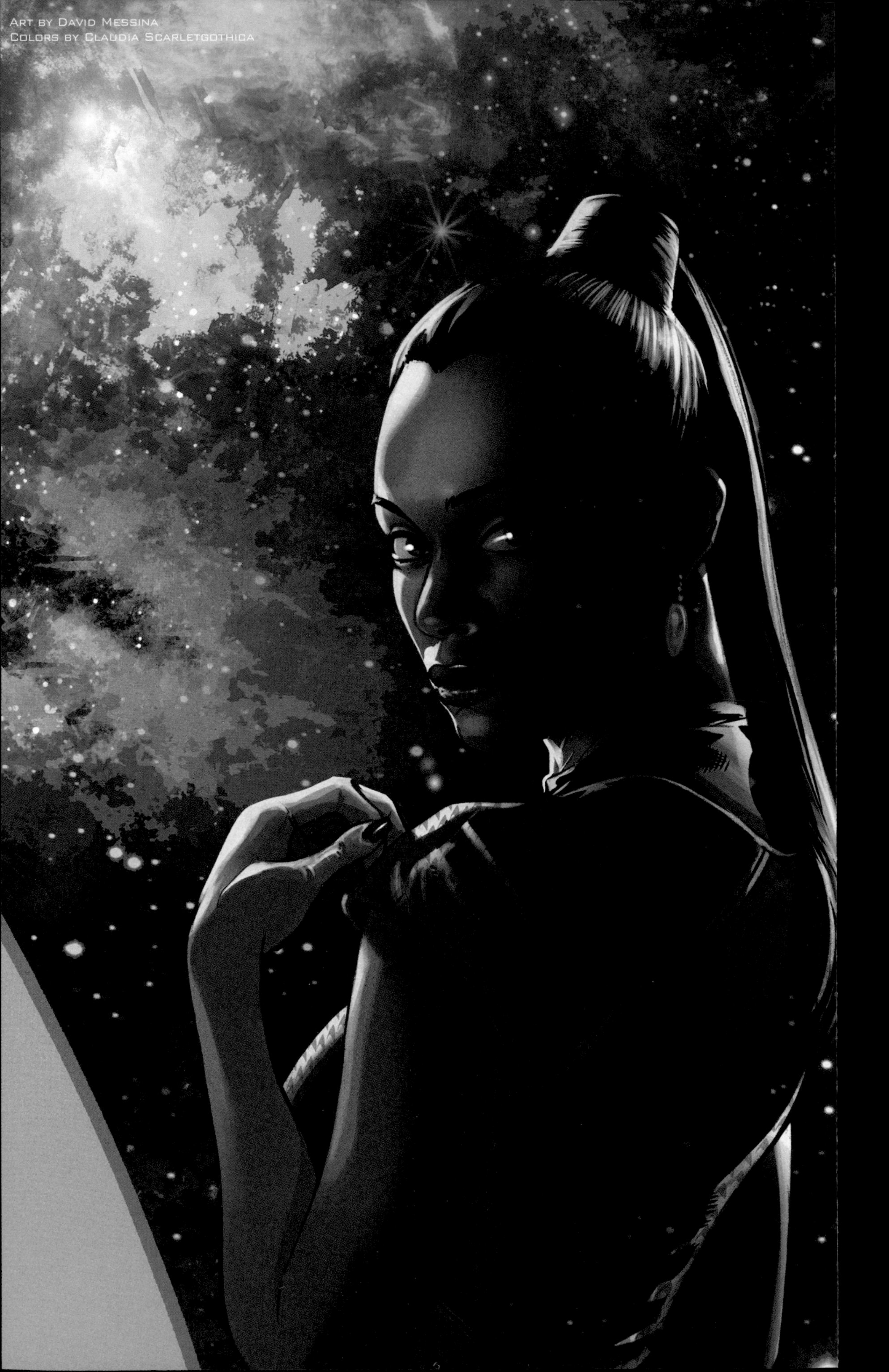

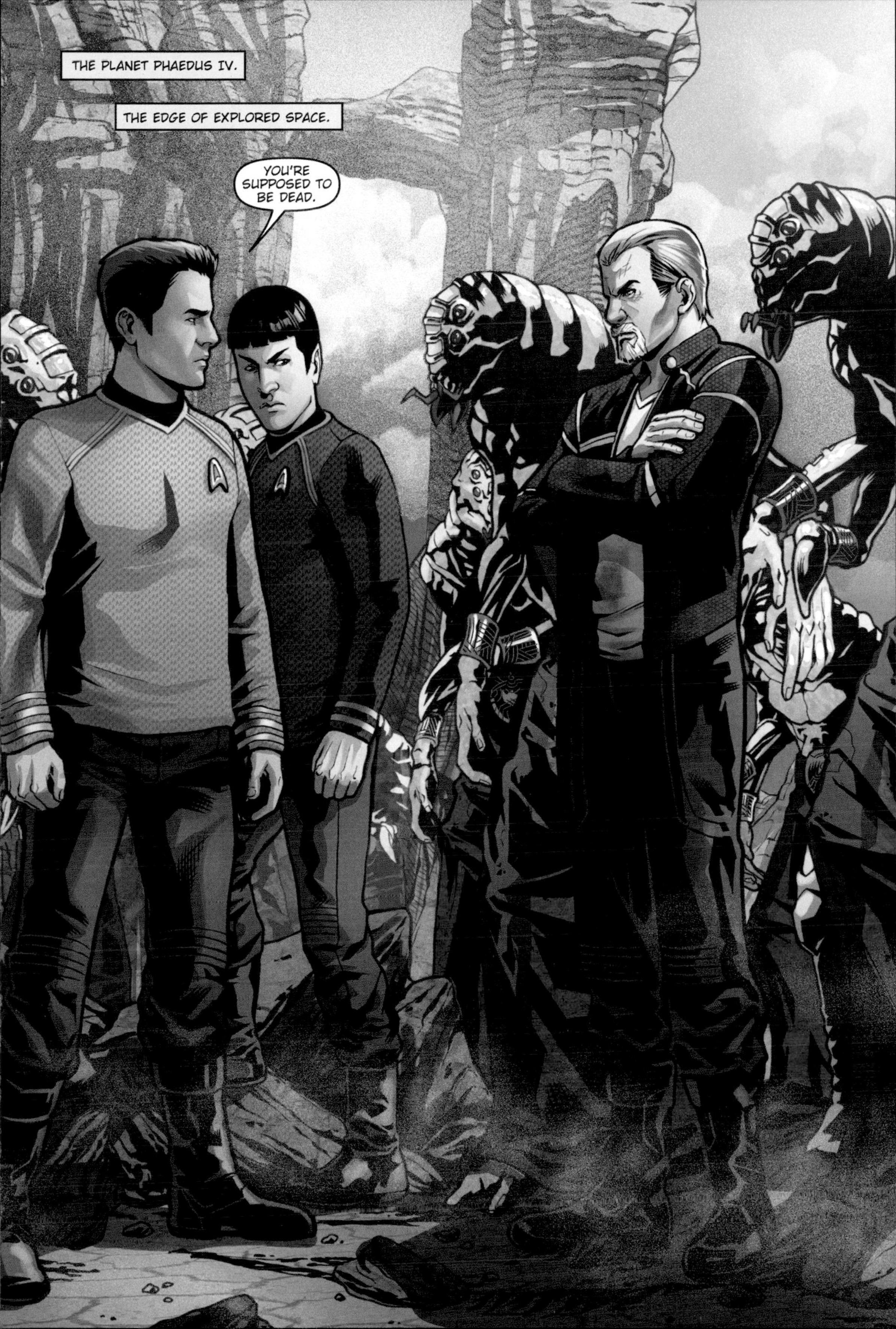
THE PLANET PHAEDUS IV.
THE EDGE OF EXPLORED SPACE.
YOU'RE SUPPOSED TO BE DEAD.

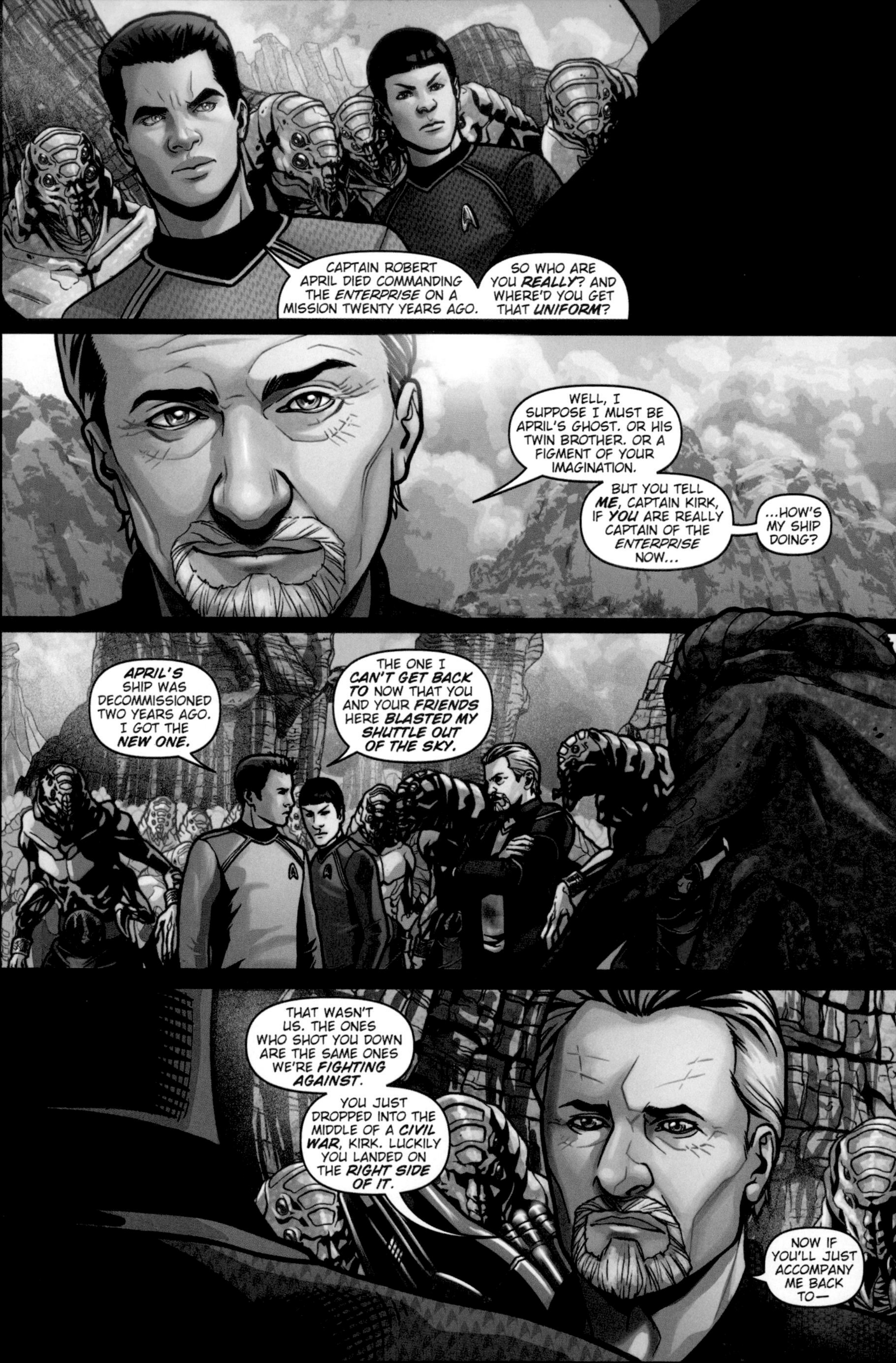
CAPTAIN ROBERT APRIL DIED COMMANDING THE ENTERPRISE ON A MISSION TWENTY YEARS AGO.
SO WHO ARE YOU REALLY? AND WHERE'D YOU GET THAT UNIFORM?
WELL, I SUPPOSE I MUST BE APRIL'S GHOST. OR HIS TWIN BROTHER. OR A FIGMENT OF YOUR IMAGINATION.
BUT YOU TELL ME, CAPTAIN KIRK, IF YOU ARE REALLY CAPTAIN OF THE ENTERPRISE NOW...
...HOW'S MY SHIP DOING?
APRIL'S SHIP WAS DECOMMISSIONED TWO YEARS AGO. I GOT THE NEW ONE.
THE ONE I CAN'T GET BACK TO NOW THAT YOU AND YOUR FRIENDS HERE BLASTED MY SHUTTLE OUT OF THE SKY.
THAT WASN'T US. THE ONES WHO SHOT YOU DOWN ARE THE SAME ONES WE'RE FIGHTING AGAINST.
YOU JUST DROPPED INTO THE MIDDLE OF A CIVIL WAR, KIRK. LUCKILY YOU LANDED ON THE RIGHT SIDE OF IT.
NOW IF YOU'LL JUST ACCOMPANY ME BACK TO—

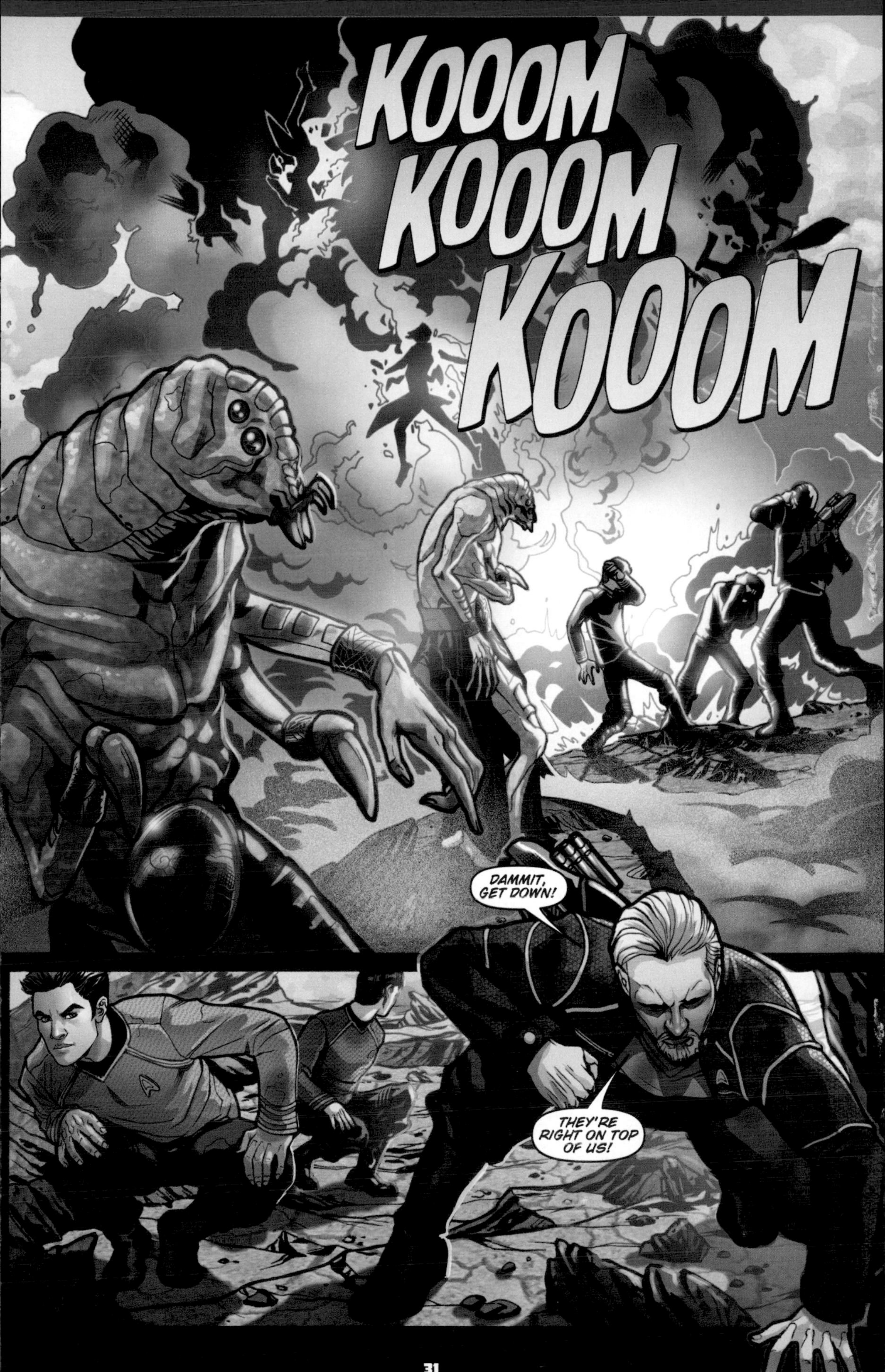
KOOOM
KOOOM
KOOOM
DAMMIT, GET DOWN!
THEY'RE RIGHT ON TOP OF US!

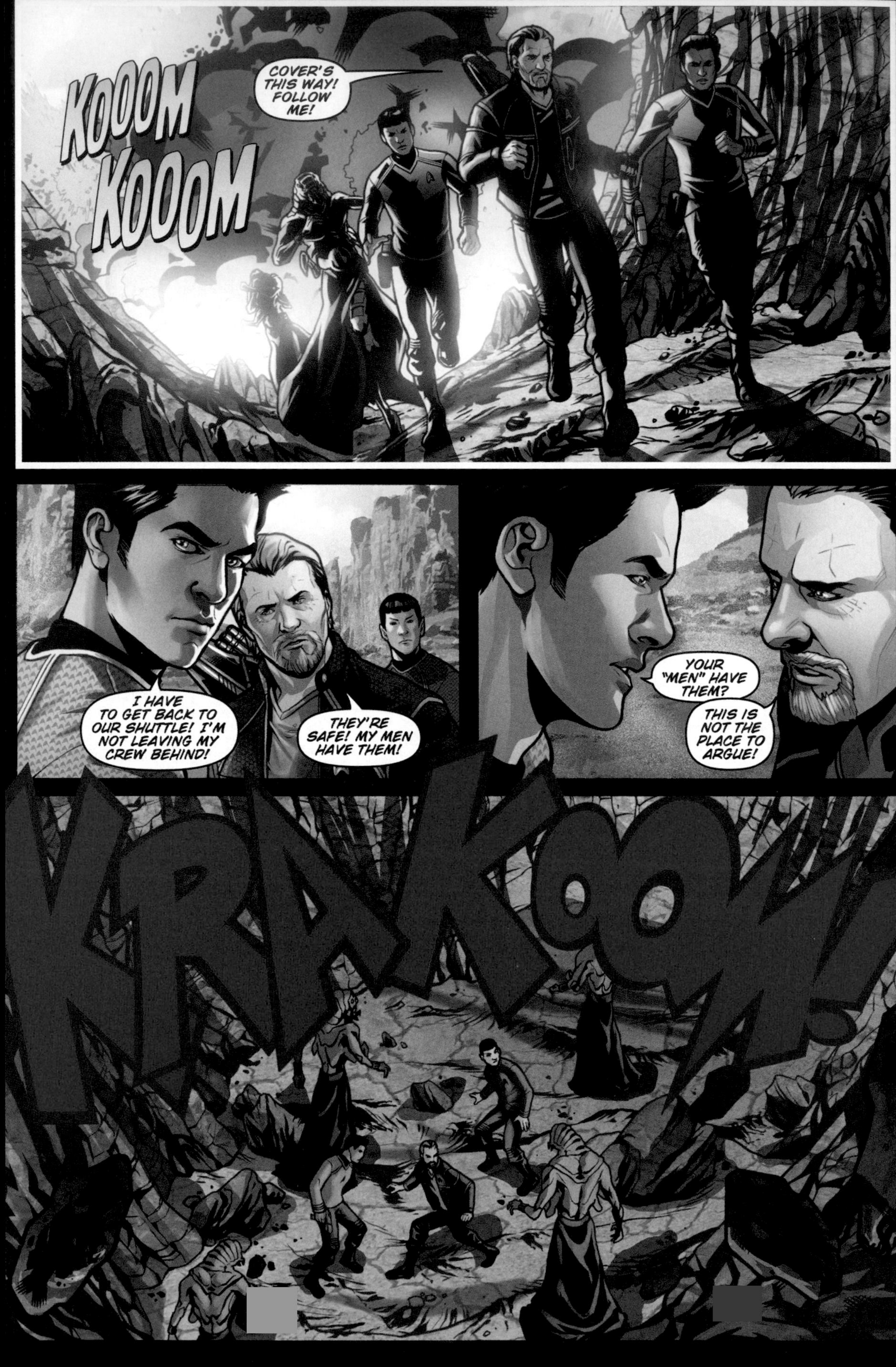
KOOOM KOOOM
COVER'S THIS WAY! FOLLOW ME!
I HAVE TO GET BACK TO OUR SHUTTLE! I'M NOT LEAVING MY CREW BEHIND!
THEY'RE SAFE! MY MEN HAVE THEM!
YOUR "MEN" HAVE THEM?
THIS IS NOT THE PLACE TO ARGUE!
KRAKOOM!

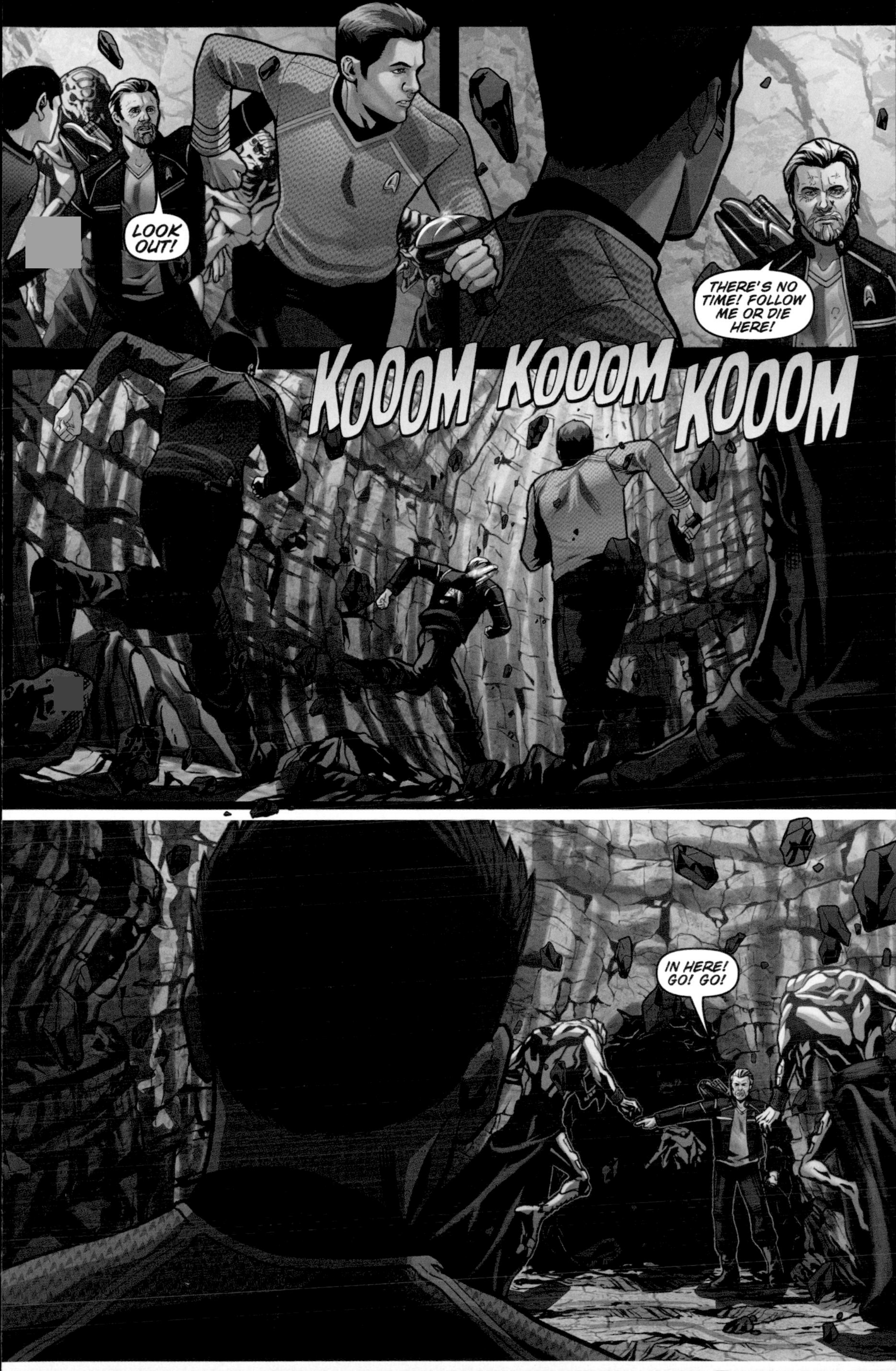
LOOK OUT!
THERE'S NO TIME! FOLLOW ME OR DIE HERE!
KOOOM KOOOM KOOOM
IN HERE! GO! GO!

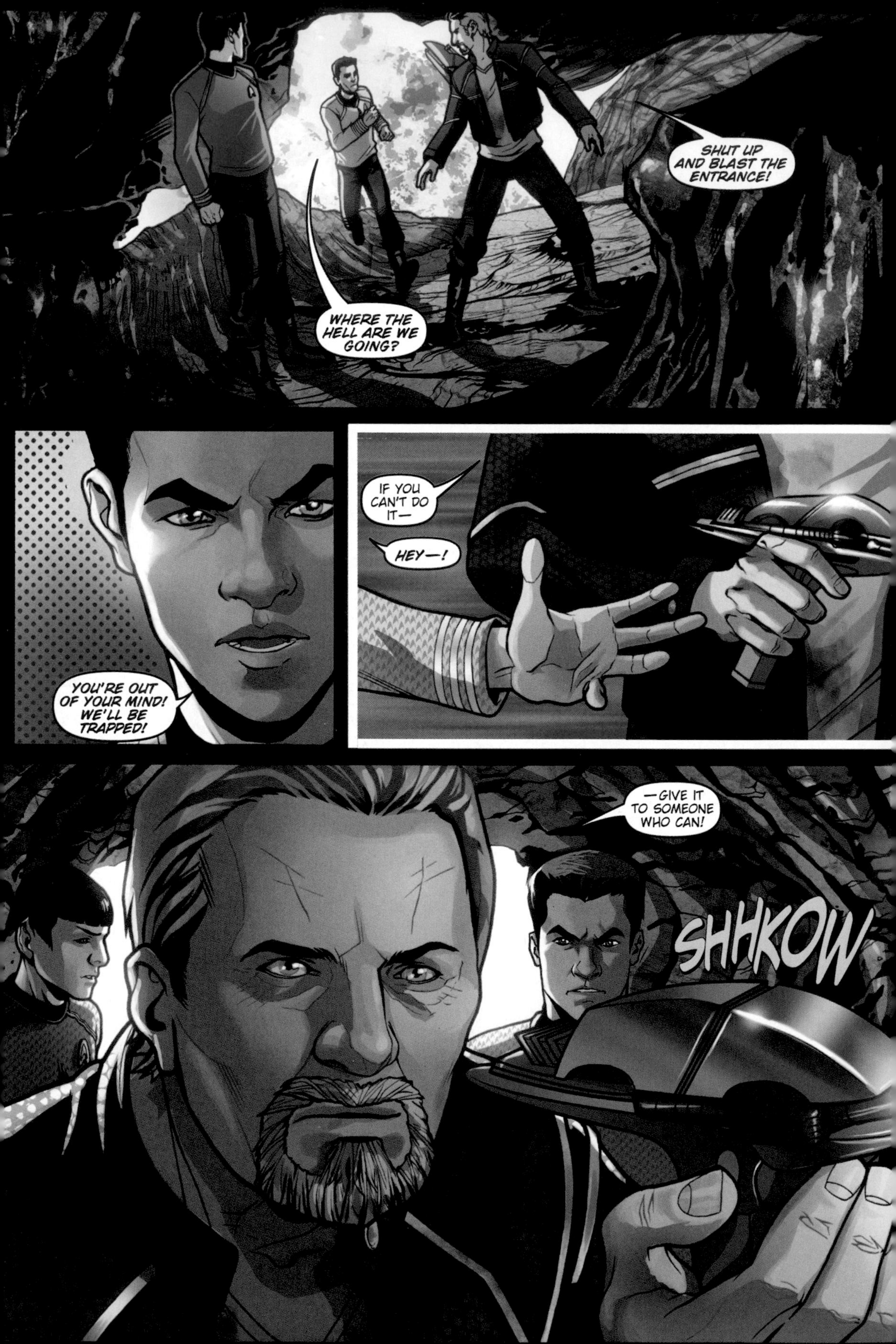
SHUT UP AND BLAST THE ENTRANCE!
WHERE THE HELL ARE WE GOING?
YOU'RE OUT OF YOUR MIND! WE'LL BE TRAPPED!
IF YOU CAN'T DO IT—
HEY—!
—GIVE IT TO SOMEONE WHO CAN!
SHHKOW

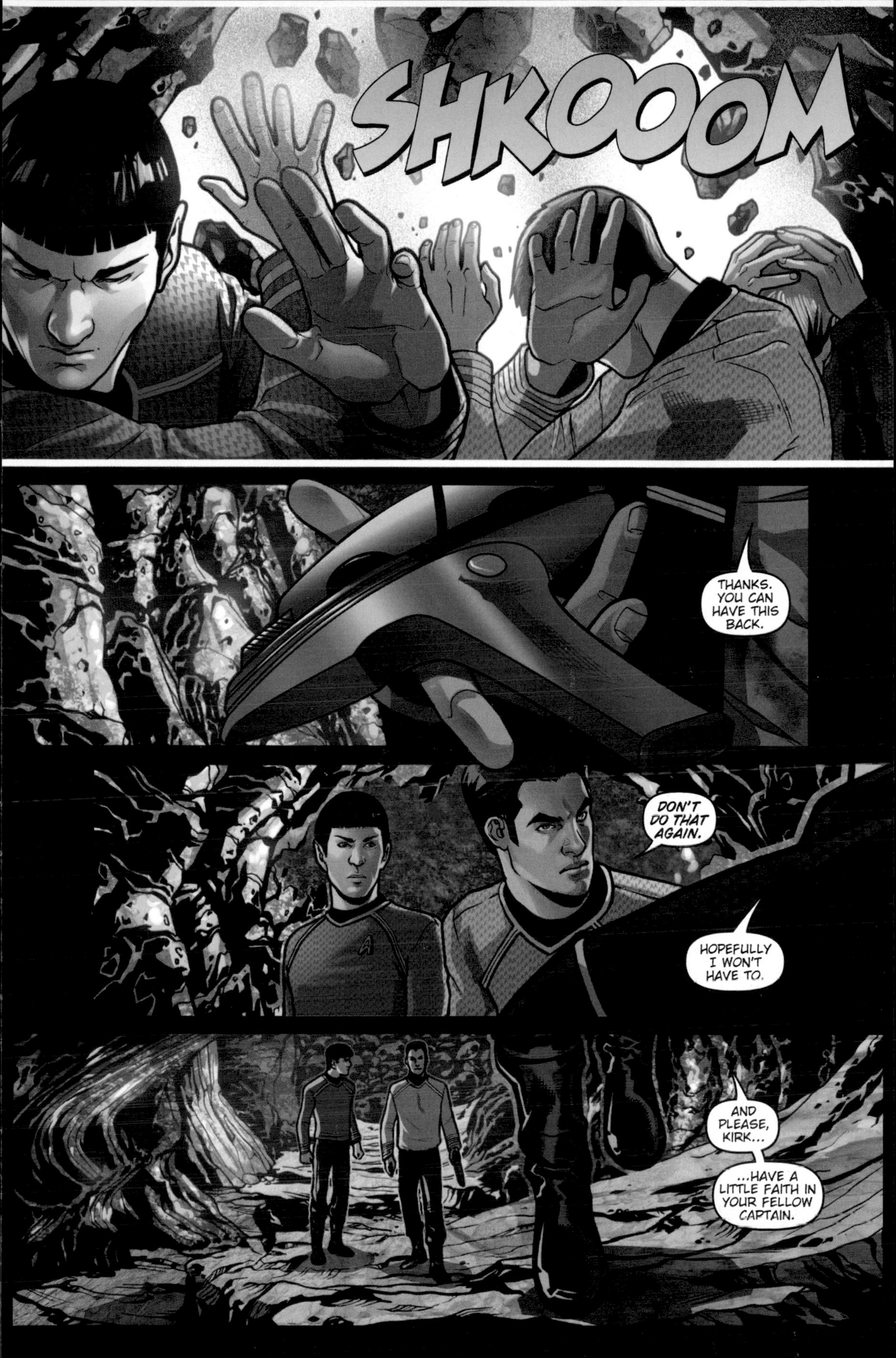
SHKOOOM
THANKS. YOU CAN HAVE THIS BACK.
DON'T DO THAT AGAIN.
HOPEFULLY I WON'T HAVE TO.
AND PLEASE, KIRK...
...HAVE A LITTLE FAITH IN YOUR FELLOW CAPTAIN.

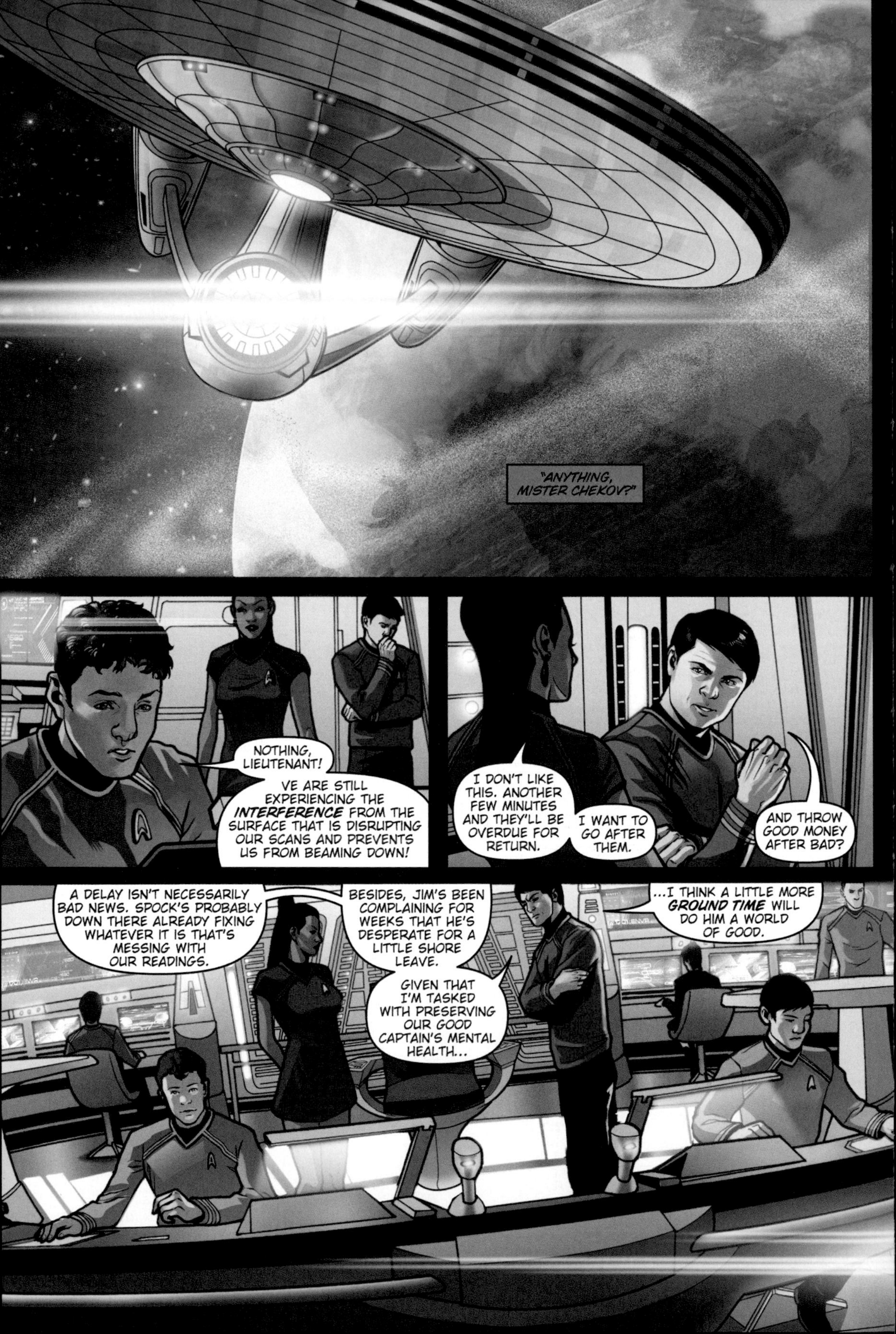
"ANYTHING, MISTER CHEKOV?"
NOTHING, LIEUTENANT!
VE ARE STILL EXPERIENCING THE INTERFERENCE FROM THE SURFACE THAT IS DISRUPTING OUR SCANS AND PREVENTS US FROM BEAMING DOWN!
I DON'T LIKE THIS. ANOTHER FEW MINUTES AND THEY'LL BE OVERDUE FOR RETURN.
I WANT TO GO AFTER THEM.
AND THROW GOOD MONEY AFTER BAD?
A DELAY ISN'T NECESSARILY BAD NEWS. SPOCK'S PROBABLY DOWN THERE ALREADY FIXING WHATEVER IT IS THAT'S MESSING WITH OUR READINGS.
BESIDES, JIM'S BEEN COMPLAINING FOR WEEKS THAT HE'S DESPERATE FOR A LITTLE SHORE LEAVE.
GIVEN THAT I'M TASKED WITH PRESERVING OUR GOOD CAPTAIN'S MENTAL HEALTH...
...I THINK A LITTLE MORE GROUND TIME WILL DO HIM A WORLD OF GOOD.

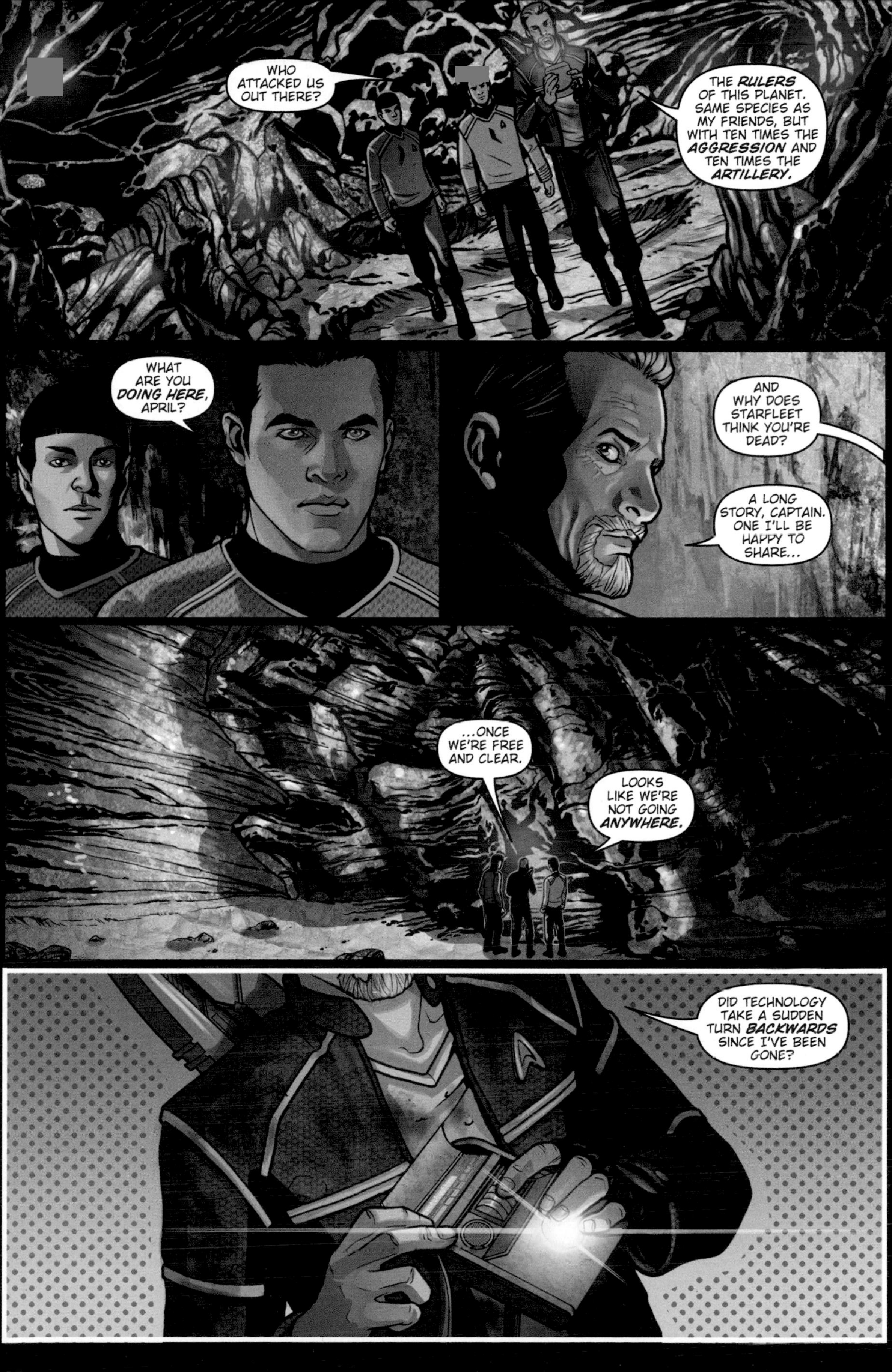
WHO ATTACKED US OUT THERE?
THE *RULERS* OF THIS PLANET. SAME SPECIES AS MY FRIENDS, BUT WITH TEN TIMES THE *AGGRESSION* AND TEN TIMES THE *ARTILLERY.*
WHAT ARE YOU *DOING HERE*, APRIL?
AND WHY DOES STARFLEET THINK YOU'RE DEAD?
A LONG STORY, CAPTAIN. ONE I'LL BE HAPPY TO SHARE...
...ONCE WE'RE FREE AND CLEAR.
LOOKS LIKE WE'RE NOT GOING *ANYWHERE.*
DID TECHNOLOGY TAKE A SUDDEN TURN *BACKWARDS* SINCE I'VE BEEN GONE?

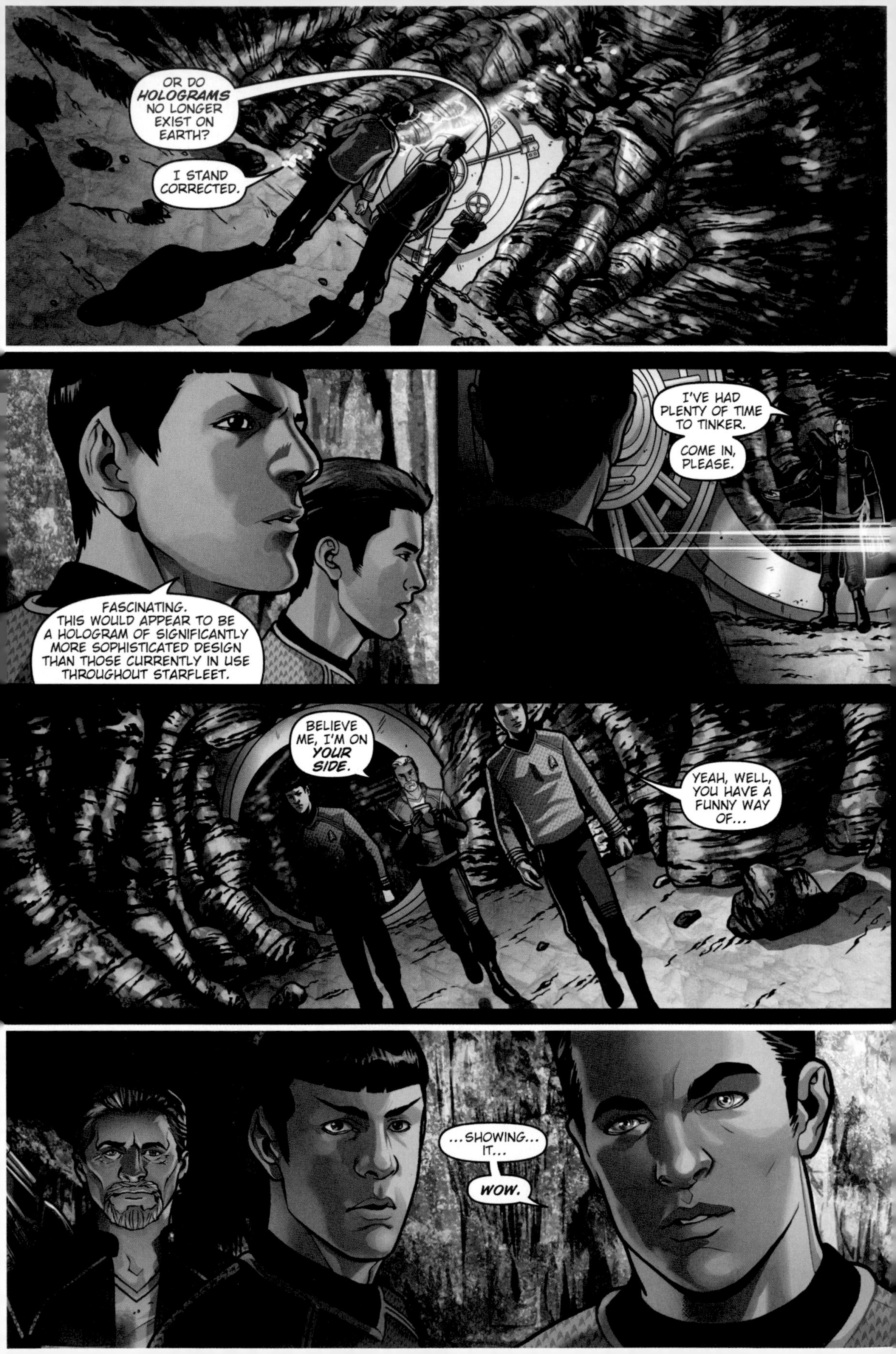
OR DO HOLOGRAMS NO LONGER EXIST ON EARTH?
I STAND CORRECTED.
FASCINATING. THIS WOULD APPEAR TO BE A HOLOGRAM OF SIGNIFICANTLY MORE SOPHISTICATED DESIGN THAN THOSE CURRENTLY IN USE THROUGHOUT STARFLEET.
I'VE HAD PLENTY OF TIME TO TINKER.
COME IN, PLEASE.
BELIEVE ME, I'M ON YOUR SIDE.
YEAH, WELL, YOU HAVE A FUNNY WAY OF...
...SHOWING... IT...
WOW.

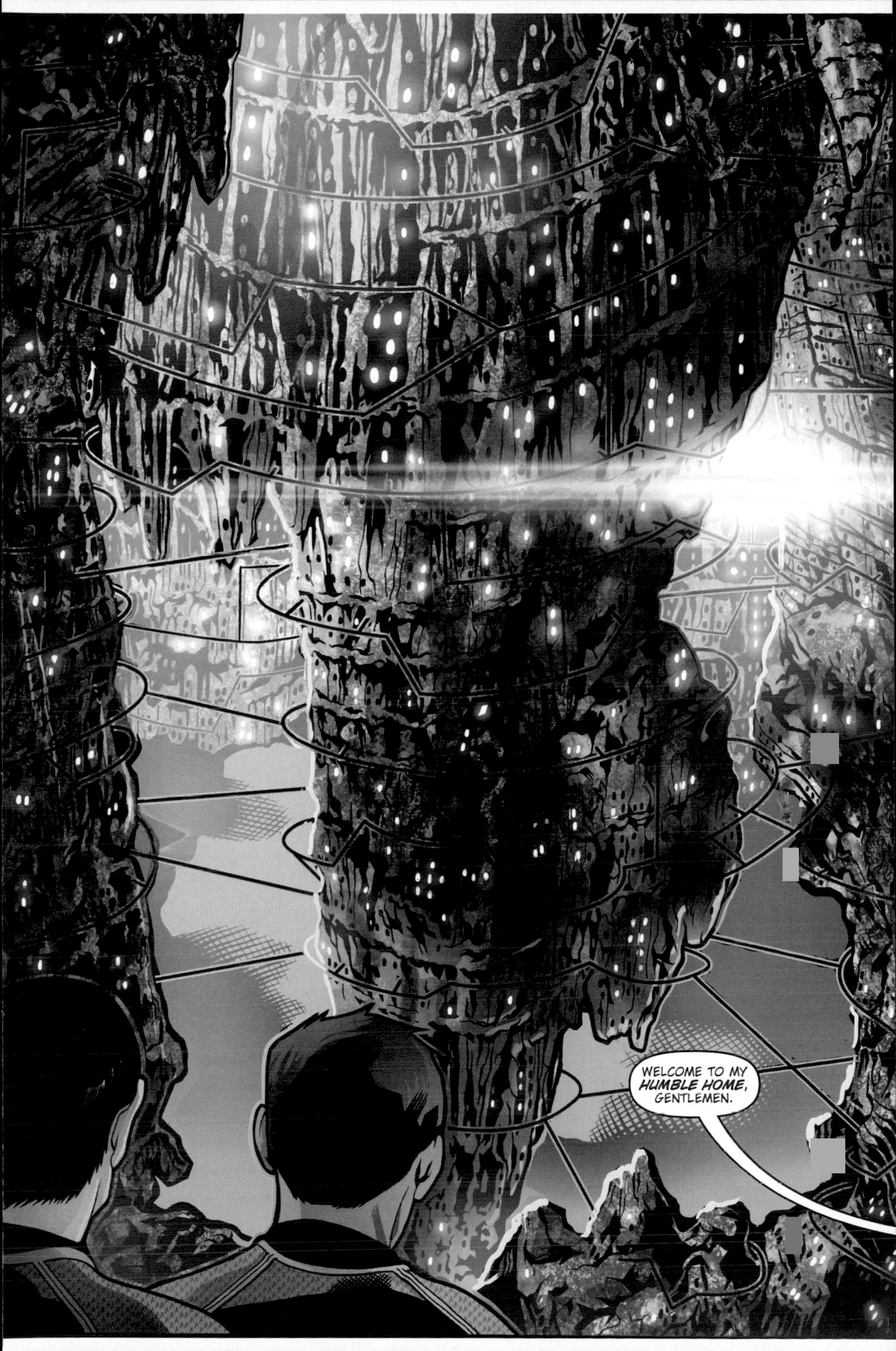
WELCOME TO MY HUMBLE HOME, GENTLEMEN.

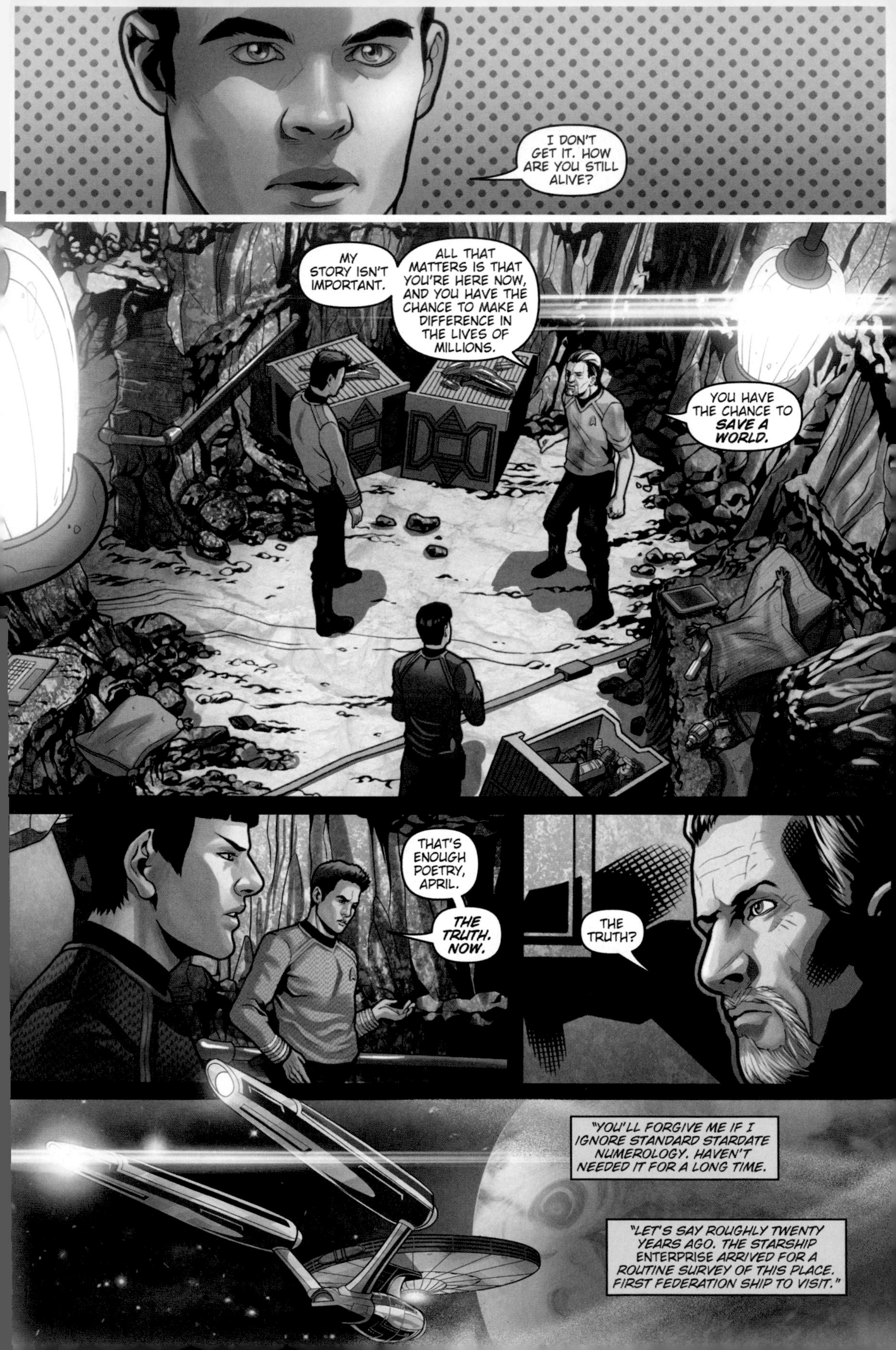
I DON'T GET IT. HOW ARE YOU STILL ALIVE?
MY STORY ISN'T IMPORTANT.
ALL THAT MATTERS IS THAT YOU'RE HERE NOW, AND YOU HAVE THE CHANCE TO MAKE A DIFFERENCE IN THE LIVES OF MILLIONS.
YOU HAVE THE CHANCE TO SAVE A WORLD.
THAT'S ENOUGH POETRY, APRIL.
THE TRUTH. NOW.
THE TRUTH?
"YOU'LL FORGIVE ME IF I IGNORE STANDARD STARDATE NUMEROLOGY. HAVEN'T NEEDED IT FOR A LONG TIME.
"LET'S SAY ROUGHLY TWENTY YEARS AGO. THE STARSHIP ENTERPRISE ARRIVED FOR A ROUTINE SURVEY OF THIS PLACE. FIRST FEDERATION SHIP TO VISIT."

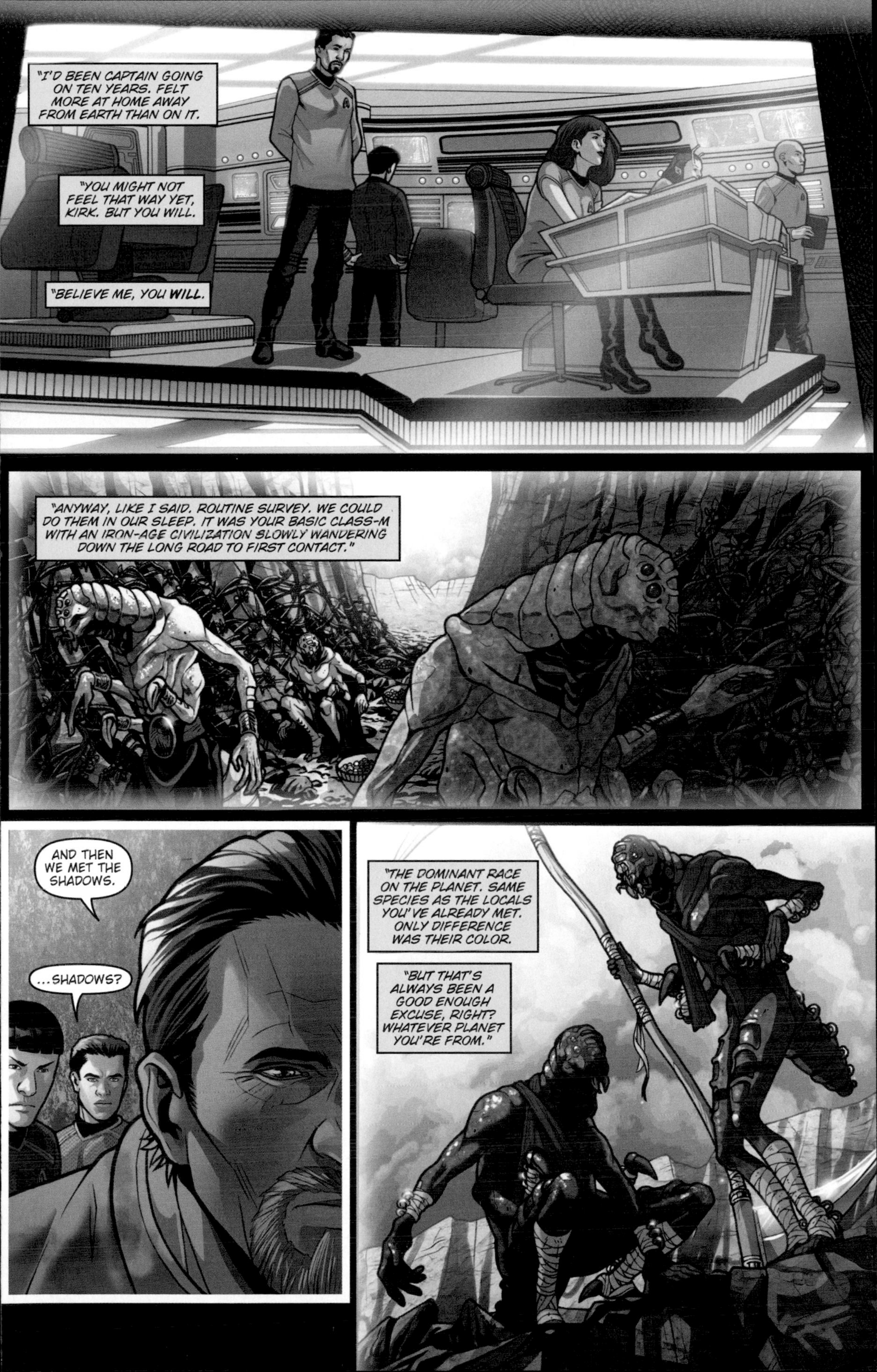
"I'D BEEN CAPTAIN GOING ON TEN YEARS. FELT MORE AT HOME AWAY FROM EARTH THAN ON IT.
"YOU MIGHT NOT FEEL THAT WAY YET, KIRK. BUT YOU WILL.
"BELIEVE ME, YOU WILL.
"ANYWAY, LIKE I SAID. ROUTINE SURVEY. WE COULD DO THEM IN OUR SLEEP. IT WAS YOUR BASIC CLASS-M WITH AN IRON-AGE CIVILIZATION SLOWLY WANDERING DOWN THE LONG ROAD TO FIRST CONTACT."
AND THEN WE MET THE SHADOWS.
...SHADOWS?
"THE DOMINANT RACE ON THE PLANET. SAME SPECIES AS THE LOCALS YOU'VE ALREADY MET. ONLY DIFFERENCE WAS THEIR COLOR.
"BUT THAT'S ALWAYS BEEN A GOOD ENOUGH EXCUSE, RIGHT? WHATEVER PLANET YOU'RE FROM."

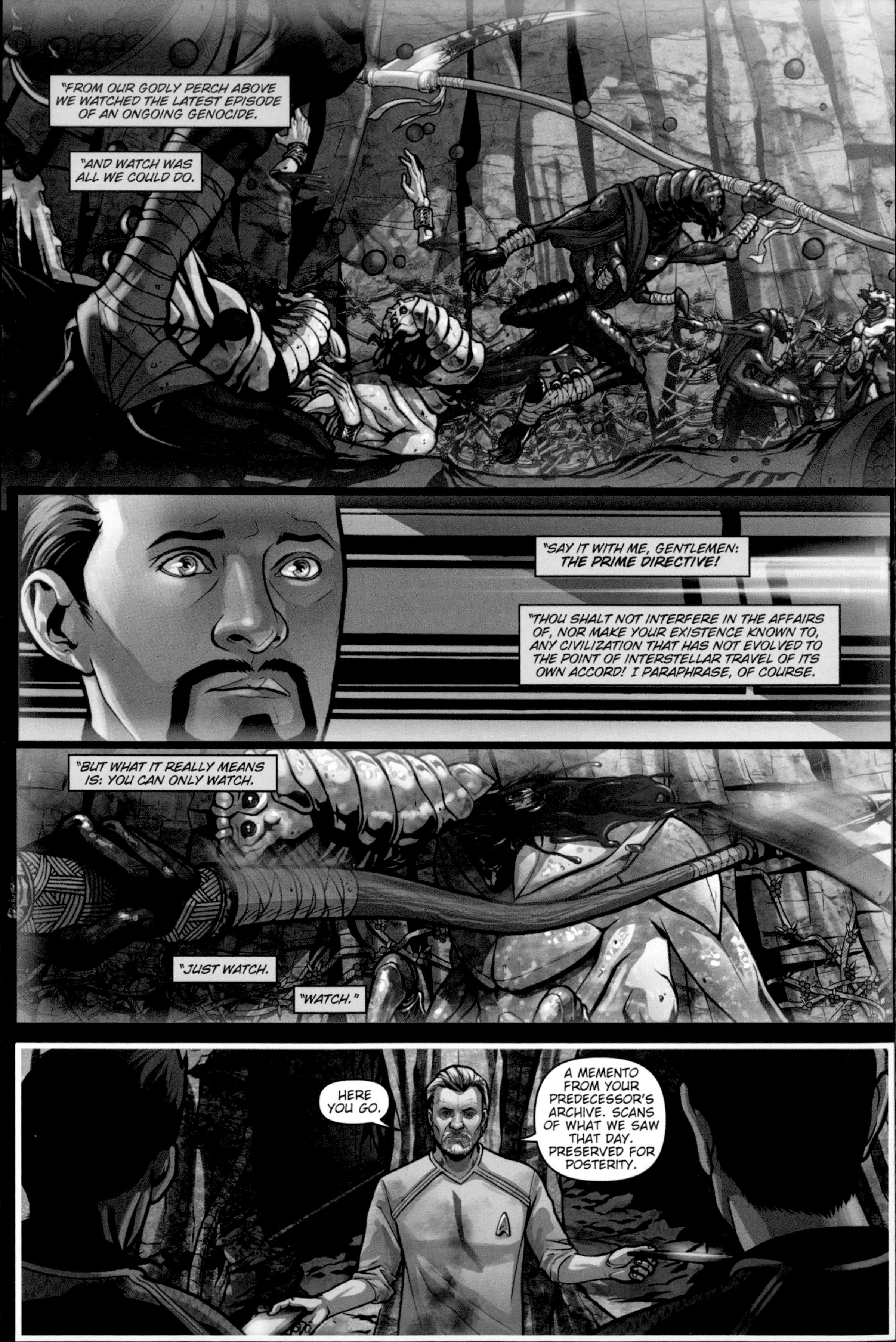
"FROM OUR GODLY PERCH ABOVE WE WATCHED THE LATEST EPISODE OF AN ONGOING GENOCIDE.
"AND WATCH WAS ALL WE COULD DO.
"SAY IT WITH ME, GENTLEMEN: THE PRIME DIRECTIVE!
"THOU SHALT NOT INTERFERE IN THE AFFAIRS OF, NOR MAKE YOUR EXISTENCE KNOWN TO, ANY CIVILIZATION THAT HAS NOT EVOLVED TO THE POINT OF INTERSTELLAR TRAVEL OF ITS OWN ACCORD! I PARAPHRASE, OF COURSE.
"BUT WHAT IT REALLY MEANS IS: YOU CAN ONLY WATCH.
"JUST WATCH.
"WATCH."
HERE YOU GO.
A MEMENTO FROM YOUR PREDECESSOR'S ARCHIVE. SCANS OF WHAT WE SAW THAT DAY. PRESERVED FOR POSTERITY.

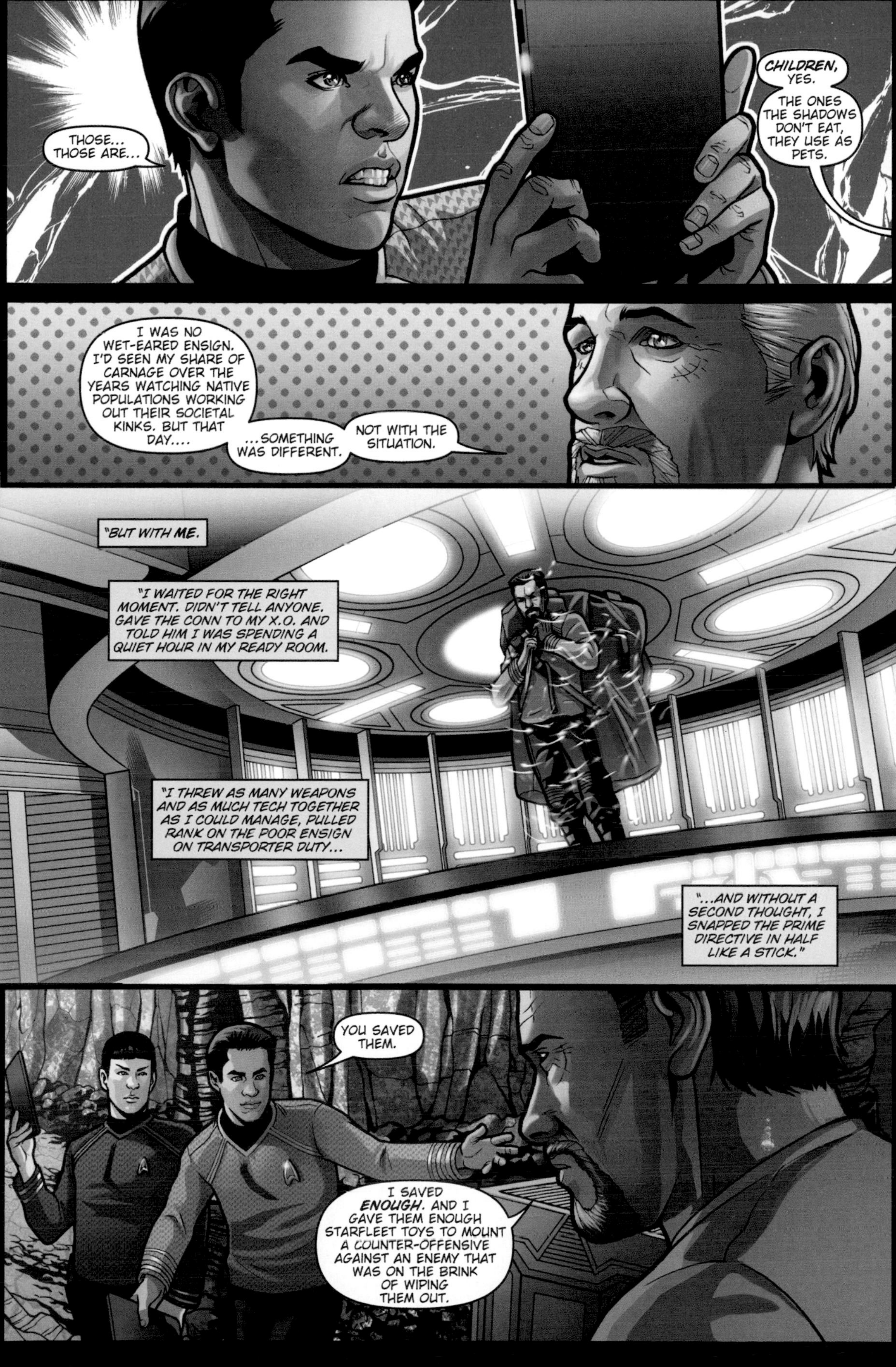
THOSE... THOSE ARE...
CHILDREN, YES.
THE ONES THE SHADOWS DON'T EAT, THEY USE AS PETS.
I WAS NO WET-EARED ENSIGN. I'D SEEN MY SHARE OF CARNAGE OVER THE YEARS WATCHING NATIVE POPULATIONS WORKING OUT THEIR SOCIETAL KINKS. BUT THAT DAY....
...SOMETHING WAS DIFFERENT.
NOT WITH THE SITUATION.
"BUT WITH ME.
"I WAITED FOR THE RIGHT MOMENT. DIDN'T TELL ANYONE. GAVE THE CONN TO MY X.O. AND TOLD HIM I WAS SPENDING A QUIET HOUR IN MY READY ROOM.
"I THREW AS MANY WEAPONS AND AS MUCH TECH TOGETHER AS I COULD MANAGE, PULLED RANK ON THE POOR ENSIGN ON TRANSPORTER DUTY...
"...AND WITHOUT A SECOND THOUGHT, I SNAPPED THE PRIME DIRECTIVE IN HALF LIKE A STICK."
YOU SAVED THEM.
I SAVED ENOUGH. AND I GAVE THEM ENOUGH STARFLEET TOYS TO MOUNT A COUNTER-OFFENSIVE AGAINST AN ENEMY THAT WAS ON THE BRINK OF WIPING THEM OUT.

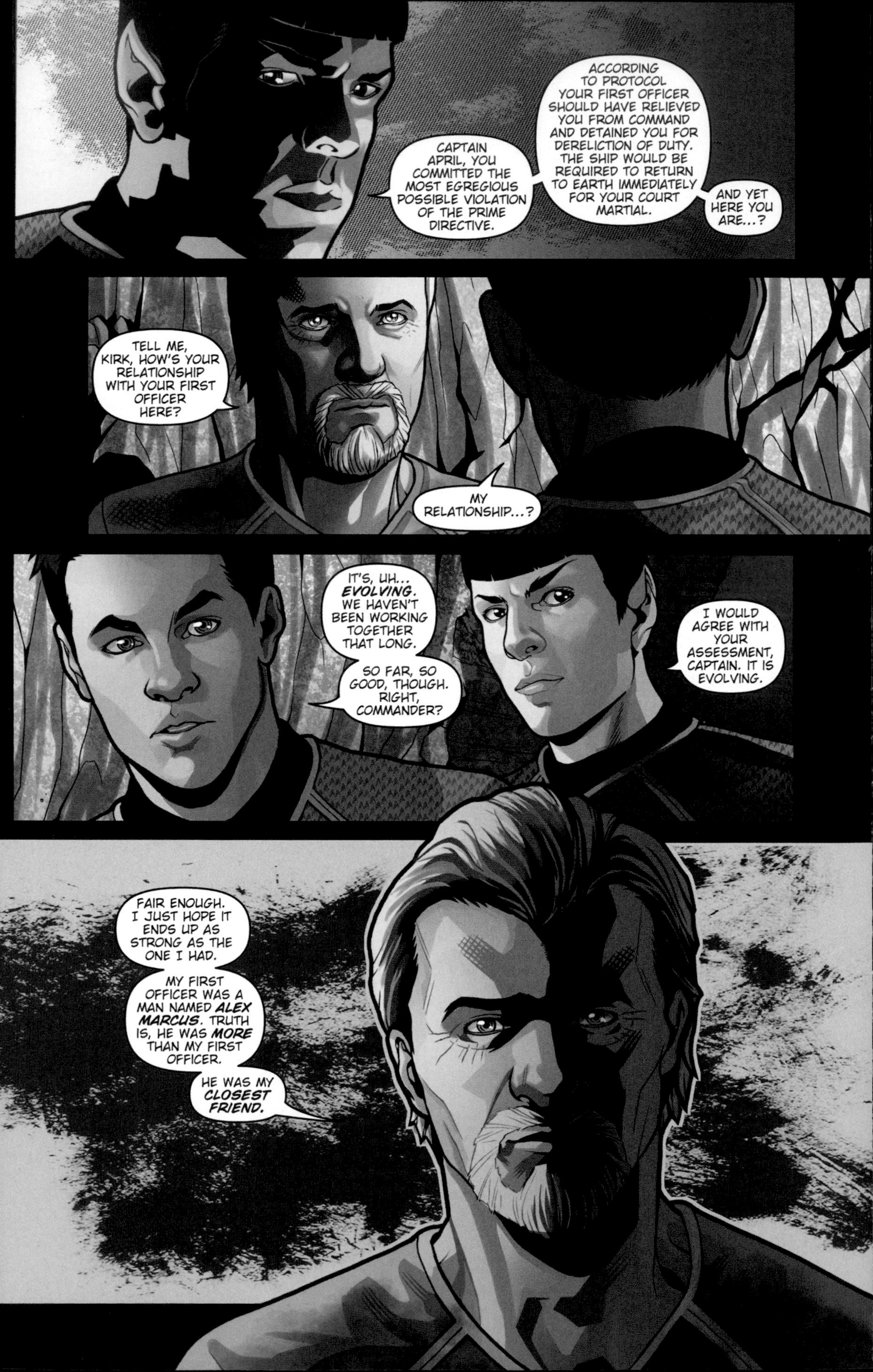
CAPTAIN APRIL, YOU COMMITTED THE MOST EGREGIOUS POSSIBLE VIOLATION OF THE PRIME DIRECTIVE.
ACCORDING TO PROTOCOL YOUR FIRST OFFICER SHOULD HAVE RELIEVED YOU FROM COMMAND AND DETAINED YOU FOR DERELICTION OF DUTY. THE SHIP WOULD BE REQUIRED TO RETURN TO EARTH IMMEDIATELY FOR YOUR COURT MARTIAL.
AND YET HERE YOU ARE...?
TELL ME, KIRK, HOW'S YOUR RELATIONSHIP WITH YOUR FIRST OFFICER HERE?
MY RELATIONSHIP...?
IT'S, UH... ***EVOLVING***. WE HAVEN'T BEEN WORKING TOGETHER THAT LONG.
SO FAR, SO GOOD, THOUGH. RIGHT, COMMANDER?
I WOULD AGREE WITH YOUR ASSESSMENT, CAPTAIN. IT IS EVOLVING.
FAIR ENOUGH. I JUST HOPE IT ENDS UP AS STRONG AS THE ONE I HAD.
MY FIRST OFFICER WAS A MAN NAMED ***ALEX MARCUS***. TRUTH IS, HE WAS ***MORE*** THAN MY FIRST OFFICER.
HE WAS MY ***CLOSEST FRIEND.***

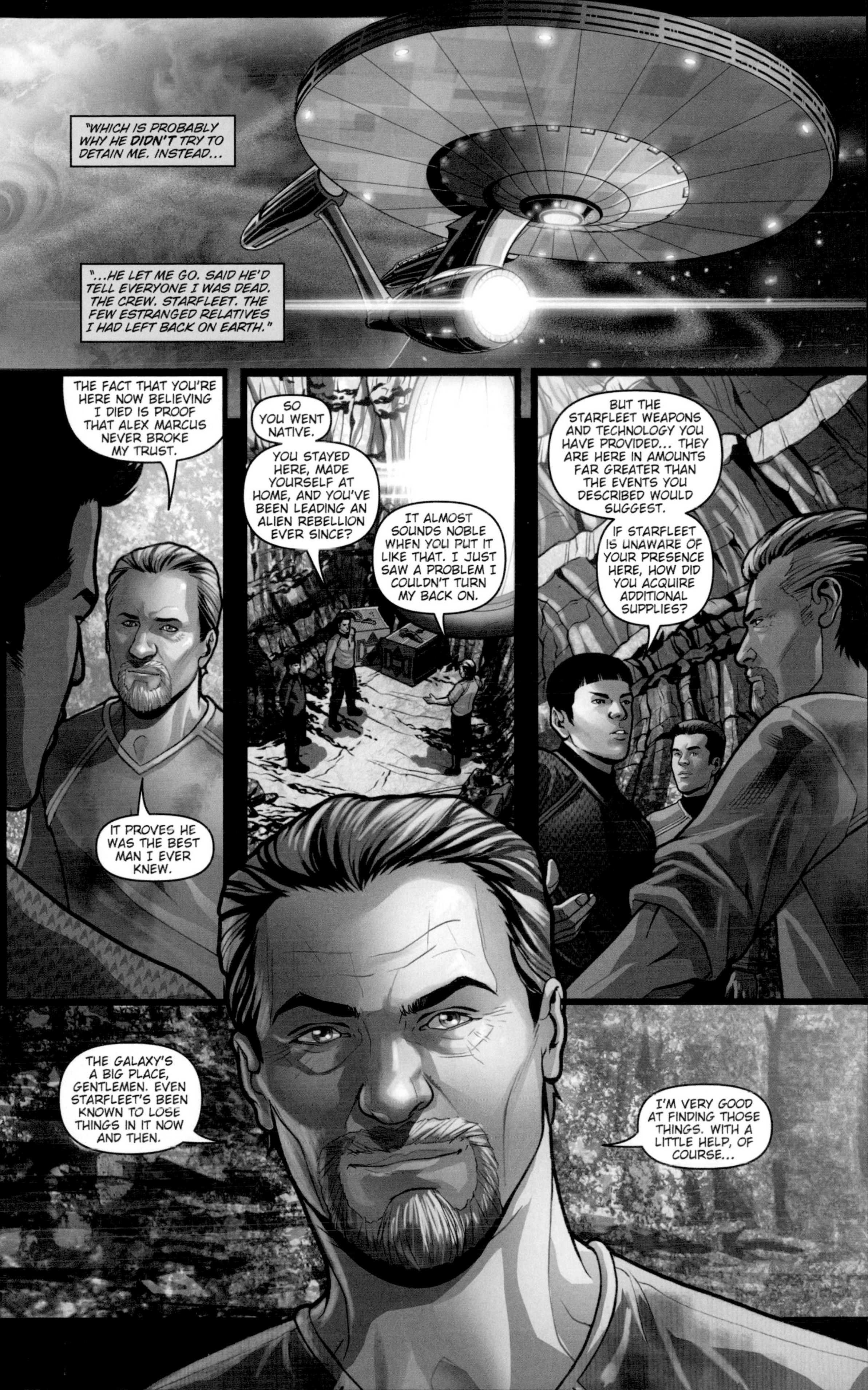
"WHICH IS PROBABLY WHY HE DIDN'T TRY TO DETAIN ME. INSTEAD...
"...HE LET ME GO. SAID HE'D TELL EVERYONE I WAS DEAD. THE CREW. STARFLEET. THE FEW ESTRANGED RELATIVES I HAD LEFT BACK ON EARTH."
THE FACT THAT YOU'RE HERE NOW BELIEVING I DIED IS PROOF THAT ALEX MARCUS NEVER BROKE MY TRUST.
IT PROVES HE WAS THE BEST MAN I EVER KNEW.
SO YOU WENT NATIVE.
YOU STAYED HERE, MADE YOURSELF AT HOME, AND YOU'VE BEEN LEADING AN ALIEN REBELLION EVER SINCE?
IT ALMOST SOUNDS NOBLE WHEN YOU PUT IT LIKE THAT. I JUST SAW A PROBLEM I COULDN'T TURN MY BACK ON.
BUT THE STARFLEET WEAPONS AND TECHNOLOGY YOU HAVE PROVIDED... THEY ARE HERE IN AMOUNTS FAR GREATER THAN THE EVENTS YOU DESCRIBED WOULD SUGGEST.
IF STARFLEET IS UNAWARE OF YOUR PRESENCE HERE, HOW DID YOU ACQUIRE ADDITIONAL SUPPLIES?
THE GALAXY'S A BIG PLACE, GENTLEMEN. EVEN STARFLEET'S BEEN KNOWN TO LOSE THINGS IN IT NOW AND THEN.
I'M VERY GOOD AT FINDING THOSE THINGS. WITH A LITTLE HELP, OF COURSE...

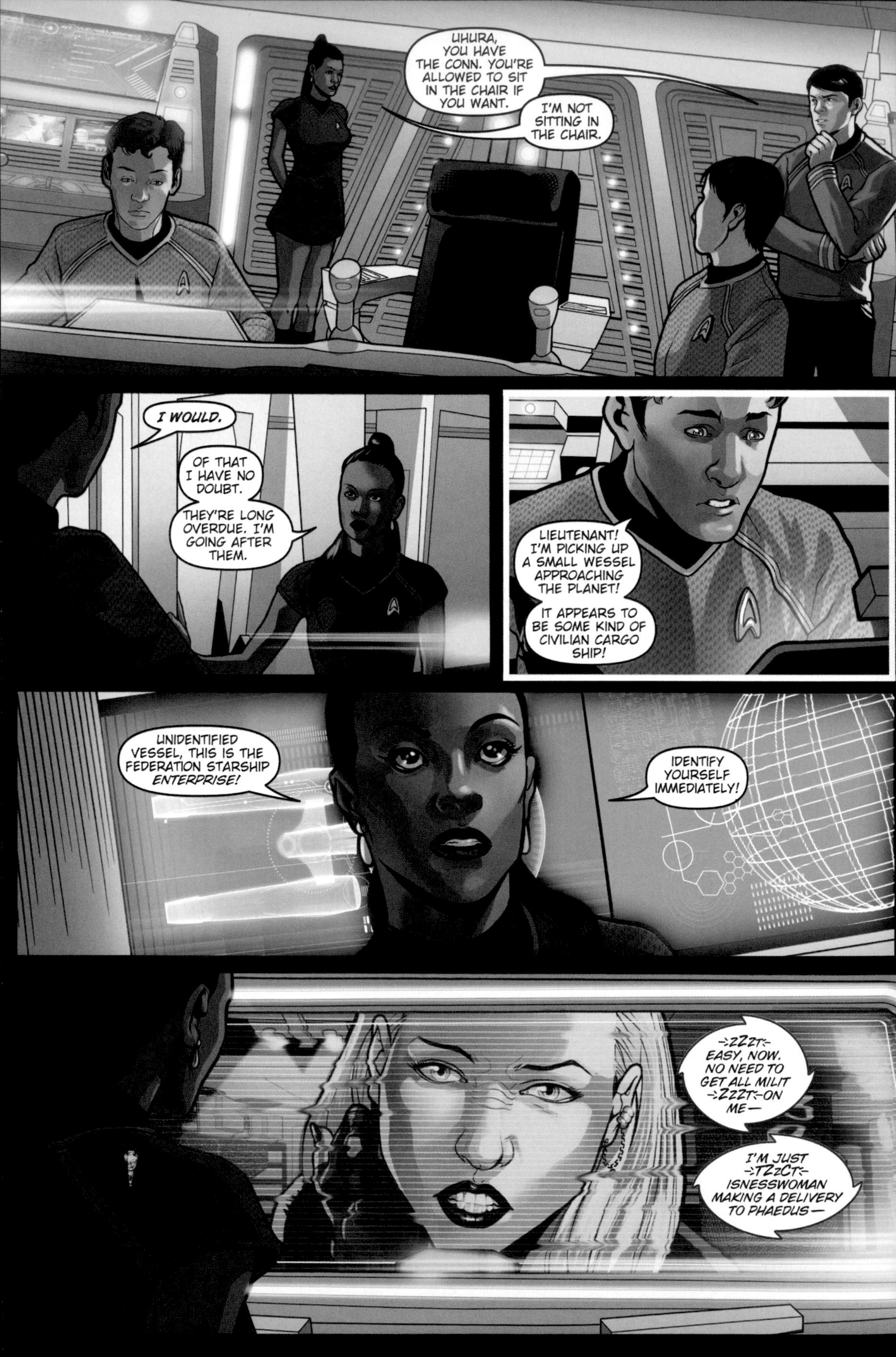
UHURA, YOU HAVE THE CONN. YOU'RE ALLOWED TO SIT IN THE CHAIR IF YOU WANT.
I'M NOT SITTING IN THE CHAIR.
I WOULD.
OF THAT I HAVE NO DOUBT.
THEY'RE LONG OVERDUE. I'M GOING AFTER THEM.
LIEUTENANT! I'M PICKING UP A SMALL WESSEL APPROACHING THE PLANET!
IT APPEARS TO BE SOME KIND OF CIVILIAN CARGO SHIP!
UNIDENTIFIED VESSEL, THIS IS THE FEDERATION STARSHIP *ENTERPRISE!*
IDENTIFY YOURSELF IMMEDIATELY!
-ZZZT- EASY, NOW. NO NEED TO GET ALL MILIT -ZZZT- ON ME—
I'M JUST -TZZCT- ISNESSWOMAN MAKING A DELIVERY TO PHAEDUS—

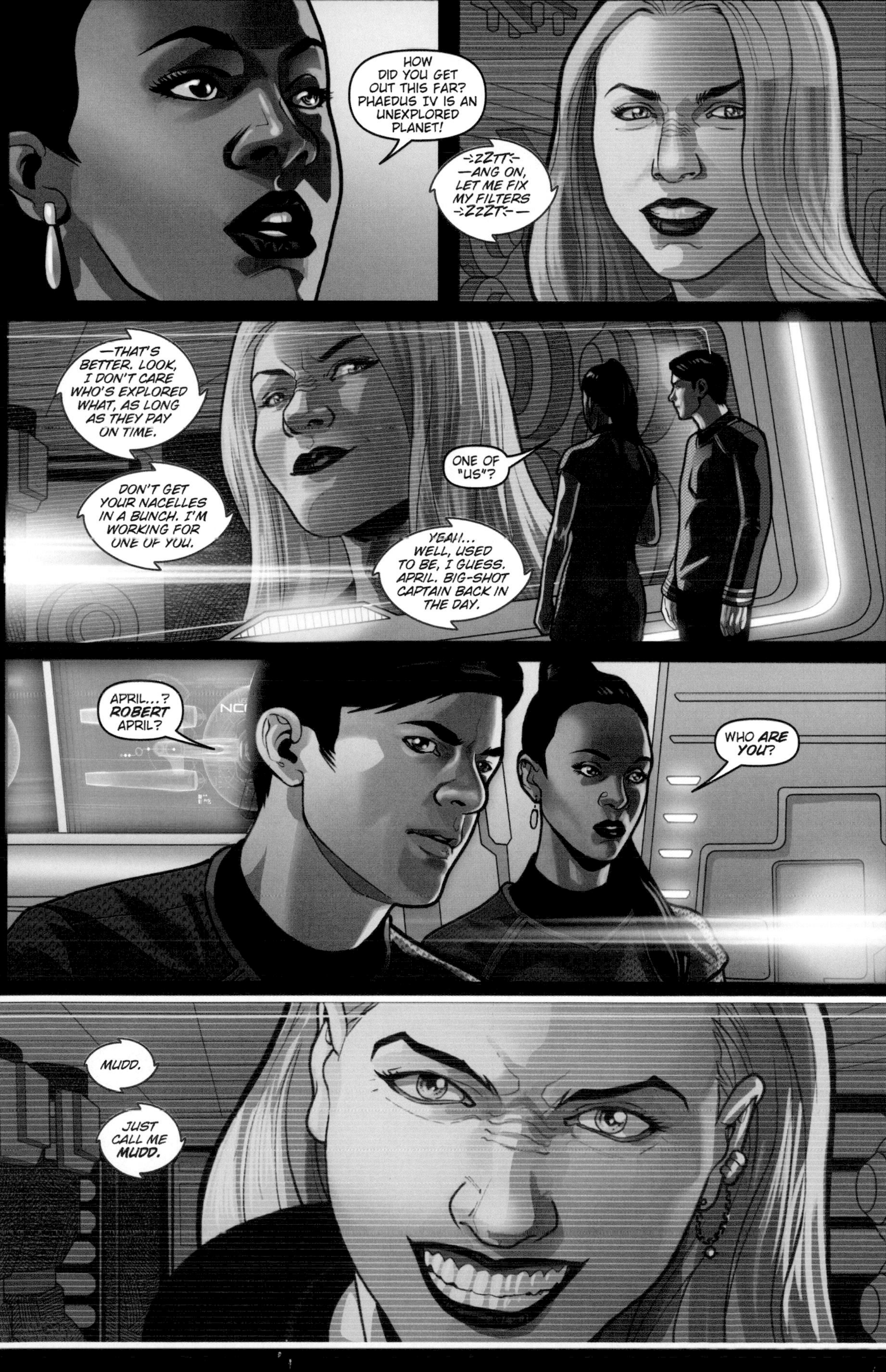
HOW DID YOU GET OUT THIS FAR? PHAEDUS IV IS AN UNEXPLORED PLANET!
-ZZTT- —ANG ON, LET ME FIX MY FILTERS -ZZZT- —
—THAT'S BETTER. LOOK, I DON'T CARE WHO'S EXPLORED WHAT, AS LONG AS THEY PAY ON TIME.
DON'T GET YOUR NACELLES IN A BUNCH. I'M WORKING FOR ONE OF YOU.
ONE OF "US"?
YEAH... WELL, USED TO BE, I GUESS. APRIL. BIG-SHOT CAPTAIN BACK IN THE DAY.
APRIL...? ROBERT APRIL?
WHO ARE YOU?
MUDD.
JUST CALL ME MUDD.

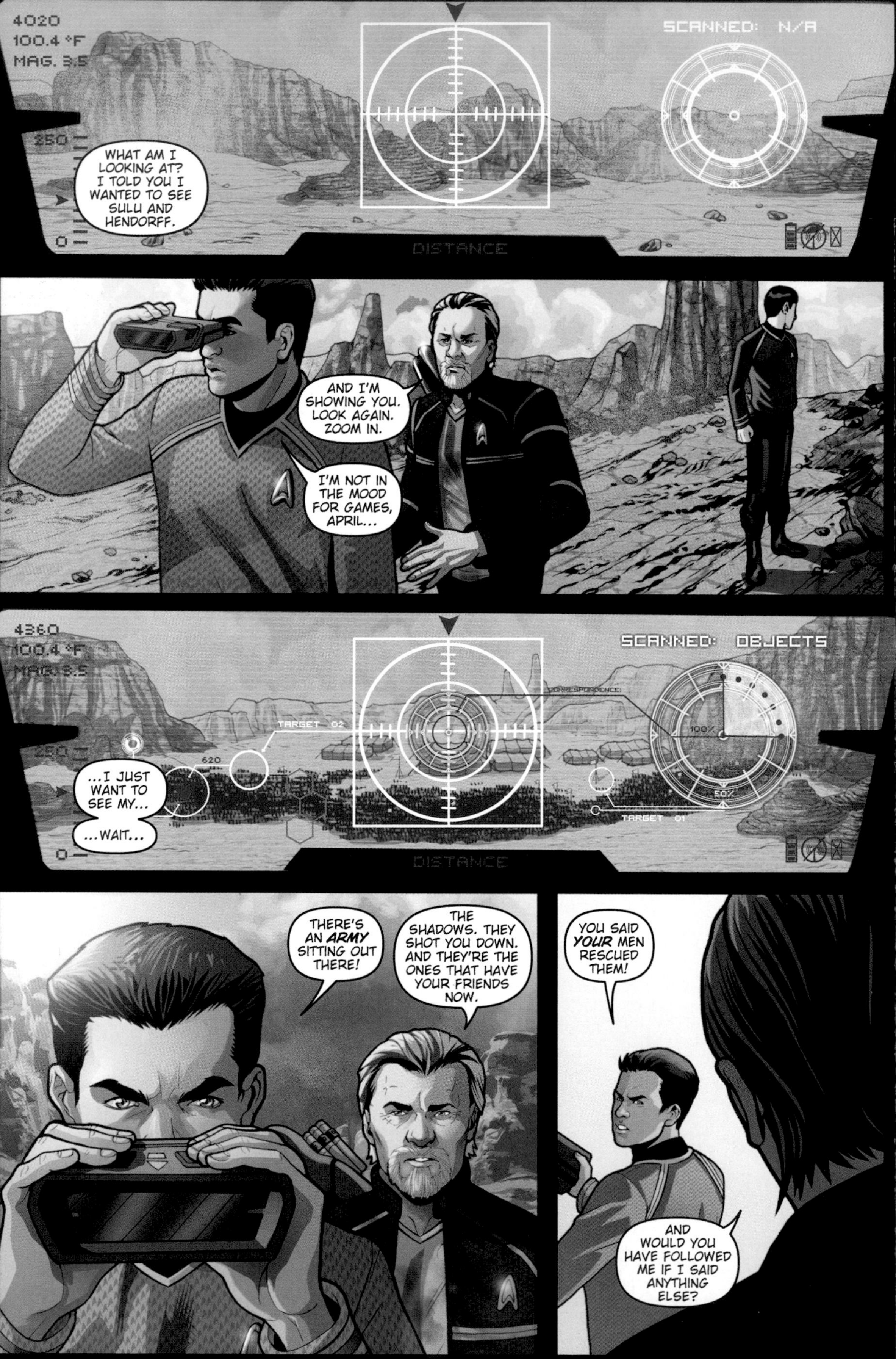

4020
100.4 °F
MAG. 3.5
SCANNED: N/A
250
WHAT AM I LOOKING AT? I TOLD YOU I WANTED TO SEE SULU AND HENDORFF.
0
DISTANCE
AND I'M SHOWING YOU. LOOK AGAIN. ZOOM IN.
I'M NOT IN THE MOOD FOR GAMES, APRIL...
4360
100.4 °F
SCANNED: OBJECTS
CORRESPONDENCE:
TARGET 02
620
100%
250
...I JUST WANT TO SEE MY...
...WAIT...
50%
TARGET 01
0
DISTANCE
THERE'S AN ***ARMY*** SITTING OUT THERE!
THE SHADOWS. THEY SHOT YOU DOWN. AND THEY'RE THE ONES THAT HAVE YOUR FRIENDS NOW.
YOU SAID ***YOUR*** MEN RESCUED THEM!
AND WOULD YOU HAVE FOLLOWED ME IF I SAID ANYTHING ELSE?

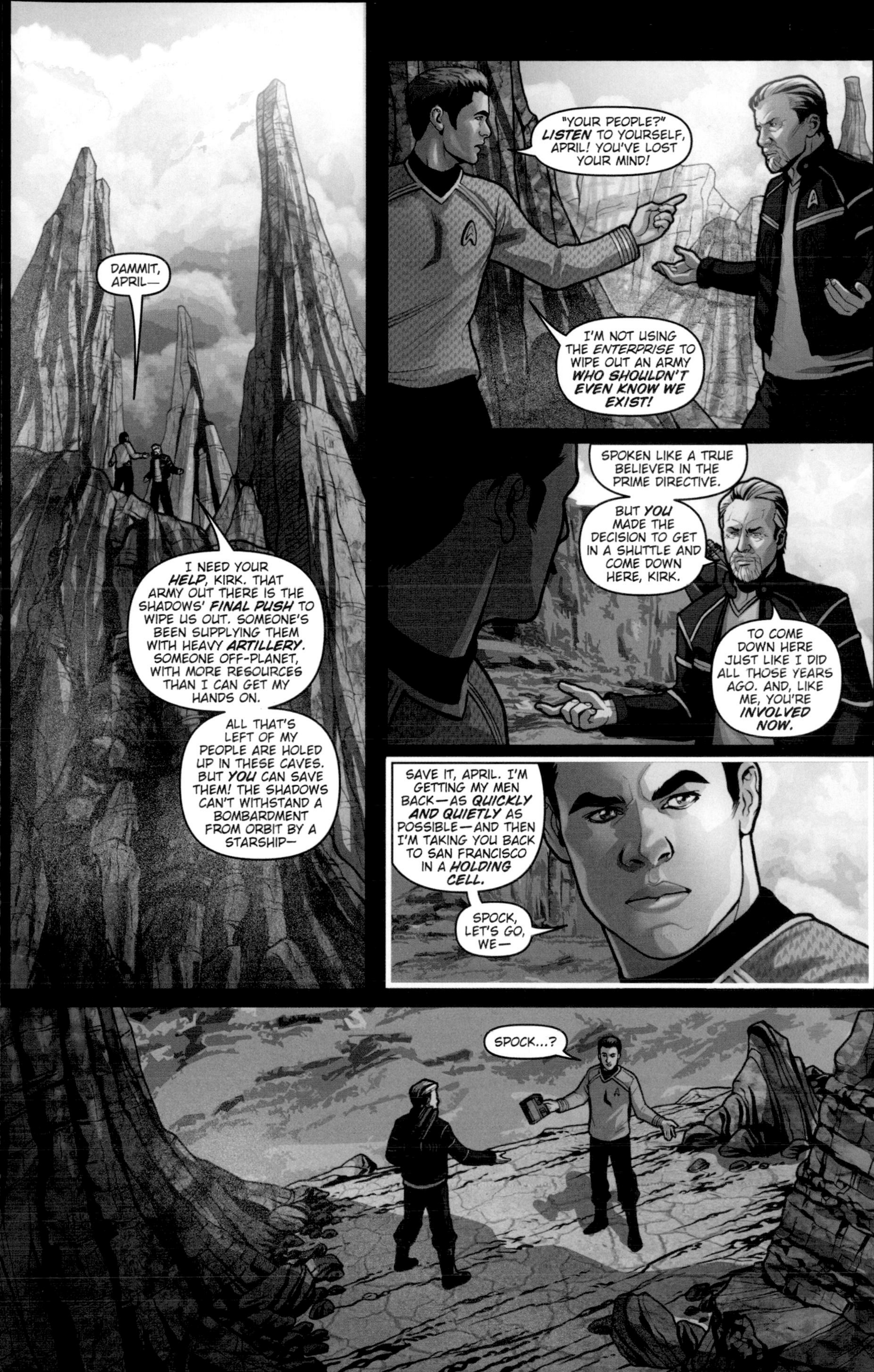
DAMMIT, APRIL—
I NEED YOUR HELP, KIRK. THAT ARMY OUT THERE IS THE SHADOWS' FINAL PUSH TO WIPE US OUT. SOMEONE'S BEEN SUPPLYING THEM WITH HEAVY ARTILLERY. SOMEONE OFF-PLANET, WITH MORE RESOURCES THAN I CAN GET MY HANDS ON.
ALL THAT'S LEFT OF MY PEOPLE ARE HOLED UP IN THESE CAVES. BUT YOU CAN SAVE THEM! THE SHADOWS CAN'T WITHSTAND A BOMBARDMENT FROM ORBIT BY A STARSHIP—
"YOUR PEOPLE?" LISTEN TO YOURSELF, APRIL! YOU'VE LOST YOUR MIND!
I'M NOT USING THE ENTERPRISE TO WIPE OUT AN ARMY WHO SHOULDN'T EVEN KNOW WE EXIST!
SPOKEN LIKE A TRUE BELIEVER IN THE PRIME DIRECTIVE.
BUT YOU MADE THE DECISION TO GET IN A SHUTTLE AND COME DOWN HERE, KIRK.
TO COME DOWN HERE JUST LIKE I DID ALL THOSE YEARS AGO. AND, LIKE ME, YOU'RE INVOLVED NOW.
SAVE IT, APRIL. I'M GETTING MY MEN BACK—AS QUICKLY AND QUIETLY AS POSSIBLE—AND THEN I'M TAKING YOU BACK TO SAN FRANCISCO IN A HOLDING CELL.
SPOCK, LET'S GO, WE—
SPOCK...?

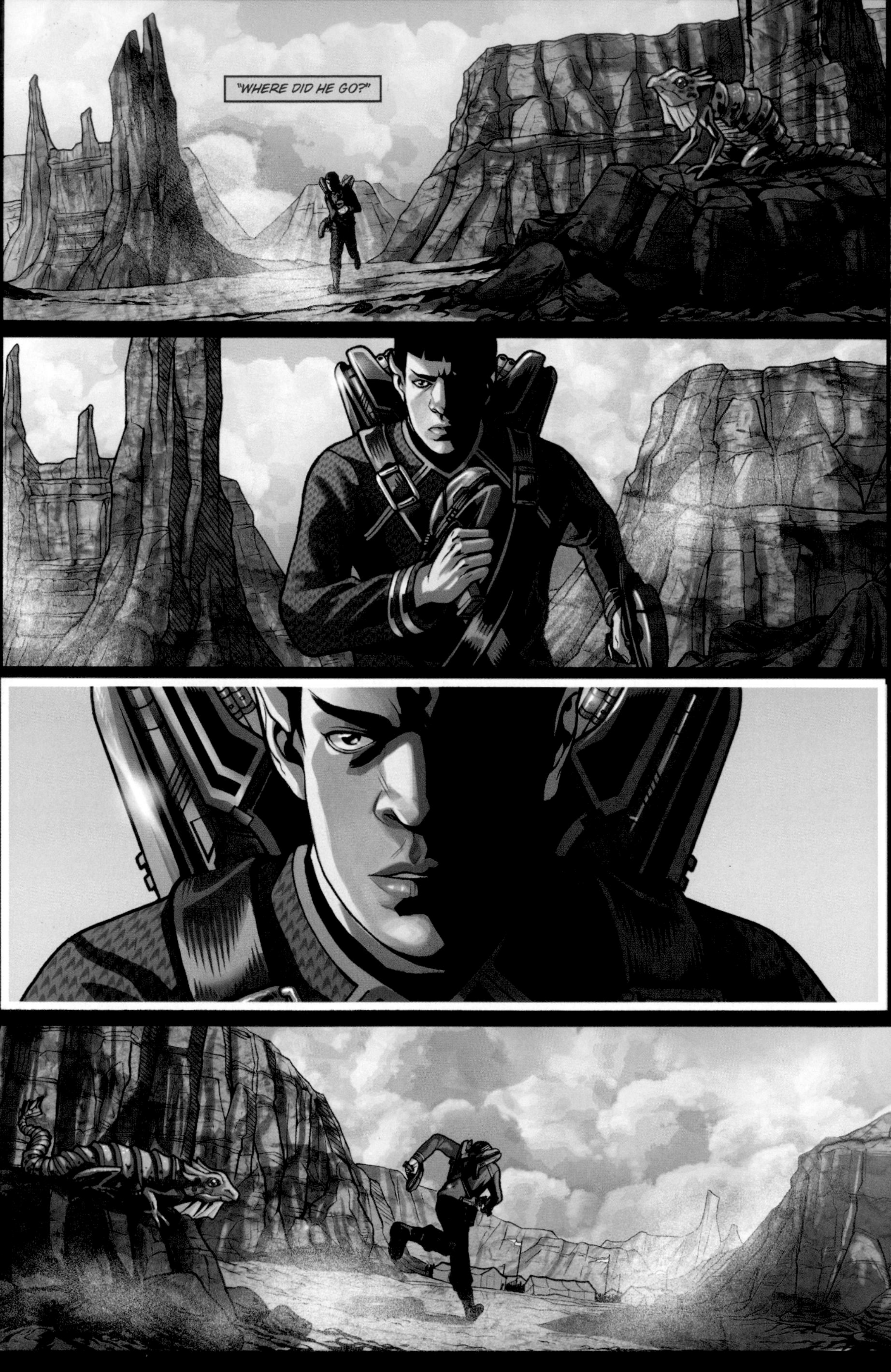
"WHERE DID HE GO?"

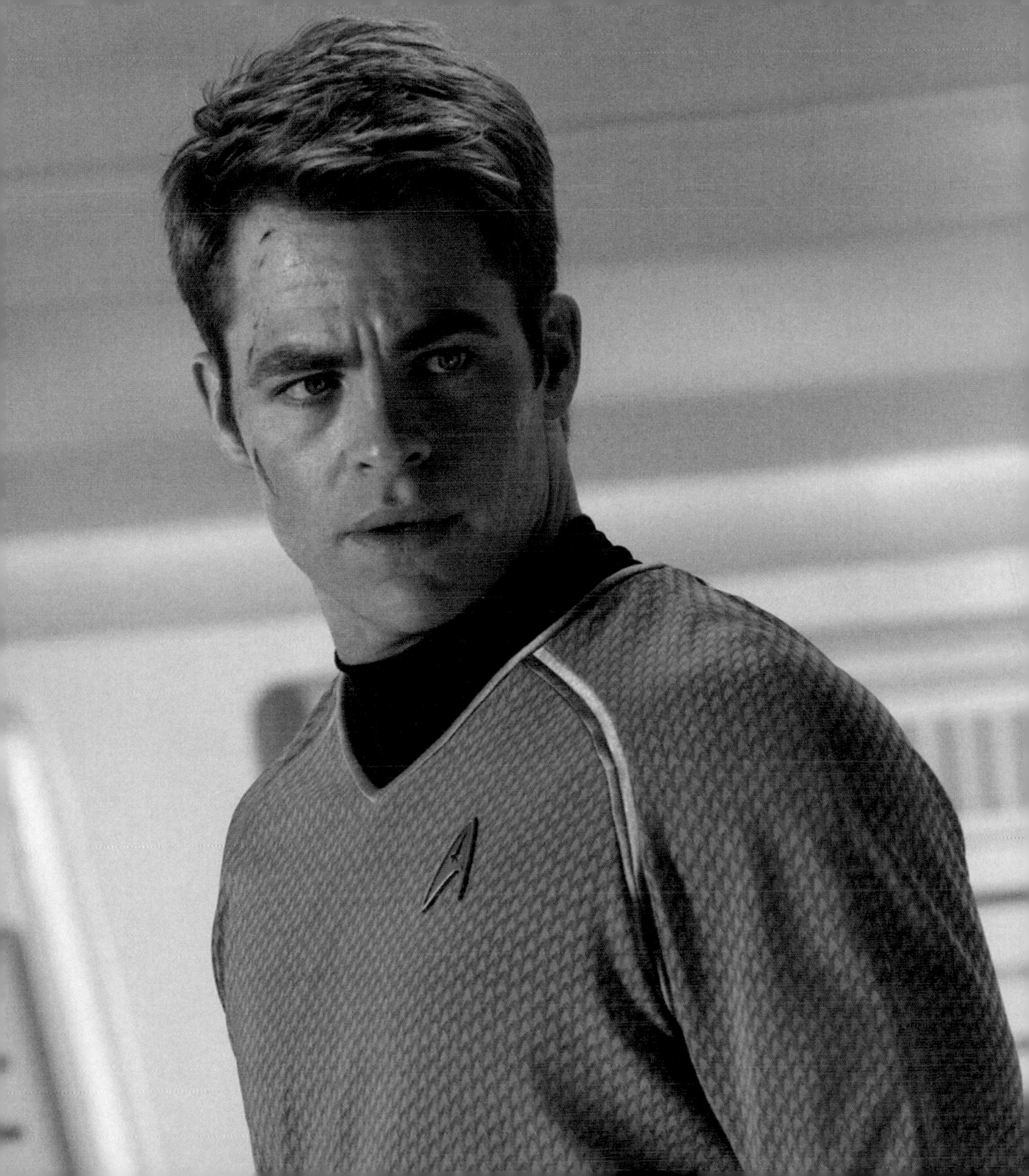

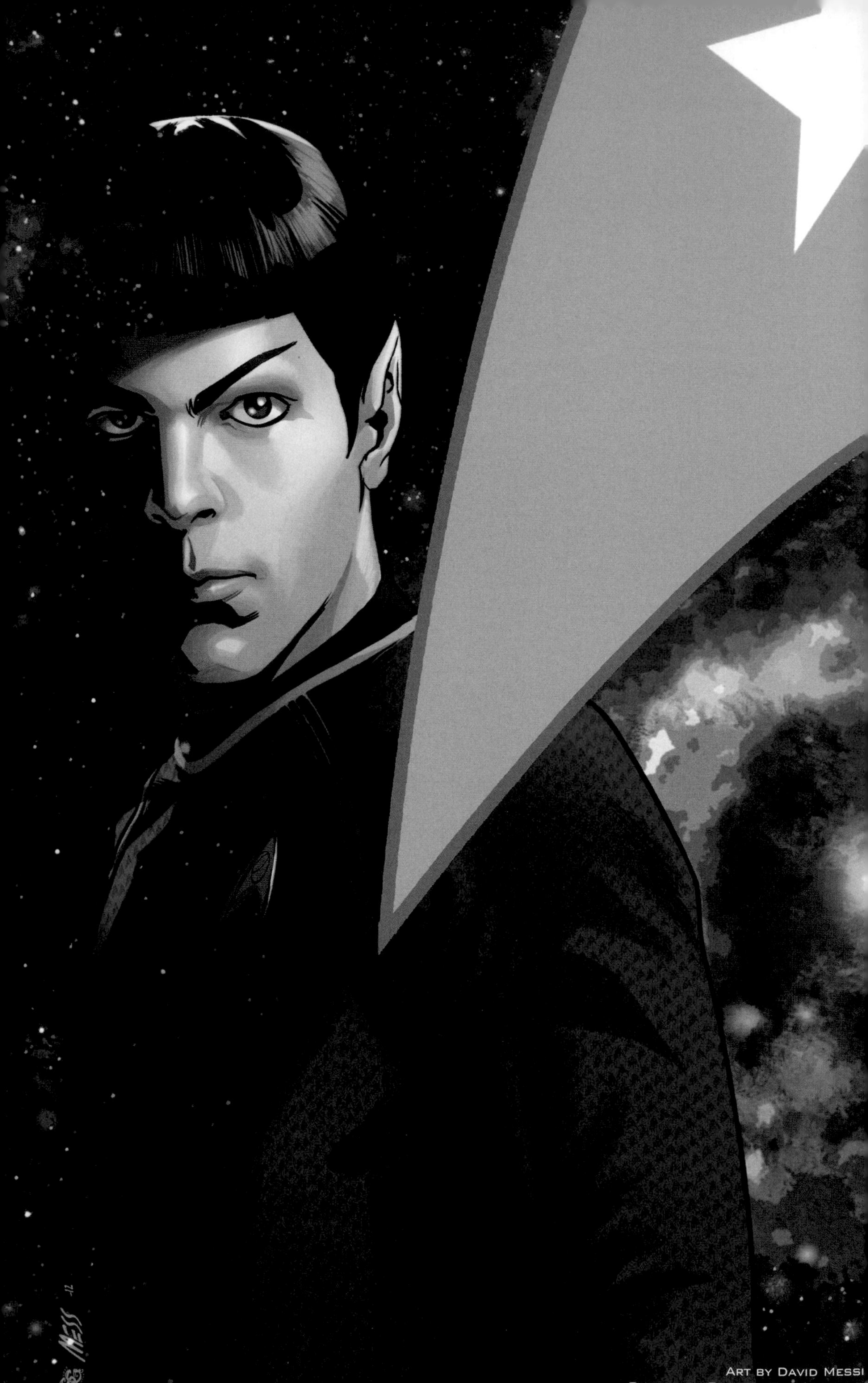

ART BY DAVID MESSI
COLORS BY CLAUDIA SCARLETGOTH

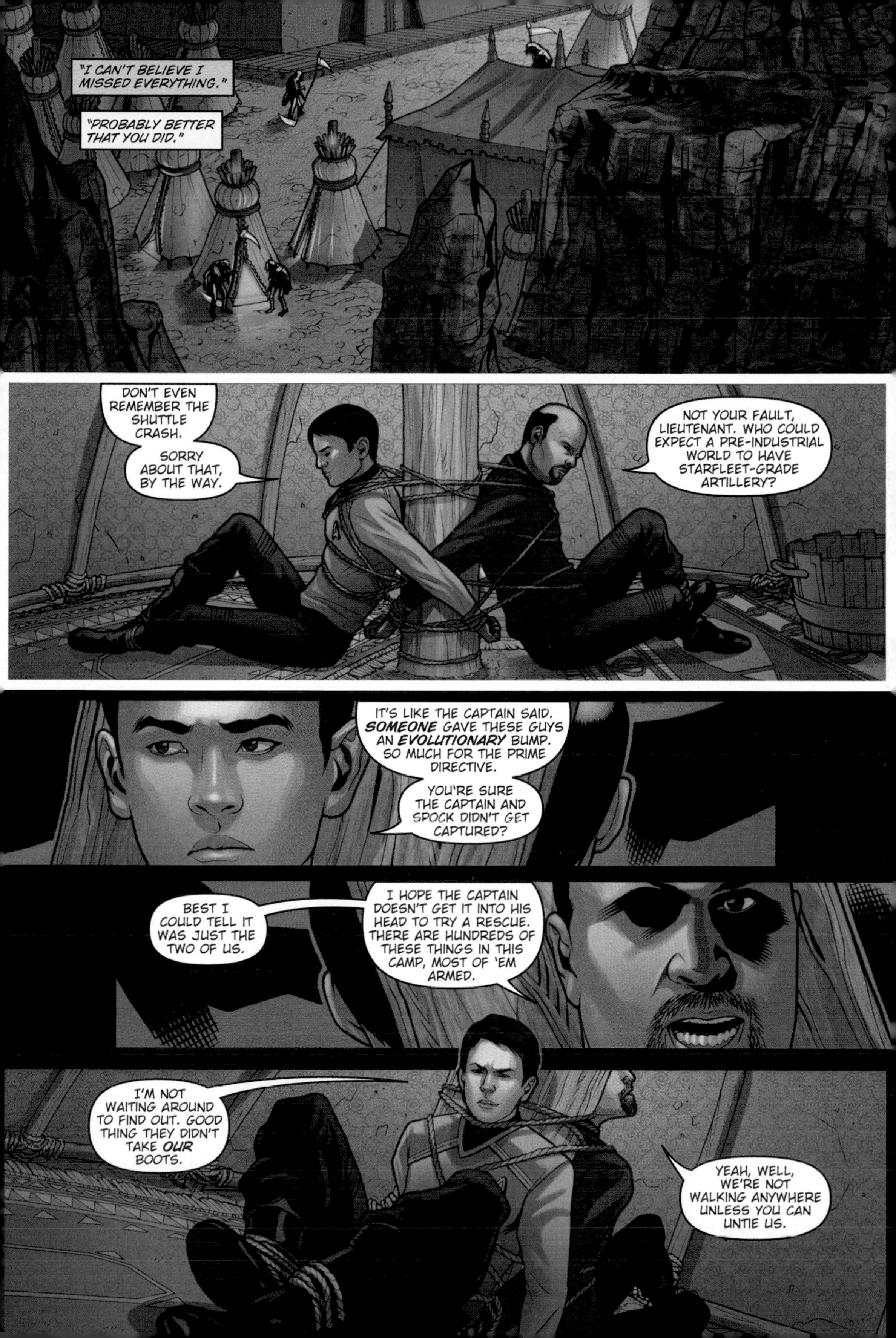
"I CAN'T BELIEVE I MISSED EVERYTHING."
"PROBABLY BETTER THAT YOU DID."
DON'T EVEN REMEMBER THE SHUTTLE CRASH.
SORRY ABOUT THAT, BY THE WAY.
NOT YOUR FAULT, LIEUTENANT. WHO COULD EXPECT A PRE-INDUSTRIAL WORLD TO HAVE STARFLEET-GRADE ARTILLERY?
IT'S LIKE THE CAPTAIN SAID. SOMEONE GAVE THESE GUYS AN EVOLUTIONARY BUMP. SO MUCH FOR THE PRIME DIRECTIVE.
YOU'RE SURE THE CAPTAIN AND SPOCK DIDN'T GET CAPTURED?
BEST I COULD TELL IT WAS JUST THE TWO OF US.
I HOPE THE CAPTAIN DOESN'T GET IT INTO HIS HEAD TO TRY A RESCUE. THERE ARE HUNDREDS OF THESE THINGS IN THIS CAMP, MOST OF 'EM ARMED.
I'M NOT WAITING AROUND TO FIND OUT. GOOD THING THEY DIDN'T TAKE OUR BOOTS.
YEAH, WELL, WE'RE NOT WALKING ANYWHERE UNLESS YOU CAN UNTIE US.

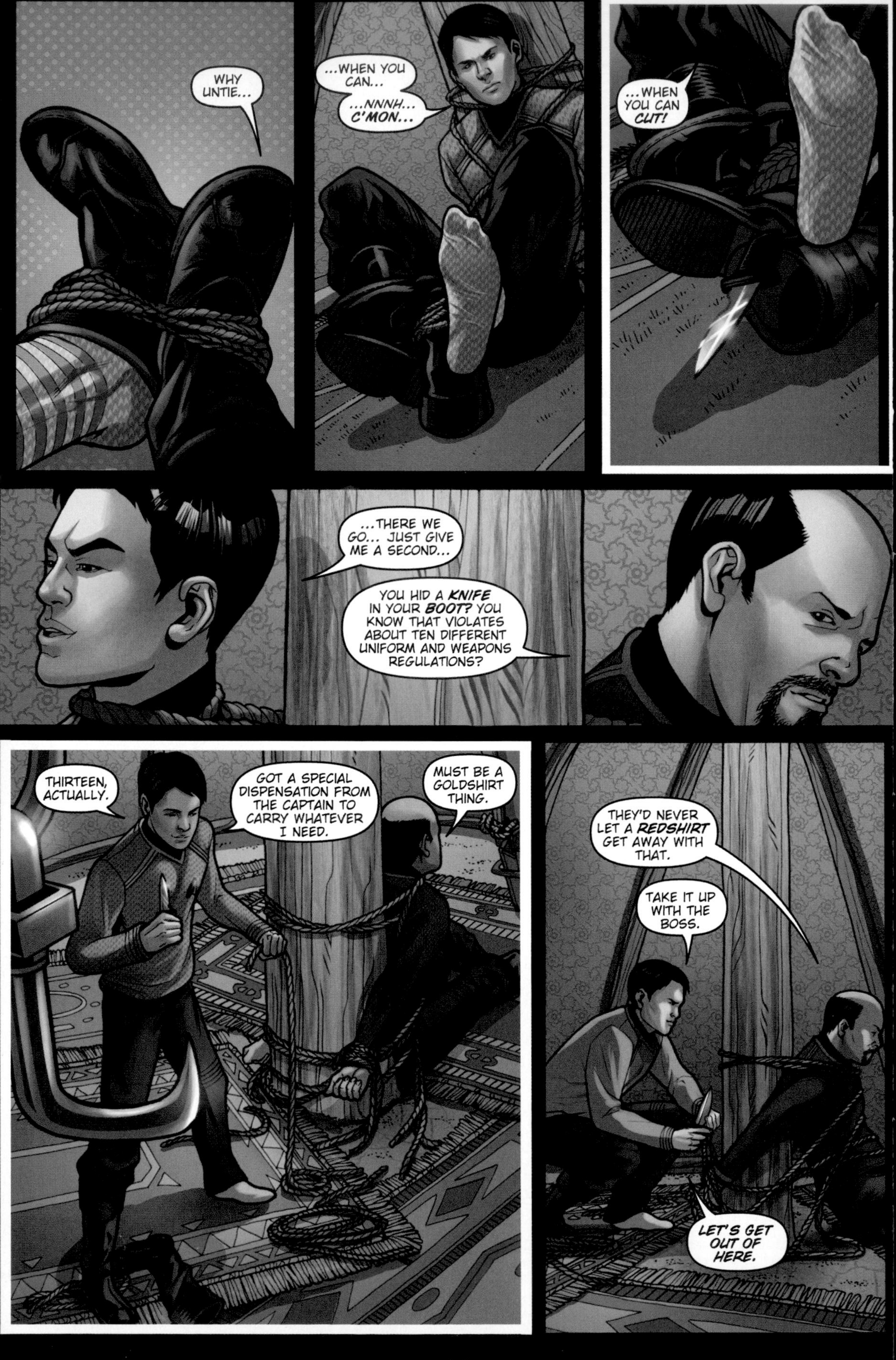

WHY UNTIE...
...WHEN YOU CAN...
...NNNH... C'MON...
...WHEN YOU CAN CUT!
...THERE WE GO... JUST GIVE ME A SECOND...
YOU HID A KNIFE IN YOUR BOOT? YOU KNOW THAT VIOLATES ABOUT TEN DIFFERENT UNIFORM AND WEAPONS REGULATIONS?
THIRTEEN, ACTUALLY.
GOT A SPECIAL DISPENSATION FROM THE CAPTAIN TO CARRY WHATEVER I NEED.
MUST BE A GOLDSHIRT THING.
THEY'D NEVER LET A REDSHIRT GET AWAY WITH THAT.
TAKE IT UP WITH THE BOSS.
LET'S GET OUT OF HERE.

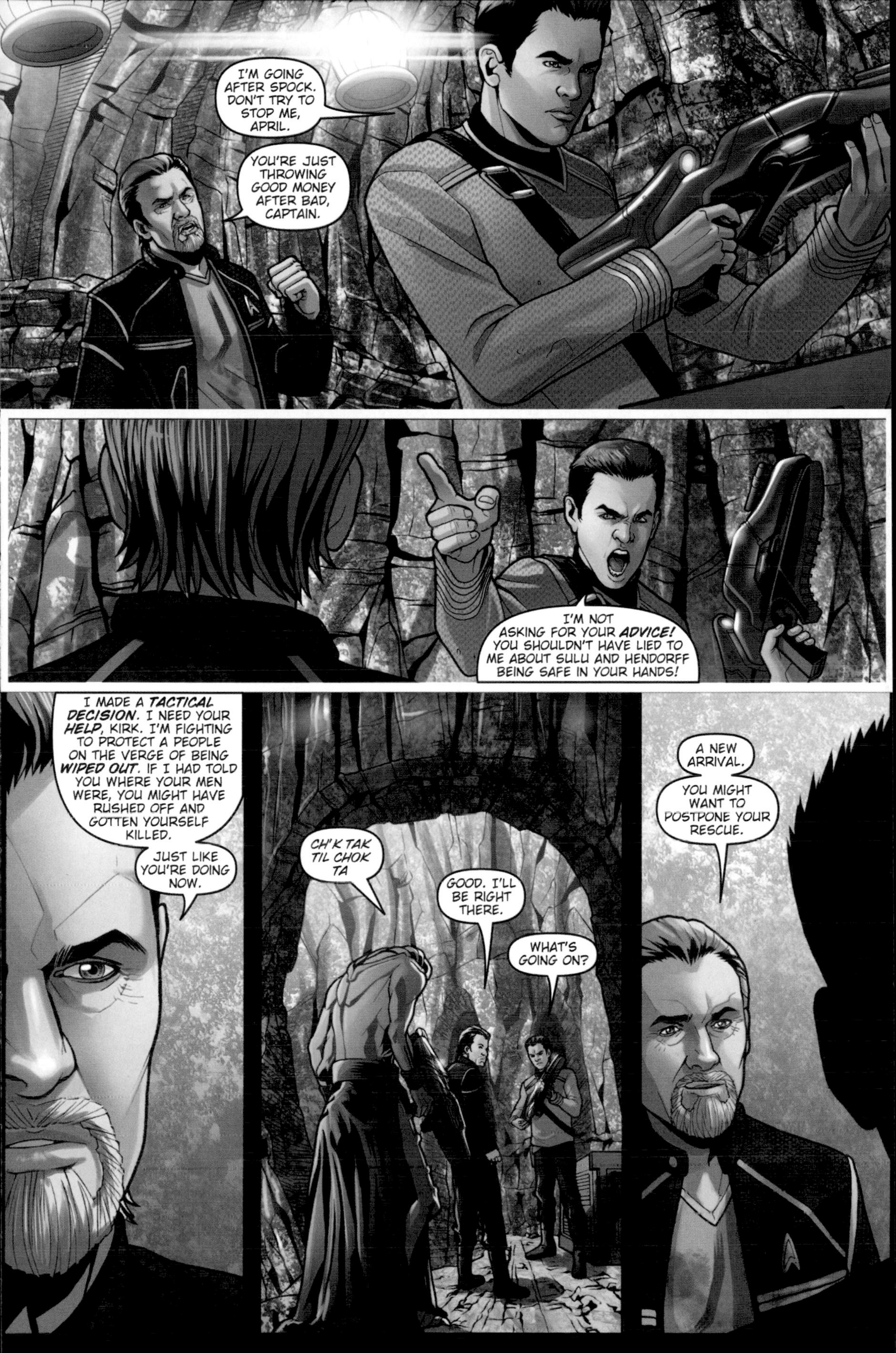
I'M GOING AFTER SPOCK. DON'T TRY TO STOP ME, APRIL.
YOU'RE JUST THROWING GOOD MONEY AFTER BAD, CAPTAIN.
I'M NOT ASKING FOR YOUR ADVICE! YOU SHOULDN'T HAVE LIED TO ME ABOUT SULU AND HENDORFF BEING SAFE IN YOUR HANDS!
I MADE A TACTICAL DECISION. I NEED YOUR HELP, KIRK. I'M FIGHTING TO PROTECT A PEOPLE ON THE VERGE OF BEING WIPED OUT. IF I HAD TOLD YOU WHERE YOUR MEN WERE, YOU MIGHT HAVE RUSHED OFF AND GOTTEN YOURSELF KILLED.
JUST LIKE YOU'RE DOING NOW.
CH'K TAK TIL CHOK TA
GOOD. I'LL BE RIGHT THERE.
WHAT'S GOING ON?
A NEW ARRIVAL.
YOU MIGHT WANT TO POSTPONE YOUR RESCUE.

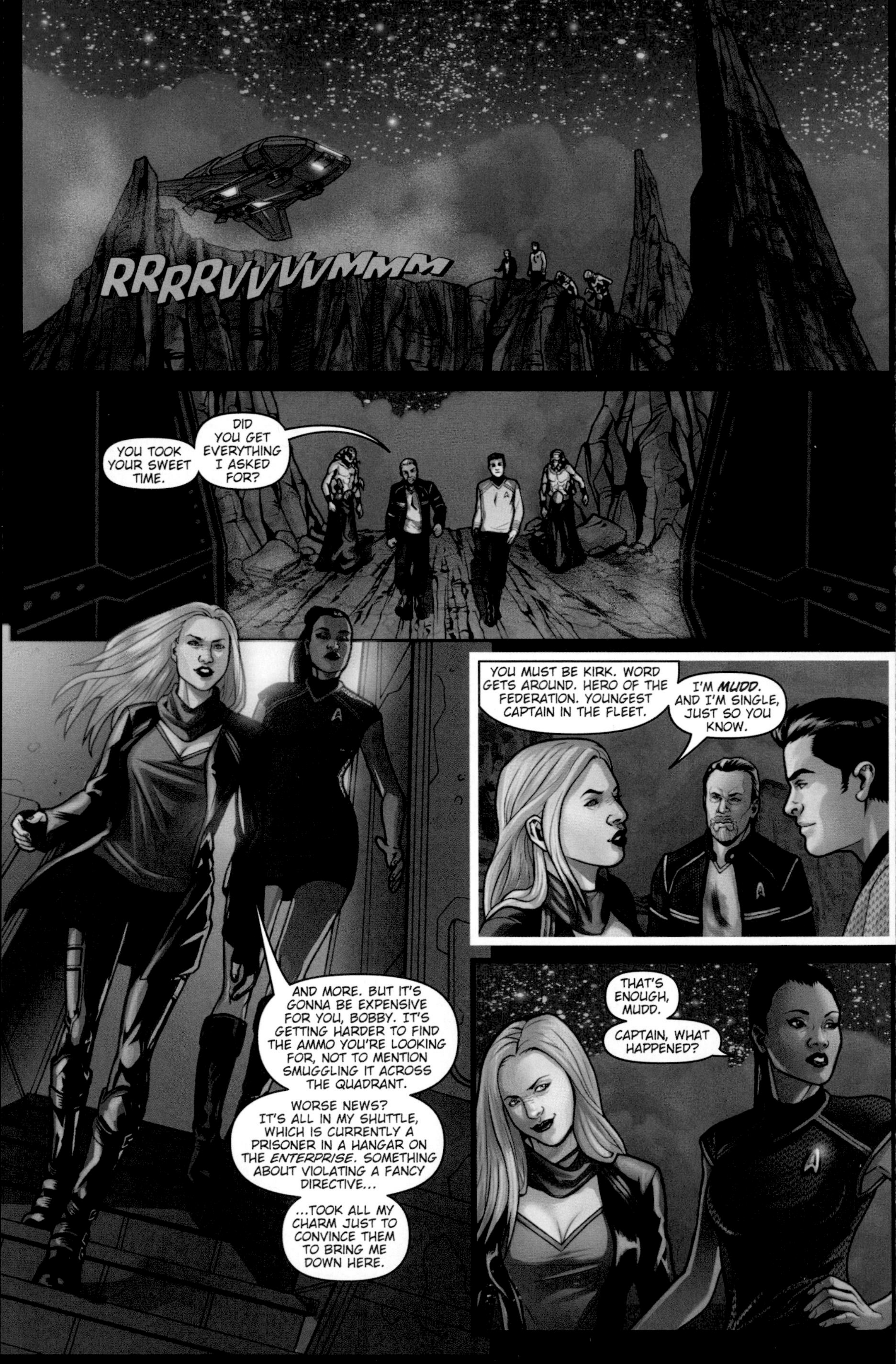
RRRRVVVVVMMMM
YOU TOOK YOUR SWEET TIME.
DID YOU GET EVERYTHING I ASKED FOR?
AND MORE. BUT IT'S GONNA BE EXPENSIVE FOR YOU, BOBBY. IT'S GETTING HARDER TO FIND THE AMMO YOU'RE LOOKING FOR, NOT TO MENTION SMUGGLING IT ACROSS THE QUADRANT.
WORSE NEWS? IT'S ALL IN MY SHUTTLE, WHICH IS CURRENTLY A PRISONER IN A HANGAR ON THE *ENTERPRISE*. SOMETHING ABOUT VIOLATING A FANCY DIRECTIVE...
...TOOK ALL MY CHARM JUST TO CONVINCE THEM TO BRING ME DOWN HERE.
YOU MUST BE KIRK. WORD GETS AROUND. HERO OF THE FEDERATION. YOUNGEST CAPTAIN IN THE FLEET.
I'M ***MUDD***. AND I'M SINGLE, JUST SO YOU KNOW.
THAT'S ENOUGH, MUDD.
CAPTAIN, WHAT HAPPENED?

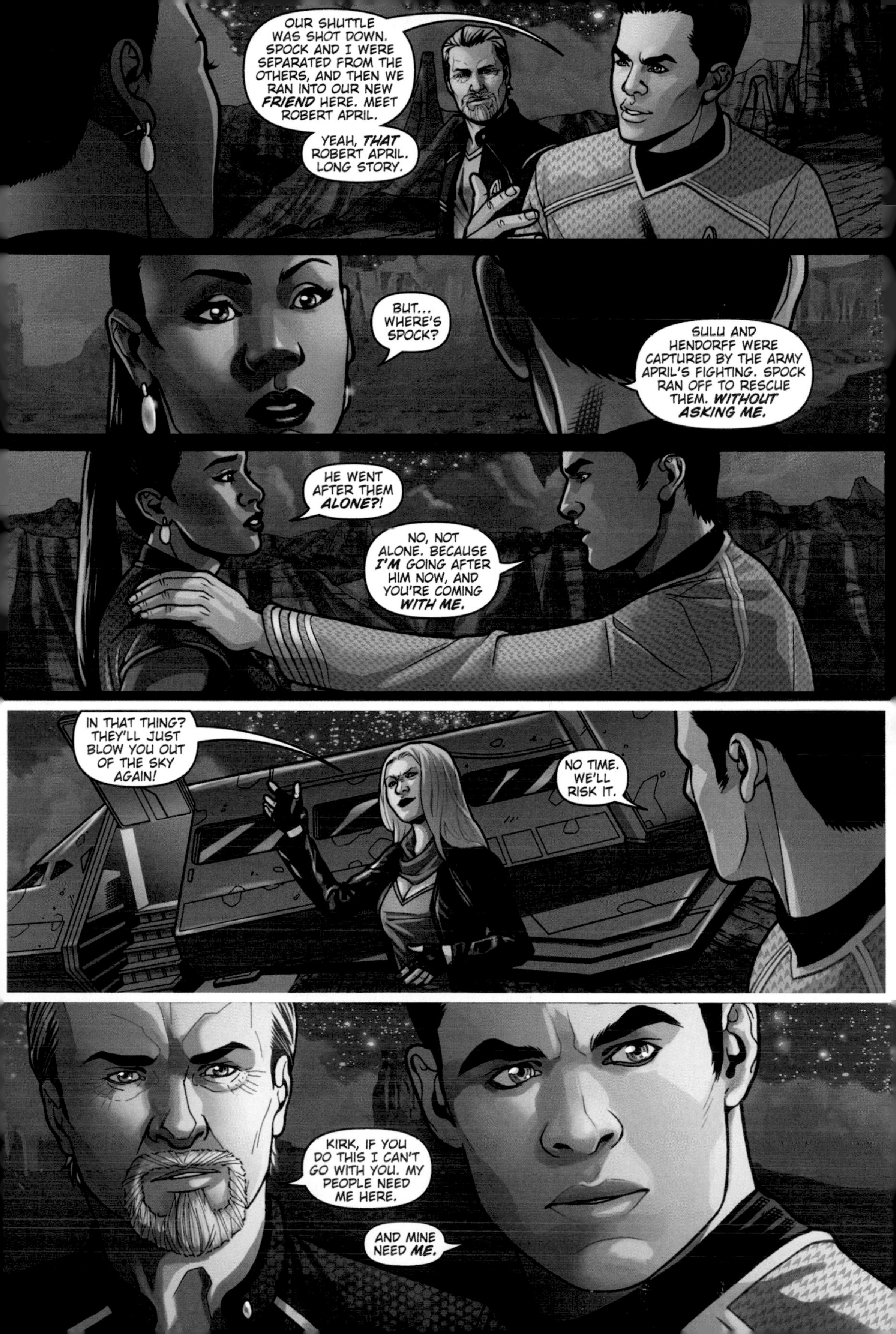
OUR SHUTTLE WAS SHOT DOWN. SPOCK AND I WERE SEPARATED FROM THE OTHERS, AND THEN WE RAN INTO OUR NEW FRIEND HERE. MEET ROBERT APRIL.
YEAH, THAT ROBERT APRIL. LONG STORY.
BUT... WHERE'S SPOCK?
SULU AND HENDORFF WERE CAPTURED BY THE ARMY APRIL'S FIGHTING. SPOCK RAN OFF TO RESCUE THEM. WITHOUT ASKING ME.
HE WENT AFTER THEM ALONE?!
NO, NOT ALONE. BECAUSE I'M GOING AFTER HIM NOW, AND YOU'RE COMING WITH ME.
IN THAT THING? THEY'LL JUST BLOW YOU OUT OF THE SKY AGAIN!
NO TIME. WE'LL RISK IT.
KIRK, IF YOU DO THIS I CAN'T GO WITH YOU. MY PEOPLE NEED ME HERE.
AND MINE NEED ME.

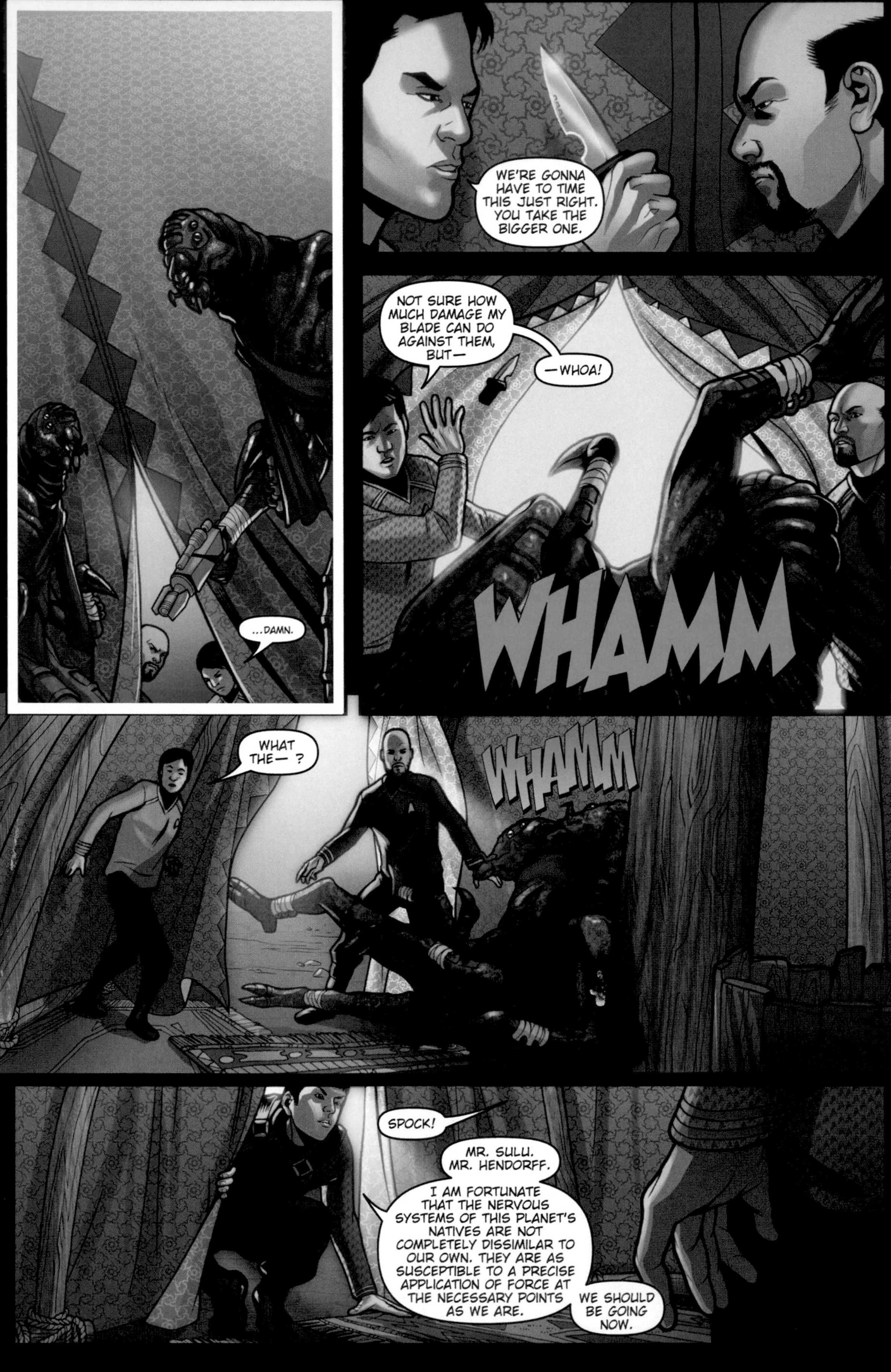
...DAMN.
WE'RE GONNA HAVE TO TIME THIS JUST RIGHT. YOU TAKE THE BIGGER ONE.
NOT SURE HOW MUCH DAMAGE MY BLADE CAN DO AGAINST THEM, BUT—
—WHOA!
WHAMM
WHAT THE— ?
WHAMM
SPOCK!
MR. SULU. MR. HENDORFF.
I AM FORTUNATE THAT THE NERVOUS SYSTEMS OF THIS PLANET'S NATIVES ARE NOT COMPLETELY DISSIMILAR TO OUR OWN. THEY ARE AS SUSCEPTIBLE TO A PRECISE APPLICATION OF FORCE AT THE NECESSARY POINTS AS WE ARE.
WE SHOULD BE GOING NOW.

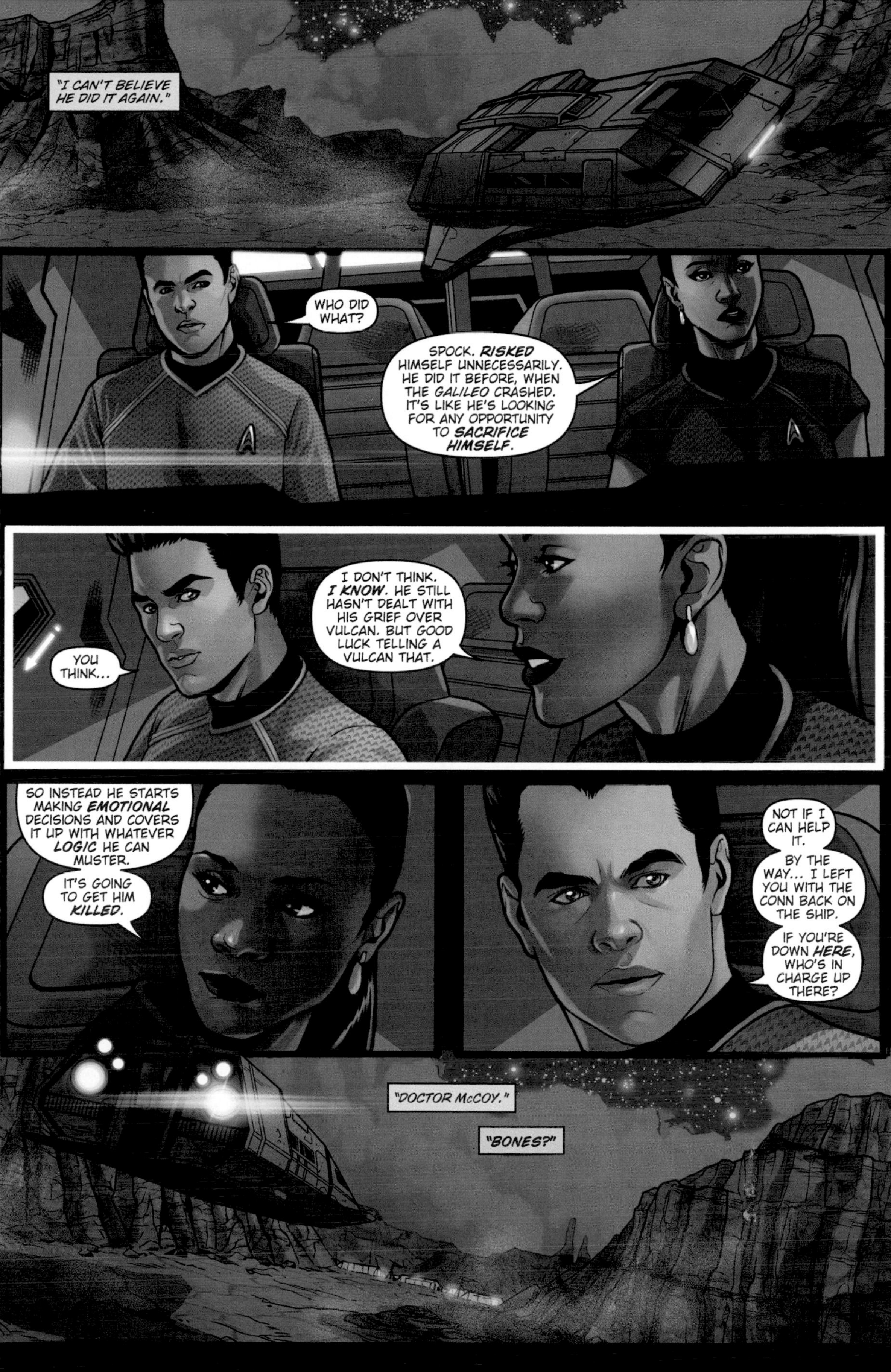
"I CAN'T BELIEVE HE DID IT AGAIN."
WHO DID WHAT?
SPOCK. RISKED HIMSELF UNNECESSARILY. HE DID IT BEFORE, WHEN THE GALILEO CRASHED. IT'S LIKE HE'S LOOKING FOR ANY OPPORTUNITY TO SACRIFICE HIMSELF.
YOU THINK...
I DON'T THINK. I KNOW. HE STILL HASN'T DEALT WITH HIS GRIEF OVER VULCAN. BUT GOOD LUCK TELLING A VULCAN THAT.
SO INSTEAD HE STARTS MAKING EMOTIONAL DECISIONS AND COVERS IT UP WITH WHATEVER LOGIC HE CAN MUSTER.
IT'S GOING TO GET HIM KILLED.
NOT IF I CAN HELP IT.
BY THE WAY... I LEFT YOU WITH THE CONN BACK ON THE SHIP.
IF YOU'RE DOWN HERE, WHO'S IN CHARGE UP THERE?
"DOCTOR McCOY."
"BONES?"

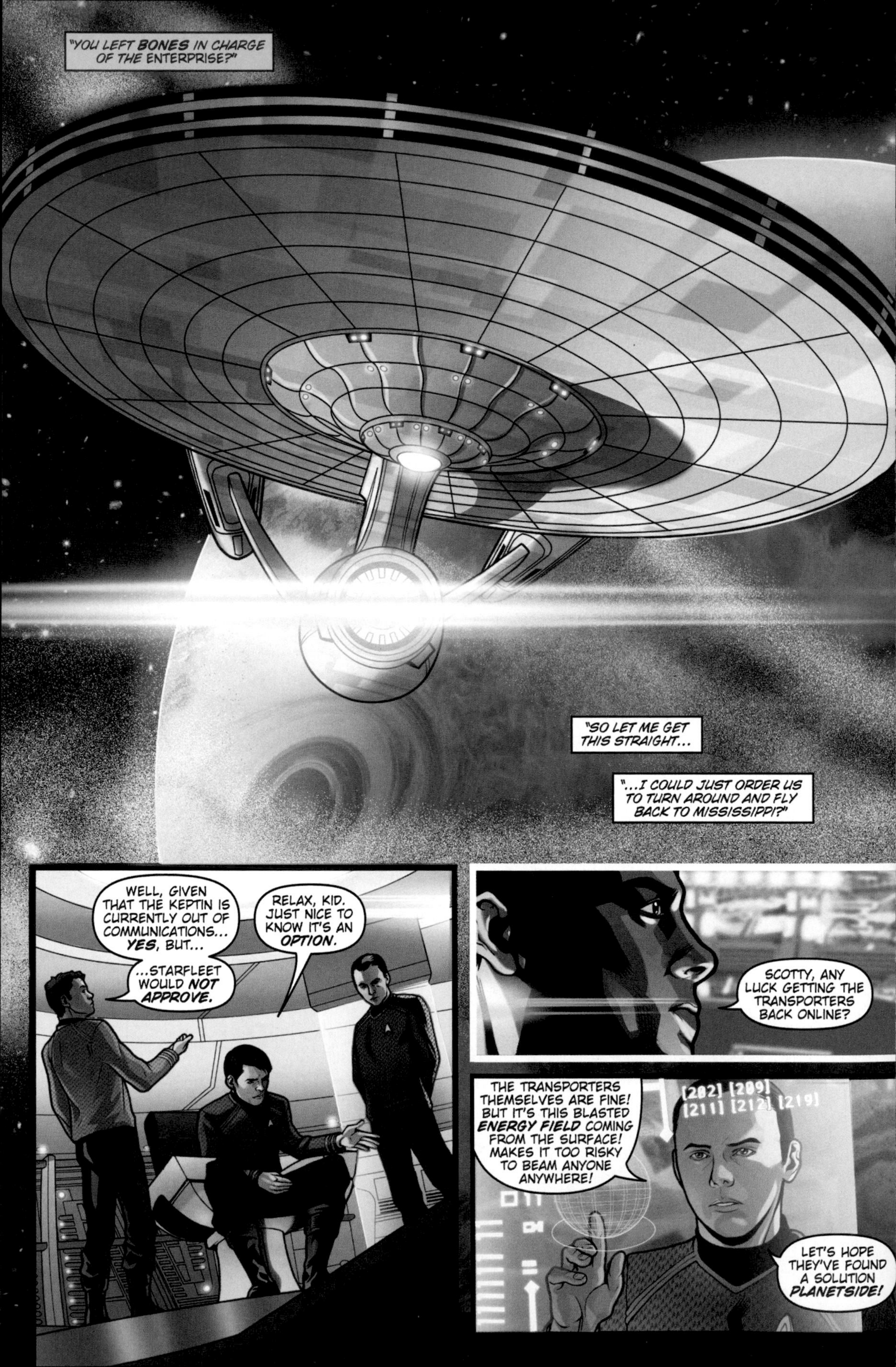
"YOU LEFT BONES IN CHARGE OF THE ENTERPRISE?"
"SO LET ME GET THIS STRAIGHT...
"...I COULD JUST ORDER US TO TURN AROUND AND FLY BACK TO MISSISSIPPI?"
WELL, GIVEN THAT THE KEPTIN IS CURRENTLY OUT OF COMMUNICATIONS... YES, BUT...
...STARFLEET WOULD NOT APPROVE.
RELAX, KID. JUST NICE TO KNOW IT'S AN OPTION.
SCOTTY, ANY LUCK GETTING THE TRANSPORTERS BACK ONLINE?
THE TRANSPORTERS THEMSELVES ARE FINE! BUT IT'S THIS BLASTED ENERGY FIELD COMING FROM THE SURFACE! MAKES IT TOO RISKY TO BEAM ANYONE ANYWHERE!
[202] [209]
[211] [212] [219]
LET'S HOPE THEY'VE FOUND A SOLUTION PLANETSIDE!

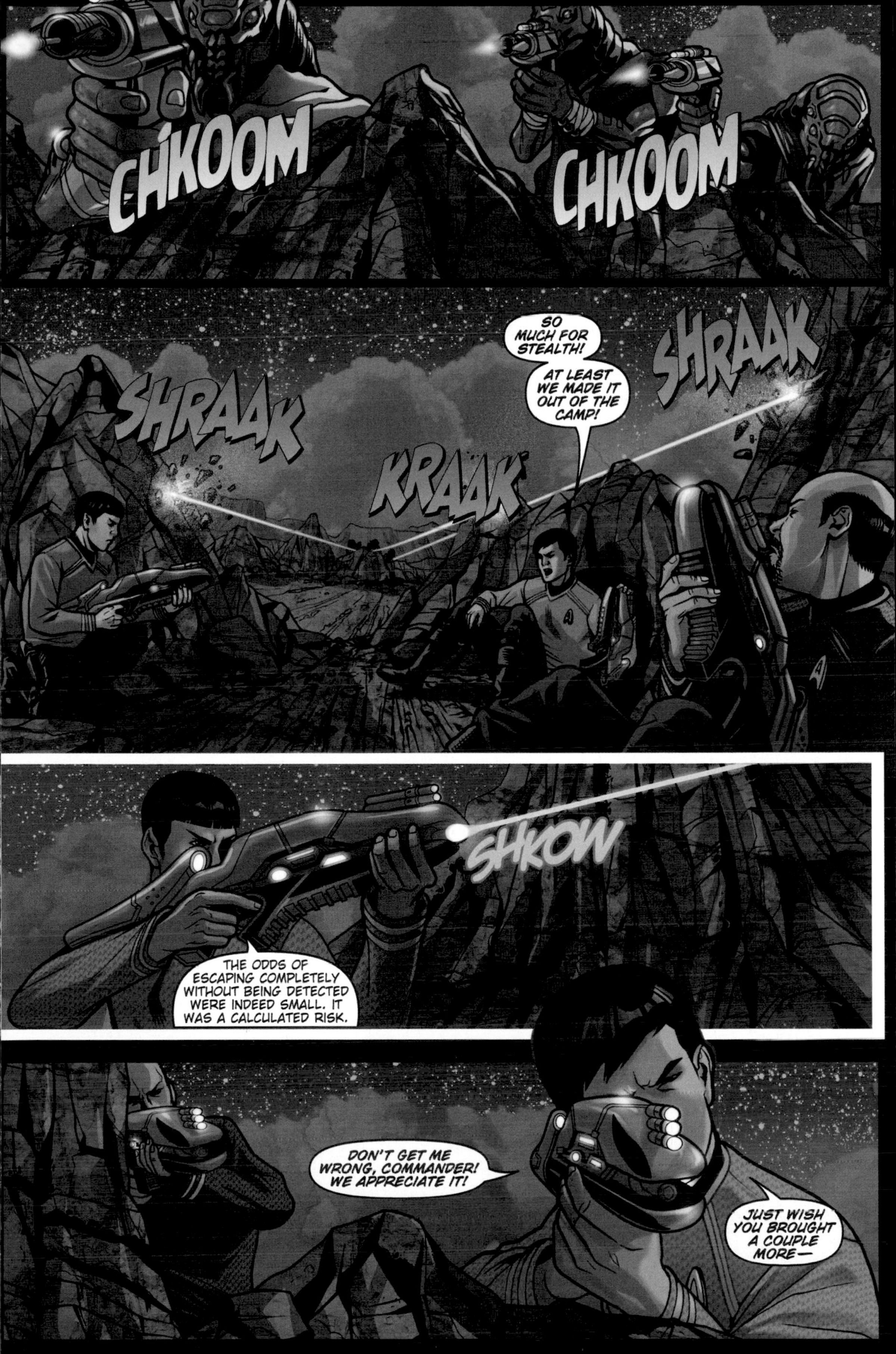
CHKOOM
CHKOOM
SHRAAK
KRAAK
SO MUCH FOR STEALTH!
AT LEAST WE MADE IT OUT OF THE CAMP!
SHRAAK
SHKOW
THE ODDS OF ESCAPING COMPLETELY WITHOUT BEING DETECTED WERE INDEED SMALL. IT WAS A CALCULATED RISK.
DON'T GET ME WRONG, COMMANDER! WE APPRECIATE IT!
JUST WISH YOU BROUGHT A COUPLE MORE—

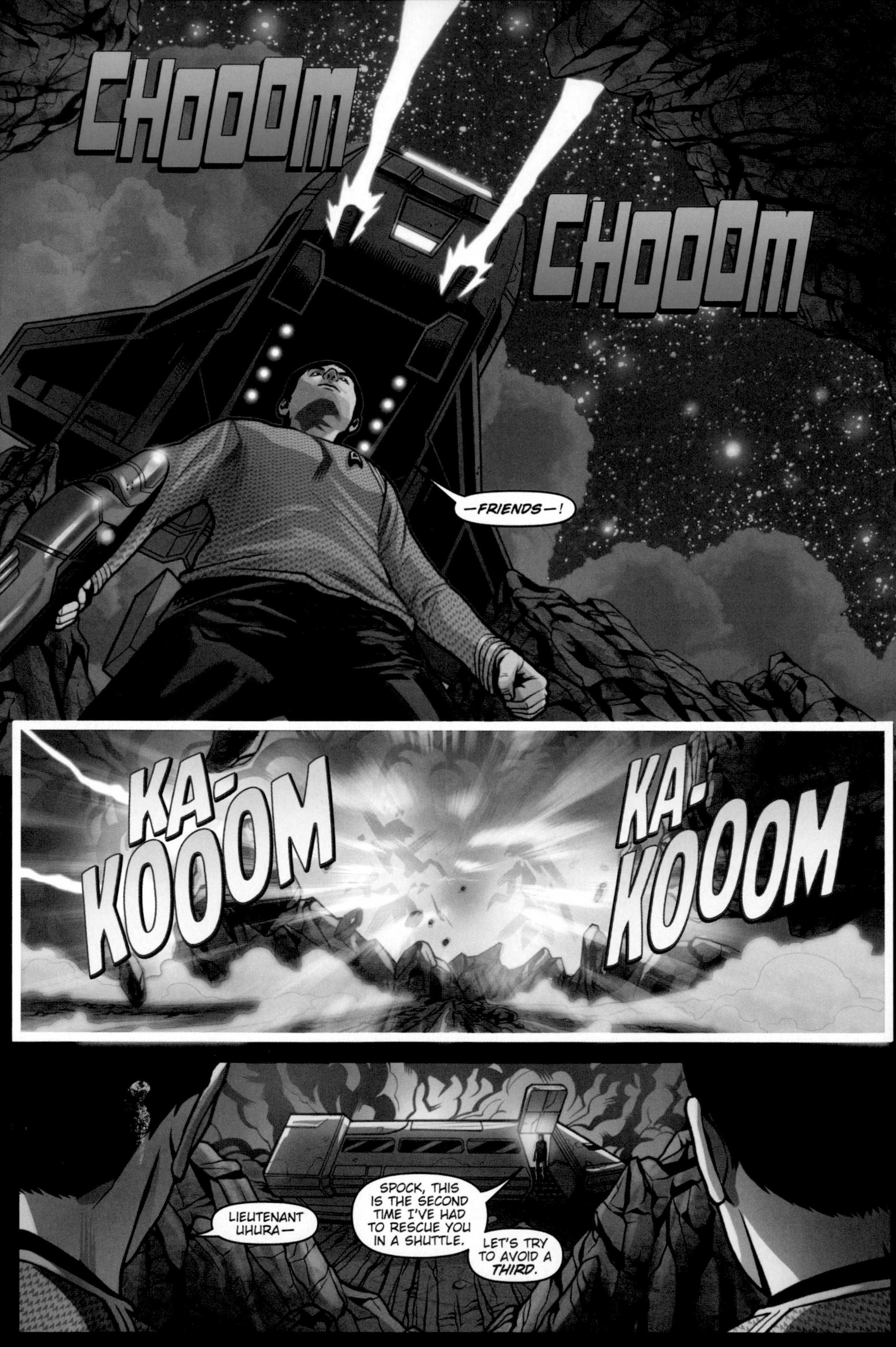
CHOOOM
CHOOOM
—FRIENDS—!
KA-KOOOM
KA-KOOOM
LIEUTENANT UHURA—
SPOCK, THIS IS THE SECOND TIME I'VE HAD TO RESCUE YOU IN A SHUTTLE.
LET'S TRY TO AVOID A THIRD.

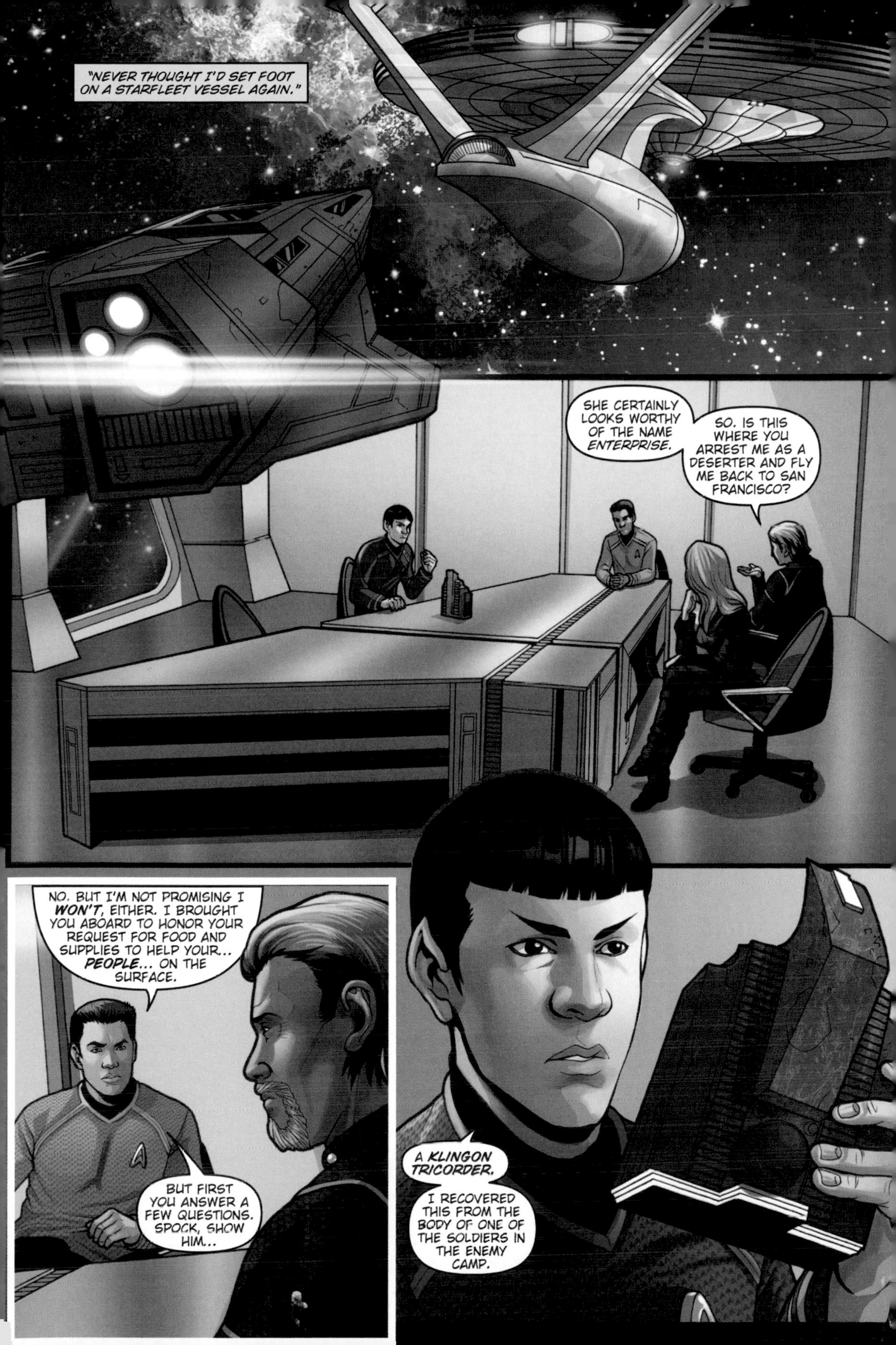
"NEVER THOUGHT I'D SET FOOT ON A STARFLEET VESSEL AGAIN."
SHE CERTAINLY LOOKS WORTHY OF THE NAME ENTERPRISE.
SO. IS THIS WHERE YOU ARREST ME AS A DESERTER AND FLY ME BACK TO SAN FRANCISCO?
NO. BUT I'M NOT PROMISING I WON'T, EITHER. I BROUGHT YOU ABOARD TO HONOR YOUR REQUEST FOR FOOD AND SUPPLIES TO HELP YOUR... PEOPLE... ON THE SURFACE.
BUT FIRST YOU ANSWER A FEW QUESTIONS. SPOCK, SHOW HIM...
A KLINGON TRICORDER.
I RECOVERED THIS FROM THE BODY OF ONE OF THE SOLDIERS IN THE ENEMY CAMP.

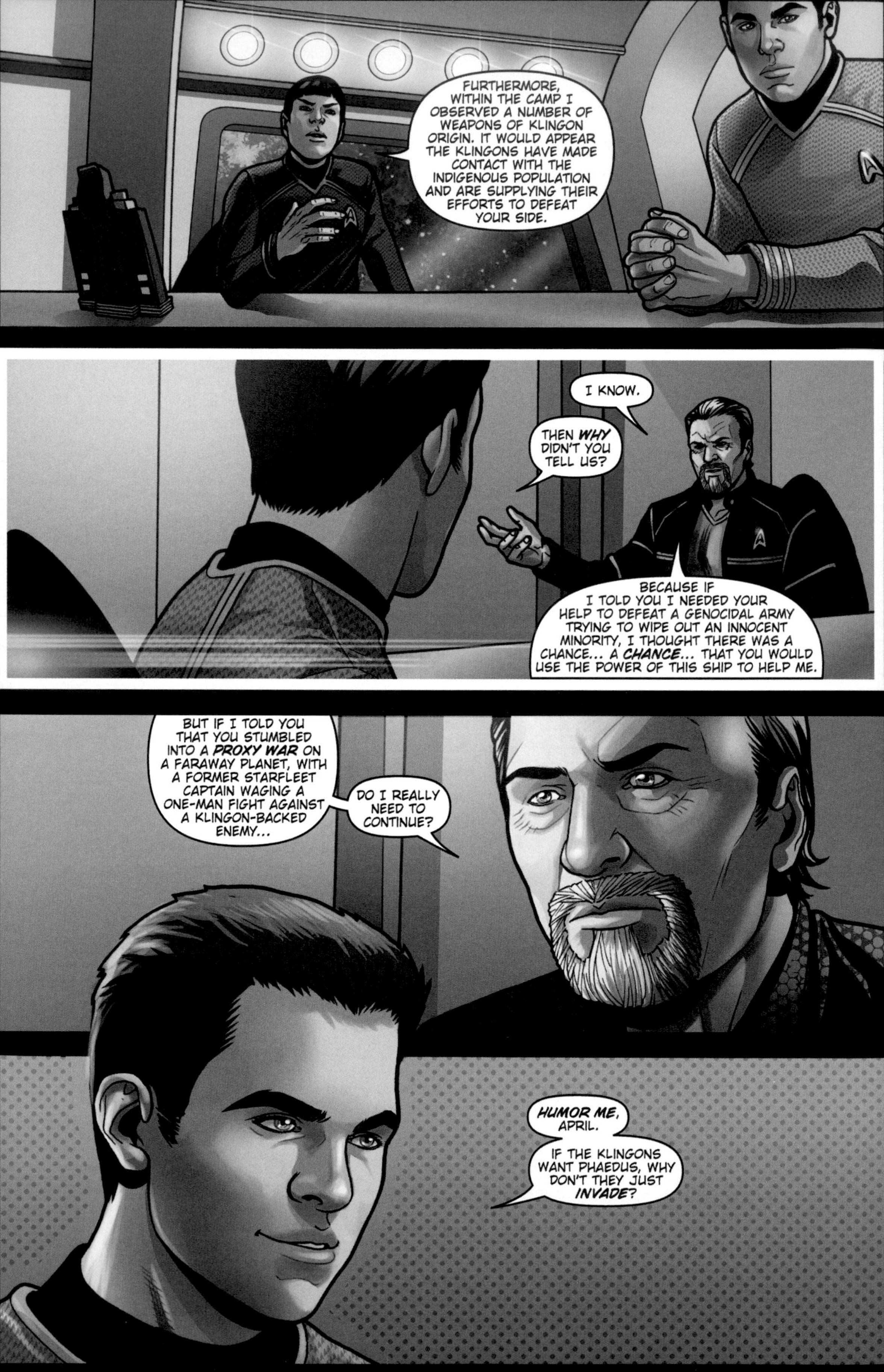
FURTHERMORE, WITHIN THE CAMP I OBSERVED A NUMBER OF WEAPONS OF KLINGON ORIGIN. IT WOULD APPEAR THE KLINGONS HAVE MADE CONTACT WITH THE INDIGENOUS POPULATION AND ARE SUPPLYING THEIR EFFORTS TO DEFEAT YOUR SIDE.
THEN WHY DIDN'T YOU TELL US?
I KNOW.
BECAUSE IF I TOLD YOU I NEEDED YOUR HELP TO DEFEAT A GENOCIDAL ARMY TRYING TO WIPE OUT AN INNOCENT MINORITY, I THOUGHT THERE WAS A CHANCE... A CHANCE... THAT YOU WOULD USE THE POWER OF THIS SHIP TO HELP ME.
BUT IF I TOLD YOU THAT YOU STUMBLED INTO A PROXY WAR ON A FARAWAY PLANET, WITH A FORMER STARFLEET CAPTAIN WAGING A ONE-MAN FIGHT AGAINST A KLINGON-BACKED ENEMY...
DO I REALLY NEED TO CONTINUE?
HUMOR ME, APRIL.
IF THE KLINGONS WANT PHAEDUS, WHY DON'T THEY JUST INVADE?

BECAUSE THEY DON'T **HAVE TO**, CAPTAIN. ALL THEY NEED TO DO IS BACK THE WINNING SIDE IN A CIVIL WAR AND THEN SWOOP IN AND PLANT THE EMPIRE'S FLAG. INSTANT COLONY.

THE KLINGONS ARE A VIOLENT, EXPANSIONIST RACE. BUT THEY AREN'T STUPID. IF THEY'RE GOING TO RULE THE GALAXY, THEY KNOW THEY CAN'T SPREAD THEIR FORCES TOO THIN. BETTER TO FIGHT PROXY WARS WHERE THEY CAN, SPREAD THEIR INFLUENCE, AND SAVE THE TIP OF THE EMPIRE'S SPEAR FOR THE **REAL FIGHT**.

THE FEDERATION.

EXACTLY.

WHAT ABOUT YOU, MUDD? WHERE DID YOU GET THE STARFLEET WEAPONS AND TECH YOU'VE BEEN SMUGGLING TO APRIL?

IT'S A BIG GALAXY, CAPTAIN. EVEN STARFLEET'S BEEN KNOWN TO LOSE THE KEYS TO AN OUTPOST WEAPONS DEPOT OR TWO, ESPECIALLY IN THE OUTER SYSTEMS WHERE THE NATIVES AREN'T QUITE AS... **FEDERATED**.

YOU'RE NOT GONNA ARREST ME TOO, ARE YOU?

HAVEN'T MADE UP MY MIND.

IN THE MEANTIME I NEED YOU BOTH TO REPORT TO SICKBAY. DR. McCOY WANTS TO MAKE SURE WE DIDN'T MISS ANYTHING WHEN YOU PASSED THROUGH QUARANTINE.

I'LL MEET YOU THERE SHORTLY.

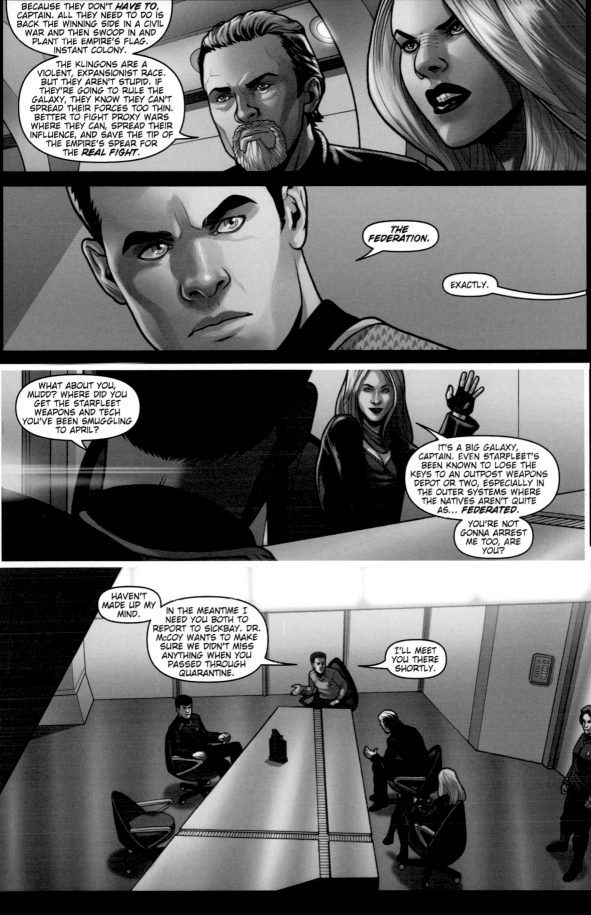

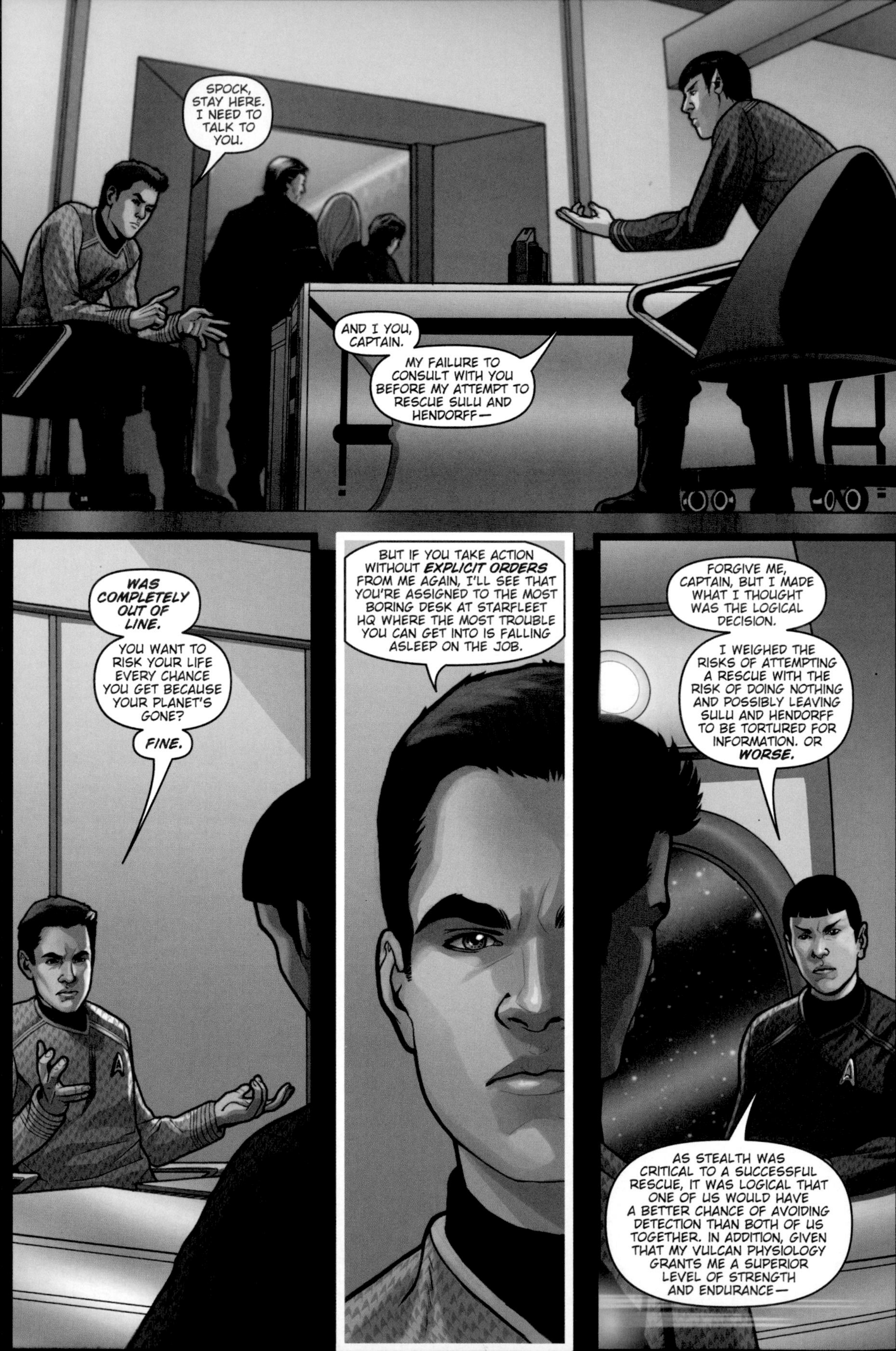
SPOCK, STAY HERE. I NEED TO TALK TO YOU.
AND I YOU, CAPTAIN.
MY FAILURE TO CONSULT WITH YOU BEFORE MY ATTEMPT TO RESCUE SULU AND HENDORFF—
WAS COMPLETELY OUT OF LINE.
YOU WANT TO RISK YOUR LIFE EVERY CHANCE YOU GET BECAUSE YOUR PLANET'S GONE?
FINE.
BUT IF YOU TAKE ACTION WITHOUT EXPLICIT ORDERS FROM ME AGAIN, I'LL SEE THAT YOU'RE ASSIGNED TO THE MOST BORING DESK AT STARFLEET HQ WHERE THE MOST TROUBLE YOU CAN GET INTO IS FALLING ASLEEP ON THE JOB.
FORGIVE ME, CAPTAIN, BUT I MADE WHAT I THOUGHT WAS THE LOGICAL DECISION.
I WEIGHED THE RISKS OF ATTEMPTING A RESCUE WITH THE RISK OF DOING NOTHING AND POSSIBLY LEAVING SULU AND HENDORFF TO BE TORTURED FOR INFORMATION. OR WORSE.
AS STEALTH WAS CRITICAL TO A SUCCESSFUL RESCUE, IT WAS LOGICAL THAT ONE OF US WOULD HAVE A BETTER CHANCE OF AVOIDING DETECTION THAN BOTH OF US TOGETHER. IN ADDITION, GIVEN THAT MY VULCAN PHYSIOLOGY GRANTS ME A SUPERIOR LEVEL OF STRENGTH AND ENDURANCE—

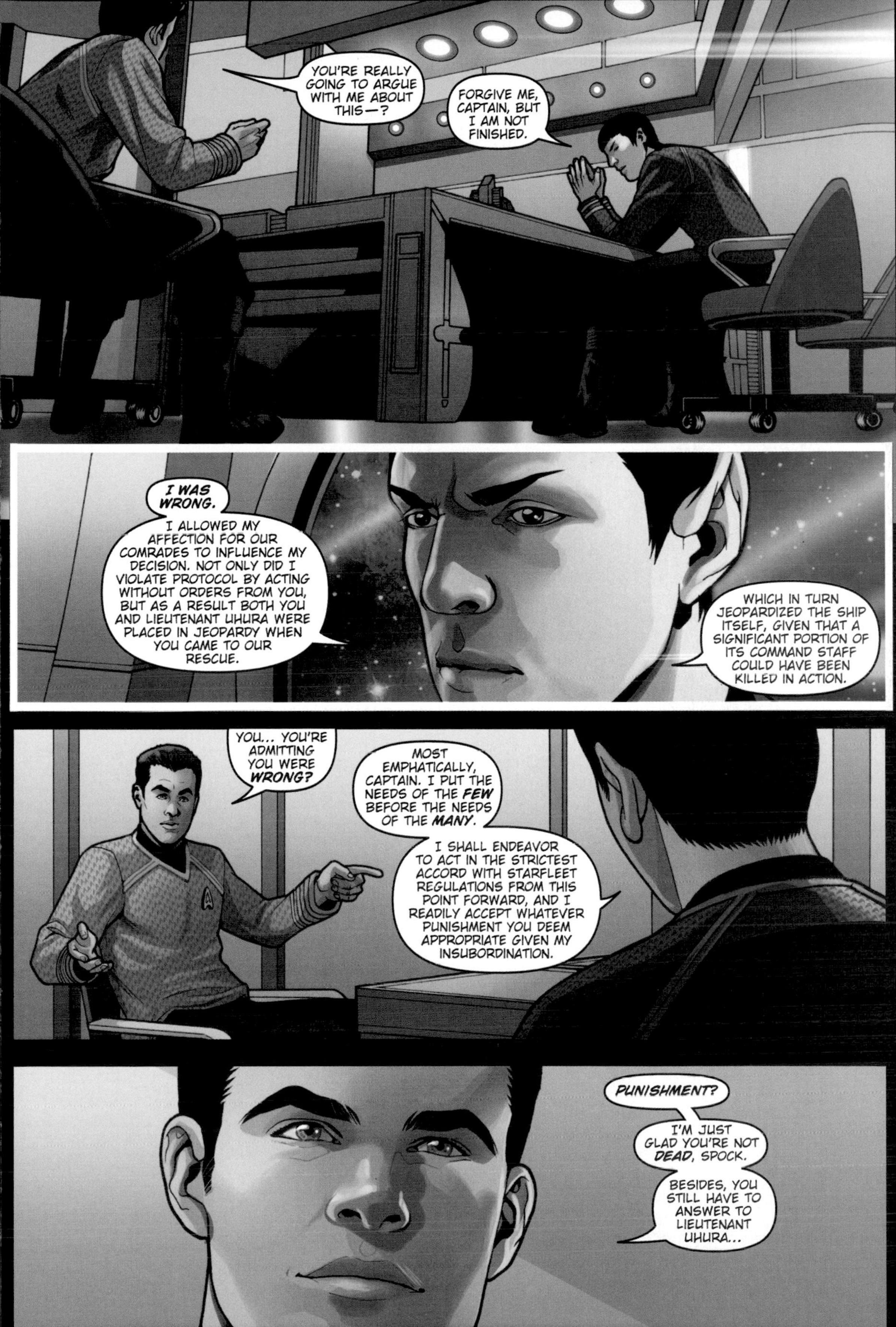
YOU'RE REALLY GOING TO ARGUE WITH ME ABOUT THIS—?
FORGIVE ME, CAPTAIN, BUT I AM NOT FINISHED.
I WAS WRONG.
I ALLOWED MY AFFECTION FOR OUR COMRADES TO INFLUENCE MY DECISION. NOT ONLY DID I VIOLATE PROTOCOL BY ACTING WITHOUT ORDERS FROM YOU, BUT AS A RESULT BOTH YOU AND LIEUTENANT UHURA WERE PLACED IN JEOPARDY WHEN YOU CAME TO OUR RESCUE.
WHICH IN TURN JEOPARDIZED THE SHIP ITSELF, GIVEN THAT A SIGNIFICANT PORTION OF ITS COMMAND STAFF COULD HAVE BEEN KILLED IN ACTION.
YOU... YOU'RE ADMITTING YOU WERE WRONG?
MOST EMPHATICALLY, CAPTAIN. I PUT THE NEEDS OF THE FEW BEFORE THE NEEDS OF THE MANY.
I SHALL ENDEAVOR TO ACT IN THE STRICTEST ACCORD WITH STARFLEET REGULATIONS FROM THIS POINT FORWARD, AND I READILY ACCEPT WHATEVER PUNISHMENT YOU DEEM APPROPRIATE GIVEN MY INSUBORDINATION.
PUNISHMENT?
I'M JUST GLAD YOU'RE NOT DEAD, SPOCK.
BESIDES, YOU STILL HAVE TO ANSWER TO LIEUTENANT UHURA...

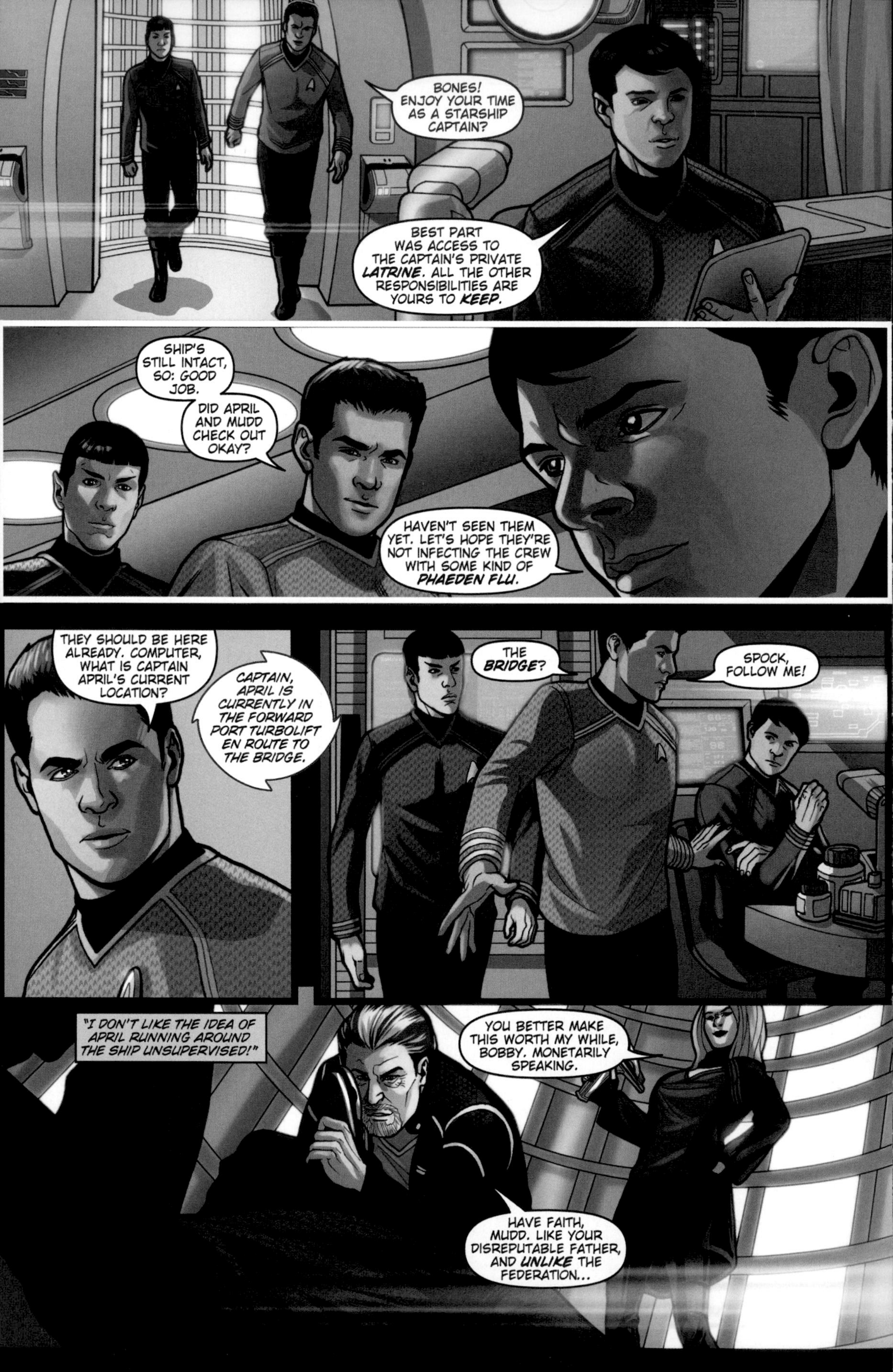
BONES! ENJOY YOUR TIME AS A STARSHIP CAPTAIN?
BEST PART WAS ACCESS TO THE CAPTAIN'S PRIVATE LATRINE. ALL THE OTHER RESPONSIBILITIES ARE YOURS TO KEEP.
SHIP'S STILL INTACT, SO: GOOD JOB.
DID APRIL AND MUDD CHECK OUT OKAY?
HAVEN'T SEEN THEM YET. LET'S HOPE THEY'RE NOT INFECTING THE CREW WITH SOME KIND OF PHAEDEN FLU.
THEY SHOULD BE HERE ALREADY. COMPUTER, WHAT IS CAPTAIN APRIL'S CURRENT LOCATION?
CAPTAIN, APRIL IS CURRENTLY IN THE FORWARD PORT TURBOLIFT EN ROUTE TO THE BRIDGE.
THE BRIDGE?
SPOCK, FOLLOW ME!
"I DON'T LIKE THE IDEA OF APRIL RUNNING AROUND THE SHIP UNSUPERVISED!"
YOU BETTER MAKE THIS WORTH MY WHILE, BOBBY. MONETARILY SPEAKING.
HAVE FAITH, MUDD. LIKE YOUR DISREPUTABLE FATHER, AND UNLIKE THE FEDERATION...

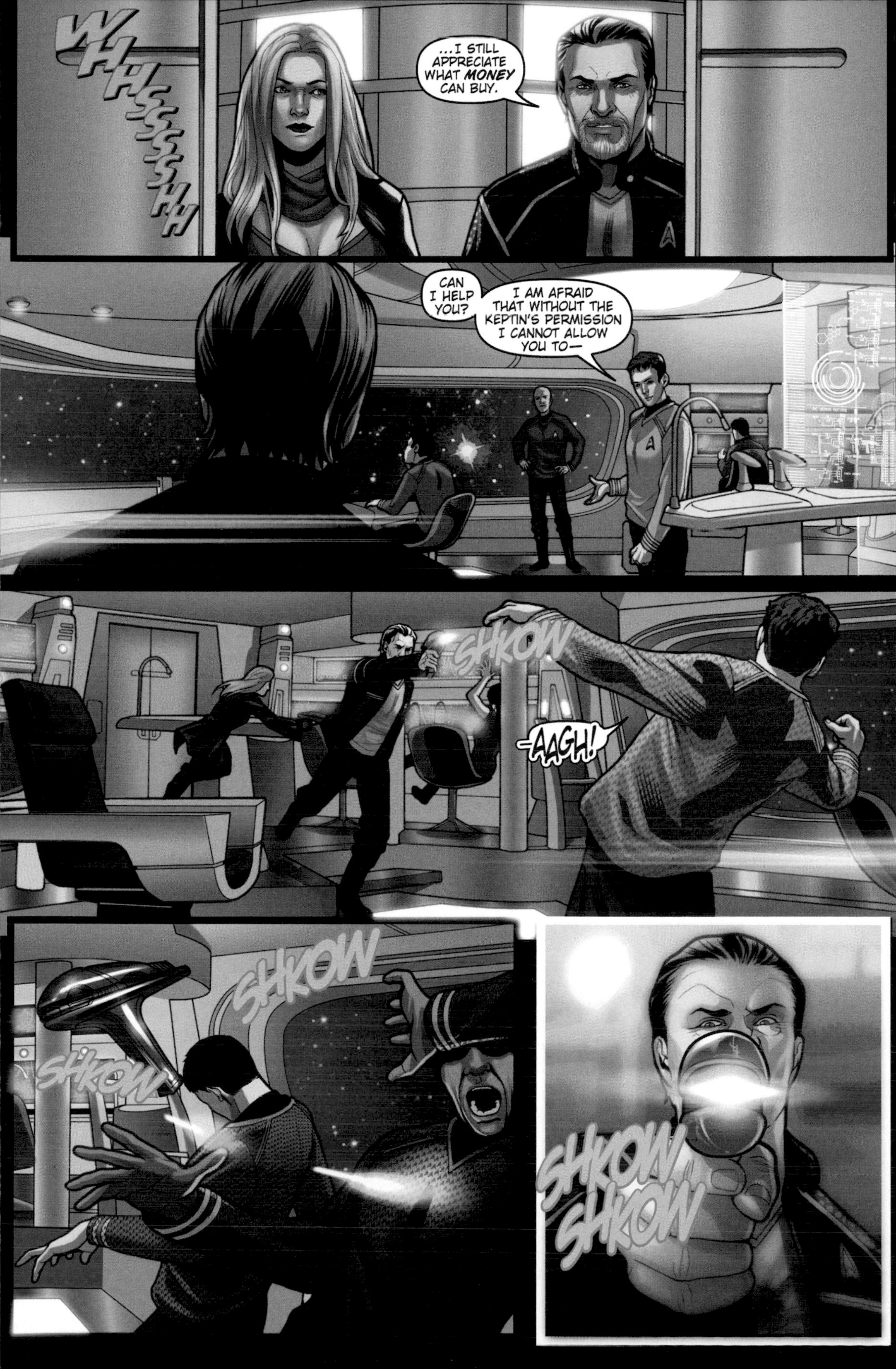
WHHSSSSHH
...I STILL APPRECIATE WHAT MONEY CAN BUY.
CAN I HELP YOU?
I AM AFRAID THAT WITHOUT THE KEPTIN'S PERMISSION I CANNOT ALLOW YOU TO—
SHKOW
-AAGH!
SHKOW
SHKOW
SHKOW
SHKOW

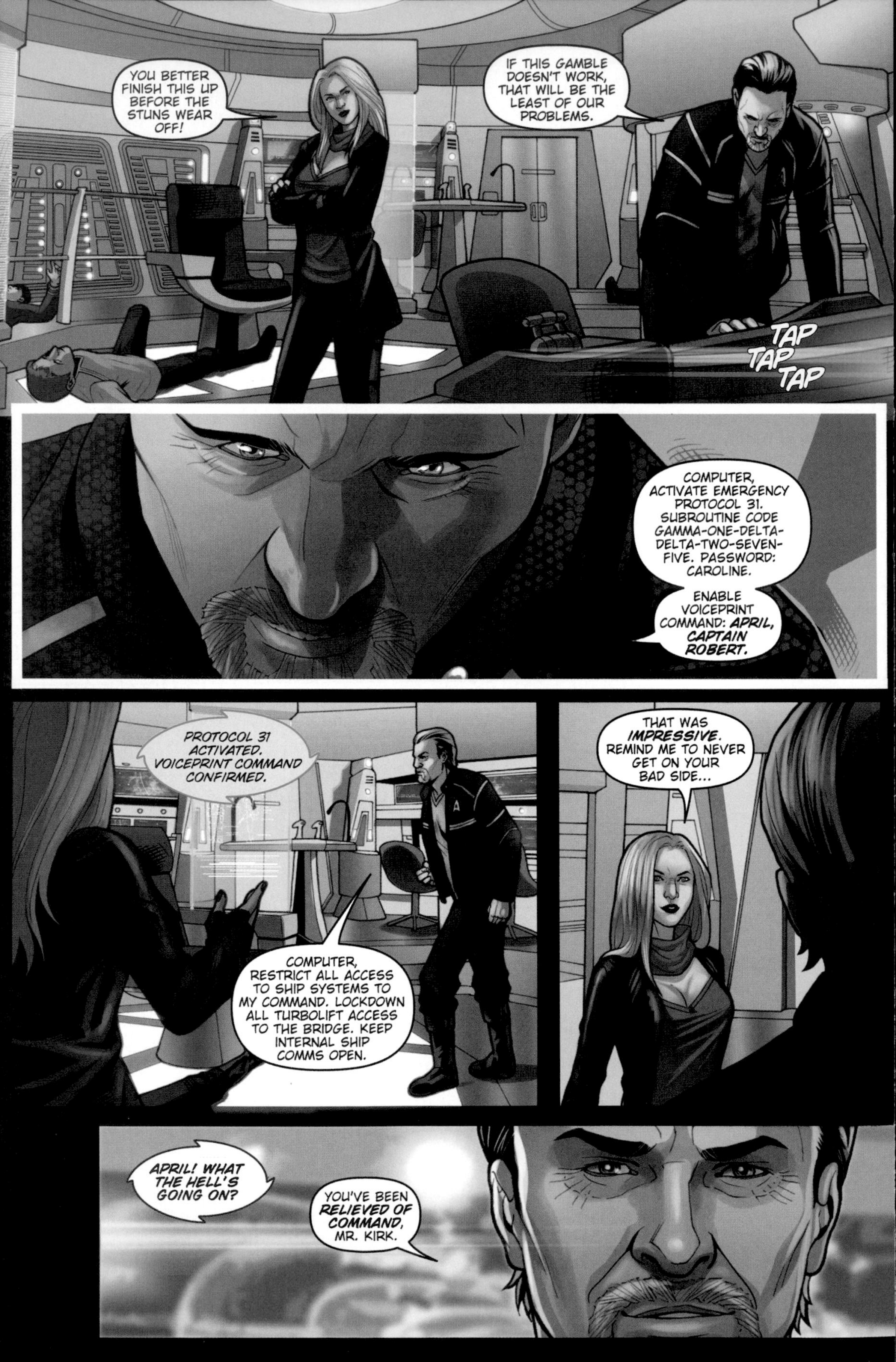
YOU BETTER FINISH THIS UP BEFORE THE STUNS WEAR OFF!
IF THIS GAMBLE DOESN'T WORK, THAT WILL BE THE LEAST OF OUR PROBLEMS.
TAP TAP TAP
COMPUTER, ACTIVATE EMERGENCY PROTOCOL 31. SUBROUTINE CODE GAMMA-ONE-DELTA-DELTA-TWO-SEVEN-FIVE. PASSWORD: CAROLINE.
ENABLE VOICEPRINT COMMAND: APRIL, CAPTAIN ROBERT.
PROTOCOL 31 ACTIVATED. VOICEPRINT COMMAND CONFIRMED.
COMPUTER, RESTRICT ALL ACCESS TO SHIP SYSTEMS TO MY COMMAND. LOCKDOWN ALL TURBOLIFT ACCESS TO THE BRIDGE. KEEP INTERNAL SHIP COMMS OPEN.
THAT WAS IMPRESSIVE. REMIND ME TO NEVER GET ON YOUR BAD SIDE...
APRIL! WHAT THE HELL'S GOING ON?
YOU'VE BEEN RELIEVED OF COMMAND, MR. KIRK.

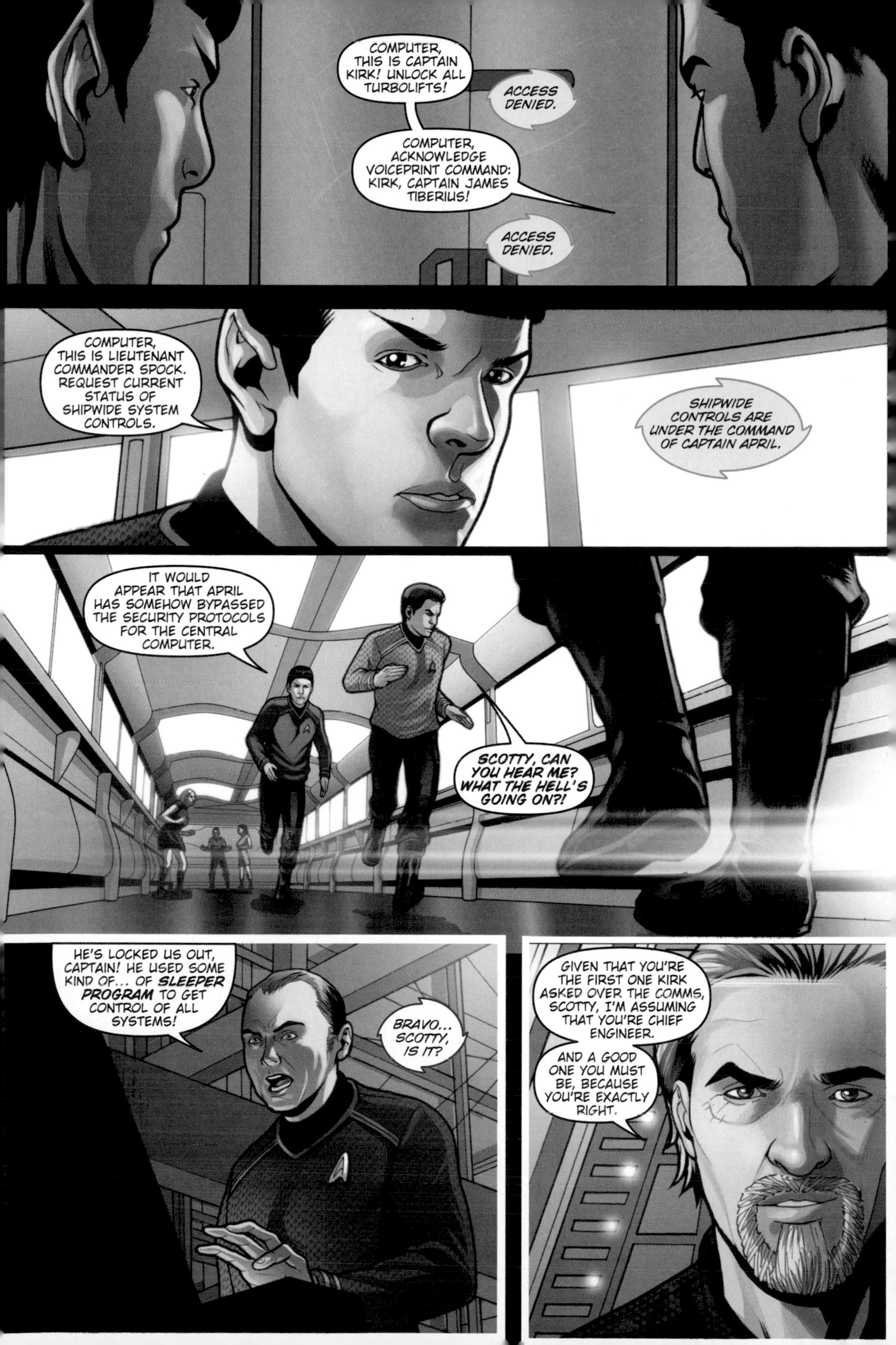
COMPUTER, THIS IS CAPTAIN KIRK! UNLOCK ALL TURBOLIFTS!
ACCESS DENIED.
COMPUTER, ACKNOWLEDGE VOICEPRINT COMMAND: KIRK, CAPTAIN JAMES TIBERIUS!
ACCESS DENIED.
COMPUTER, THIS IS LIEUTENANT COMMANDER SPOCK. REQUEST CURRENT STATUS OF SHIPWIDE SYSTEM CONTROLS.
SHIPWIDE CONTROLS ARE UNDER THE COMMAND OF CAPTAIN APRIL.
IT WOULD APPEAR THAT APRIL HAS SOMEHOW BYPASSED THE SECURITY PROTOCOLS FOR THE CENTRAL COMPUTER.
SCOTTY, CAN YOU HEAR ME? WHAT THE HELL'S GOING ON?!
HE'S LOCKED US OUT, CAPTAIN! HE USED SOME KIND OF... OF SLEEPER PROGRAM TO GET CONTROL OF ALL SYSTEMS!
BRAVO... SCOTTY, IS IT?
GIVEN THAT YOU'RE THE FIRST ONE KIRK ASKED OVER THE COMMS, SCOTTY, I'M ASSUMING THAT YOU'RE CHIEF ENGINEER.
AND A GOOD ONE YOU MUST BE, BECAUSE YOU'RE EXACTLY RIGHT.

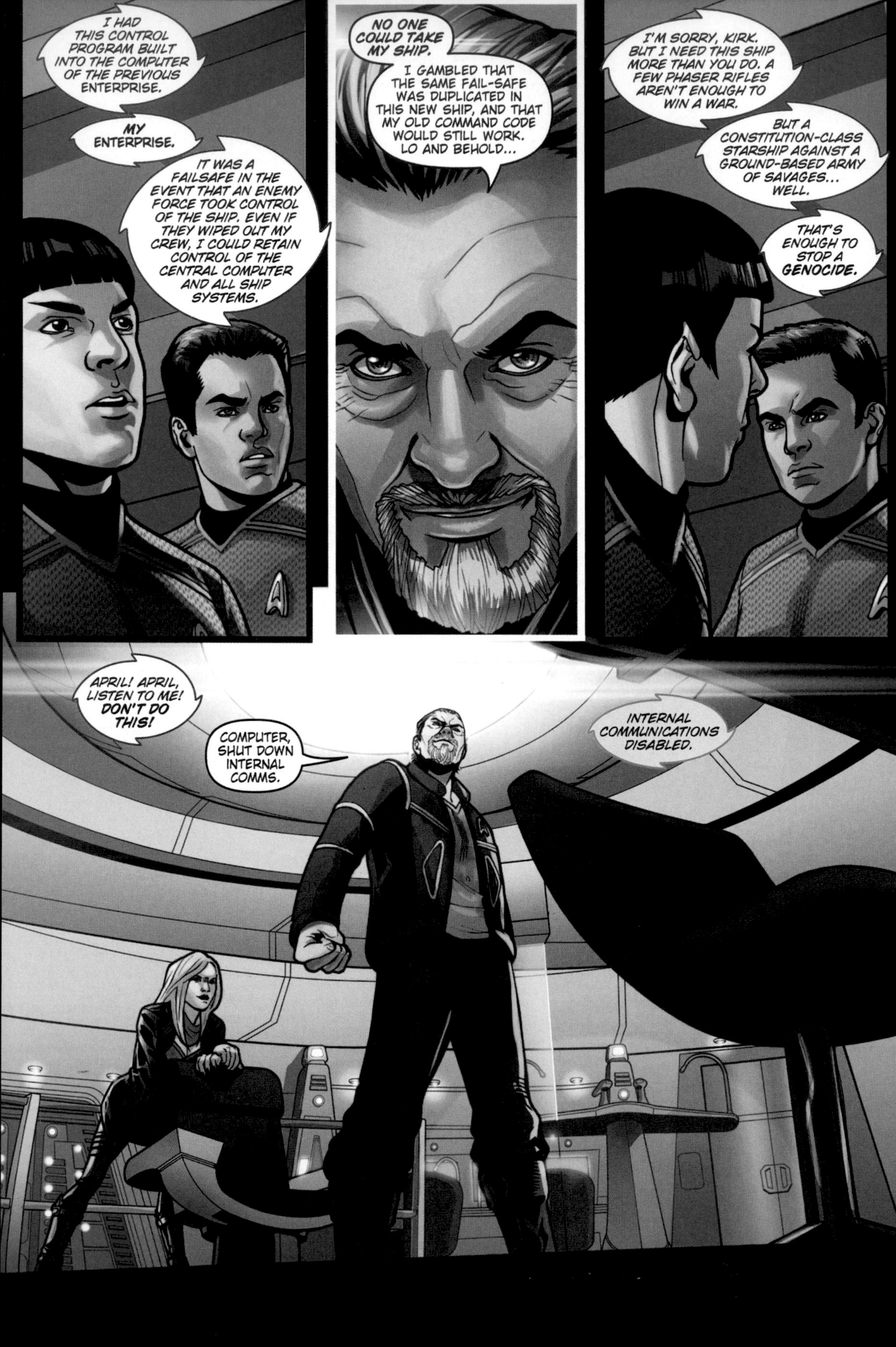
I HAD THIS CONTROL PROGRAM BUILT INTO THE COMPUTER OF THE PREVIOUS ENTERPRISE.
MY ENTERPRISE.
IT WAS A FAILSAFE IN THE EVENT THAT AN ENEMY FORCE TOOK CONTROL OF THE SHIP. EVEN IF THEY WIPED OUT MY CREW, I COULD RETAIN CONTROL OF THE CENTRAL COMPUTER AND ALL SHIP SYSTEMS.
NO ONE COULD TAKE MY SHIP.
I GAMBLED THAT THE SAME FAIL-SAFE WAS DUPLICATED IN THIS NEW SHIP, AND THAT MY OLD COMMAND CODE WOULD STILL WORK. LO AND BEHOLD...
I'M SORRY, KIRK. BUT I NEED THIS SHIP MORE THAN YOU DO. A FEW PHASER RIFLES AREN'T ENOUGH TO WIN A WAR.
BUT A CONSTITUTION-CLASS STARSHIP AGAINST A GROUND-BASED ARMY OF SAVAGES... WELL.
THAT'S ENOUGH TO STOP A GENOCIDE.
APRIL! APRIL, LISTEN TO ME! DON'T DO THIS!
COMPUTER, SHUT DOWN INTERNAL COMMS.
INTERNAL COMMUNICATIONS DISABLED.

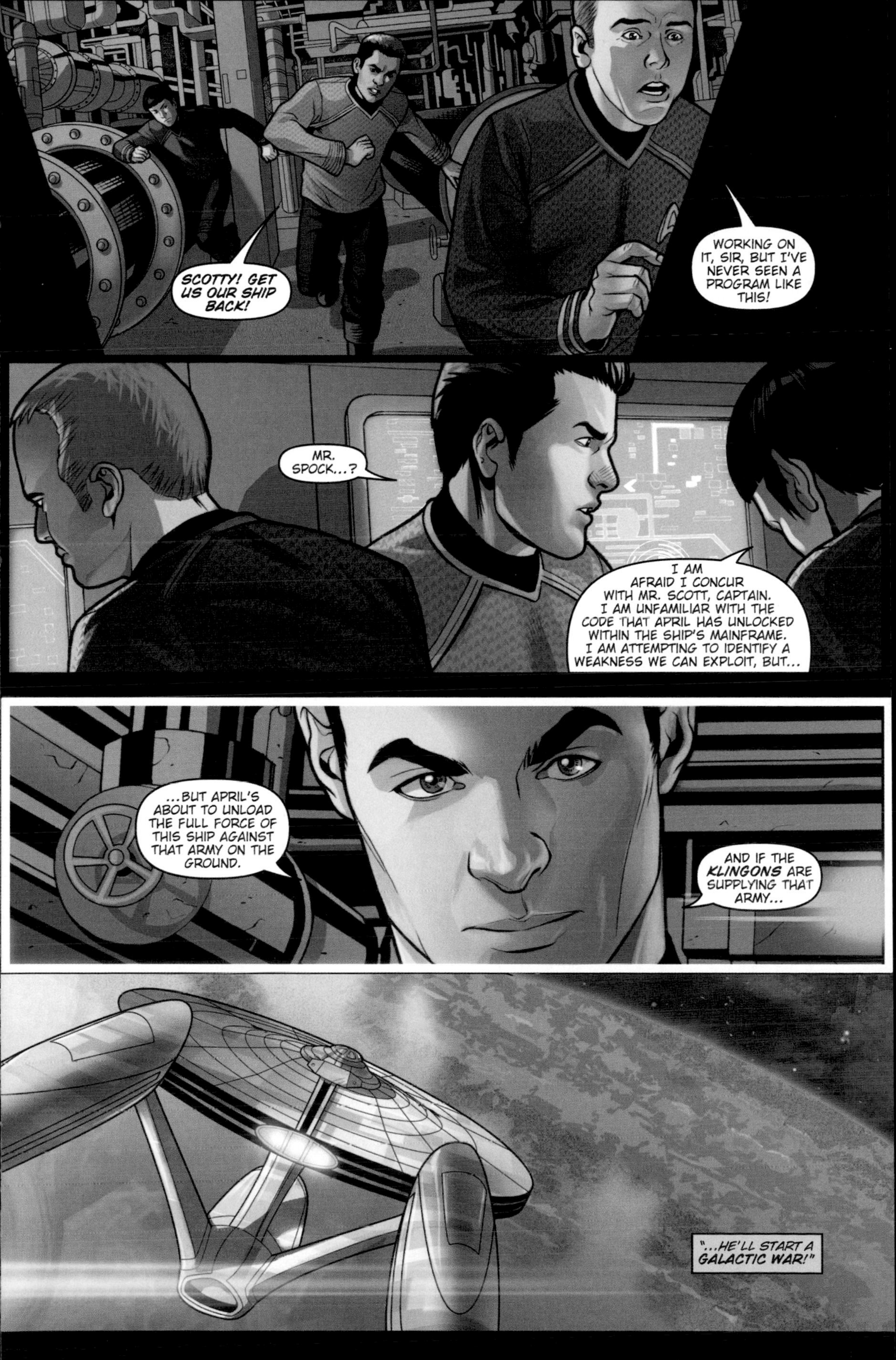
SCOTTY! GET US OUR SHIP BACK!
WORKING ON IT, SIR, BUT I'VE NEVER SEEN A PROGRAM LIKE THIS!
MR. SPOCK...?
I AM AFRAID I CONCUR WITH MR. SCOTT, CAPTAIN. I AM UNFAMILIAR WITH THE CODE THAT APRIL HAS UNLOCKED WITHIN THE SHIP'S MAINFRAME. I AM ATTEMPTING TO IDENTIFY A WEAKNESS WE CAN EXPLOIT, BUT...
...BUT APRIL'S ABOUT TO UNLOAD THE FULL FORCE OF THIS SHIP AGAINST THAT ARMY ON THE GROUND.
AND IF THE KLINGONS ARE SUPPLYING THAT ARMY...
"...HE'LL START A GALACTIC WAR!"

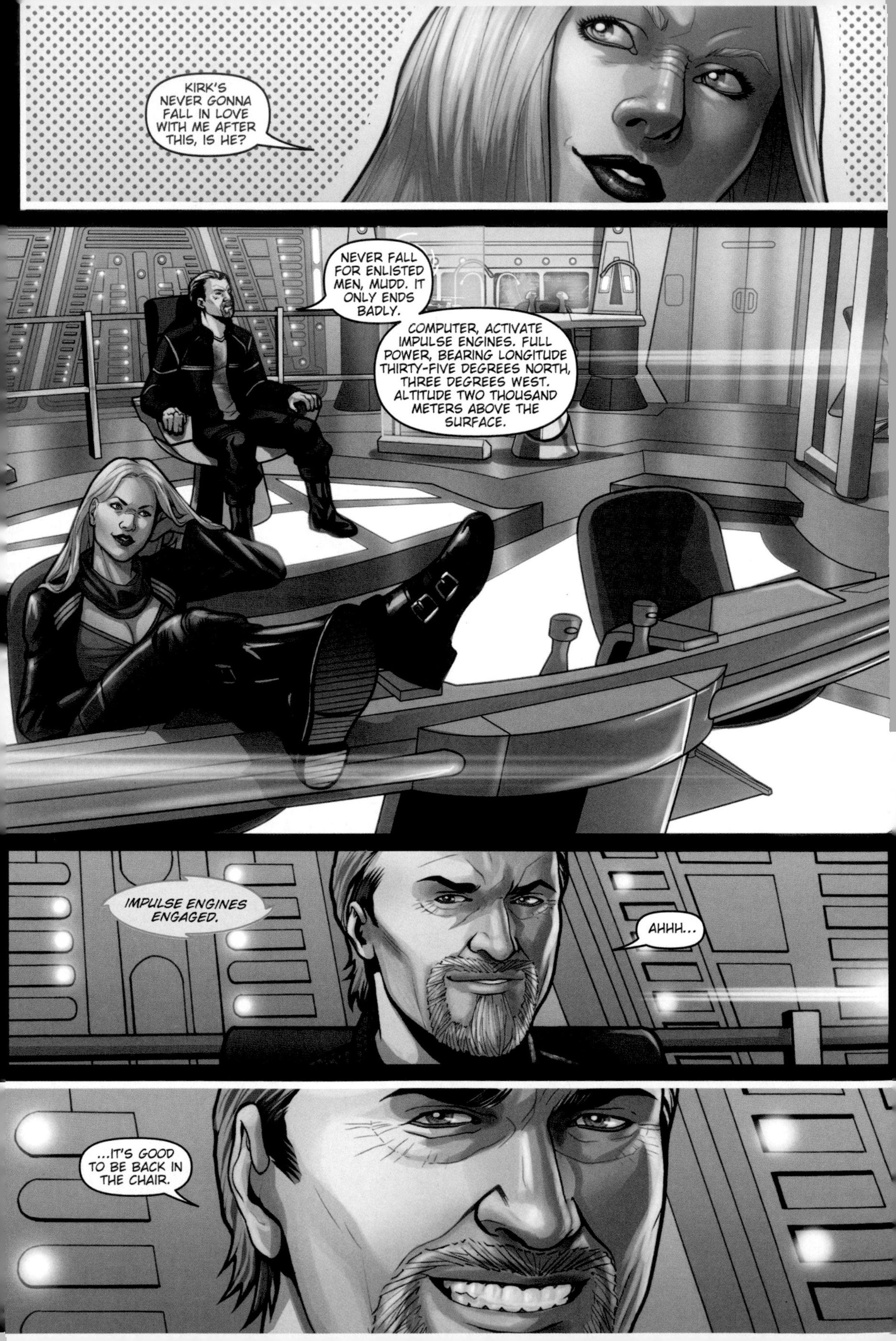
KIRK'S NEVER GONNA FALL IN LOVE WITH ME AFTER THIS, IS HE?
NEVER FALL FOR ENLISTED MEN, MUDD. IT ONLY ENDS BADLY.
COMPUTER, ACTIVATE IMPULSE ENGINES. FULL POWER, BEARING LONGITUDE THIRTY-FIVE DEGREES NORTH, THREE DEGREES WEST. ALTITUDE TWO THOUSAND METERS ABOVE THE SURFACE.
IMPULSE ENGINES ENGAGED.
AHHH...
...IT'S GOOD TO BE BACK IN THE CHAIR.

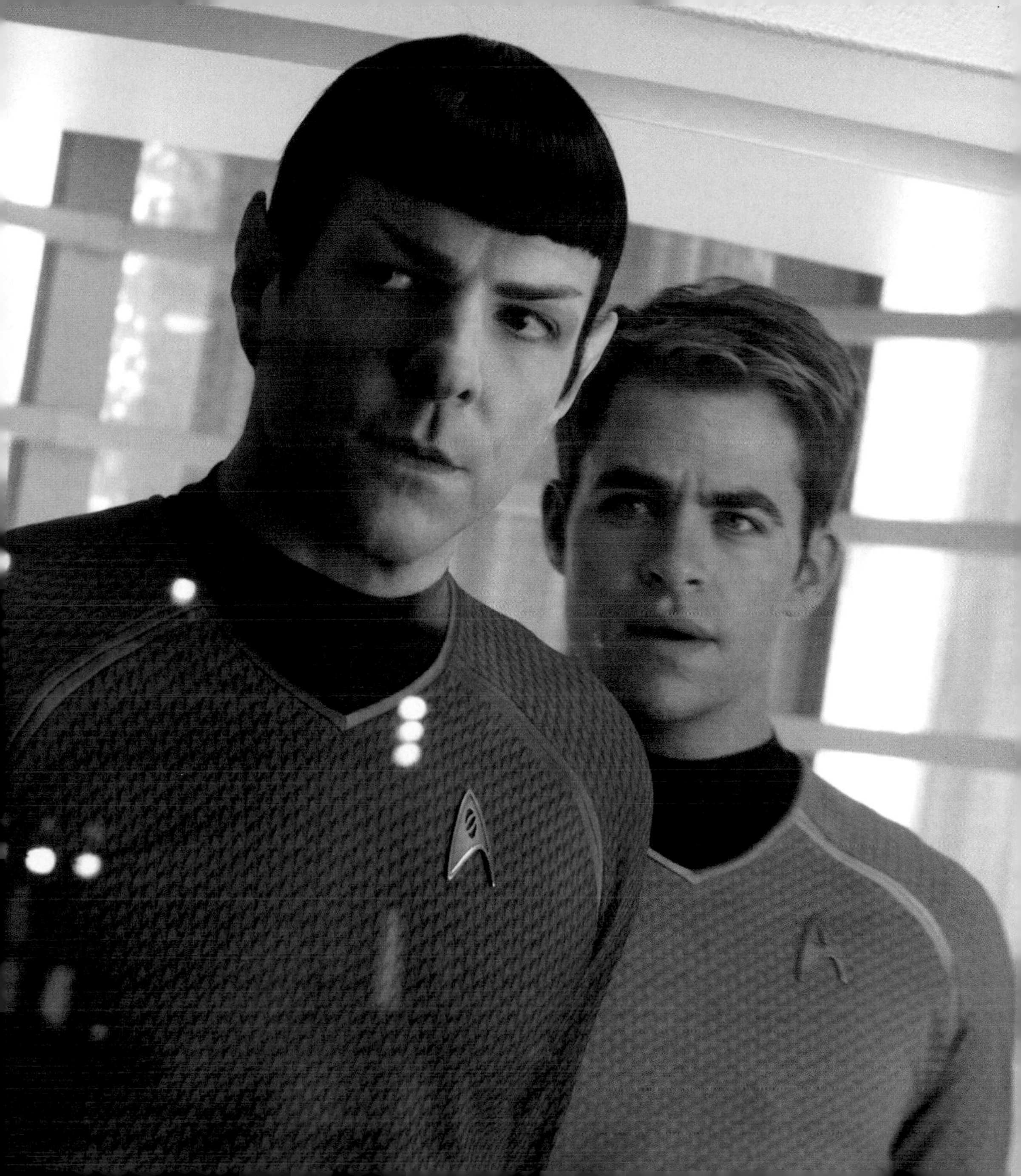

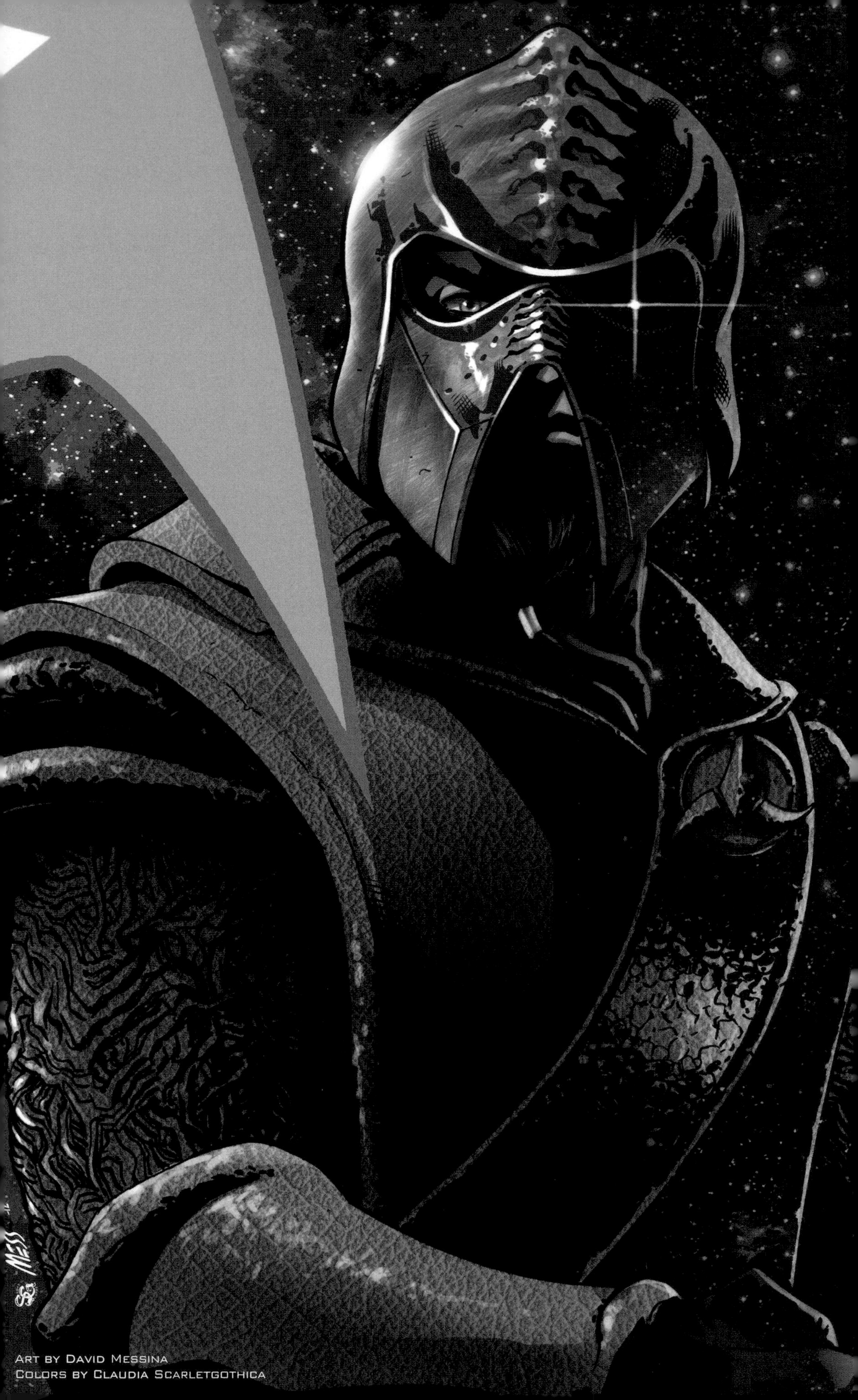

Art by David Messina
Colors by Claudia Scarletgothica

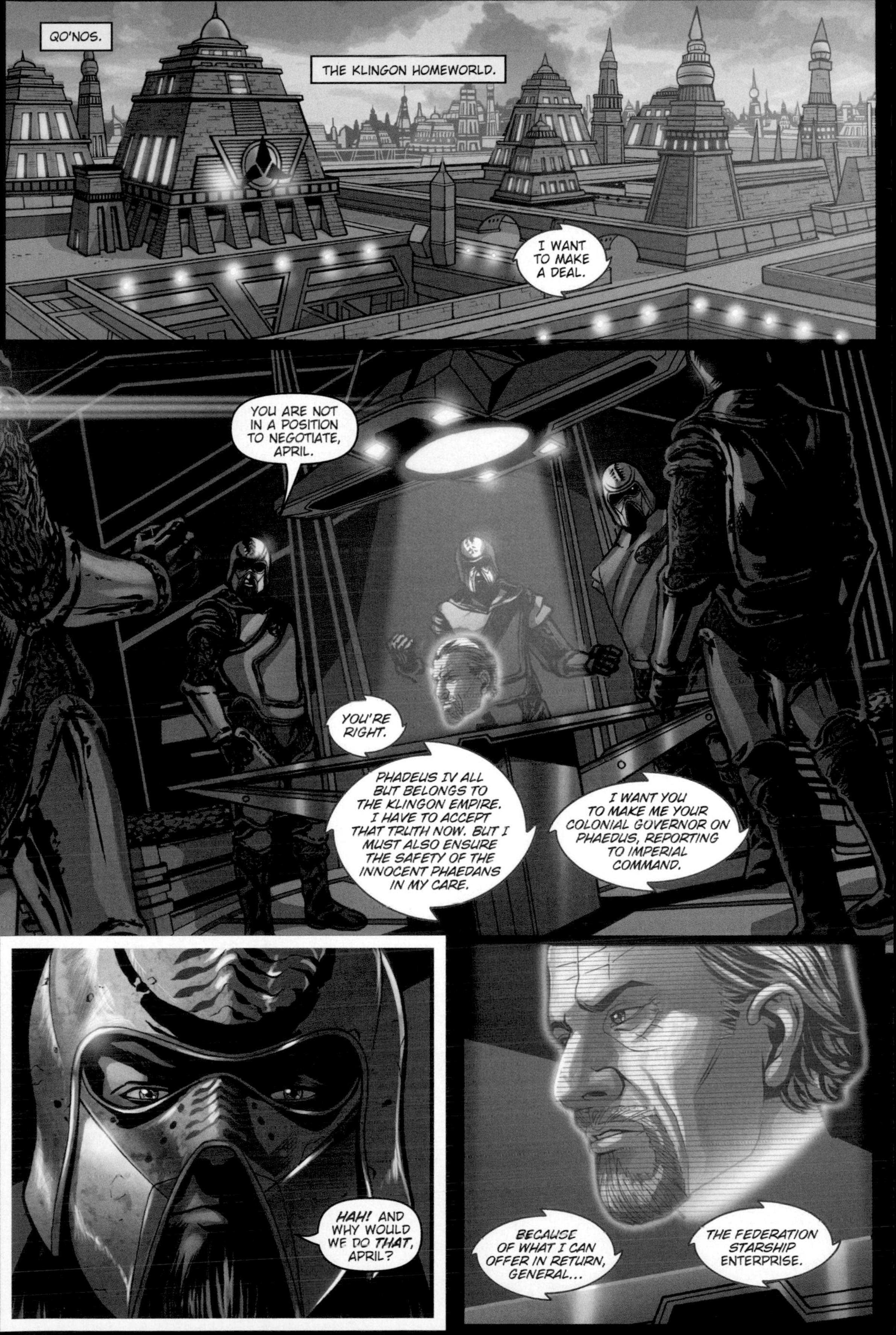
QO'NOS.
THE KLINGON HOMEWORLD.
I WANT TO MAKE A DEAL.
YOU ARE NOT IN A POSITION TO NEGOTIATE, APRIL.
YOU'RE RIGHT.
PHADEUS IV ALL BUT BELONGS TO THE KLINGON EMPIRE. I HAVE TO ACCEPT THAT TRUTH NOW. BUT I MUST ALSO ENSURE THE SAFETY OF THE INNOCENT PHAEDANS IN MY CARE.
I WANT YOU TO MAKE ME YOUR COLONIAL GOVERNOR ON PHAEDUS, REPORTING TO IMPERIAL COMMAND.
HAH! AND WHY WOULD WE DO THAT, APRIL?
BECAUSE OF WHAT I CAN OFFER IN RETURN, GENERAL...
THE FEDERATION STARSHIP ENTERPRISE.

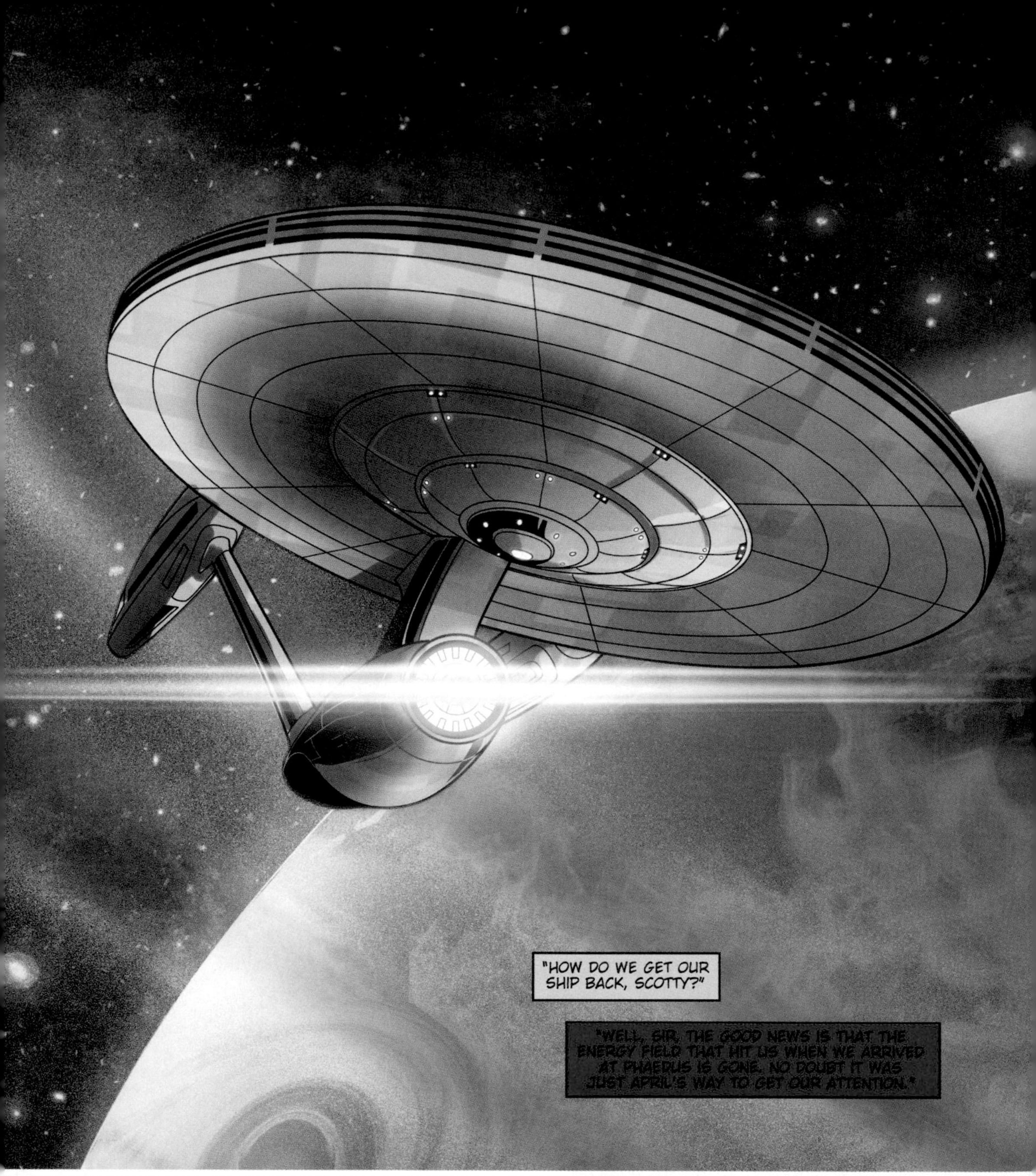
"HOW DO WE GET OUR SHIP BACK, SCOTTY?"
"WELL, SIR, THE GOOD NEWS IS THAT THE ENERGY FIELD THAT HIT US WHEN WE ARRIVED AT PHAEDUS IS GONE. NO DOUBT IT WAS JUST APRIL'S WAY TO GET OUR ATTENTION."

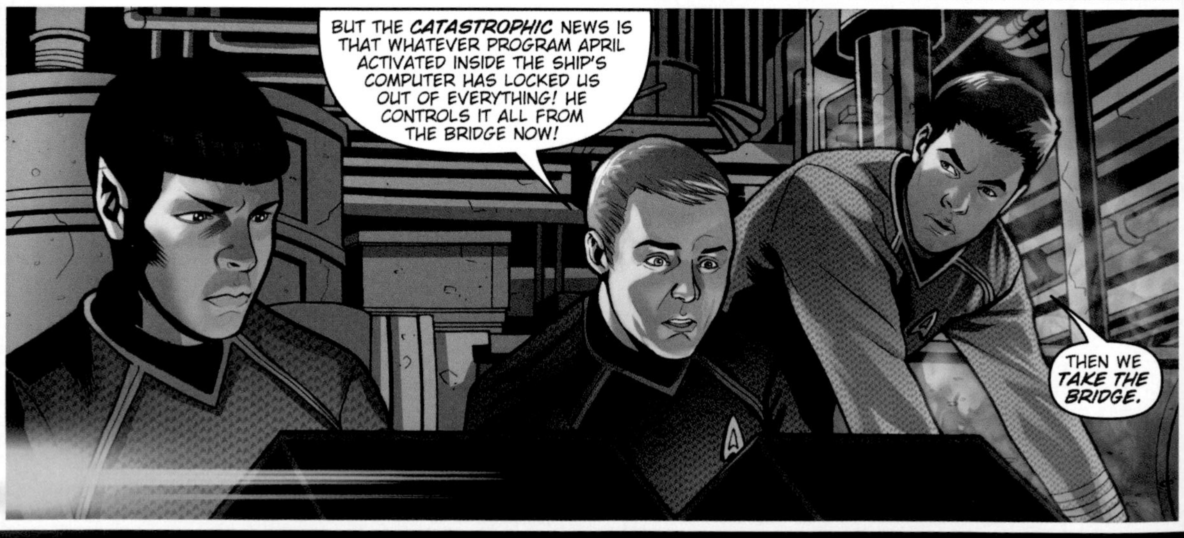
BUT THE CATASTROPHIC NEWS IS THAT WHATEVER PROGRAM APRIL ACTIVATED INSIDE THE SHIP'S COMPUTER HAS LOCKED US OUT OF EVERYTHING! HE CONTROLS IT ALL FROM THE BRIDGE NOW!
THEN WE TAKE THE BRIDGE.

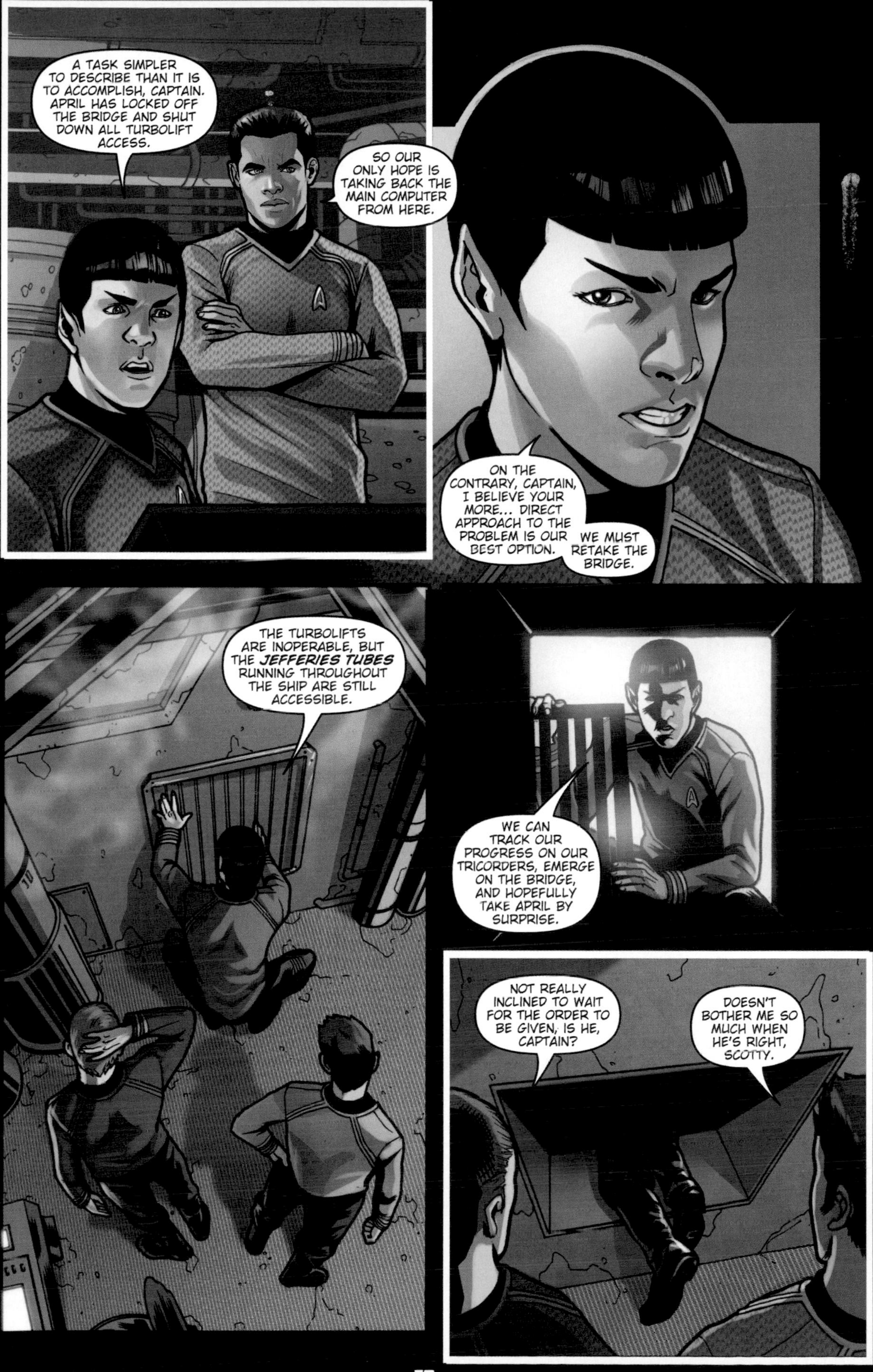
A TASK SIMPLER TO DESCRIBE THAN IT IS TO ACCOMPLISH, CAPTAIN. APRIL HAS LOCKED OFF THE BRIDGE AND SHUT DOWN ALL TURBOLIFT ACCESS.
SO OUR ONLY HOPE IS TAKING BACK THE MAIN COMPUTER FROM HERE.
ON THE CONTRARY, CAPTAIN, I BELIEVE YOUR MORE... DIRECT APPROACH TO THE PROBLEM IS OUR BEST OPTION.
WE MUST RETAKE THE BRIDGE.
THE TURBOLIFTS ARE INOPERABLE, BUT THE *JEFFERIES TUBES* RUNNING THROUGHOUT THE SHIP ARE STILL ACCESSIBLE.
WE CAN TRACK OUR PROGRESS ON OUR TRICORDERS, EMERGE ON THE BRIDGE, AND HOPEFULLY TAKE APRIL BY SURPRISE.
NOT REALLY INCLINED TO WAIT FOR THE ORDER TO BE GIVEN, IS HE, CAPTAIN?
DOESN'T BOTHER ME SO MUCH WHEN HE'S RIGHT, SCOTTY.

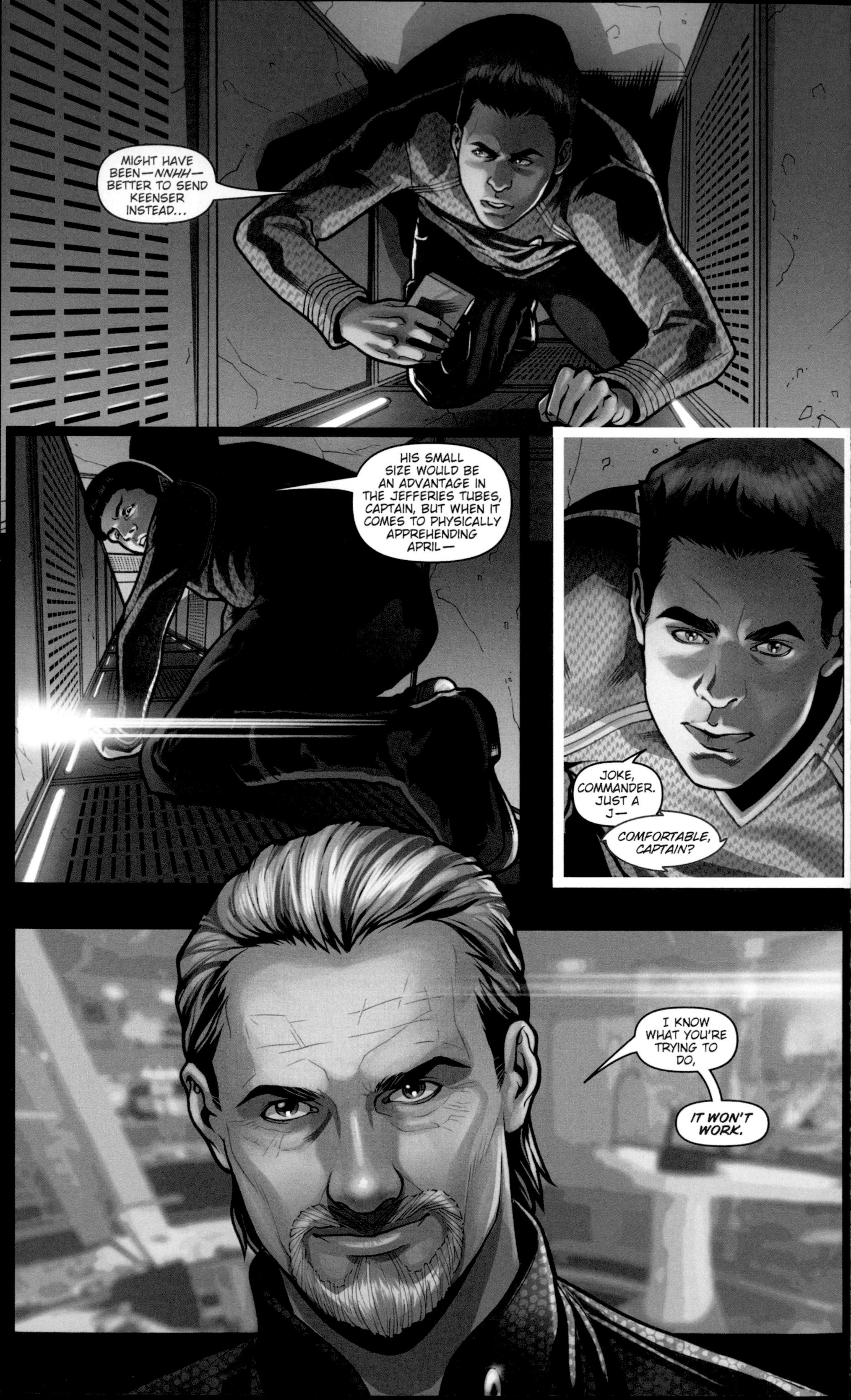
MIGHT HAVE BEEN—*NNHH*—BETTER TO SEND KEENSER INSTEAD...
HIS SMALL SIZE WOULD BE AN ADVANTAGE IN THE JEFFERIES TUBES, CAPTAIN, BUT WHEN IT COMES TO PHYSICALLY APPREHENDING APRIL—
JOKE, COMMANDER. JUST A J—
COMFORTABLE, CAPTAIN?
I KNOW WHAT YOU'RE TRYING TO DO,
IT WON'T WORK.

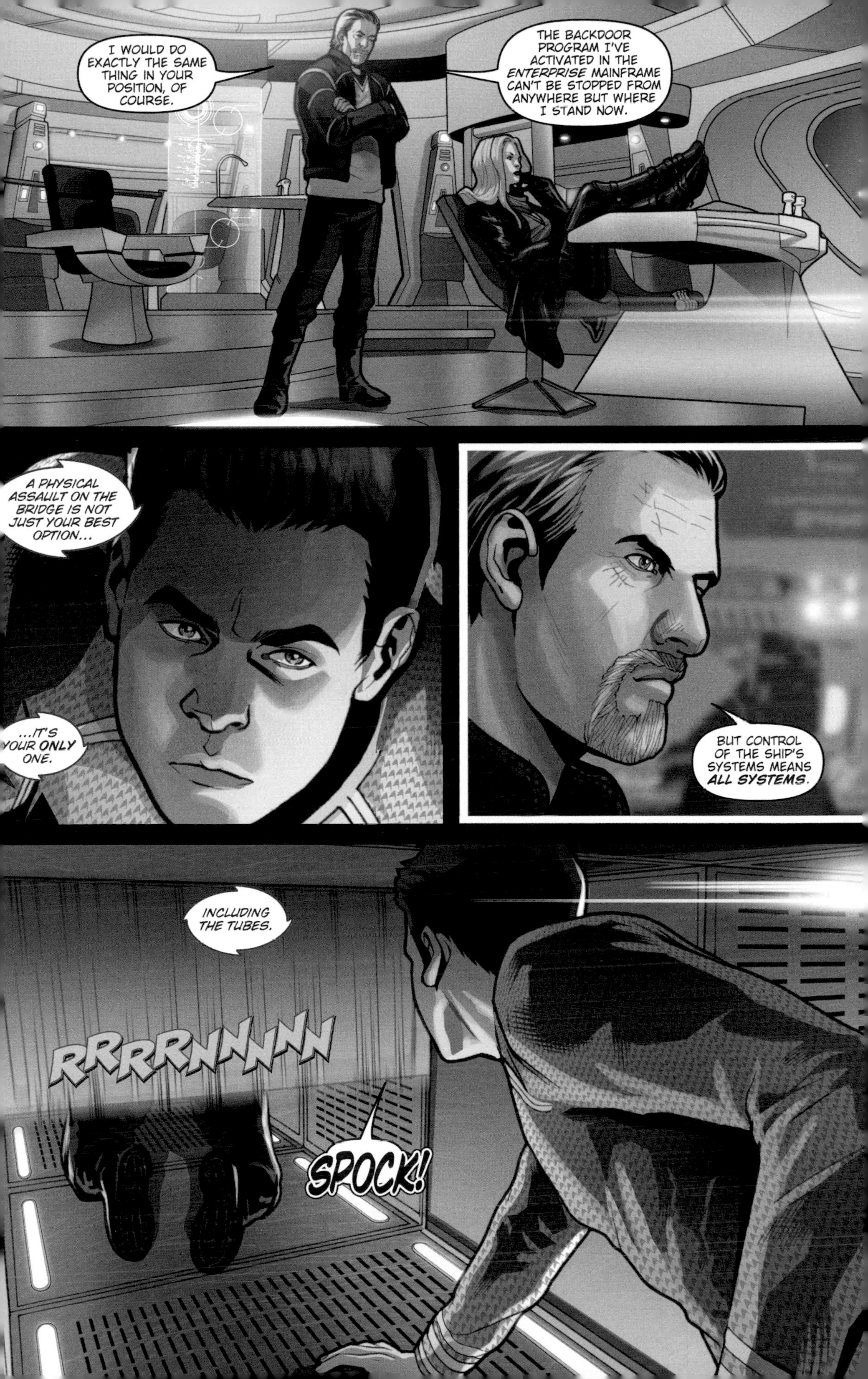
I WOULD DO EXACTLY THE SAME THING IN YOUR POSITION, OF COURSE.
THE BACKDOOR PROGRAM I'VE ACTIVATED IN THE ENTERPRISE MAINFRAME CAN'T BE STOPPED FROM ANYWHERE BUT WHERE I STAND NOW.
A PHYSICAL ASSAULT ON THE BRIDGE IS NOT JUST YOUR BEST OPTION...
...IT'S YOUR ONLY ONE.
BUT CONTROL OF THE SHIP'S SYSTEMS MEANS ALL SYSTEMS.
INCLUDING THE TUBES.
RRRRNNNNN
SPOCK!

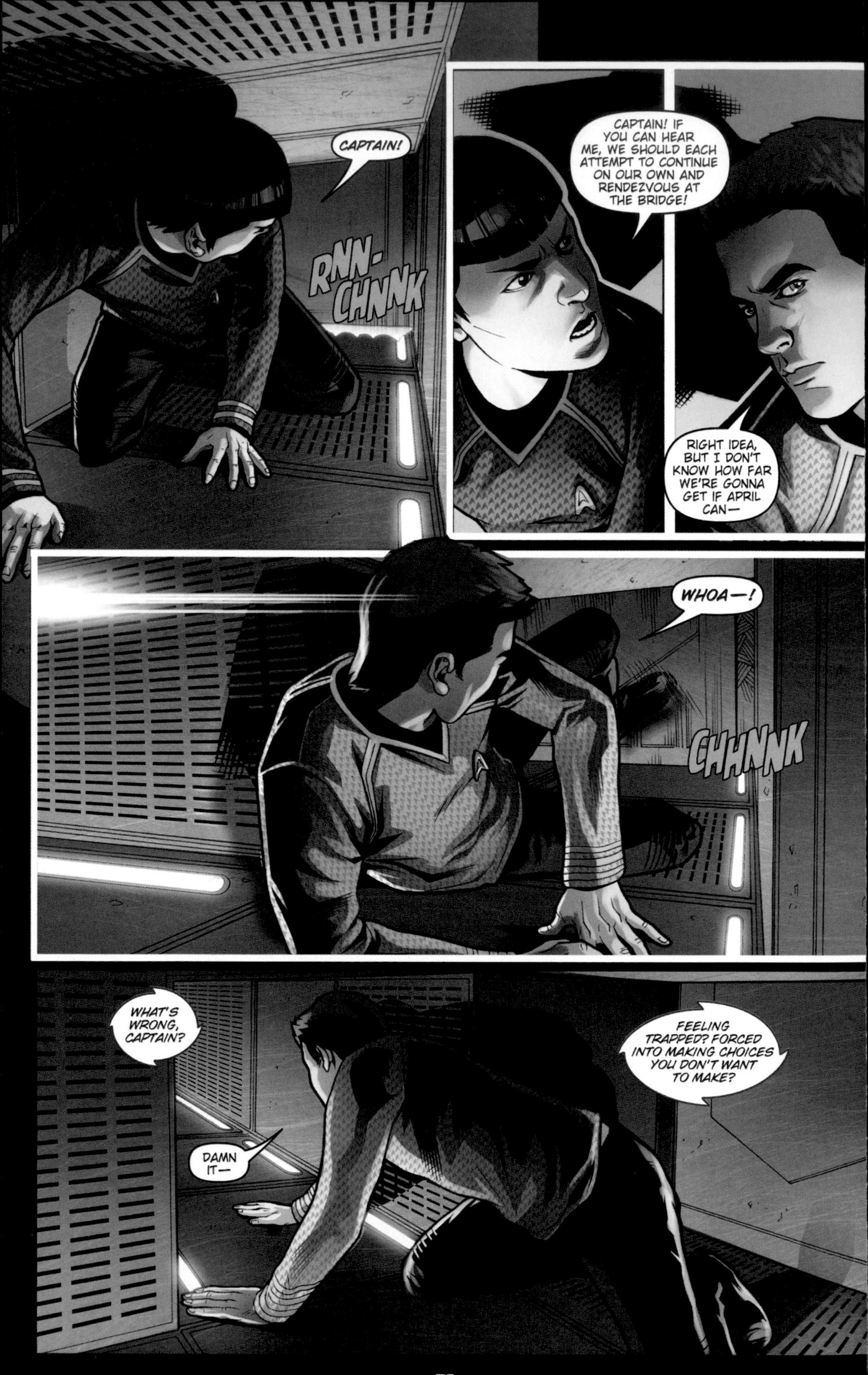
CAPTAIN!
RNN-CHNNK
CAPTAIN! IF YOU CAN HEAR ME, WE SHOULD EACH ATTEMPT TO CONTINUE ON OUR OWN AND RENDEZVOUS AT THE BRIDGE!
RIGHT IDEA, BUT I DON'T KNOW HOW FAR WE'RE GONNA GET IF APRIL CAN—
WHOA—!
CHHNNK
WHAT'S WRONG, CAPTAIN?
FEELING TRAPPED? FORCED INTO MAKING CHOICES YOU DON'T WANT TO MAKE?
DAMN IT—

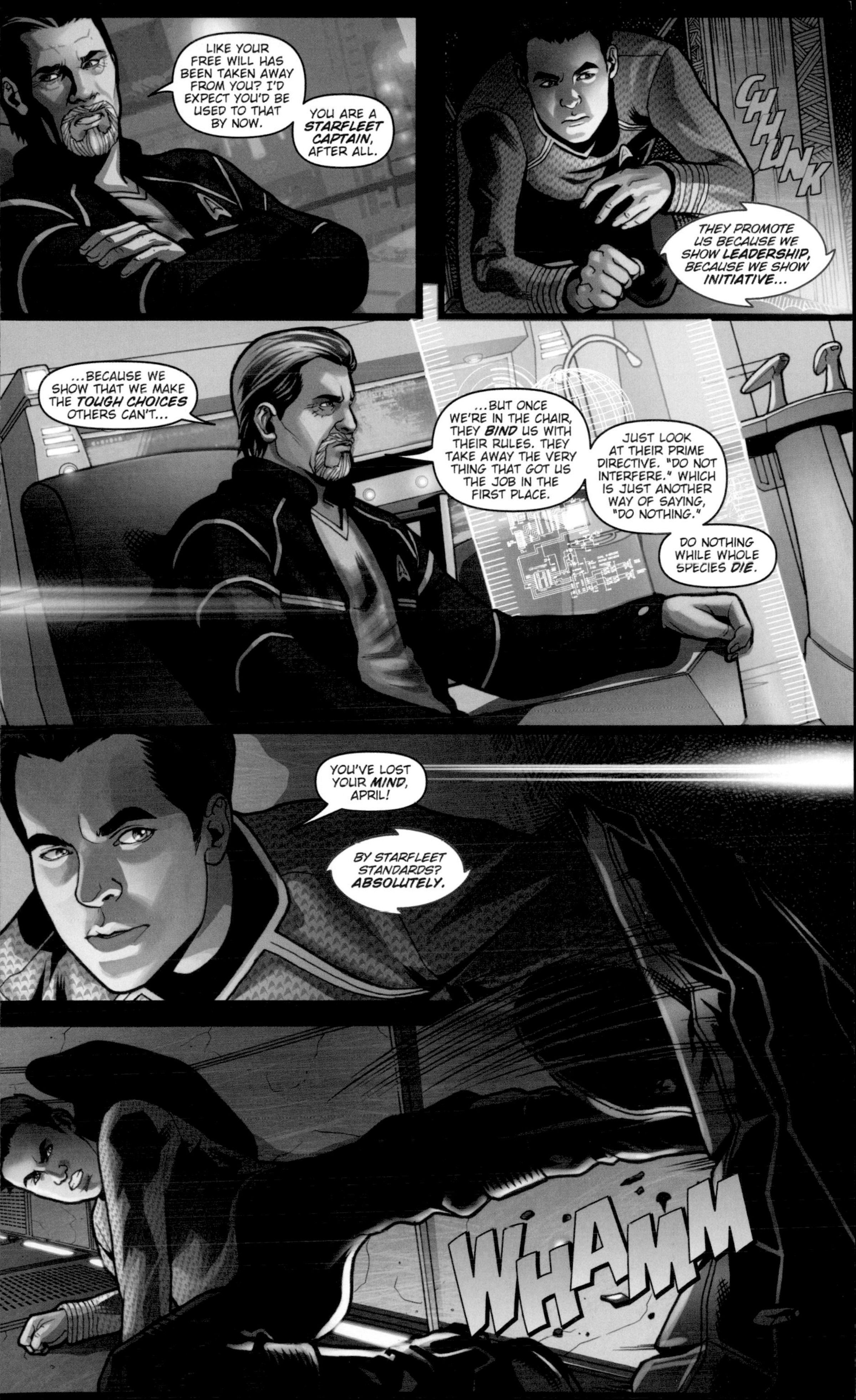
LIKE YOUR FREE WILL HAS BEEN TAKEN AWAY FROM YOU? I'D EXPECT YOU'D BE USED TO THAT BY NOW.
YOU ARE A **STARFLEET CAPTAIN**, AFTER ALL.
CHHUNK
THEY PROMOTE US BECAUSE WE SHOW **LEADERSHIP**, BECAUSE WE SHOW **INITIATIVE**...
...BECAUSE WE SHOW THAT WE MAKE THE **TOUGH CHOICES** OTHERS CAN'T...
...BUT ONCE WE'RE IN THE CHAIR, THEY **BIND** US WITH THEIR RULES. THEY TAKE AWAY THE VERY THING THAT GOT US THE JOB IN THE FIRST PLACE.
JUST LOOK AT THEIR PRIME DIRECTIVE. "DO NOT INTERFERE." WHICH IS JUST ANOTHER WAY OF SAYING, "DO NOTHING."
DO NOTHING WHILE WHOLE SPECIES **DIE**.
YOU'VE LOST YOUR **MIND**, APRIL!
BY STARFLEET STANDARDS? **ABSOLUTELY.**
WHAMM

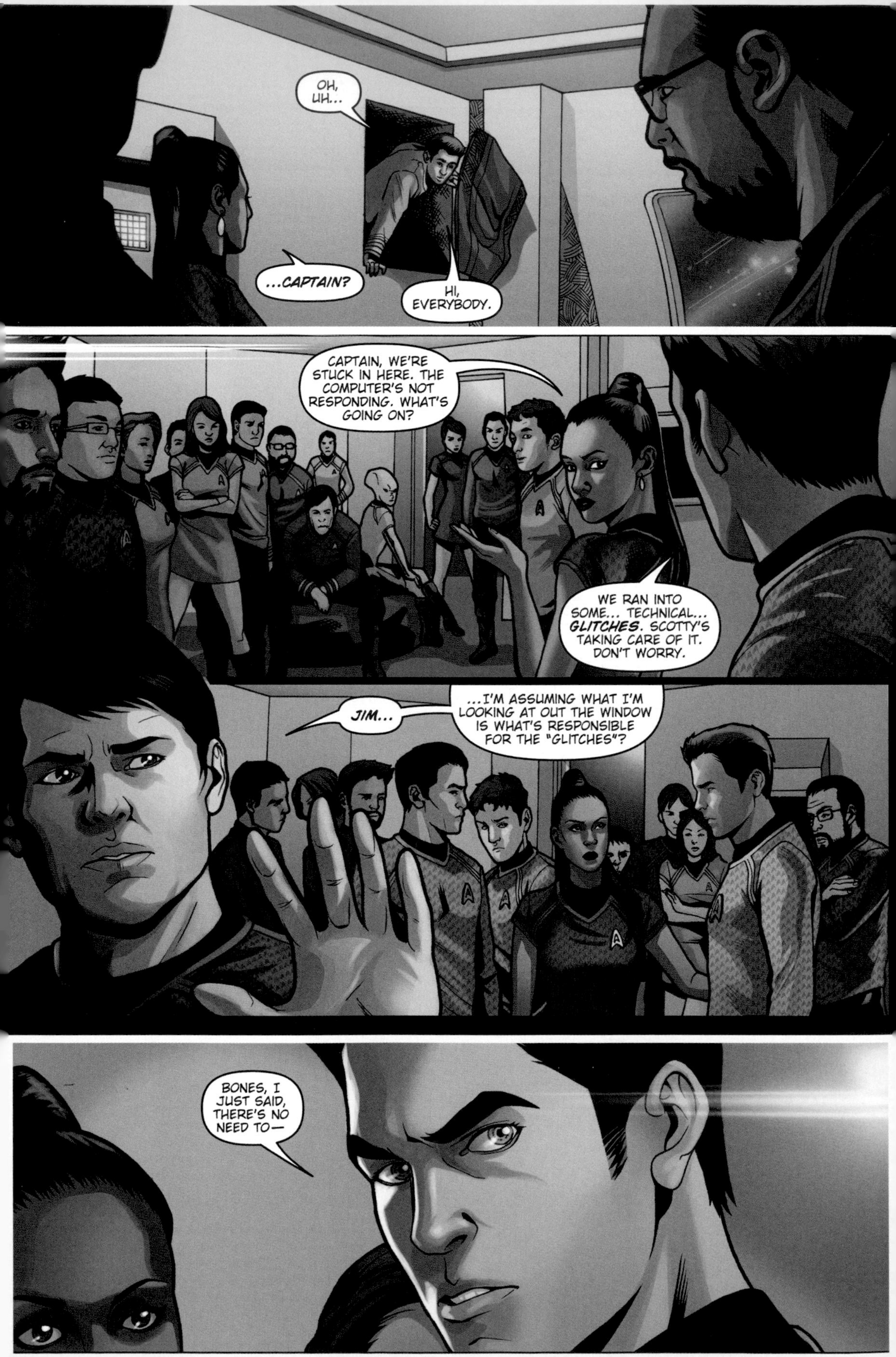
OH, UH...
...CAPTAIN?
HI, EVERYBODY.
CAPTAIN, WE'RE STUCK IN HERE. THE COMPUTER'S NOT RESPONDING. WHAT'S GOING ON?
WE RAN INTO SOME... TECHNICAL... GLITCHES. SCOTTY'S TAKING CARE OF IT. DON'T WORRY.
JIM...
...I'M ASSUMING WHAT I'M LOOKING AT OUT THE WINDOW IS WHAT'S RESPONSIBLE FOR THE "GLITCHES"?
BONES, I JUST SAID, THERE'S NO NEED TO—

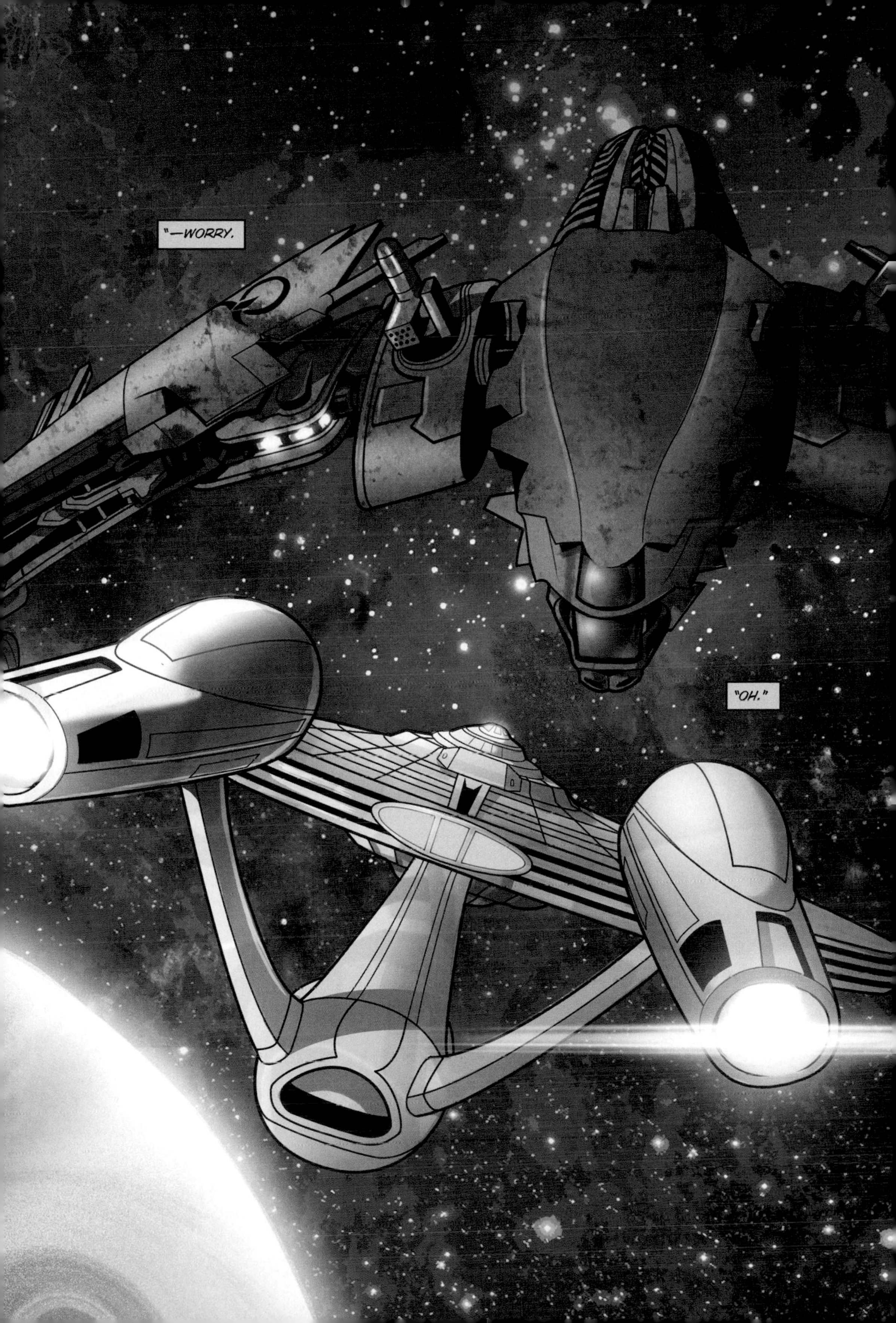
"—WORRY.
"OH."

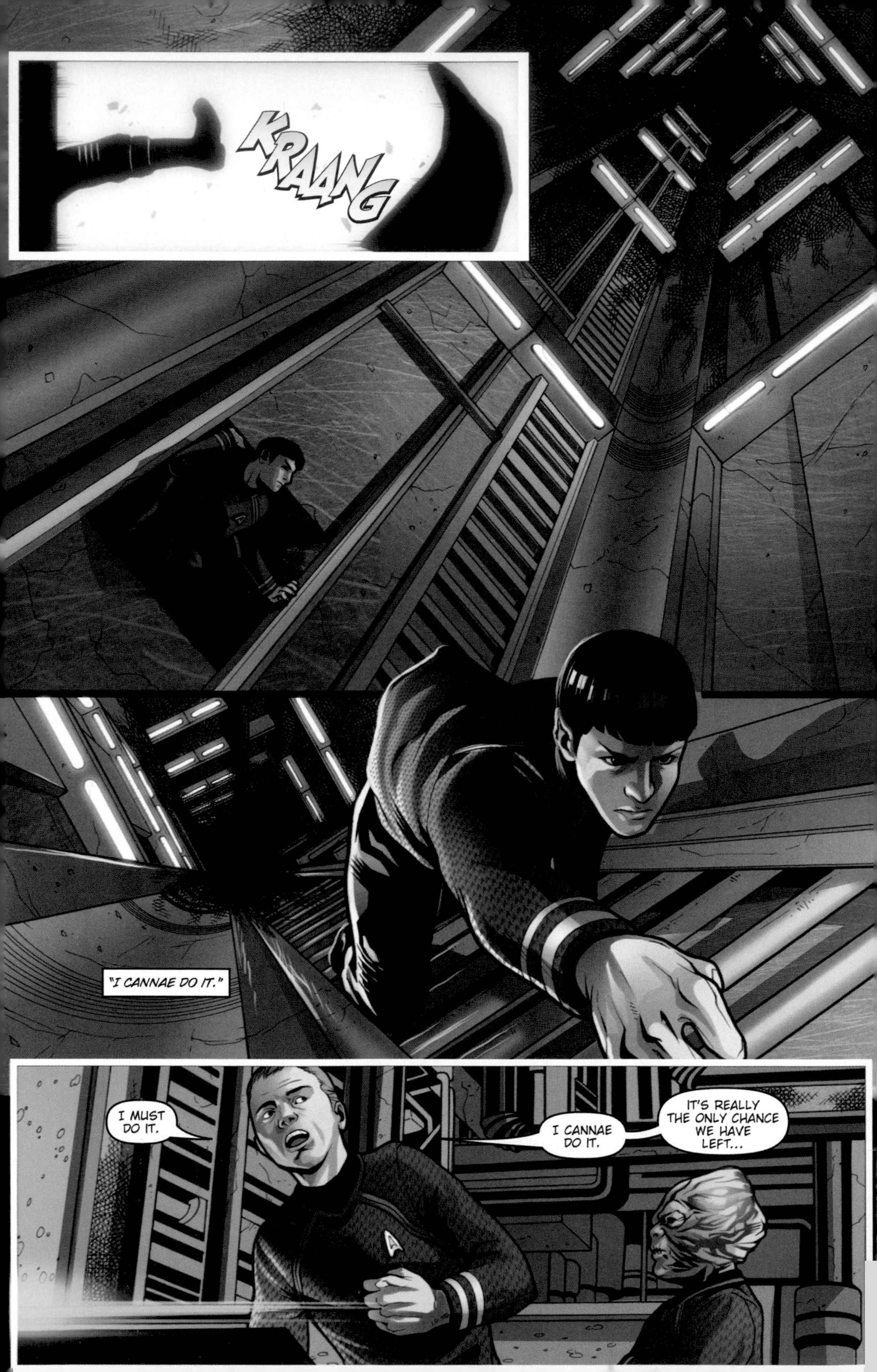
KRAANG
"I CANNAE DO IT."
I MUST DO IT.
I CANNAE DO IT.
IT'S REALLY THE ONLY CHANCE WE HAVE LEFT...

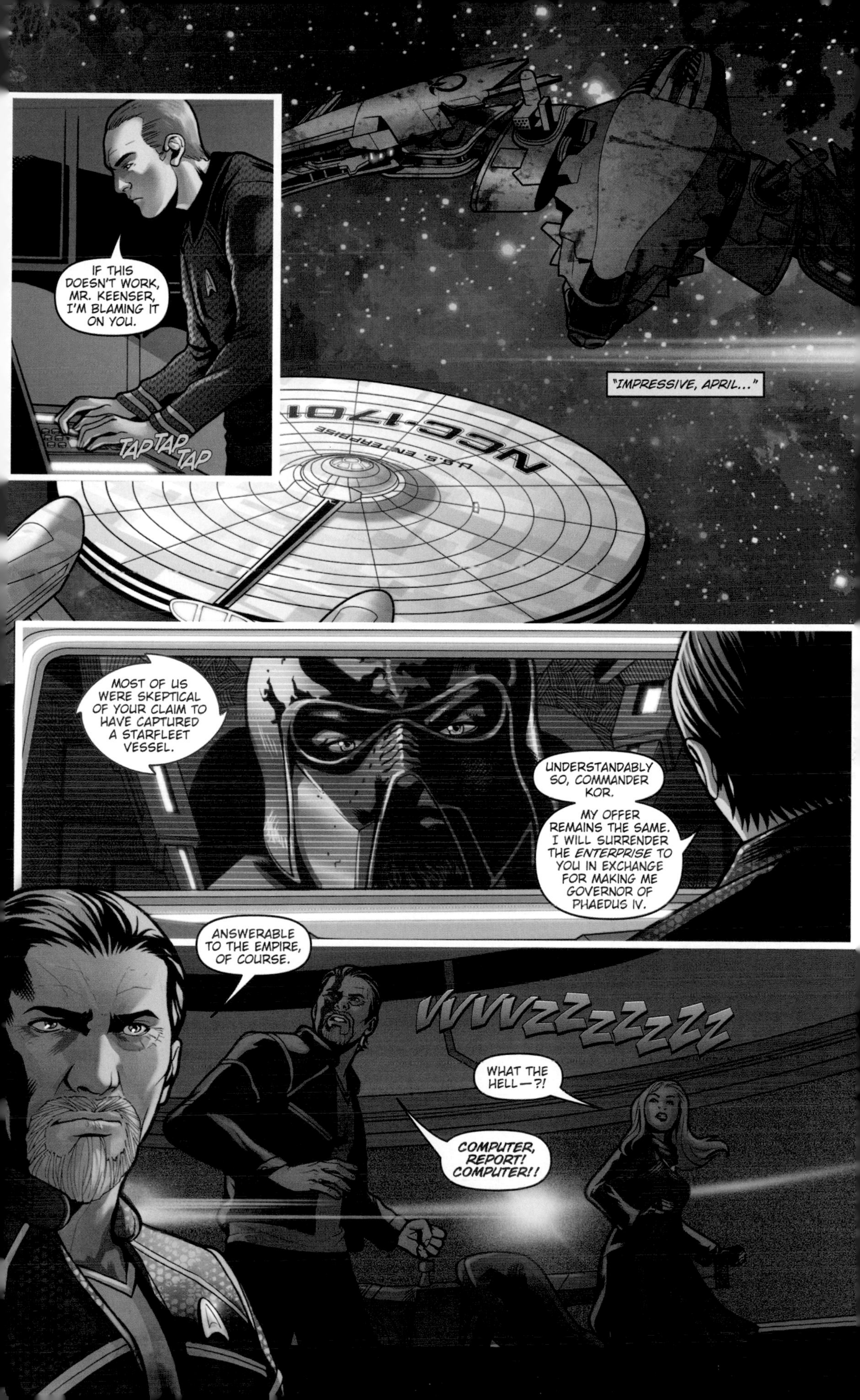
IF THIS DOESN'T WORK, MR. KEENSER, I'M BLAMING IT ON YOU.
TAP TAP TAP
NCC-1701
U.S.S. ENTERPRISE
"IMPRESSIVE, APRIL..."
MOST OF US WERE SKEPTICAL OF YOUR CLAIM TO HAVE CAPTURED A STARFLEET VESSEL.
UNDERSTANDABLY SO, COMMANDER KOR.
MY OFFER REMAINS THE SAME. I WILL SURRENDER THE *ENTERPRISE* TO YOU IN EXCHANGE FOR MAKING ME GOVERNOR OF PHAEDUS IV.
ANSWERABLE TO THE EMPIRE, OF COURSE.
VVVVZZZZZZZ
WHAT THE HELL—?!
COMPUTER, REPORT! COMPUTER!!

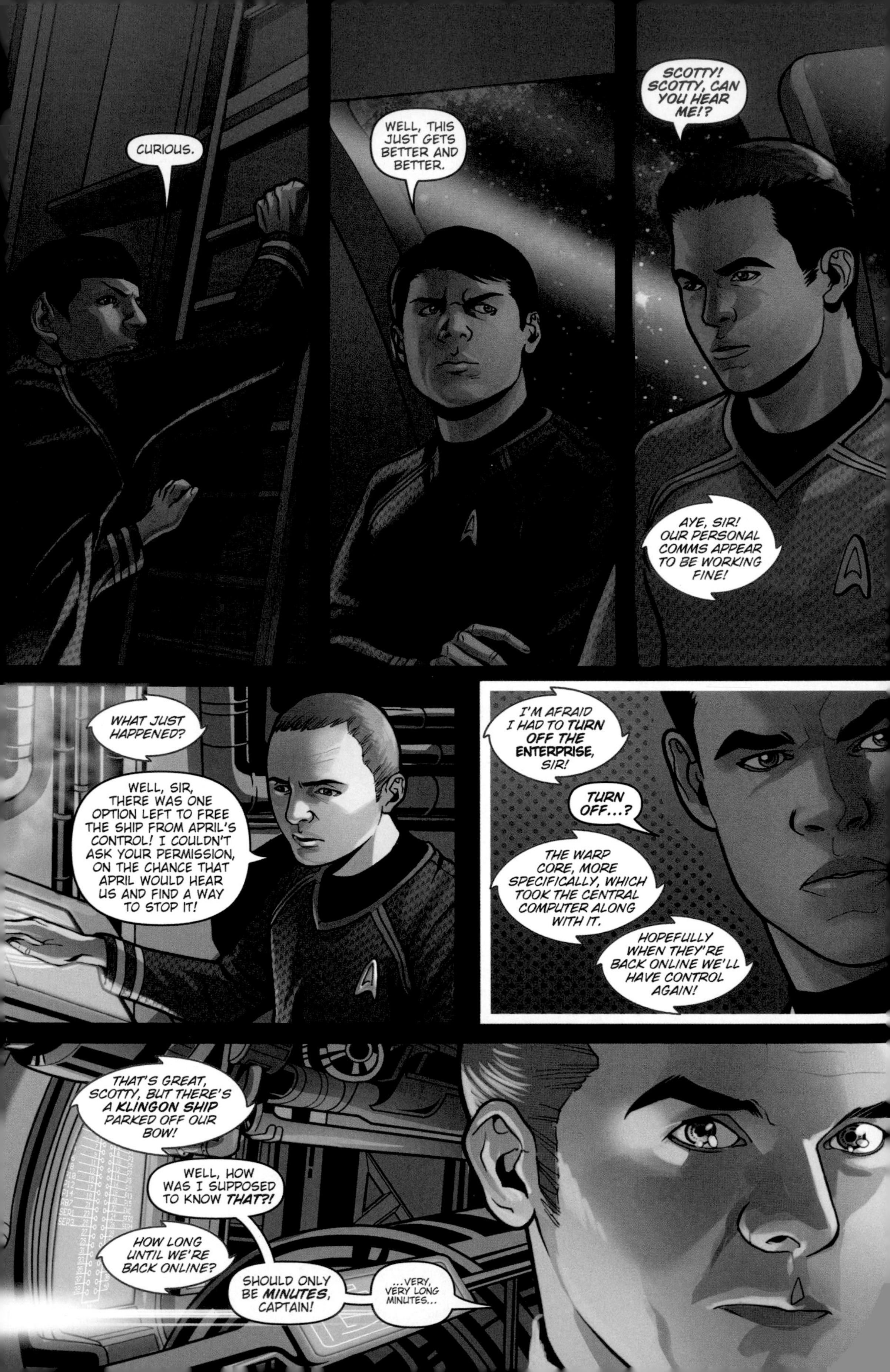
CURIOUS.
WELL, THIS JUST GETS BETTER AND BETTER.
SCOTTY! SCOTTY, CAN YOU HEAR ME!?
AYE, SIR! OUR PERSONAL COMMS APPEAR TO BE WORKING FINE!
WHAT JUST HAPPENED?
WELL, SIR, THERE WAS ONE OPTION LEFT TO FREE THE SHIP FROM APRIL'S CONTROL! I COULDN'T ASK YOUR PERMISSION, ON THE CHANCE THAT APRIL WOULD HEAR US AND FIND A WAY TO STOP IT!
I'M AFRAID I HAD TO TURN OFF THE ENTERPRISE, SIR!
TURN OFF...?
THE WARP CORE, MORE SPECIFICALLY, WHICH TOOK THE CENTRAL COMPUTER ALONG WITH IT.
HOPEFULLY WHEN THEY'RE BACK ONLINE WE'LL HAVE CONTROL AGAIN!
THAT'S GREAT, SCOTTY, BUT THERE'S A KLINGON SHIP PARKED OFF OUR BOW!
WELL, HOW WAS I SUPPOSED TO KNOW THAT?!
HOW LONG UNTIL WE'RE BACK ONLINE?
SHOULD ONLY BE MINUTES, CAPTAIN!
...VERY, VERY LONG MINUTES...

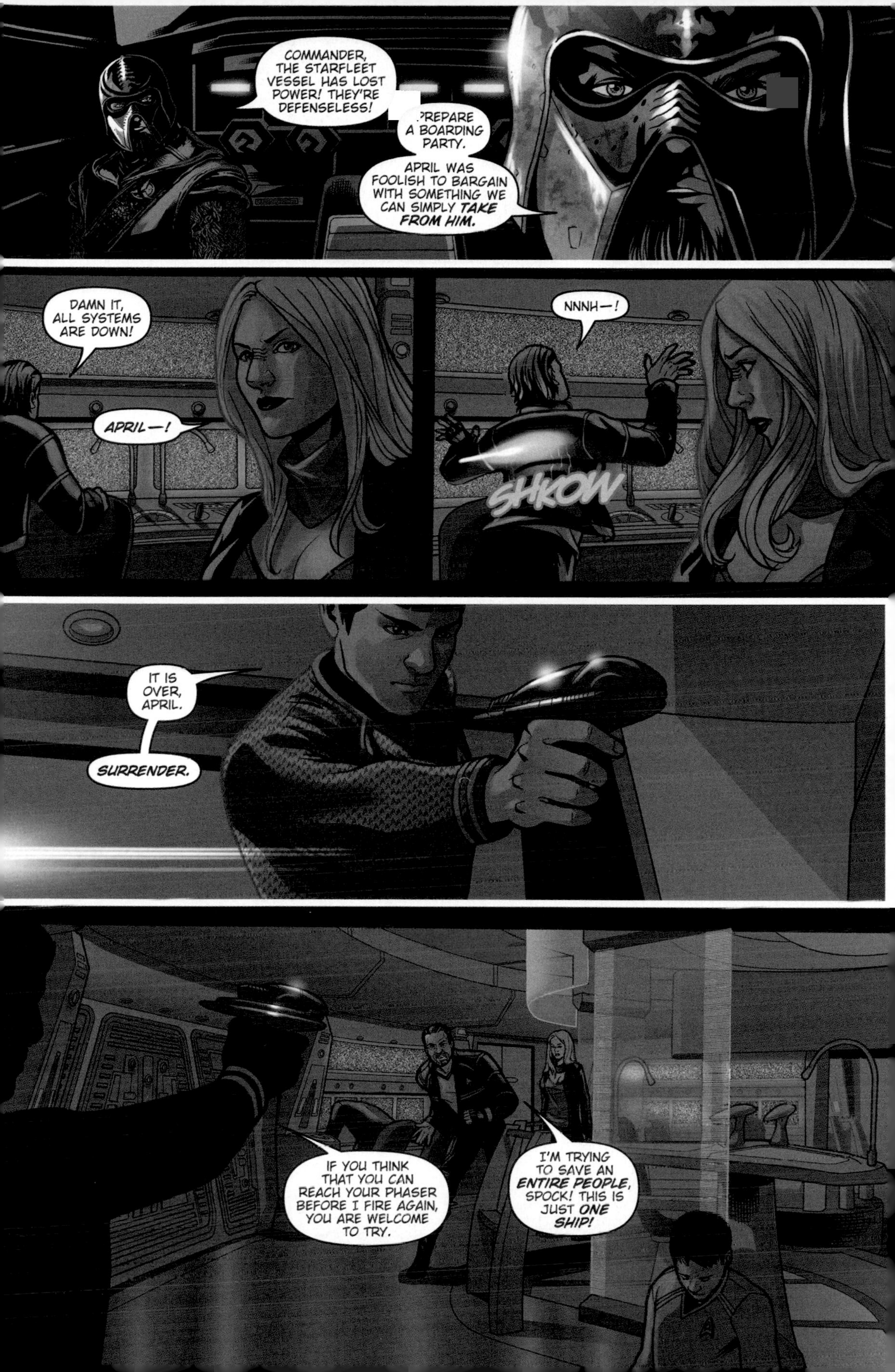
COMMANDER, THE STARFLEET VESSEL HAS LOST POWER! THEY'RE DEFENSELESS!
PREPARE A BOARDING PARTY.
APRIL WAS FOOLISH TO BARGAIN WITH SOMETHING WE CAN SIMPLY TAKE FROM HIM.
DAMN IT, ALL SYSTEMS ARE DOWN!
APRIL—!
NNNH—!
SHKOW
IT IS OVER, APRIL.
SURRENDER.
IF YOU THINK THAT YOU CAN REACH YOUR PHASER BEFORE I FIRE AGAIN, YOU ARE WELCOME TO TRY.
I'M TRYING TO SAVE AN ENTIRE PEOPLE, SPOCK! THIS IS JUST ONE SHIP!

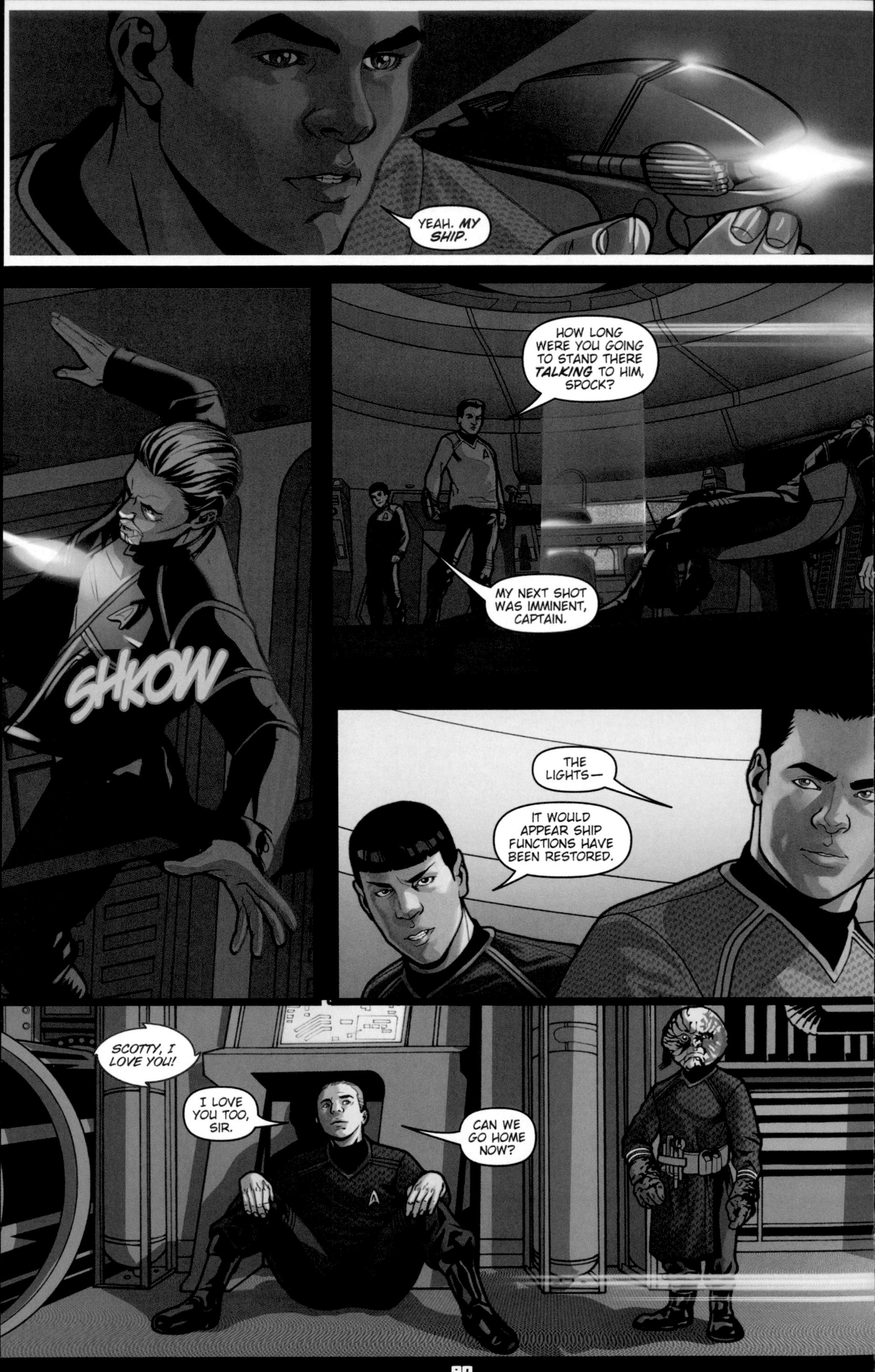

YEAH. *MY SHIP.*
SHKOW
HOW LONG WERE YOU GOING TO STAND THERE *TALKING* TO HIM, SPOCK?
MY NEXT SHOT WAS IMMINENT, CAPTAIN.
THE LIGHTS—
IT WOULD APPEAR SHIP FUNCTIONS HAVE BEEN RESTORED.
SCOTTY, I LOVE YOU!
I LOVE YOU TOO, SIR.
CAN WE GO HOME NOW?

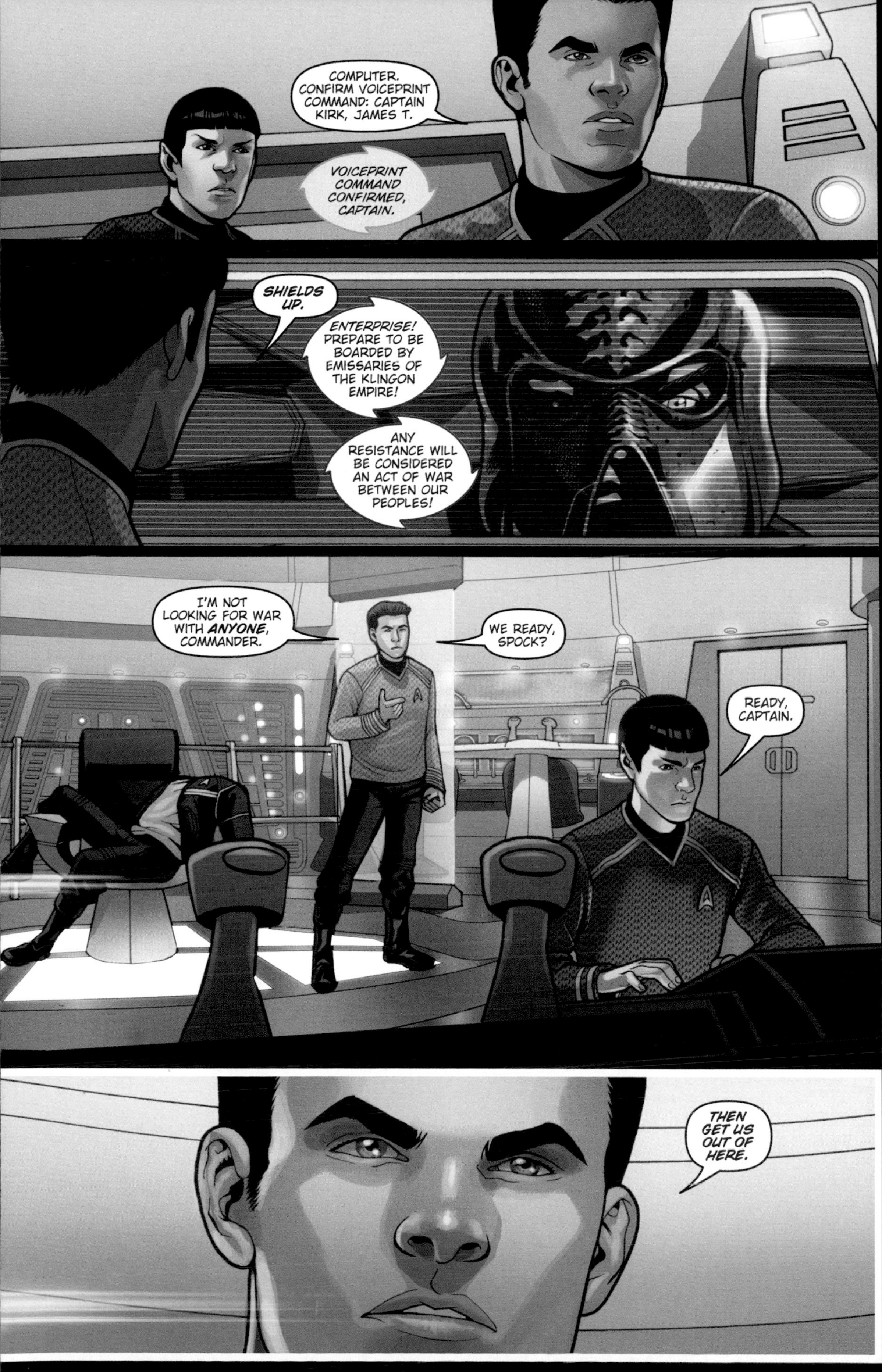

COMPUTER. CONFIRM VOICEPRINT COMMAND: CAPTAIN KIRK, JAMES T.
VOICEPRINT COMMAND CONFIRMED, CAPTAIN.
SHIELDS UP.
ENTERPRISE! PREPARE TO BE BOARDED BY EMISSARIES OF THE KLINGON EMPIRE!
ANY RESISTANCE WILL BE CONSIDERED AN ACT OF WAR BETWEEN OUR PEOPLES!
I'M NOT LOOKING FOR WAR WITH ANYONE, COMMANDER.
WE READY, SPOCK?
READY, CAPTAIN.
THEN GET US OUT OF HERE.

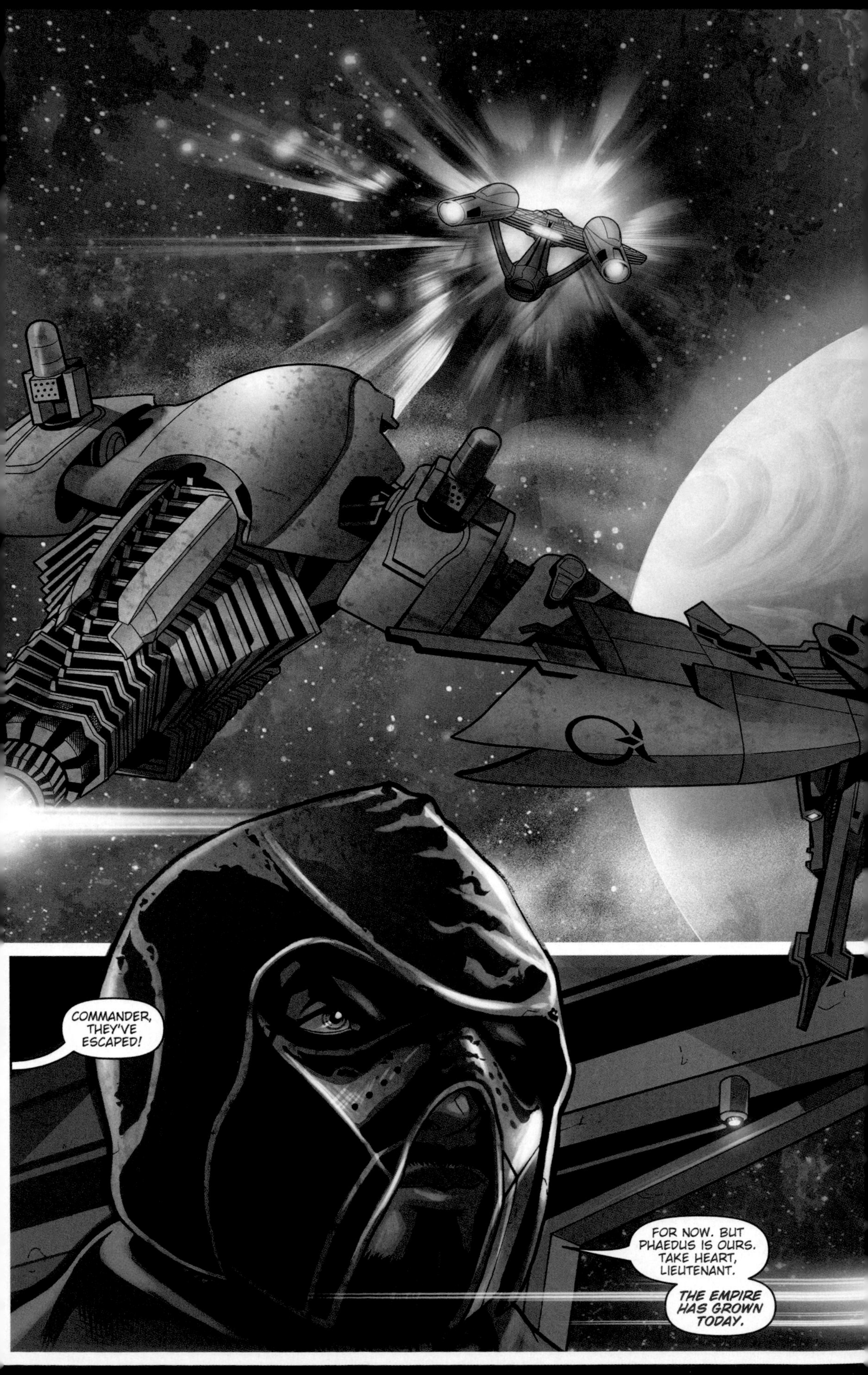
COMMANDER, THEY'VE ESCAPED!
FOR NOW. BUT PHAEDUS IS OURS. TAKE HEART, LIEUTENANT.
THE EMPIRE HAS GROWN TODAY.

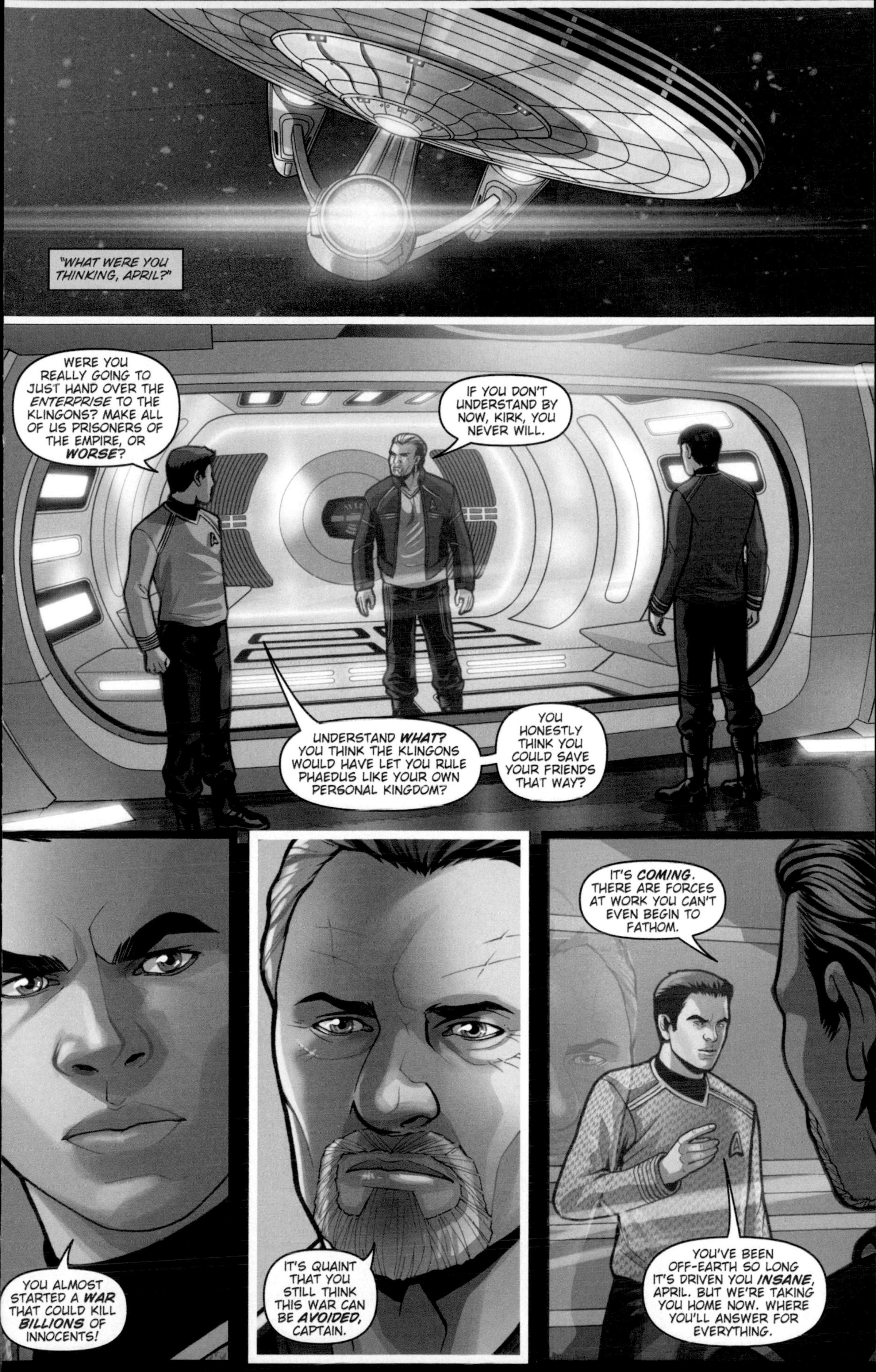
"WHAT WERE YOU THINKING, APRIL?"
WERE YOU REALLY GOING TO JUST HAND OVER THE *ENTERPRISE* TO THE KLINGONS? MAKE ALL OF US PRISONERS OF THE EMPIRE, OR **WORSE**?
IF YOU DON'T UNDERSTAND BY NOW, KIRK, YOU NEVER WILL.
UNDERSTAND **WHAT?** YOU THINK THE KLINGONS WOULD HAVE LET YOU RULE PHAEDUS LIKE YOUR OWN PERSONAL KINGDOM?
YOU HONESTLY THINK YOU COULD SAVE YOUR FRIENDS THAT WAY?
YOU ALMOST STARTED A **WAR** THAT COULD KILL **BILLIONS** OF INNOCENTS!
IT'S QUAINT THAT YOU STILL THINK THIS WAR CAN BE **AVOIDED**, CAPTAIN.
IT'S **COMING**. THERE ARE FORCES AT WORK YOU CAN'T EVEN BEGIN TO FATHOM.
YOU'VE BEEN OFF-EARTH SO LONG IT'S DRIVEN YOU **INSANE**, APRIL. BUT WE'RE TAKING YOU HOME NOW. WHERE YOU'LL ANSWER FOR EVERYTHING.

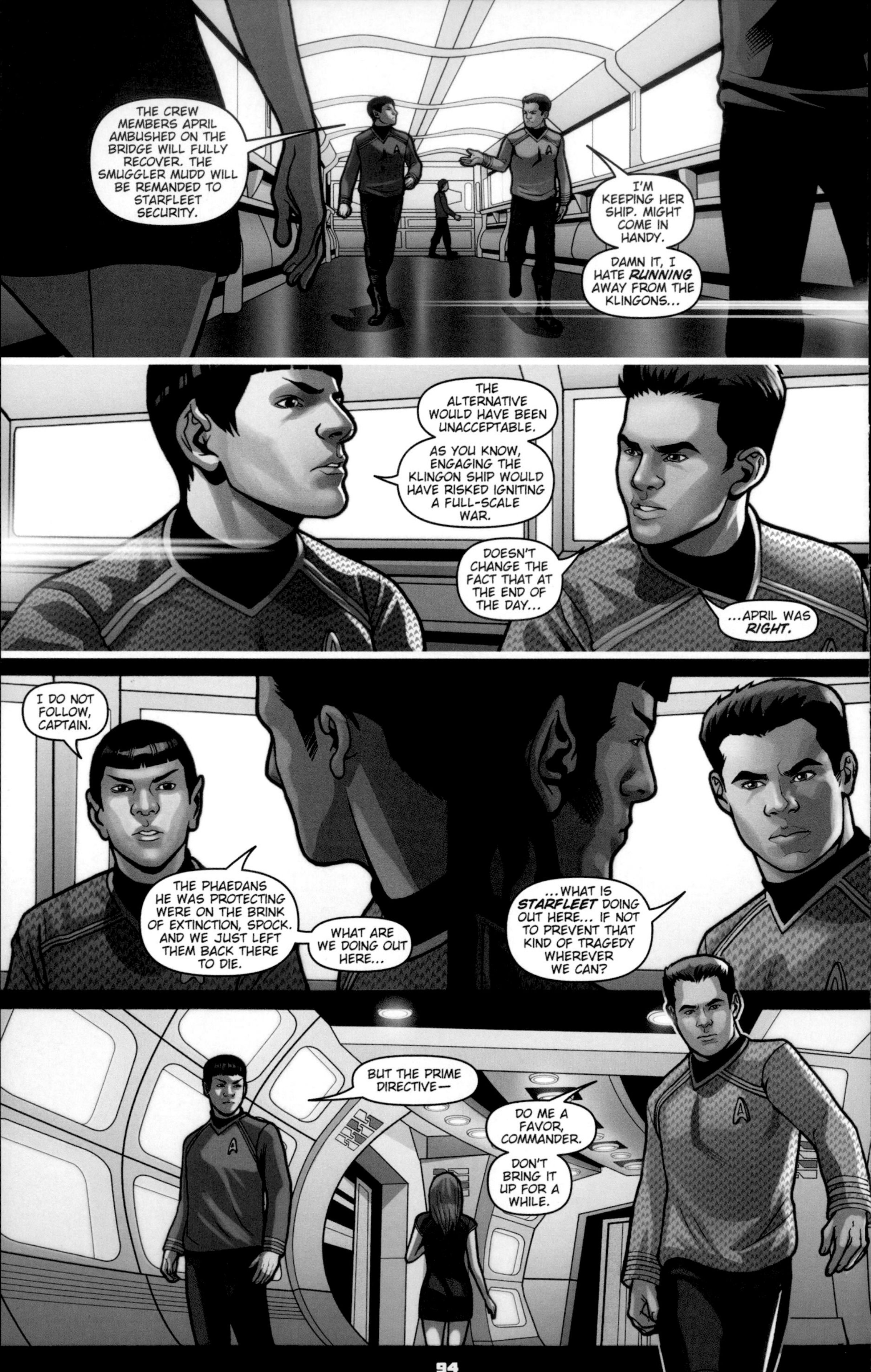
THE CREW MEMBERS APRIL AMBUSHED ON THE BRIDGE WILL FULLY RECOVER. THE SMUGGLER MUDD WILL BE REMANDED TO STARFLEET SECURITY.
I'M KEEPING HER SHIP. MIGHT COME IN HANDY.
DAMN IT, I HATE *RUNNING* AWAY FROM THE KLINGONS...
THE ALTERNATIVE WOULD HAVE BEEN UNACCEPTABLE.
AS YOU KNOW, ENGAGING THE KLINGON SHIP WOULD HAVE RISKED IGNITING A FULL-SCALE WAR.
DOESN'T CHANGE THE FACT THAT AT THE END OF THE DAY...
...APRIL WAS *RIGHT.*
I DO NOT FOLLOW, CAPTAIN.
THE PHAEDANS HE WAS PROTECTING WERE ON THE BRINK OF EXTINCTION, SPOCK. AND WE JUST LEFT THEM BACK THERE TO DIE.
WHAT ARE WE DOING OUT HERE...
...WHAT IS *STARFLEET* DOING OUT HERE... IF NOT TO PREVENT THAT KIND OF TRAGEDY WHEREVER WE CAN?
BUT THE PRIME DIRECTIVE—
DO ME A FAVOR, COMMANDER.
DON'T BRING IT UP FOR A WHILE.

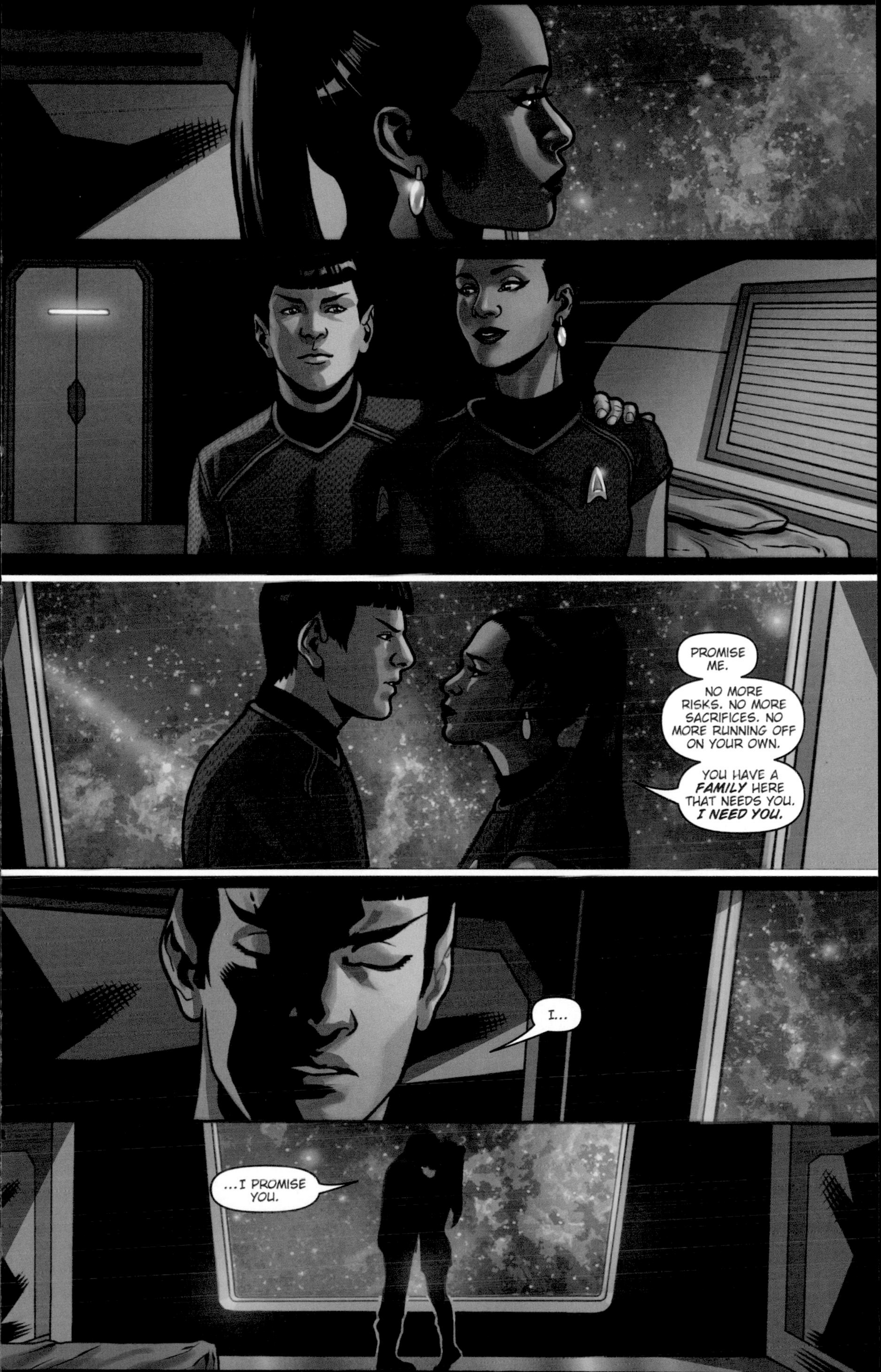
PROMISE ME.
NO MORE RISKS. NO MORE SACRIFICES. NO MORE RUNNING OFF ON YOUR OWN.
YOU HAVE A **FAMILY** HERE THAT NEEDS YOU. ***I NEED YOU.***
I...
...I PROMISE YOU.

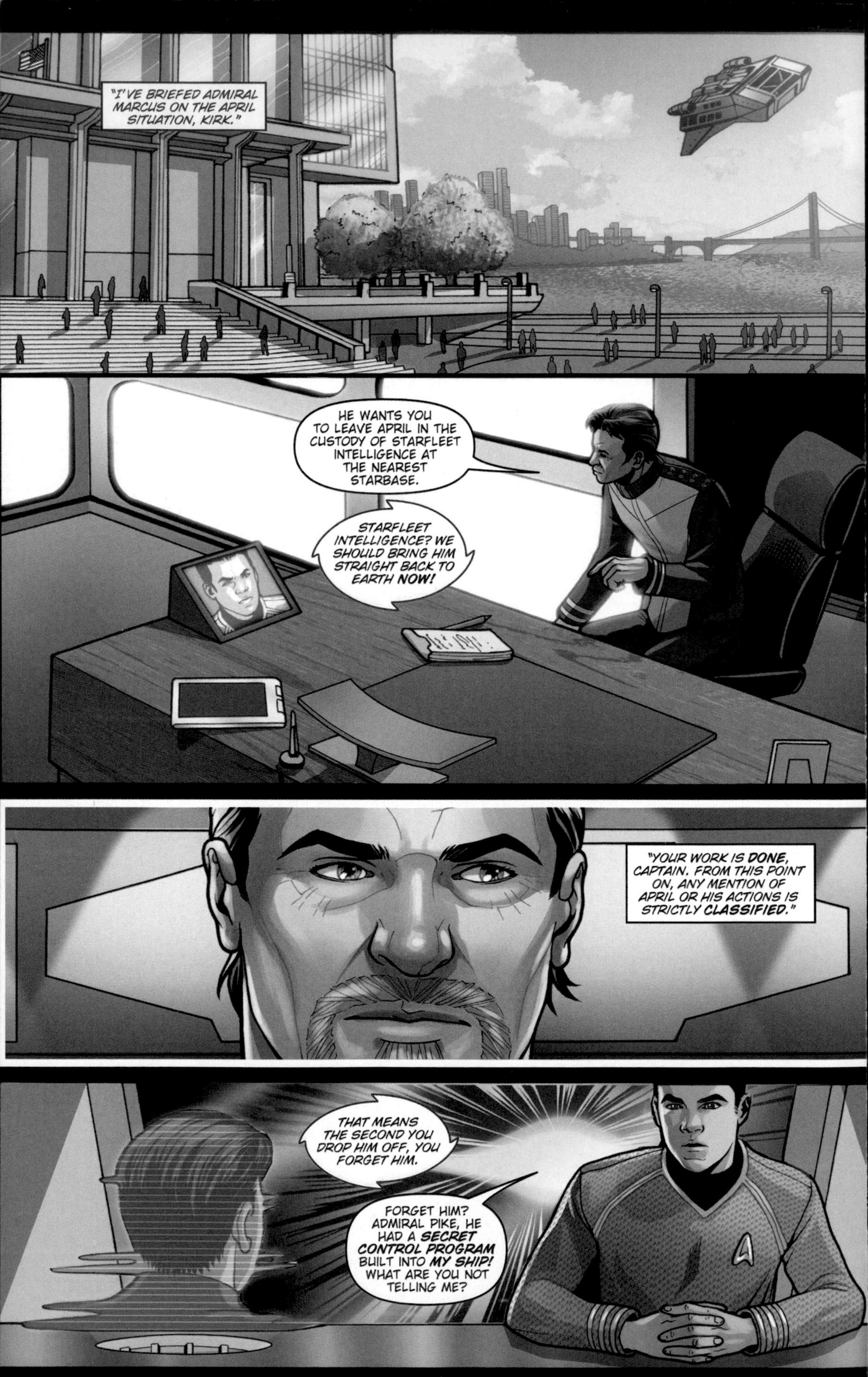
"I'VE BRIEFED ADMIRAL MARCUS ON THE APRIL SITUATION, KIRK."
HE WANTS YOU TO LEAVE APRIL IN THE CUSTODY OF STARFLEET INTELLIGENCE AT THE NEAREST STARBASE.
STARFLEET INTELLIGENCE? WE SHOULD BRING HIM STRAIGHT BACK TO EARTH NOW!
"YOUR WORK IS DONE, CAPTAIN. FROM THIS POINT ON, ANY MENTION OF APRIL OR HIS ACTIONS IS STRICTLY CLASSIFIED."
THAT MEANS THE SECOND YOU DROP HIM OFF, YOU FORGET HIM.
FORGET HIM? ADMIRAL PIKE, HE HAD A SECRET CONTROL PROGRAM BUILT INTO MY SHIP! WHAT ARE YOU NOT TELLING ME?

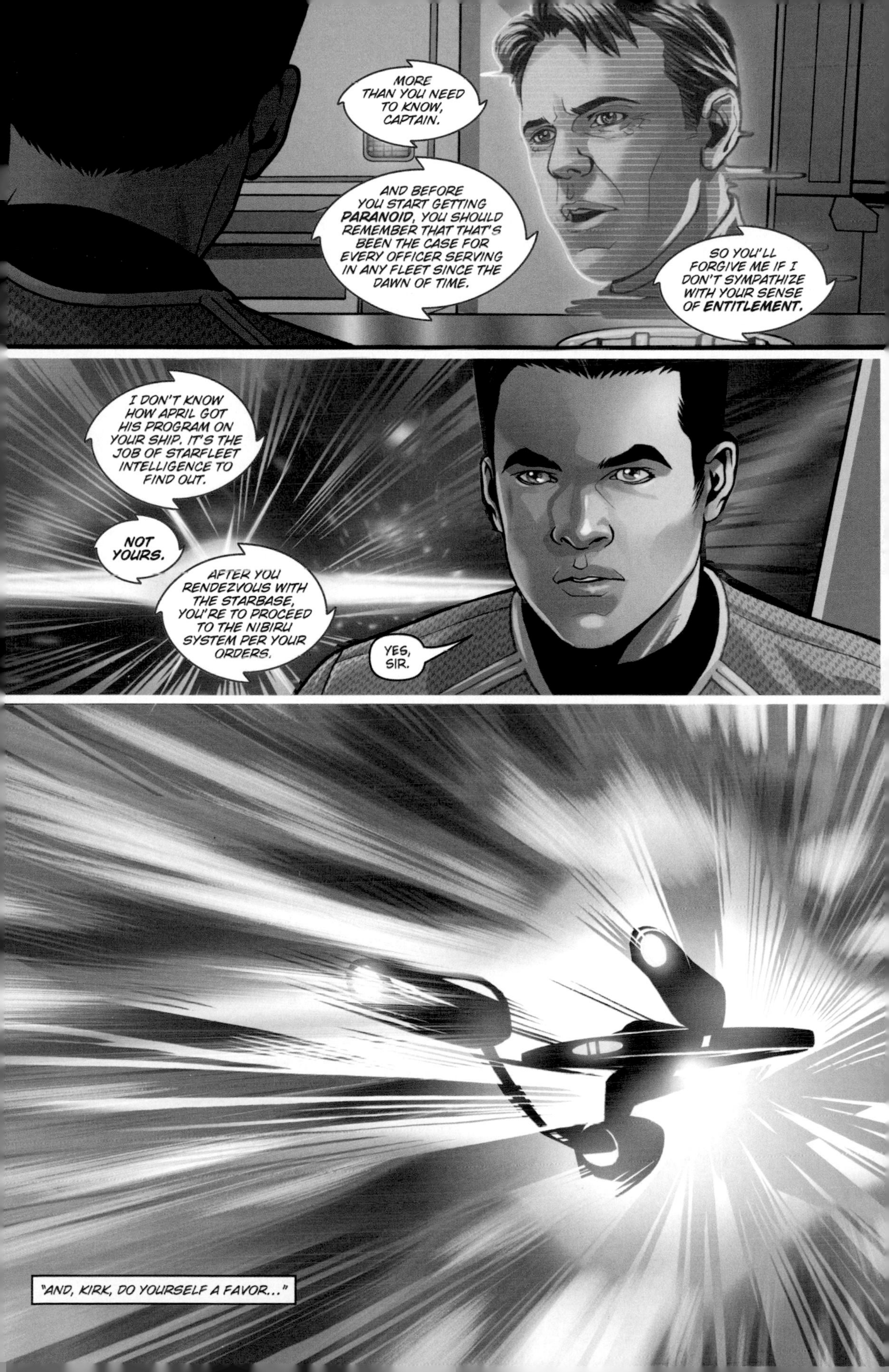
MORE THAN YOU NEED TO KNOW, CAPTAIN.
AND BEFORE YOU START GETTING **PARANOID**, YOU SHOULD REMEMBER THAT THAT'S BEEN THE CASE FOR EVERY OFFICER SERVING IN ANY FLEET SINCE THE DAWN OF TIME.
SO YOU'LL FORGIVE ME IF I DON'T SYMPATHIZE WITH YOUR SENSE OF **ENTITLEMENT.**
I DON'T KNOW HOW APRIL GOT HIS PROGRAM ON YOUR SHIP. IT'S THE JOB OF STARFLEET INTELLIGENCE TO FIND OUT.
NOT YOURS.
AFTER YOU RENDEZVOUS WITH THE STARBASE, YOU'RE TO PROCEED TO THE NIBIRU SYSTEM PER YOUR ORDERS.
YES, SIR.
"AND, KIRK, DO YOURSELF A FAVOR..."

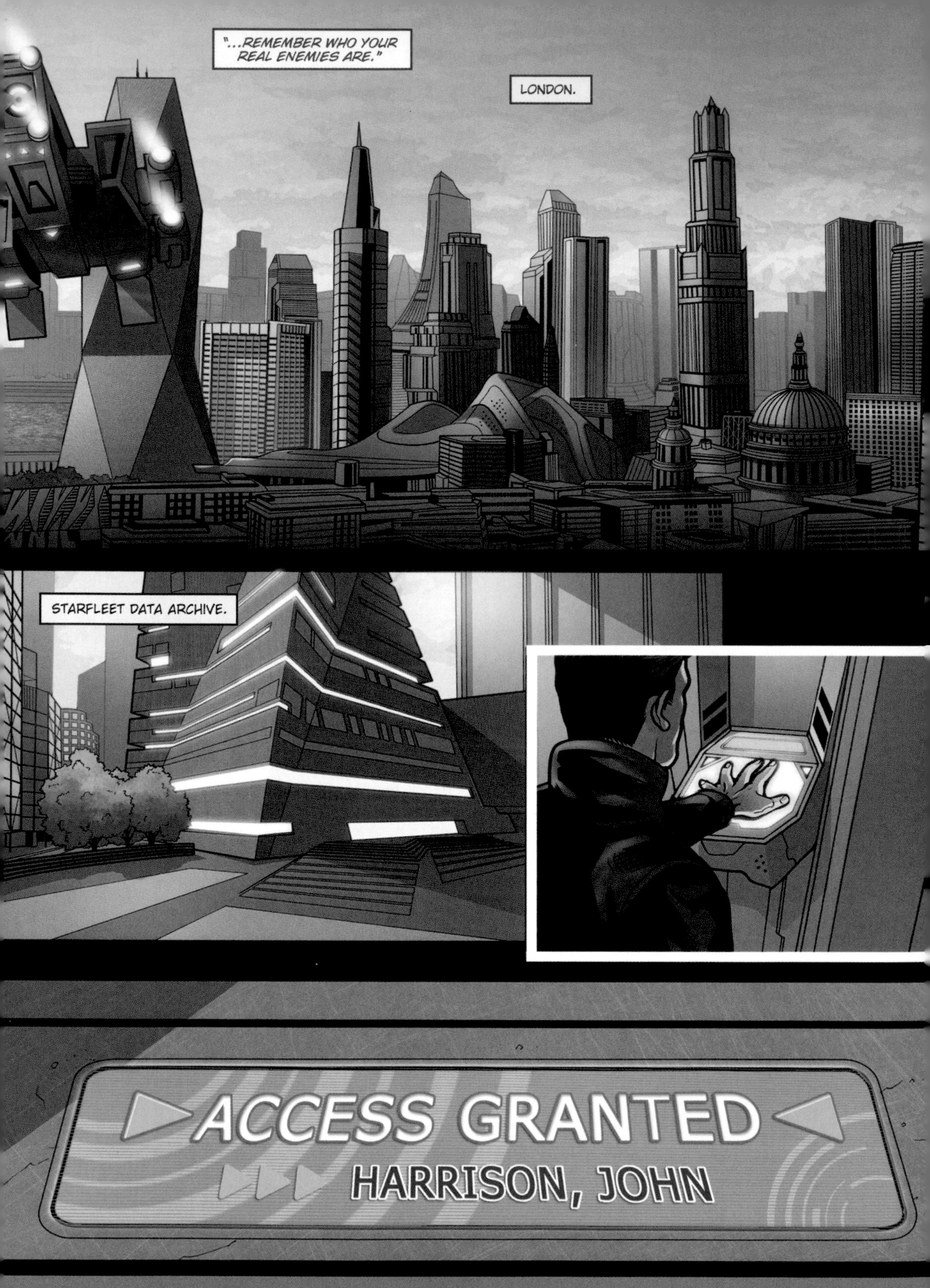
"...REMEMBER WHO YOUR REAL ENEMIES ARE."
LONDON.
STARFLEET DATA ARCHIVE.
ACCESS GRANTED
HARRISON, JOHN

TO BE CONTINUED ONSCREEN IN
STAR TREK
INTO DARKNESS
05.17.13

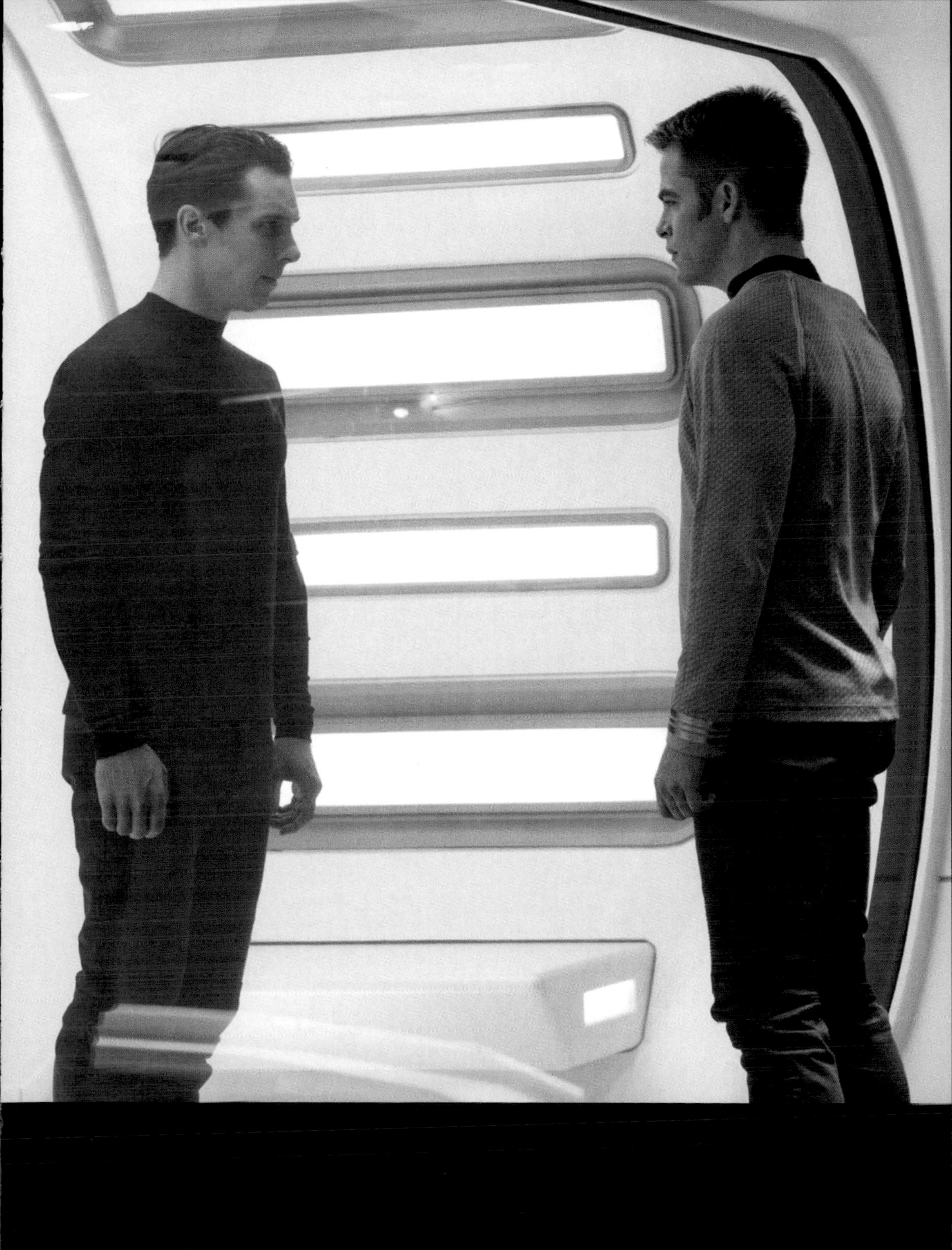

ALIEN DESIGNS by DAVID MESSINA

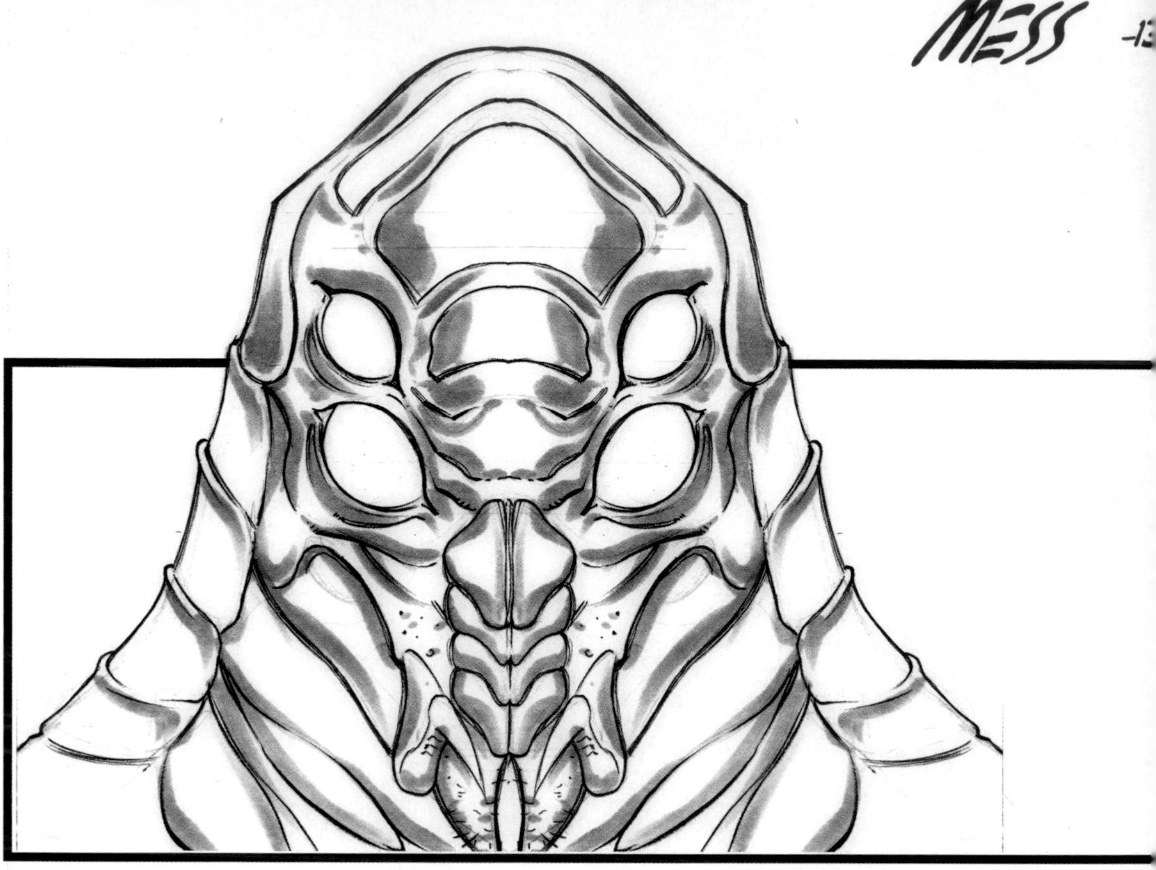
MESS

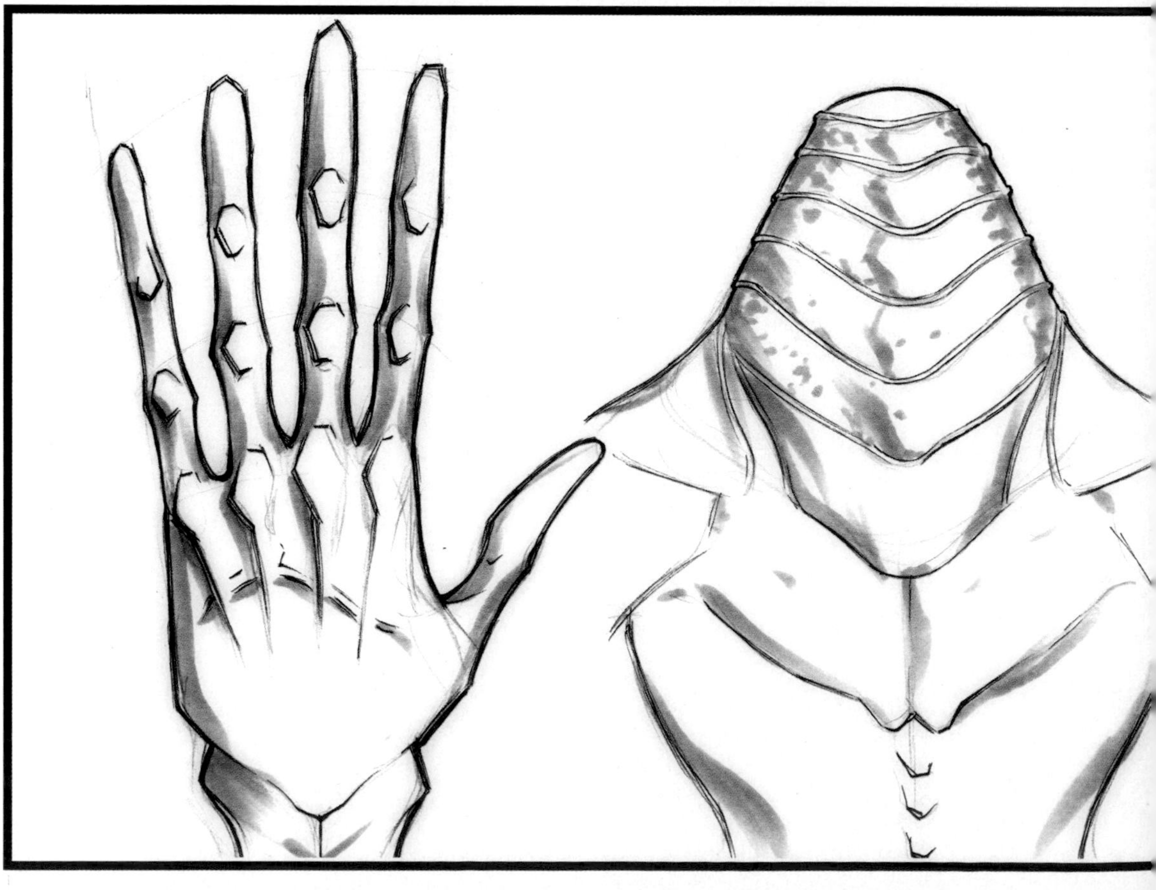

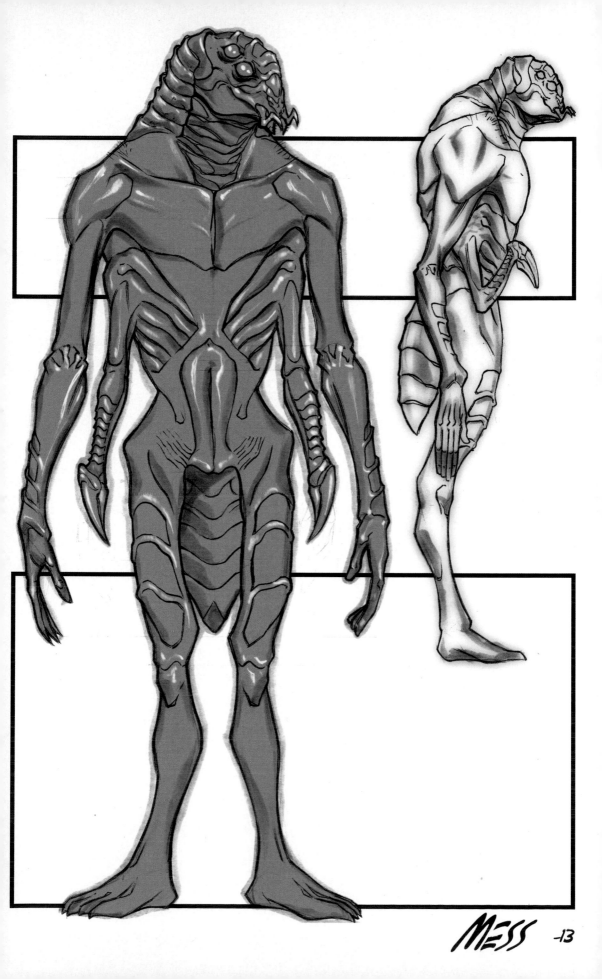

MESS -13

3D models by LINO GRANDI

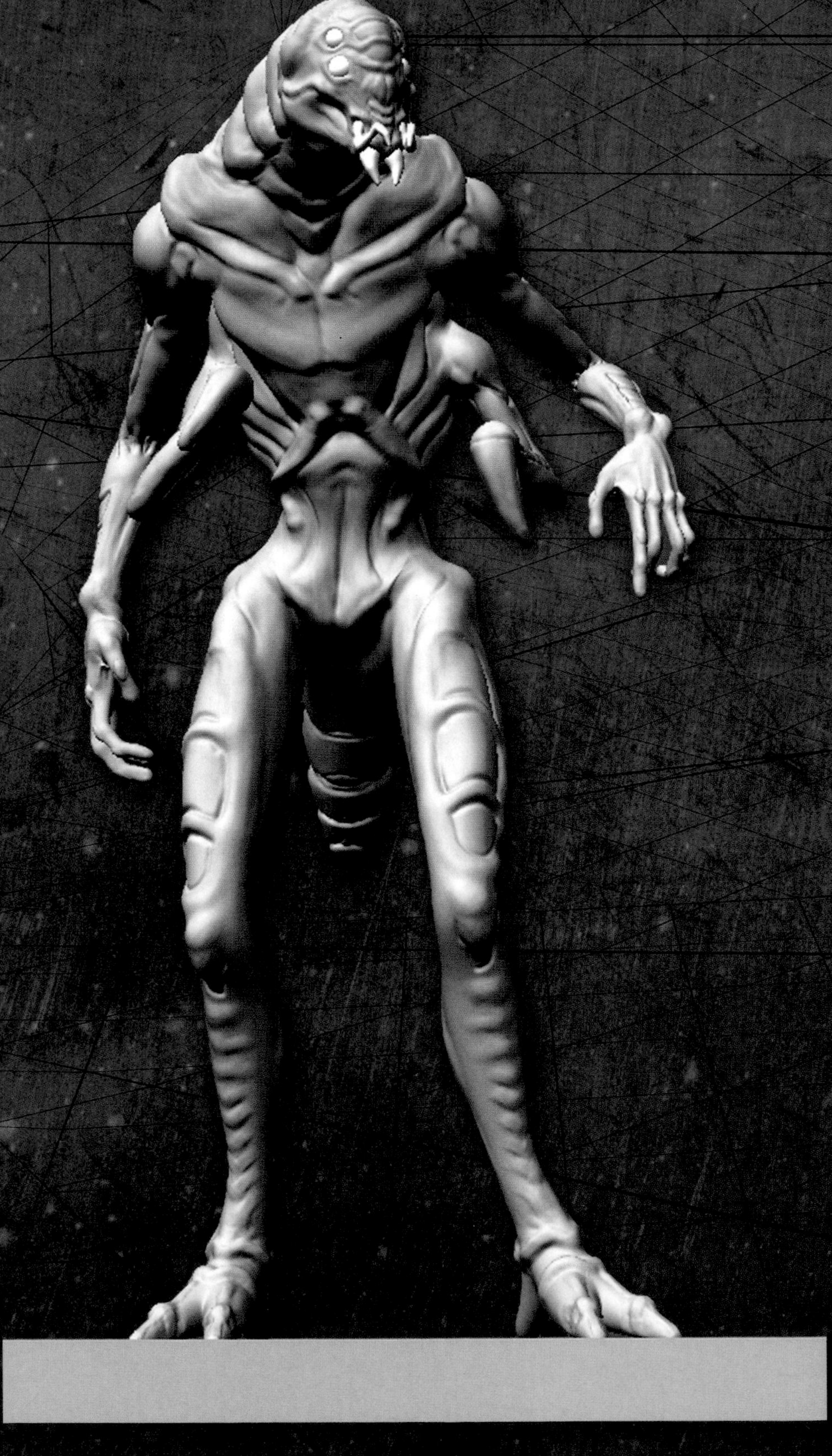

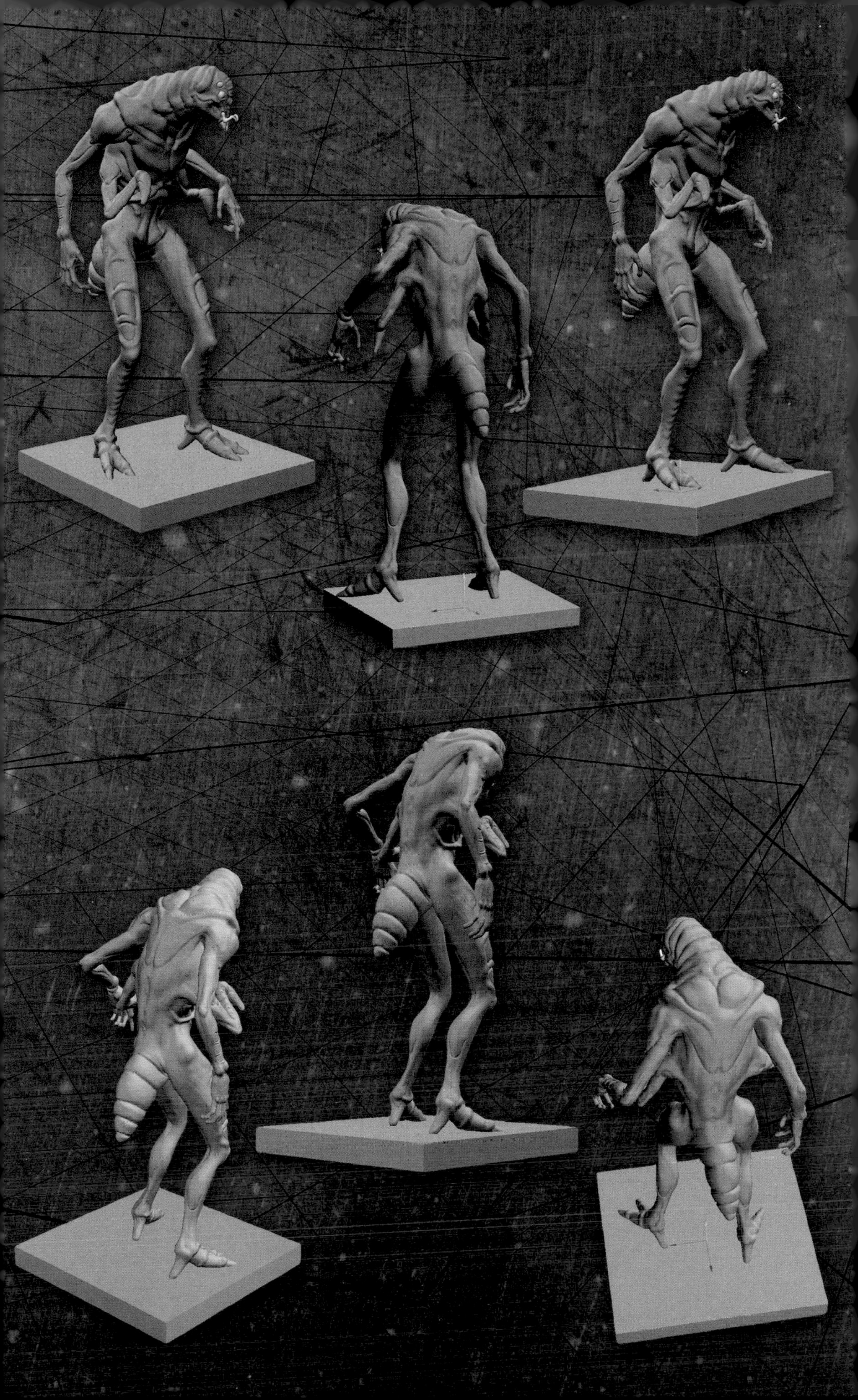

AFTERWORD

Movies are the best.

There's nothing better than settling into your seat in front of the biggest screen imaginable and being transported into an adventure that blows your mind. Thanks to amazing advances in visual effects, anything a filmmaker dreams up can be brought to cinematic life.

On behalf of the COUNTDOWN team, we hope this story whets your appetite for STAR TREK INTO DARKNESS. We feel grateful to work on Gene Roddenberry's epic creation in any capacity, and we hope our love for the characters comes through on every page.

Comics have a unique ability to portray both the grand scope of the STAR TREK universe and the more personal moments that are a hallmark of the series, without the need to pack it all into two hours.

Making comics means that we don't have to deal with the constraints of a movie's schedule and budget, or the pressure of launching a worldwide marketing campaign, or the headaches of dealing with everything that can go wrong at any moment on a massive soundstage. Making comics is the most direct way to get from the spark of an idea to a finished product that fans can enjoy.

Come to think of it...

Comics are the best.

Mike Johnson